"Startling imagery, deft
engaging writing make S
Tim

"John Wyndham meets *Black Mirror* in Tim Major's
scintillating novel, a parallel world thriller, which takes
as its themes duplicity, paranoia and what it truly means
to be human. *Snakeskins* wrapped its coils around
me and wouldn't let go."
Mark Morris

"A premise worthy of Wyndham becomes a twisty political
SF thriller in the hands of Major. *Snakeskins* is full of action
and surprise, keeping me reading, but the real hook lies
in the rich seam of humanity within."
Aliya Whiteley

"Another great page-turner from Tim Major! We follow
Caitlin, a teenage girl, whose ability to produce 'snakeskin'
clones causes emotional ripples that spread more widely than
she'd ever anticipated. It's a gripping and thought-provoking
tale, with Major exploring the wider implications of cloning
and extended life-spans in the growth of a corrupt new
government which has consequences for all."
Alison Littlewood

"The world-building is subtle and convincing, a plausible
alternate UK where isolationist foreign policy has retarded the
country's technological and economic progress. A cautionary
tale for our times."
James Brogden

"Whether as page-turning thriller, coming of age story, or
timely satire on a broken Britain, *Snakeskins* is a delight."
Robert Shearman

"Tim Major has a talent for combining big ideas to create
something exciting. With *Snakeskins* he gives us an SF thriller
brimming with questions about identity."
Priya Sharma

### Praise for Tim Major

"Tim Major is an exceptional writer."
Adam Roberts

"Once I started reading it, I couldn't put it down
until I reached the end."
Lynda Rucker on *Carus and Mitch*

"That perfect blend of cautionary tale, psychological horror
and introspective character study."
The Eloquent Page on *You Don't Belong Here*

"It has freshness and it's fluently written entertainment."
Rising Shadow

"Strongly recommended for fans of original
and uniquely weird fiction."
Ginger Nuts of Horror on *Blighters*

# SNAKESKINS

**BY TIM MAJOR AND AVAILABLE FROM TITAN BOOKS**

*Snakeskins*
*Hope Island* (May 2020)

# SNAKESKINS

## TIM MAJOR

**TITAN** BOOKS

Snakeskins
Print edition ISBN: 9781789090789
E-book edition ISBN: 9781789090796

Published by Titan Books
A division of Titan Publishing Group Ltd
144 Southwark Street, London SE1 0UP
www.titanbooks.com

First edition: May 2019
10 9 8 7 6 5 4 3 2 1

This is a work of fiction. Names, places and incidents are either products of the
author's imagination or used fictitiously. Any resemblance to actual persons,
living or dead (except for satirical purposes), is entirely coincidental.

© 2019 Tim Major

No part of this publication may be reproduced, stored in a retrieval system, or
transmitted, in any form or by any means without the prior written permission
of the publisher, nor be otherwise circulated in any form of binding or cover
other than that in which it is published and without a similar condition being
imposed on the subsequent purchaser.

A CIP catalogue record for this title is available from the British Library.

Printed and bound by CPI Group (UK) Ltd, Croydon, CR0 4YY

**For Mum**

# ONE

Caitlin gasped at the cold sting of the wind. Gusts had licked at her cagoule the entire way, but now whistled at high speed through narrow gaps between the rock columns. It felt as though her skin was bare.

The sky had cleared during the last half an hour as dusk fell. Caitlin enjoyed seeing the stars – low cloud cover made her claustrophobic – but tonight she would have preferred being less aware of the umbrella of bright speckles above. The pale moon and the imagined constellations, planets and distant galaxies all contributed to her sense of being watched.

Her dad, Ian, turned on the path ahead. His cheeks shone. "It's just around this outcrop. But we'll have to hurry."

Caitlin jogged to reach his side. She took his hand and squeezed. He nodded and they set off along the gravel track and around the copper-coloured rock formation.

She had been here before, when she was around seven or eight. Her memories of the rocks were indistinct, but she could recall the gift shop in vivid detail. Her mum had bought her a Red Riding Hood doll which, when turned inside out, became the wolf.

"There," Ian said. He raised their joined hands to point.

Caitlin squinted against the gloom. They ought to have brought torches. When he had grudgingly opened the gates after subjecting their ID cards to absurd scrutiny, the gatekeeper had warned them that there were no lamps to light the paths.

The Idol was a shocking white as if the moonlight illuminated only that single formation out of all of the Brimham Rocks. It was twice as wide as Caitlin was tall. Its lumpen, curved shape reminded her of an enormous molar. It balanced precariously on a tiny hillock of stone which had eroded over centuries to become an unlikely base for the monolith above it.

She placed both her hands on the lower, bulbous section of the rock, expecting it to shift under her weight. A single slender cloud knifed across the moon and she drew away sharply. The movement had tricked her. The Idol seemed to be tipping.

"It's actually smaller than I expected," she said.

Her dad flinched. Immediately, Caitlin regretted her comment. The Idol had been her mum's favourite. A postcard image of it was still Blu-Tacked to their kitchen wall.

Ian sucked in air, clapped his hands and spun slowly on the spot. "Strange. She's not here."

"What?" Caitlin said, still lingering on thoughts of her mum. "What did you say?"

"The lady. Where is she?" Ian said. "And for that matter, where's your uncle?"

Despite the circumstances, Caitlin had almost forgotten that they weren't alone.

After a minute or so, Tobe emerged from the darkness. He had pulled his sweatshirt hood up; the grey expanse of cotton made him look as though he had been produced by the same weathering processes as the lumpy rock formations.

Ian bent down. He slung his rucksack from his shoulders and began rifling through its contents.

"Guys!" Tobe shouted.

Caitlin winced. She felt instinctively that they ought to keep their voices down. She didn't reply.

Tobe plodded over. He glanced up at the Idol, unimpressed.

"Guys," he said again, still loud. "There's a better one back there. It's up high, as if it's looking down on the whole place. The map calls it the Eagle and it's true, it really is like one, ready to swoop down or shit out an egg or something. What could be more rock and roll than an *eagle*?" He looked up again. "Speaking of which, this rock looks like it's ready to roll, any second."

He launched himself at the Idol. Both of his hands slapped against the stone surface. It didn't shift.

Caitlin grinned at his undisguised disappointment.

Ian stood up, now holding a crimson velour-covered notebook. Caitlin had seen it before, on the shelves in her mum's old study.

"No, Tobe," Ian said. "We're doing this here."

Tobe stretched to his full height, towering over Ian, a visual echo of the Idol. "Because why? This is my night, isn't it?"

3

The notepad shook in Ian's grip. Caitlin stepped between the two men. Sometimes she had to remind herself that Tobe really was an adult, that he was seven-and-a-bit years older than her. That this was his *second* shedding.

Tobe had wanted the ceremony to take place at a stone circle somewhere down south, after he'd seen it on a heavy metal album sleeve. He'd even gone to the trouble of buying a T-shirt with the band's logo printed on it. Caitlin knew for a fact that he was wearing it today, beneath his hoody.

"You know why," Ian replied.

Tobe's shoulders slumped. "It's not right, Janet still getting to call the shots."

"Don't, Tobe."

Tobe continued, "If my sister liked all this crap so much, why didn't she hang around long enough to be here? Some Charmer she turned out to be."

"She didn't have any say about that, did she?" Caitlin whispered. Tobe was always shooting his mouth off. It didn't mean anything.

"Dunno," Tobe replied. He stole a glance at Ian. "Maybe she did."

Caitlin grasped at her father's arm, a second too late.

"I warned you!" Ian hissed as he threw himself at his brother-in-law.

Ian Hext had never been a fighter. His first punch missed Tobe entirely; on the second, his hand tangled with the hood of Tobe's sweatshirt. The third made contact, though. Caitlin gasped as her dad's knuckles crunched into Tobe's right eye.

She pulled her father away. He stumbled, almost toppling on top of her.

Tobe staggered, too. The back of his head smacked against the Idol.

She half expected him to attack her father. Instead, Tobe looked as though he might cry. "I'm telling you," he said. "That's all. That's the last time I'm telling you."

Out of the corner of her eye, Caitlin noticed something moving on the path.

The woman was walking in fits and starts, alternately sprinting for a few seconds and then hobbling awkwardly. Her shoes crunched on the gravel; the sharp sounds echoed from the rock surfaces on either side of the track. Her unbuttoned jacket made dark wings behind her.

When she finally reached them she was almost breathless. "Toby Hext?" She turned from Ian to Tobe and back again.

Reluctantly, Tobe raised his hand, as though he were being asked a question in school, as though he was the sixteen-year-old rather than Caitlin. A red swell had already appeared beneath his right eye where Ian had hit him.

"Blaine," the woman said. At first Caitlin wondered if she was trying to clear her throat, until she extended her hand towards Tobe. "Ms Blaine. From the department."

Tobe shook her hand limply, then jammed both hands into his pockets.

"You didn't wait for me," Ms Blaine said.

"That's exactly what we were doing, right here," Ian said.

She glared at him, as though he ought not to be there at all. "I mean in town. You were supposed to give me a lift. I told you I don't drive. Why you people choose such out-of-the-way spots, I'll never know. I had to get a taxi and of course then there was this whole godforsaken park to tramp around before I—"

Caitlin glared at her. "What the hell do you mean, '*you people*'?"

"Cait," Ian said softly.

Caitlin wriggled, shrugging him off even though he hadn't put a hand on her. "No. Seriously. Ms Blaine? Explain to me what you meant by 'you people'. Right this minute."

Ms Blaine looked at each of the men in a silent appeal for help. Neither responded. "I— It's not that I—" Her face crumpled. "I apologise. I don't know why I said that. This is my first time."

With a touch of guilt, Caitlin realised that she was enjoying this sense of righteous anger. "Yeah, well you ought to know better. And I tell you now, when it comes to my turn to shed, I'll be making bloody clear that I don't want a Ms Blaine coming anywhere near me or my Skin. Understand?"

"Understand. Yes, I do." The woman shuddered. She turned her attention to the oversized handbag looped over her arm. She pulled out a clipboard with a single A4 sheet attached, though on the first attempt she dropped it through trembling fingers.

Ian checked his watch. "It's very nearly time."

Ms Blaine came to life again. "The regulations state a minimum of five metres. Mr Hext – may I call you Toby? Where would you most like to be?"

"In bed."

"No, I mean…"

6

"I know what you mean. I'll be over here." Tobe gestured towards the Idol. "You all piss off over there, on the path."

Ian pulled a bundle of dark green cloth from the rucksack. He held it out to Tobe. When Tobe didn't take it, Ian pressed it into his hands. Tobe pushed the fabric under his arm without unfolding it.

Ms Blaine's eyes were fixed on her clipboard. "There are a few housekeeping rules, of course. Have you eaten or drunk within the last hour? Have you relinquished all electronic devices? And, of course, you must remove your clothes before it begins."

Tobe brandished a crinkled chocolate bar wrapper and his brand-new pager. "You can fuck off if you think I'm going to do a strip show for you all."

"Oh! But you must—"

Caitlin pushed Ms Blaine backwards the few paces to the path, with more force than she had intended, and had to tug on the lapels of the woman's jacket to keep her from falling. Something about this whole situation was bringing out the worst in her.

"Ms Blaine," Ian said. "It's straightforward, it really is. I'm sure that most of those rules are only for reassurance. We've done this before and none of it matters. More to the point, there really isn't time."

Ms Blaine relented with a deep sigh. "Well, in that case it remains only for me to say—" She peered at the clipboard, raising it to her face.

"No you bloody well don't," Caitlin said. "Dad will take over from here, thanks all the same."

Ian nodded. His fingers slid along the edge of the crimson notebook and opened it at the page marked with a ribbon. He cleared his throat and began to read. "Toby Richard Hext, son of Colin and Juliet Hext, grandson of Ezra and Maria and before them Ingrid and Oscar. Then others, all the way back to Madeleine and David…"

"Faster," Ms Blaine whispered. She shivered and pulled her jacket tighter around her. Caitlin's mother would have tutted and told her she'd catch her death, coming out into the night dressed like that.

Ian glanced at his watch and nodded. His finger traced down the page, moving past chunks of notes. "On this, the fourteenth day of June of the year 2020, we witness this shedding of skin, and with it we honour this momentous event, this defining point in your life."

Caitlin turned her attention to Tobe. He stood inert beside the Idol, which seemed to totter in the shimmering moonlight. He still had his hands jammed into his pockets and Caitlin could hear his teeth chattering.

She realised that her dad was nearing the end of the speech. It hardly mattered that she had missed it, though. She'd be hearing it again before long.

"Any second," Ms Blaine said.

"Five," Ian said.

Tobe pulled himself upright, having slouched more and more during Ian's speech.

"Four… three…"

Ms Blaine pulled her clipboard close as if it might stop her shivering.

"Two."

Caitlin looked at her father, then at Tobe again.

"One."

Tobe cleared his throat. So did Ms Blaine.

Nothing happened.

And then it began.

All of a sudden, Tobe looked petrified. Was the shuddering part of the shedding? His pained expression made him look as though he was trying to keep his bladder in check.

A green light appeared behind him. No, not behind. Around. Caitlin had seen pictures and videos of sheddings before, but up close it was different. It reminded her of videos she'd seen of the Northern Lights. The green halo moved constantly, shifting and licking out from Tobe's body – not flames exactly, more like projected images of flames.

It lasted for about thirty seconds.

And then there he was.

There they were.

Tobe gazed out at them, then to his right to see what they were seeing. He cleared his throat again.

Beside him stood Tobe. Another Tobe, naked. Just like the first, this Tobe's rust-coloured hair was plastered down on one side, sticking up on the other. A red swelling made an island blotch under his right eye. Caitlin looked at the original Tobe. His injured eye was as good as new. The swelling had healed instantly.

The new Tobe – the Snakeskin – blinked several times. He shivered.

Caitlin felt suddenly ashamed at seeing his nakedness.

9

She shivered too. Abruptly, she recognised her own fear. Not fear of Tobe and his twin, but fear for herself, for her own future. She rubbed her eyes. *Grow up.*

One of the Snakeskin's hands darted downwards to cover his genitals. The other hand stretched out towards his twin.

The original Tobe didn't respond at first. He stared at his Skin, at the grasping fingers. Then he realised what the gesture meant. He passed the bundle of green cloth over, careful not to let his hand touch his twin's. The Skin let the cloth billow out in the wind, then pulled the thick green cape around his body. It covered his flesh from his neck almost to his toes. He kept shuffling from side to side. The ground beneath his feet was smooth, cold rock.

Tobe – the real Tobe, the 'originator' – pointed at his twin. His top lip curled, perhaps in disgust. "Can I talk to him?"

Caitlin reminded herself that Tobe had been seventeen the only other time he had shed, only slighter older than she was now. Seven years was a long time. For all his bravado, he must be terrified. Perhaps no Charmer ever got used to it.

It was Ian who answered. "If you want. There aren't any rules about that."

Out of the corner of her eye, Caitlin noticed Ms Blaine writing something on her clipboard form.

"All right?" Tobe said, addressing the Snakeskin.

The new Tobe looked a little shell-shocked. The licks of green halo carried on shimmering around him for a few moments more, before dissipating.

"Yeah," he said.

"You know what's happening? You know you're a Skin?"

"Yeah."

Caitlin hadn't considered beforehand what the Skin might say. It made sense that it might not be particularly interesting. She remembered a phrase from IT class about computer coding in BASIC: *Garbage in, garbage out.* Not that Uncle Tobe was garbage, but he had never been the sparkiest conversationalist either.

Caitlin edged forwards. Ian put his hand on her arm: no closer.

She felt a sudden determination. She couldn't let the moment pass without participating. Surely it was her right to ask a question. She was next in line.

The wind picked up again. Caitlin had to raise her voice to speak to the Skin. "Are you scared?"

"Yeah." The Skin gazed at her. Even at that distance, she saw something different there, something she had never seen before in Tobe's eyes. "Yeah," he said again. "I fucking am."

Ms Blaine checked her watch. Caitlin felt like hitting her, as her dad had hit Tobe.

Ian clucked his tongue, then turned his attention to the notebook. "We honour you," he said, his voice cracking a little. "And with your arrival we acknowledge this important milestone in the life of Toby Richard Hext. With your passing, he will learn and grow. You are the instrument of his maturation. We thank you."

He closed the book. Nobody said anything. The only sound Caitlin could hear was the chattering of teeth – the

Skin's, this time. Beside him, Tobe hugged himself tight, only sneaking quick looks at his twin.

"Any second now," Ms Blaine said.

The Skin looked down at his hands. The green halo reappeared, rippling around his fingers. The aurora snuck underneath the cloak, then reappeared at his neck.

Abruptly, the light disappeared. Caitlin squinted, forcing her eyes to adjust to the darkness.

"Oh shit," the Snakeskin said. "I don't—"

The cape dropped to the ground. It was almost too fast for Caitlin to process what had happened, exactly, but she was certain that it had started at his feet, then crept upwards. In her alarm, Caitlin fixated on a trivial detail: what was holding him up for those few seconds or milliseconds, when the lower part of his body had disappeared?

Then ash, or smoke, or perhaps skin cells, drifted away. It floated northwards away from the Idol.

Caitlin replayed the scene in her mind. It was impossible to be sure whether the Skin's face really had lasted longer than the rest of him, or whether it was only that the look in his eyes had imprinted on her retina. But she found that if she closed her eyes, she could still picture his expression with absolute clarity. The look on his face suggested that he felt no sense of acceptance about what was happening. Just terror.

After nearly a minute of silence, Ms Blaine said, "Right, then."

"Can we go now?" Tobe said.

Ian nodded. Caitlin followed the rest of the group along

the gravel track, past the looming rocks, back to the car.
Nobody said a word.

# TWO

Gerry Chafik fidgeted within the curves of the soft leather chair, trying to find a posture that was comfortable but that kept her feet on the floor. The chair seemed to have been designed to lull people into drowsiness. She hooked her ankles around the chair legs and perched on the tip of the seat. It hurt her calves, but that would keep her alert.

The door to the office crashed open. "Geraldine!"

Gerry scowled. The only people who called her Geraldine were those who didn't know her, or those who were trying to needle her. Zemma Finch had been her editor for eight years.

She stood, wiped her hand on her skirt and held it out. "Zemma. Good to see you. I can't believe it's taken me this long to visit the new place."

Zemma looked around, as if she too were seeing her surroundings for the first time. She was as immaculate as ever. Her honey-coloured hair fell in loose waves, a straight-from-the-salon appearance, like in the ads. Gerry resisted the urge to tug at her own tight braids.

"It'll do," Zemma said.

Beyond the glass wall of Zemma's corner office, heads bobbed in a sea of bulbous CRT screens and low partition walls. Most of these people were project managers and editorial assistants, Gerry knew. The real journalists were all out in the field. She snorted even as she thought the phrase. *In the field.* Out to pasture, more like.

Zemma sauntered to her desk. Behind it was a low counter, the walls decorated with a mosaic of computer keyboards. During her long wait, Gerry had checked that the keys really could be pressed. Zemma pushed the Enter key on one of the keyboards and a hidden door swung open. She retrieved a bottle of tonic and two glasses and placed them on the desk. Then she sat in an oversized armchair, more like a throne than an office chair. Gerry noticed for the first time that there was no desktop computer upon Zemma's vast desk. This was an office for displaying authority rather than for performing actual work.

Zemma poured tonic into the glasses. "I'd add gin, but it's rather…"

Gerry eased herself into her ludicrous chair. She nodded. Clearly the time of day wasn't an issue – Zemma's long delay in showing up meant that it was already well after five. Alcoholic drinks were reserved for more important people.

Zemma pushed a glass towards Gerry, leant back and steepled her fingers. Her manicured nails tapped together. "So."

Gerry took a breath. "So. Thanks for agreeing to this meeting, Zemma."

"It's always a pleasure. You're the wheels that keep this newspaper running. All of you are, I mean."

Gerry's buttocks tensed. She was in danger of slipping into the cup of the chair, at the precise moment she needed to remain in control.

"I need to know where I stand," she said.

Zemma arched an eyebrow. Her eyes flicked down to Gerry's chair.

"The takeover," Gerry continued, speaking more quickly. "The changes. It's all been far more profound than we were led to believe – more than just a new owner and a new tabloid format. I need to know… Is *Folk* still *Folk*, beneath the flashy new red-top banner? I need to know that we're still about news. It doesn't matter than it's given out for free at tube stations. It doesn't matter that it's rammed full of adverts. People still want news when they read a newspaper. Right?"

Zemma sipped her drink. "That's a lot of questions, Geraldine. Perhaps you should pick just one."

"I'll pick a different one, then. Where do I fit in?"

"I'd say… current affairs."

"That could be anything."

"Current affairs with a lifestyle hook."

"What does that even mean?" Gerry paused, then shook her head. "No. That's not my question, after all. My question is, why haven't my last five stories been printed anywhere in the newspaper? And the one before, the only one you've actually published since the Cormorant buyout, why did you bury it just before the sport?"

Zemma offered a sickening smile. "We don't care."

"You—" Gerry blinked. "You don't care? You, meaning Zemma Finch, or you, meaning *Folk*?"

"Neither. Both. I mean the readers, Geraldine. And I still class myself as one, an avid one, regardless of my exalted position. We readers simply don't care about the stories you've written."

Gerry leapt to her feet; her chair spun slowly across the carpet. She leant on Zemma's desk. Its marble surface was ice cold.

"Gerry," she hissed. "My name is Gerry."

Zemma's eyelashes fluttered in a display of surprise. Even so, she appeared more amused than alarmed.

"Our readers," she said in a slow voice, as though speaking to a child, "want short, sharp stories. For their dreary commute, you see. This isn't an issue of the takeover, or the new format. It's a matter of entertainment, Geraldine. *Gerry*."

"It's not supposed to be entertainment."

"It isn't? So it's supposed to be about the dry facts, is that right? That's all well and good, but put it this way: if there's a factual article in the woods and there's nobody there to read it…"

Gerry stared at her. She wished she had the nerve to hold her tongue, to force Zemma to complete the idiotic analogy. She lasted only a few seconds. "I've been doing important work. These are stories that people would read, if only you actually published them. More to the point, they're stories that people need to know about."

"You've become rather a specialist."

17

"That's what journalists do, Zemma. They find a subject and they follow it."

"Some might say obsessively."

Gerry gave an exasperated sigh. "We're talking about Snakeskins, Zemma. Charmers and Snakeskins. The most important and least understood development of the last two hundred years, eclipsing the Industrial Revolution, world peace, the founding of Great British Prosperity. It would be a crime not to investigate further, to try and comprehend. People want that."

"Oh, people want it, all right."

"I have a new report," Gerry said, aware that she was gabbling. "I wanted to bring it to you personally. A first-hand account by a Charmer. He talks about the psychological discomfort involved in shedding. Wait, that's not all. He's outraged by the levels of secrecy in Charmer society. He has family members in the Party, and if I could follow up on those leads… I swear, Zemma, people don't know a fraction of the ways in which Charmers wield power. We could serialise this thing for weeks."

Zemma opened a desk drawer and produced a purple cardboard folder. "It all sounds terribly conspiratorial. My assessment would be that this source of yours is overstating his hand in order to be noticed. As for the report you *have* written… it's simply the angle that you're getting wrong. This is 2020, not the Victorian era. People don't want dry 'accounts' of sheddings. I assume this source of yours is pretty average, is that right? Just a 'bloke', like you and me and our readers?"

Gerry's lips tightened. She nodded.

"Now *these* are what people want." Zemma opened the folder and spread a handful of documents across the gleaming surface of the desk.

They were photos. The images were almost entirely black, with only faint sources of light that illuminated the handful of figures. In the first photos the people were all in one corner, as if the photographer had been far away, or as if he or she hadn't known quite where to point the camera. The people were arranged in a semicircle.

Despite herself, Gerry bent closer. In each successive picture, the figures grew in size. The photographer must have been sneaking towards them, hidden in the darkness.

All but one of the figures had their backs to the camera. Gerry realised that she recognised the woman facing the camera, standing before a fire in an ornate iron brazier. Her build was slighter than the people around her. Her shoulder-length hair shone white.

"That's Rebecca Verne," Gerry said.

Zemma nodded.

"And she's a—"

Another nod.

"She turned fifty-two last week," Zemma said. "You'd never know it, would you?"

"Seriously? Rebecca Verne's a Charmer?" Gerry already felt foolish for caring. "How has she kept it secret all this time?"

"You know what that industry's like. Ever since she began as a Pinewood starlet – at a more advanced age than you might expect – she's been surrounded by an entourage, protected from the real world. Who's going to let on?"

Throughout Rebecca Verne's acting career, and despite her glamorous red carpet appearances at premieres and awards ceremonies, she had specialised in down-to-earth roles. She was loved for her empathy and her ability to hold a mirror to people in all strata of society. And all this time, she had been a Charmer. The British public would be outraged. But any sense of unfairness would be overwhelmed by fascination.

"It gets better," Zemma said. She pushed a few photos aside to reveal the ones at the bottom of the pile.

Now the photographer had reached a position close enough to be able to frame Rebecca Verne perfectly. She wore a long, loose, grey gown studded with pinpricks of bright white – probably sequins, but the effect was that it looked as though her own body were the source of illumination, rather than the fire. Her face was that of somebody half her age. There were no creases or any hint of looseness to the skin.

In the next photo Rebecca was looking up at the sky. Her mouth was open, perhaps in speech.

"Why did she do it outside?" Gerry wondered aloud.

"Basic hygiene, darling," Zemma replied. "All that dust."

Gerry glanced at the next picture. Now Rebecca's body really was glowing, but with a greenish light rather than the white of her sequins or the yellow of the fire. The photographer kept her framed within the left-hand side of the image. The right-hand side was empty and black.

Zemma pulled another photo from the pile.

Gerry couldn't stop herself from gasping.

Rebecca Verne stood beside Rebecca Verne. The originator still faced the sky. The newcomer looked to her right, at the first woman.

And, of course, the Snakeskin Rebecca was naked. Either she was unashamed, or she hadn't yet the presence of mind to care, but her arms hung at her sides, displaying a taut, pale body. She was beautiful. They were both beautiful.

In the next photo, one of the entourage had already placed a cape around the Snakeskin's shoulders. The cape still revealed a wide V of the Snakeskin's flesh, as though it were a designer gown.

"This is the one," Zemma said, pointing at the next image.

The man with the cloak had retreated again. Now the original Rebecca Verne, the Charmer, had turned to face the newcomer. They regarded each other levelly. Though one wore a shimmering gown and the other a plain black cape, in every other respect they were identical. Even their blond hair was styled in exactly the same manner. Gerry peered at the two faces. If there was a difference, it was in their expressions. The Charmer's nose tilted upwards very slightly, making her look a touch imperious. The Skin held her head fractionally further back, as if mid-flinch. It was only a faint hint, but she appeared afraid.

"Tomorrow's front page," Zemma said.

"Not that one, then?" Gerry pointed at the photo of the naked Rebecca.

"It's glorious, isn't it? But no. We couldn't afford the court battle. Never fear, the picture won't be wasted. Miss Verne will pay for that one herself."

Gerry pushed the front-page image to one side. In the next photo, the framing of the two Rebeccas had gone askew. By the next one, they were barely visible at the corner of the image. The photographer must have turned and run.

No matter how illicitly the photos had been gained, they were undeniably fascinating. Gerry hated herself for what she was about to say. "Zemma, if you want I could—"

Zemma shook her head. "We have all the details we need. The story writes itself, or at least a junior assistant will write it, which amounts to the same thing. Frankly, the photos speak for themselves."

Gerry scolded herself for the distraction. "So we're back to my first question, then. Where do I fit in, Zemma?"

The editor gazed up, her chair swaying slightly.

"I'm not going to beg," Gerry said, though she felt on the cusp of doing exactly that.

Zemma turned to look through the floor-to-ceiling window into the main office. Gerry suddenly realised what had been alien about the newsroom when she had passed through it earlier – the lack of phones ringing or any voices in discussion.

"I think I can answer the question myself," Gerry said.

Resisting a last look at the photos on Zemma's desk, she turned and left.

*

Despite his hurry, Russell Handler forced himself to walk at a steady pace, checking and rechecking the heavy box to ensure it didn't tip. He staggered past the stone steps

of the overgrown botanic gardens and across Magdalen
Bridge, which divided the town centre, with its ancient
college buildings emblazoned with Great British Prosperity
Party banners, from the grubby East Oxford suburbs. The
dawn sunlight skidded across the surface of the river and
through the gaps between the stone balustrades, blinding
him intermittently.

He scowled at an express supermarket. The shelves were
only half-full of stock, but even so the shop could have
provided equivalents of everything in the cardboard box
he was carrying. But his boss had his particular tastes.
Ellis insisted that Russell buy groceries from the St Giles
delicatessen in North Oxford – a shop that Ellis himself
passed on his journey to work each day. Still, perhaps it
was this kind of choosiness that marked somebody out as
suitable for the highest ranks of politics. Perhaps, if and
when Russell reached the higher levels of the GBP, he would
demand such things from his subordinates.

"Hey, chum!"

Russell saw the man lurch out of the doorway of a
boarded-up shop. Russell veered away, staggering with the
momentum produced by the heavy box.

"Anything in there for me, chum?"

The man hadn't blocked Russell's way, not quite. His
expression was good-natured enough and his dark stubble
emphasised his smile. Still, there was no telling whether
he might suddenly become dangerous. One of his front
teeth was missing. Beneath his duffel coat Russell glimpsed
a black shirt emblazoned with the red bull of the Morris

23

Motors logo. Perhaps the man had worked at the Cowley plant before he fell on hard times. Or perhaps he still worked there.

"It's just paperwork," Russell said. He shuddered involuntarily as something within the box clinked loudly. He thought of the six glass jars of chutney, the two bottles of freshly squeezed apple juice, the horrendously expensive jar of boiled sweets. He winced.

The man tilted his head to read the printed text on the box. "Says it's food. I'm proper hungry."

Might he attack Russell in public, in daylight? The side road that led to the office was only a hundred metres away. Not for the first time, Russell cursed Ellis for locating the office in East Oxford, with its early-morning drunks, its sick-puddle evidence of last night's debauchery. Reputable businesses tended to be in the town centre or Jericho. Closer to the deli.

The man studied his face. "Got a couple of quid, then?"

Russell shook his head.

"Fifty pee?"

"Look, I'm going to call for help if you don't leave me alone. All right?"

The man reached forward. When Russell jerked away, he held up his hands in surrender.

"Types like you shouldn't come here," the man said.

"I couldn't agree more."

The man scratched his beard. "What's your business, then?"

"Party. I mean, I'm a government employee."

"Shit. Really? GBP, round here? What the hell for?"

"We only moved in three months ago. It's a new department, still setting up. Redevelopment and Funding."

The man glanced at the faded newspaper pasted in the window of the abandoned premises beside them, then at the heaps of litter piled against the shopfront. Somebody had spray-painted onto a nearby wall the words *SKINS GO HOME* followed by a large upward-pointing arrow. He looked down at himself and seemed surprised at the filth on his jeans. "You going to help us, then? Fund us? We going to get some redevelopment round here?"

"No. I mean, yes. Not straight away. There are some greenfield sites, north of the city. And the retail park's going to be—"

"I get it," the man said. "It's not for us. I get it all, now, the way you're looking at me. It's not just that you're loaded, is it? You're one of them."

Russell felt his cheeks glow.

The man backed away. "Wouldn't have got up close and personal if I'd known. Okay?"

Russell didn't dare speak for fear of changing the man's opinion of him. The man's sense of deference was appropriate, of course – if he'd been correct. Russell felt guilty contentment at the thought of being assumed 'one of them'. He held his breath and pushed past.

Behind him, the man muttered, "Tight-arse. Fucking tight-arse Charmers."

By the time Russell reached the office complex on Marston Street, his fingers felt as though they might uncurl at any moment, spilling his precious cargo onto the filthy pavement. He balanced the box on his knee to fish out his ID pass.

The door to the complex burst open before he reached it.

Russell's fall felt like slow motion; he managed to half-support the box all the way to the ground. A snap of glass accompanied its landing. Something wet seeped through the cardboard and into Russell's cupped hands.

A woman backed out of the building. She wore a smart grey suit, though her hair was unkempt. She didn't acknowledge Russell sprawled on the floor.

"I know your name, you know!" she shouted at somebody inside the building. Russell saw the office security guard standing behind his counter. He looked distraught.

The woman didn't let the security guard interrupt. "If he's having an affair, and if I find out you've been covering for him, you're done for. So just think about that the next time you tackle a woman from behind."

She turned and finally saw Russell. Her freckled face now showed only curiosity. She hesitated – and in the moment their eyes were fixed on one another Russell lost all sense of the passing of time – and then she simply stepped over the leaking box and its growing puddle of juice. As she walked towards the gated exit, her walk slowed from an angry stride to a stroll.

Gingerly, Russell lifted one of the flaps of the cardboard box. Apple juice sloshed around inside and one corner of the box had turned black with oil from a cracked jar of chutney. He heaved himself to his feet and opened the door.

"Mrs Blackwood, I—" the security guard began, before he realised that it was Russell. "Oh, it's you. Sorry."

Russell glanced out into the car park. "That was Minister Blackwood's wife?"

The security guard said sheepishly, "Rules are rules. Nobody without access rights preloaded onto their ID gets in."

"She can't visit her own husband at work?"

The guard shrugged. "She didn't even say she wanted to. Said she was organising a kid's party." He pointed towards the nearest door within the office complex. There was no business name on the door, only a faint photocopied picture of three balloons. "But rules are rules, especially if it means sneaking past me when I'm busy." His eyes flicked down to the counter. Russell saw the corner of a newspaper page filled with tiny print – the racing results.

They stood in awkward silence for a moment. Russell had never known how to talk to working-class people, despite having been brought up by honest, proletarian parents. He coughed. "There's a bit of a mess out there. A box. Could you bring it into Minister Blackwood's office? Any time that's convenient to you. Although, actually, he'll want it quite soon."

Without waiting for the guard's response, Russell strode inside. He glanced again at the door to the children's party suppliers. Until now, he had never really paid much attention to the other businesses in the shared office complex, though when he had been hired three months ago he had been surprised that any government department might need to share a building at all. He studied each door as he passed: a freelance photographer, a small historical publisher, a banner-printing service, three separate accountants. The door marked *Redevelopment and Funding* was at the end. He shoved it open, making the smoked-glass door rattle.

The minister refused to allow entry to the cleaner who serviced the rest of the building, so Russell's first task of each day was to rescue crockery from Ellis's study, a room of generous proportions that jutted into the far smaller main office area. Russell pushed open the door to the study. Inside, something on the wide wooden desk spasmed.

Ellis Blackwood lifted his head from the desk. His hair was ordinarily untidy but today it was wild, with the frontmost curls glued to his forehead. His grey suit was crumpled. There was still grandeur about him, though whether it was only his status – both as a Charmer and a member of the Party – Russell couldn't tell. A few months ago Russell had come across some meeting minutes that referred to him and the minister together as 'Russellis', a compound nickname that he had never heard repeated but which continued to fill him with secret pride.

"Russell," the minister said, his voice cracking. "Does this mean that it's morning?"

"Six forty-five," Russell said, without needing to check the clock. He was nothing if not punctual.

"Then I've missed my chance to sleep."

"I wasn't expecting you so early, sir. It's not normally how things are."

Ellis smiled. "You're rather a stickler, aren't you?"

"That's my job, sir." Russell began gathering coffee cups and plates from the desk. "Your groceries will be here in a moment. I could bring you some muesli?"

Ellis hesitated, glanced over Russell's shoulder at the door, then waved a hand. "No, no. Nell goes in for all that stuff, not me. Do you know what I'd really like? A bacon sarnie, from the greasy spoon. Five doors down. Perhaps after we discuss the diary you could fetch me one."

Russell's nails dug into his palms. Each day that passed, he was less a personal assistant and more a delivery boy. His mother had been so proud when he had told her about his new government role. "Of course, Minister."

"And might there be a fresh suit somewhere within this cavernous space?"

Russell sidestepped past the desk and slid open the wardrobe door that Ellis had had installed. Six identical grey suits hung beside shelves of neatly folded shirts.

"You're a wonder, Russell," Ellis said, beaming, as he retrieved the change of clothes. "Now give me two minutes and we'll proceed."

More than fifteen minutes later – and still without a cup of coffee, though he had provided Ellis with his – Russell wheeled his swivel chair into the minister's office and sat with his knees touching the desk. Ellis had removed his crumpled jacket but had then either forgotten about or decided against replacing his suit.

"Your first is an eleven o'clock," Russell began, turning the diary sideways for Ellis to see. "The opening of the new hospital in Bicester. I've booked the driver for ten-thirty and he'll wait to bring you back again at eleven-fifteen."

Ellis rolled his eyes.

"And then your only other appointment is at three. At the Randolph again."

"Lovely. Who with?"

"I'm sorry, Minister. I wasn't informed." Russell pointed to the faint question mark he had drawn beside the appointment booking.

"Ah. Good."

"Good, sir?"

"Three o'clock is good, I mean. We'll be offered afternoon tea. The Randolph lays on a certain level of spread. You really must try it."

Russell looked up. Did Ellis really imagine that a personal assistant's salary would allow him to eat at the Randolph whenever he felt like it? Perhaps one day, though, if he played his cards right.

Ellis had stopped paying attention. He stared above Russell's head.

"Sir?"

Ellis blinked as though waking from a dream. "Goodness. Look at me. I may fall asleep even whilst holding the giant scissors. At the hospital opening, I mean."

Russell cleared his throat. "Ah. I'm afraid they've not asked you to actually conduct the opening, Minister. I believe it's due to be a local celebrity, a young man. He won a talent show on TV. Say anything to him, and he can repeat it instantly, backwards. To music. The organisers felt that—"

Ellis nodded sagely. "That a fuddy-duddy Party minister

wouldn't be a glamorous enough attraction. I understand. Who can compete with the spectacle of a spotty teenager speaking backwards?"

Russell paused before nodding. That wasn't quite the reason, he suspected. The organisers hadn't said it out loud, but it had been clear enough that they didn't want a Charmer to formally open the hospital. They had only grudgingly agreed that Ellis should be named publicly as the minister responsible for locating the funds for the project.

Ellis's head bowed. His eyes closed before he jolted upright again.

"Sir?"

Ellis stared at him stupidly.

"Do you need more coffee, sir?"

Ellis's mouth twitched. "Don't believe everything you hear about us, Russell. Charmers need to sleep as much as the next man. And I'm rather lacking in the sleep department, these days. The mind plays tricks." He nodded slowly, as if that explained everything.

In the silence that followed, Russell felt more awkward than ever. He had no idea what might be the appropriate response.

Abruptly, Ellis leapt to his feet. "D'you know what? I think I'll make that trip to the greasy spoon myself. And then perhaps a stroll to South Park. You can hold the fort." He beamed. "Russell Handler, handling things with aplomb. I rather like that."

Without pulling on his jacket, he strode to the smoked-glass door and into the corridor. Moments later, Russell heard the minister's muffled voice. Russell dashed to the doorway, gripped by a sudden anxiety that the security guard might be complaining about his impertinence regarding the groceries. The security guard stood at the end of the corridor, facing the exit. Ellis was nowhere to be seen.

Russell sighed. None of this was what he had expected when he had taken the job. Not yet thirty, and the right-hand man of a Great British Prosperity Party minister! For a long time he had held off telling his mother that the job wouldn't be located in Westminster, but rather Oxford, or that he wouldn't be working in a formal office, but instead this tiny room in a rented complex. In part, this was because he didn't understand the reasons himself. His mother had been no less impressed when the truth was out, though. Compared to her work as a seamstress, and his father's work on a production line at a factory producing components for radio sets, Russell's current lifestyle was unimaginably high-flying. Furthermore, the unstated truth was that, unlike them, he would be unlikely to be forced to continue working into his seventies.

He downed Ellis's untouched cup of coffee. The trill of a phone made him splutter liquid back into the cup.

He grabbed the diary out of habit and ran back to his desk, then stopped himself moments before he attempted to sit on the missing chair, which was still in Ellis's study. He crouched awkwardly to answer the phone. "Ellis Blackwood, Minister for Redevelopment and Funding." He coughed. Some of the coffee must have gone down the wrong way.

"Russell Handler?"

"Sorry, yes. I normally say that. 'Russell Handler speaking' is what I say."

"Are you alone?"

The voice sounded familiar, though the line was bad.

"Minister?" Russell said. "Is that you? Are you in the greasy spoon?"

The line went silent for a moment. "The minister is not present?"

"I'm afraid he's popped out. A morning meeting." He paused. "In a local establishment."

"Listen to me, Russell." The voice was deep and the poor line made it flat, like the compressed sound of old home videos. "I need to tell you something. And I need you to tell me something."

"I'm sorry. If you're from the *Daily Counsel*, then there are proper channels. Who's speaking, please?"

"Somebody who knows a great deal more than you."

Almost everybody knew more than Russell knew. It might as well be part of the job description.

"You may call me Ixion," the voice continued. "I am in a position close to the heart of government. I and my colleagues have observed something occurring. And it is not something good."

"Why are you calling me?"

"Ellis Blackwood cannot be trusted. You control the minister's diary. You are best placed to monitor his actions and you alone can identify unusual behaviour, unusual appointments. You are vital, Russell. It must be you."

Russell had no idea how to end the call. "Look, if this is

something to do with the minister being a Charmer, that's all public record. There are no secrets—"

"You're wrong. There are secrets. The Party is on the verge of disintegration, and Ellis Blackwood will play a key role. Mark this: you will not be rewarded for assisting him."

Russell noted the implication that, if he collaborated with 'Ixion' and his colleagues, a reward would be in the offing.

"I'm going to hang up," he said hurriedly.

"Let me explain—"

"This is a crank call. I'm hanging up."

"We must meet."

"Absolutely not."

"I will contact you again."

"Please don't."

Russell jammed the receiver onto its cradle. His hands were shaking.

He looked down at the question mark drawn in Ellis's diary.

# THREE

Evie toppled inside Ivy Cottage the moment Caitlin opened the front door. She must have been pressing on it with her full weight, eager to be let in. In her text message, Caitlin had demanded that Evie come as soon as possible, but that was less than ten minutes ago – a new record. Evie's elder brother's canary-yellow Mini was parked askew on the driveway, its front wheels in the flower bed.

Evie planted a wet kiss on her cheek. "My darling! I've so missed you!"

Caitlin pushed her away, laughing. Evie always knew when to go over the top.

Evie kicked the door shut with her heel. "You look crappy."

Instinctively, Caitlin put her hand up to tug at her red hair. Evie's was almost black, and cropped short – a style that Caitlin would adopt herself if she had the nerve.

Evie rolled her eyes. "You're ravishing as usual, you flame-haired goddess. I'm talking about *this*." She drew a circle with her finger, encompassing Caitlin's face. "You're proper mardy this morning. What gives?"

Caitlin shrugged. She wished she knew. She hadn't exactly cried herself to sleep last night, but she'd come close. She hadn't been this despondent since she was a kid. At sixteen, surely that sort of thing should be behind her?

"So this is about a guy?" Evie stood on tiptoes to peer around Caitlin and into the dark hallway.

"I've sworn off men."

Evie snorted. "You've said that a thousand times. I'm not talking about a conquest, anyway. I'm talking about your uncle. Let me at him."

"Why would you want to talk to Tobe?"

"Bloody hell, you're a dope sometimes. Fine. I'll find him myself."

Evie pushed past and prowled along the hallway, peering into each doorway. Not for the first time, Caitlin felt a twinge of embarrassment about the size of the house. In theory it was a cottage, but over the generations her ancestors had added wings to both sides and to the rear, the original building a tree trunk with rooms sprouting from it like branches. She supposed that the increased longevity as a result of the Hexts' Charmer abilities meant that more family members had to be housed here, once upon a time. Not now. She couldn't remember the last time anyone had used any of the ground-floor rooms along this hallway. The largest sitting room, at the eastern end of the house, was now permanently dark and used only to house her dad's telescope, which was fixed pointing out of the bay windows that overlooked the fields behind the house.

"Aha!" Evie cried as she pushed open the door to the

kitchen. Orange light bloomed to illuminate the hallway, turning its parquet flooring into a mesh of glittering gold.

Caitlin's dad and uncle turned to face them. Tobe sat at the wide farmhouse table, nursing a cup of coffee, while Ian busied himself at the small electric oven, despite the fact that the enormous Aga alongside it was already belching out heat. He had never got to grips with using the Aga for anything other than heating the house. Caitlin's mum had always been the more enthusiastic cook.

"If you're making pancakes, Ian?" Evie called out.

Ian bowed. "Certainly, your ladyship. You too, Cait?"

Caitlin shook her head. She tugged on Evie's leather jacket. Evie was supposed to be here to give her support, let her moan a bit, not to hang out with her family. Evie brushed her away and took the seat opposite Tobe, who watched her warily. He rubbed at the skin under his right eye, even though there had been no evidence of a bruise since his rejuvenation at the shedding.

"So," Evie said, thumping her elbows on the tabletop, "tell me everything."

Tobe swigged his coffee and shrugged.

"Come on, Evie," Caitlin whispered. "Come upstairs. I'm not going to say please."

Evie ignored her. She kept her eyes on Tobe. "How long did he last?"

"Who?" Tobe replied after a pause.

"The Snakeskin, genius."

Tobe waved his cup vaguely. "Not long."

"Was it more or less than the last time around?"

"Dunno. About the same."

Caitlin's dad had been bending before the oven, trying to decipher the numerals on the dials. Now he stood and turned. "I don't think so, Tobe. I reckon it was about half the time. Thirty seconds, if that."

Tobe shot a look at Ian's back.

Evie giggled. "You know what they say about the length of a Charmer's Skin."

"What do they say?" Tobe said, scowling.

Evie pushed back her chair and tilted her head to look at Tobe beneath the table. "You know, the shorter the Skin lasts, the shorter the—"

"Evie!" Caitlin hissed.

Evie held up both hands in surrender. Tobe looked at the door, maybe judging his ability to escape. These days, he spent most of his time in the oversized garden shed at the foot of the garden, with his Commodore 64 games and his porn mags. He'd never been a people person.

With a sigh, Caitlin slumped down in her chair. Ian placed a cup of coffee before her. He squeezed her shoulders and then retreated to the stove.

Evie leant forward. "Did it hurt?"

Tobe shook his head.

"Not a tickle?"

Another shake.

"How about in here?" Evie put a hand over her heart.

Tobe stared at her breasts.

Evie gave Ian a thumbs-up as he passed her a cup of coffee. "You know what, Tobester? You're going to be a big help when it's Cait's turn. Your support and understanding will mean a ton to her."

Caitlin stiffened.

Ian swore at the frying pan, which had begun to spit oil. He called over his shoulder, "We don't need to talk about that yet. Don't rush her, Evie."

Evie glanced at Caitlin. "It's only like four days from now."

"The paperwork's all sorted," Caitlin said. "There's nothing I need to do but wait."

"Paperwork's hardly the issue here. I'm talking about making yourself ready. I might be charmless, so to speak, but I know sheddings are a big deal. And your first one? You're not going to tell me that you're not fretting about it. I've seen those self-portrait sketches you've been doing up in your room, Cait. It's been on your mind for months."

Caitlin blushed furiously. As usual, Evie had read her immediately. It was true that her bad mood was directly linked to Tobe's shedding yesterday evening, and to her own shedding too. But Evie had got one thing wrong: her seventeenth birthday – and therefore her first shedding – was only three days from now and counting.

"I'm not worried," she said, trying to hide the quaver in her voice. "Shedding's no big deal. If my whole family can do it, so can I." She glanced over at her dad, who continued pouring batter into the frying pan. "Sorry, Dad. You know what I mean."

He turned. "It's all right." He flipped the pancake high and caught it in a single smooth motion. He looked absurdly pleased with the achievement. "We all have our skills. Not everyone needs to be a Charmer." He slipped the pancake onto a plate and handed it to Caitlin. "And you know your mother would be feeling so proud of you right now."

Caitlin thought of her mum's handwriting in the crimson notepad. In a faraway voice she said, "My earliest memory of Mum is of her telling me about Hexts going all the way back. Just names, but it was her tone of voice that I remember. I must have been only about five or six. She was trying to hold it together but I swear she was crying. I guess being from a line of Charmers was the most important thing in the world to her."

Ian shook his head. "Important, yes. The most important thing in the world? Not even close."

His eyes were glistening. Caitlin bit her lip and wished that Evie and Tobe weren't there.

Tobe yawned noisily. "She's right, Ian. Janet played it down for your sake. You should have seen her at uni, before she met you. Charmer rights were all she talked about. Bloody shame how it all turned out."

Caitlin caught her dad's eye. She shook her head.

Nevertheless, Ian rose to the bait. "Tobe. You've had enough warnings. Don't go making insinuations."

"Oh, I'll insinuate all I like." Tobe pushed back his chair. He rubbed at his healed eye. "And I'll be ready for you if you try to sucker punch me again. You hear?"

The two men looked ridiculous, glowering at each other with the full length of the kitchen table keeping them apart. Evie started a slow handclap, until Caitlin froze her with a look.

"I'm just saying," Tobe grumbled, "Janet was a live wire until she lowered her standards. And now she's not a live anything. No offence." He patted his pockets, picked up his pager, nodded and plodded through the back door, as if no argument had taken place.

Caitlin could always tell when her dad was rattled. He turned to the kitchen window and gazed at the field behind the house, where blue tarpaulins marked the site of the proposed Blenheim retail park development. Her dad's and her uncle's relationship had been icy since Caitlin's mum died, but it had never boiled over into anger before. Things were changing. She realised that her hands were balled into fists.

Evie let out a low whistle. "You know what? It should be a party."

Caitlin nodded.

"For your mum," Evie continued. "And for the others. You owe it to the rest of you to make a big thing of it."

Caitlin glared at her. *The rest of you.* She'd had a few comments like that at college, too. More and more, the closer she got to the shedding, her friends had actually started referring to her in passing as a Charmer, first and foremost. There was no escaping the fact that her life was inevitably going to end up on a different track to theirs. She was a different breed.

"We're *people*, Evie, not another species, or aliens, or whatever." Abruptly, everything seemed desperately unfair, this pressure of expectation that built up more every day. Evie and her other friends at college could never understand.

"Don't you fucking dare start making it all 'us and them', Evie. I won't stand for it." The last part was something her mum might have said, which only made her feel worse.

"Cait!" her father snapped. "We don't use that kind of language here. All right?"

Caitlin gritted her teeth. The phrase 'us and them' repeated in her mind. If it *was* 'us and them', then the only person she really had on her team was her uncle. The thought made her feel sick.

"Well, we fucking well should use that kind of language," Caitlin said. She ignored her dad's look of dismay. "We're dying out and it sure as hell isn't our fault. So, Evie, you can take your snooping and your Charmer-wannabe curiosity and you can shove it up your arsehole. I'm the way I am and I'm stuck with it—" she tugged at her ginger hair "—and I'll deal with it the way I need to."

She pushed away her uneaten pancake, rose and stormed to the door. She turned before leaving.

"But you're right about one thing. I'm going to have the mother of all shedding ceremonies. I'm proud of who I am. And I'm going to make sure nobody can ignore it."

\*

Gerry rested her chin on her folded arms and let out a deep groan. A couple of the other pub customers looked her way, but only for a moment. Each of them was sitting in a separate snug. Anyone who drank alone at five-thirty on a Tuesday afternoon had plenty on their mind already.

"This seat taken, miss?"

Without looking up, Gerry freed her right arm and swept it across the beer-puddled table to indicate the seat opposite.

"I think I know why you invited me here," the voice continued. "You realise you adore me and you want me back. Am I close?"

Gerry raised her head and managed a weak smile. "Thanks for coming, Drew."

"Always on call."

She looked up. Drew was dishevelled, as always. His stubble never quite became a beard. He had let himself go a little – maybe working from home just did that to people – and his neck had thickened. His dense mass of curls gave him a dark halo. Seeing him made her feel instantly better.

"So," Drew said.

"So." She sucked in a deep breath. "So it's finally over. I'm out. Gerry Chafik and *Folk* no longer enjoy a professional relationship."

Drew snorted. "I'd say that ship sailed months ago. Still, I'm sorry, Gerry. Is that the right response? Or should I be congratulating you?"

Gerry chewed her lip. Part of her did feel a little happier for having at least clarified the situation with Zemma. Deep down, she had known that this would happen, sooner or later.

Drew pointed at the drinks on the table. "Using my powers of deduction, I'd say that a pint of bitter and a – what? – coffee liqueur doesn't signify a celebratory mood."

Gerry sat upright and downed the liqueur in two gulps. "That one doesn't count. I thought it might help with the

43

heartburn that strip-lit sweatshop of an office gave me."

"I always said the trick was to keep as far away from any workplace as humanly possible. That, and being so inoffensive as to be impossible to sack."

"It's all right for you. *Folk* will always need a cartoonist. Good career move."

"Yeah. Well, no. I was a crappy journalist, Gerry. You knew it, our first editor – McKendrick? – knew it. Anyone could see it. And I'm not much of a cartoonist either, especially now. Zemma would be happier with illustrated 'knock, knock' jokes than anything that threatens to appear satirical."

"It's true," Gerry said. "You were crappy." She reached across the table and squeezed his hand.

Drew sipped his pint of Guinness. "So who was it who pulled the trigger in the end?"

"Me." She paused. "Zemma. Oh, who the hell knows."

"And it was about…" He held up a hand. "No, let me guess. Snakeskins."

Gerry exhaled and nodded. "I'm that predictable?"

"Some people would say so, but not me. This is what I'm talking about, Gerry. I was crappy because I never cared all that much. I don't have the fire in me. I'm happier watching soaps than the ten o'clock news, and my main research tool for my cartoons is what I overhear at the bus stop outside my bathroom window. You, on the other hand, you can't let it lie. In most professions that's a liability, but in journalism it's a necessity. You're tenacious. You're a bulldog."

Gerry pulled a screwed-up face. "Firstly, if you ever wondered why we never lasted longer than two one-night stands, then you could do worse than analysing that statement. A bulldog? Cheers. Secondly, in what way is my tenacity not a liability, given that it just lost me the only regular work I've ever had?"

"Fair point. But don't beat yourself up. You don't want to be working for Cormorant."

"Ah, the mysterious Cormorant."

"Mysterious? Depends who you talk to. The word is that it's a government proxy, and not all that well disguised." Drew finished his pint and shuffled sideways along the bolted-down table. "I'll get a round in. I've got some catching up to do."

Gerry groaned. That would explain a lot. So *Folk* would simply become the tabloid equivalent of the *Daily Counsel*, another mouthpiece for Party-approved information. No wonder Zemma was so incurious about the machinations of Charmers in the government. The GBP would tolerate the front-page images of sheddings – it would be fruitless to try and stifle interest in Charmers entirely – but would itself remain immune to scrutiny.

Drew returned and slumped into his seat, slamming down two fresh pints and producing twin fountains of froth. "Right. If you'd like to recline on the couch, then we can begin today's session."

With a sigh, and after another slurp of bitter, Gerry spun and lay down on the bench.

Drew's voice continued from above. "So, how long have

you been experiencing this fixation?"

"Sod off."

"I'm serious. The first of those one-night stands, when I first saw inside your flat? I was a bit taken aback by the books on your shelves. I figured you must be a Charmer yourself."

"I'm just interested. It's interesting."

"Answer the question please, Miss Chafik."

Gerry huffed theatrically. "All right. You've got me. Since I was a kid. I mean, everyone's been fixated on Charmers at some point or other in their life, right? The concept, at least. There was this cartoon on LWT—" She swivelled and sat up again. "What was it called? *Champions of Eternity*, something like that. Ever see it?"

"Didn't have a TV. Principled parents."

"Poor sod. That probably explains your current addiction to VHS box sets. Anyway, these Champions of Eternity were superheroes, doing good, the usual. Except they lived nearly forever, and each episode would follow one or two of them – there were hundreds by the end – through different eras. Helping a single family across the generations, or guiding far-flung nations through wars and out again. That sort of thing. It was pretty thinly veiled. I looked into it a few years ago, and of course the lead writer was a Charmer. It was propaganda, though hardly what you'd call corrosive, but it was the best they could do in those days when Charmers and Snakeskins were something you just didn't discuss on TV."

"Yeah. I preferred those days, all things considered."

Gerry leant forwards. "But don't you see? We're right

back there again. Except now everything's theoretically 'out in the open', yet nobody's talking about Charmers, not in any meaningful way. You can interpret that in one of two ways. Maybe everybody got sick of hearing about them as soon as we hit the twenty-first century, sick of the chat-show confessions, sick of the equal-rights campaigns, sick of the dawning realisation that not only were Charmers real, they were basically running the whole bloody country. What proportion of the Great British Prosperity Party are Charmers? Three-quarters? More? All of them?" She took a gulp of her drink. "Or alternatively, nowadays people are being affected in more subtle ways. Investigations suppressed, communication prevented, no access to the technology that I swear must be out there somewhere. And the ban on mass gatherings is a huge deal, Drew. If you're right about Cormorant, it only goes to show the hypocrisy. I mean, what's the use of a theoretically free press if the free press is owned by the government? Capitalism is doing the dirty work of a totalitarian government that prefers to keep its head down."

"And you think people shouldn't be tired of hearing about Charmers and Skins?"

"I think both are endlessly fascinating. And yes, like all bores, I think that everyone else ought to be as fascinated as I am."

"And you always wished you were one. A Charmer." It wasn't even a question.

Gerry puffed out her cheeks. "Who doesn't wish that?"

"It's more than that, though. Everyone wishes they could

win the lottery, but not as many people spend every penny of their wages on scratch cards."

"You think that's what I'm doing? That I'm trying to capture some dream by chasing the story, as if that'd make me the same as them somehow? It doesn't make any sense."

Drew leant back and put his index fingers to his lips. "I'm not here to judge. I'm here to listen."

"Oh, piss right off, Drew. It's important. Somebody has to report what's actually happening. Take the Party truism about Britain inspiring a global peacetime of a hundred and fifty years. It's utter, utter bollocks. Sure, there might have been no wars right here on our soil – nobody would ever get past the coastal defences. But there have been wars, and I mean big ones."

"Is this the point where you trot out the urban myth about the European war?"

She glared at him. "I happen to think it's not a myth and that 'European war' might even be underselling it. Call me a conspiracy nut if you like. Anyway, there's the odd source that has an inkling about the world beyond the British Isles. Non-Charmer pilots who occasionally take ministers out of the country on jaunts, that sort of thing. And they won't talk, but you still end up with hints of what's out there. And those hints are the truth, because otherwise why would I have faced prison time for chasing sources with access to Europe or America? Anyway, the common denominator is the suggestion that there are dozens of conflicts going on *right now*. There is no world peace. It's only here in Britain – and even that's a mirage entirely dependent on the total suppression of civil unrest every couple of decades. The reality is simply that Britain is isolated from the world. Who knows what everyday life is like in other countries, what kinds of developments they've achieved while we've been navel-gazing? But of course we have our Charmers and we're not letting them or anyone else out of the country, for fear of… what? Losing some competitive advantage? Utter bullshit. The Charmers in power are afraid, that's all. And they're letting the world pass us all by in their determination not to lose that power. The *Counsel* likes to bang on about Britain being the 'policeman of the world', but I bet you anything it's a lie. This idea of British naval fleets squatting off the coasts of foreign countries, maintaining the peace… all lies. We're being left alone not because we're powerful, but because we're irrelevant."

She gazed up at the nicotine-yellow ceiling. "I just think that Charmers need to be made public, that's all. No group should be allowed to hold such sway over society without being called to account. Or at least, without being visible."

Drew abandoned his neutral expression. "They're not some shadowy cabal, Gerry. They're just not. You're deliberately conflating Charmers and the Party to suit your own ideology. My brother-in-law's a Charmer. There was a bit of trouble when they got married, and it had to be a pretty functional wedding, just the two of them, but Theo is— well, he's all right. Oh, that reminds me that I didn't have a chance to tell you: my sister's pregnant. She'll finish up her producer role at *Rise and Shine* in September, then she's due in October. I'm going to be the uncle to a little

Charmer baby boy. There's nothing sinister. They're just people. People with a few tricks up their sleeves, I grant you, but who can begrudge a kid a better start in life?"

Gerry watched him for a moment, then let her head drop into her hands. "Point taken."

"I'm known for my insight. That's why 'Drawn by Drew' is hotly anticipated every day by as many as three *Folk* readers."

"So I'll give it up. Stick to dietary advice columns and gossip."

"Don't be melodramatic. You haven't got the acting chops for it."

"I'm serious. Zemma wants entertainment."

"You know you can't go back there, not now."

"The rest are all the same."

"Shall I change hats? From therapist to job opportunities adviser?"

Gerry shrugged.

"Don't give up. That's my advice. I know you're not overflowing with cash, but I also know you've been saving, and I *also* know you're incapable of taking a holiday and you have no interest in the usual metrics and milestones of progress that other people crave. So given that you're never going to be able to afford to buy a house and you don't enjoy travelling for the sake of it, then use that money for something you actually care about."

"I could buy a gun."

"Seriously, stop. You're no good at being self-involved. Use the money to buy you time. Follow the story. Follow the Charmers and the Snakeskins and see where it all leads. Without the shackles of a disapproving editor, you'll be freer. And when you've put the story together, they'll all be battering down your door to print it, or even to serialise the bestselling book."

Gerry blinked, less from surprise and more to stop tears coming to her eyes. She gripped Drew's hand in both of hers, squeezing his fleshy fingers tight. "You know, we really should've made it work, you and me."

Drew smiled and shook his head. "Much as I wanted it, no. If we'd had a relationship we'd have lasted six months, maybe a year or even two, and then I'd have been so reasonable and you so unreasonable throughout, it'd all have gone to pot and then we'd have been reluctant exchangers of Christmas cards and nothing more. I prefer this. I prefer actually knowing you, Gerry. For keeps."

Gerry wiped her eyes on the sleeve of her jacket. "You're right, as always. About everything. But I—"

Drew held up a hand. "That's where my advice ends. I'm not going to tell you how to do your job."

"But I think I'm up against a dead end. I've been chasing Charmer confessions, mainly, but it's only the oddballs who'll talk, and by that I mean Charmers who, for whatever reason, don't have wealth or power. Any Charmers that might have interesting stories to tell keep shtum."

"So don't try and talk to them."

"But you just said—"

Drew rolled his eyes. "You really are off form. All right. One more piece of advice, though it's nothing I'd claim credit for. I might have forgotten pretty much everything I learnt during my glory days of journalism, in the mentor programme. But I do remember the one simple piece of advice old McKendrick gave us, every bloody day. 'When you hit a dead end…'"

Gerry beamed. She stood, downed her drink, then planted a beery kiss on Drew's cheek.

"Go back to the source."

\*

Caitlin munched on the remainder of her baked potato and watched Evie stretch and yawn. The food was already long cold – the two of them had been putting the world to rights for the entire lunch break. The canteen was almost empty and most of the students were outside in the common area between the rows of college classrooms. The hum of their chatter was loud enough for Caitlin and Evie to have to raise their voices to be heard, even here, inside. It had rained for pretty much the last week and the appearance of the sun had energised everyone.

Evie made pistol shapes with her fingers, pointing at Caitlin. "Got it! Do it at the town hall. Smack bang in Oxford centre. We could hand out fliers beforehand, get passers-by to come in. And then inside it'd be all formal and flashy at the same time, like a wedding. We'd give everyone top hats and bouquets at the door. No. One bouquet for you and then— Ooh, ooh! No, two! One bouquet for you and one for your Skin. The moment she shows up, we give her the second bouquet and you both throw them up as though you're two brides, but without any need for a groom, obviously."

As Caitlin considered this she traced a finger along the doodles on her science folder. Ringed planets, meteors and constellations of stars drawn in silver marker pen made its cover shine with reflections of the canteen strip lights. "And what does all that actually mean?"

"Mean? What do you mean, 'mean'?"

"Well, it's not a wedding, is it? My Skin'll be there for a minute, then she'll disappear in a puff of smoke. It's more like Cinderella at the ball than any wedding."

Evie waved a hand dismissively. "Details. It's all about the spectacle, Cait."

Caitlin tapped her fork on her chin. "No. You've got part of it right. The in-your-face-ness of it. But it shouldn't be formal. That's what they want us to do – the Party."

"What party? Will there be a party?"

"The Great British Prosperity Party, dummy. The government. My dad's been ploughing through the book of rules and regulations they sent us, and it's as thick as your arm."

"Oi. No digs about my weight."

"Don't be a dick. I'm saying that they love the idea of us getting buried under formality. It gets rid of the magic of the whole thing. Tobe's shedding might have been a marvel of the natural world... but to be honest, it was as if he was doing a blood test or something. The government lady killed the fun. You know that tone that nurses have? All bored and seen-it-all-before?"

"So don't invite her. Them."

"Obviously. That's for starters. But I swear I'm not going to hide away in the town hall either. That way, only people who want to see the shedding would actually see it. The important thing is showing the people who *don't* want to see, people who'd prefer it if us Charmers all piss off and live on an island together. The shouty protesters and the people who suck their teeth and talk about the unnaturalness of it all, or the selfishness, as if we're doing it on purpose. We're an endangered species."

"That's only because Charmers hardly ever shack up with non-Charmers. Your parents were the odd ones out. The rest are keeping the gift to themselves. I'm not going to say the word inbred, but—" When Evie glanced up and saw Caitlin's expression, she clammed up. "So anyway, what are you suggesting? Climb up onto one of the college buildings?"

Caitlin shook her head. "Wouldn't work. We set up like we're doing a street performance. On Cornmarket, where there are the most people. My birthday's on a Saturday so there'll be a ton of randoms all wandering around. We gather the crowds under false pretences—"

"To watch what?"

"Doesn't matter. You. You're hot. You can be my magician's assistant and draw the crowds. Or you can wear a leotard and tell them you're going to do the splits and they can ogle your arse cheeks. Anyway, so the crowd are all there, but then instead of you doing gymnastics or whatever, suddenly I announce that I'm a Charmer and I'm proud of it and I'm not going to hide away."

"So then you undo your belt and your silken dressing gown drops to the floor and you're stark naked…"

"Yeah. Maybe. No, actually you're right! The Skin will be naked when she arrives, so I should be too. Solidarity. Right. There's me in the street, naked and proud of it. So of course everyone's looking now, and then you do the countdown—"

"And set off the fireworks."

"Yup. And then there she is, suddenly, right beside me. My spontaneous duplicate. My Snakeskin."

"Naked."

Caitlin nodded. "And I won't cover her up."

"Won't she mind? I mean, I know you'll already be naked, but it's not as if there'll be time to get her consent or anything. And you're the one who's always banging on about Charmers' rights and surely that means Skins, too?"

"Of course she won't mind. She'll be my Snakeskin, Evie. As close to being me as anyone could be. With all my memories, so they reckon. Of course she'll be in on the plan. In fact, just by me deciding right here and now that I'm okay with it, then that means she is too, because she'll remember this conversation and the fact that she agreed to it."

"It sounds iffy, from a legal point of view."

Caitlin rolled her eyes. One citizenship module and suddenly Evie thought she was a lawyer. "The point is that this isn't about the law. This is about pride in who we are. And saying sod everyone else."

"Everyone else meaning me." Evie scowled. Caitlin couldn't tell whether or not she was joking.

"Of course not you."

"Me, the magician's assistant, forever labelled a Charmer-lover."

"You say that like it's a bad thing."

"Oh, don't be a diva. I love you, don't I? But the scale of what you're talking about… well, it's illegal, for one thing. And maybe I want to keep my options open. You know, not messing up my life before I get going."

Caitlin felt a sudden sense of being caught out. There was no way she really wanted to strip naked in the high street and force people to watch her shedding. But if she *had* wanted to do it, she wanted to know that Evie had her back. Was she actually going to go through with the whole thing, just to prove a point?

"Don't come, then," she said, her voice cracking a little.

"Oh, get real, Cait. I'll be there, whatever you decide to do. All of us will."

"All of us who?"

"Me, Amy, Jacko, Jane, Flip… everyone."

In a quiet voice, Caitlin said, "I only wanted you. I don't need all the rest of them. Just you."

"Don't be daft. You said you want everyone in the world to see you. You don't have to be naked really. But you need our support."

"I need *your* support. Not you and your whole gang. I'm serious. If you can't do this for me without everyone else in tow, I don't want you to come."

"I'm your best friend in the whole world."

"Doesn't feel like it. You've got Amy and Jacko and Jane and Flip and a thousand other people."

Evie's expression hardened. "Non-Charmers, you mean. Not special types like you."

"Normal people."

Evie shrugged. "Same difference. It's a bloody shame, that's what it is. You of all people. I'd never have expected you to be all up yourself about being a Charmer. Maybe you lot can't help it."

As if responding to the mention of her name, Jane Rowntree appeared, carrying a tray. "Scrag ends," she said, nodding down at her plateful of hardened bits of lasagne scraped from the sides of pans. She looked at Evie, at her quivering lip, her fidgeting that suggested she was on the verge of tears. "What're you fighting about?"

Evie rubbed at an eye. "Turns out Caitlin hates us lot. Us normal people."

Jane thumped her tray onto the table before Caitlin. "Leave Evie alone."

"Oh, so you're Evie's mummy now, are you? Trust you to come and wipe her tears away."

"Don't be a twat. Leave her alone, skinflint."

Caitlin's cheeks reddened immediately. She had always suspected that Jane disliked her and that their friendship relied on Evie, as though Evie were the pivot of a seesaw. "What did you call me?"

"Skinflint. You're just like the rest. Living up there in Woodstock in your bloody castle. Bathing in money, same as all Charmers. Waiting for your turn to get your claws into the country, then wait for the rest of us to get sick and die off so you can take our money and our jobs."

Rationally, Caitlin knew that Jane probably didn't feel that way about her, not really. Those were probably someone else's words. Her dad had been an influential anti-prosperity campaigner. He had once been on the news, arguing with low-level government ministers, and soon afterwards he had been in prison for a year or so. But Caitlin saw the effect Jane's words had on Evie, who had fallen silent. Perhaps she was thinking of the vast, unused rooms in Ivy Cottage, compared to her own small tenement house, her own bedroom shared with her brother.

There was a flurry of movement outside the canteen. A crowd of students had gathered, making a horseshoe around the double doors. Their hoots and cheers sounded ghostly as they echoed from the bare walls of the canteen. The students were watching three boys in the middle of the half-ring. Caitlin knew only one of them by name, but she had seen the two larger, stockier boys before, swaggering around the small campus, hollering at girls. Just last week, the gurning one with the barely-there goatee had made a crack about Caitlin having ginger pubes. The other, even uglier boy wore a black denim jacket with the words *FUCK SAKE* written on it in white electrical tape.

The smaller boy was called Spencer. Caitlin barely knew him, only enough to know that he was quiet and that he was a Charmer. In fact, he was the only other Charmer at the sixth-form college – Charmer kids tended to attend posh private schools. Caitlin had always made a point of not gravitating to Spencer, in order to demonstrate that their shared gift was no common ground at all.

The bigger boys were goading Spencer, spinning him around between them. The one with the goatee tried to grab for his rucksack. Spencer stumbled to one side and Goatee snatched the bag. The strap caught on the smaller boy's arm and sent him crashing to the ground.

Caitlin had reached the doorway before she even realised she had left her seat. Her hands were fists again. The bewildered Spencer sat on his bottom like a well-behaved toddler at nursery. The howling, ape-like Goatee and Fucksake held his rucksack aloft between them, like a trophy or a weapon. The crowd of watching students had become even denser.

It was the other students that really scared her. A few were obviously concerned, but most had gleaming eyes and were calling out or chanting nonsensical insults. "Finish him off!" "Skinflint!" "He deserves it." "Snakeshit!"

Blackness crept in at the edges of Caitlin's vision. If she didn't do something, she was certain she'd pass out from rage.

"Leave him alone!" She was surprised at the volume of her voice.

Everybody turned to look at her – everybody except Spencer, who was watching Goatee and Fucksake calmly, blinking slowly as though their only crime was to have woken him up.

At first nobody said anything, but Caitlin heard a hum of disappointment. The students had been promised a spectacle and now it had been stopped abruptly. If a teacher had called a halt there would have been a general scurry away from the fight. Caitlin's interruption had only served to ruin the momentum.

Goatee and Fucksake watched her, too.

It was Jane Rowntree's voice that broke the silence. It came from somewhere behind her. "Of course she wants them to stop. Charmers always stick together."

Something jabbed into Caitlin's spine. She staggered forward, then turned to see that it was Jane who had pushed her. The semicircle closed, blocking Caitlin's way out.

Evie stood at Jane's side. Her face was pale and she was chewing her cheek.

Caitlin forced herself to face Goatee and Fucksake. She held out a hand. "Give me the bag."

Fucksake held it inches away from her fingers. His lip curled, making his face more grotesque than should have been possible. Caitlin resisted the temptation to make a grab and, as she had expected, he snatched it away again.

He unzipped the rucksack, making a show of peering inside. "Let's see what kind of kinky shit Charmers lug around with them, hey?" He pulled out a book. It wasn't a college textbook, but a computer-programming guide of some sort. Fucksake adopted a theatrical voice, loud enough for everyone in his audience to hear. "What's this? Some kind of self-help guide. Called, 'How to fuck over normal people'."

Everyone laughed. Fucksake might be a total meathead, but he knew how to work a crowd.

Goatee nudged him in the ribs. He had the mannerisms of someone much younger and much less confident than he at first appeared. All bullies were cowards, up close. "Careful you don't catch a disease. Charmer stuff's riddled with germs."

"Excellent point," Fucksake boomed. He dropped the book, keeping hold of one corner of the paperback cover so that it ripped clean off. The book and the loose cover fell to the ground. Spencer scurried over, crablike on his haunches, to rescue them.

"Give the bag to me," Caitlin said again. She took a step forwards and Fucksake took a step back.

"I wouldn't let you near me if you were the only woman in the world," he shouted. Then, in a lower voice, perfectly judged to be audible to all, "I know about you – your mum's a Charmer but your dad's a normal human, isn't he? Shacked up with a Charmer, the fucking traitor. My mum says they should have strung him up."

He turned slowly, brandishing the bag above his head again, and announced, "I guess I'd better play safe and not touch anything else in here."

The crowd fell silent.

Then Fucksake upturned the bag. A pencil case, a notebook, crisp packets and two more books dropped out. Something large jammed in the opening.

Caitlin leapt forwards with a roar, but not fast enough to catch anything. Fucksake swung the bag away as though she were a bull in the ring. The final item fell from the rucksack. It landed with a crash on the gravel before Caitlin could identify what it was. Spencer leapt upon it. In each hand he held a plastic object shimmering with circuitry. It had been a computer, judging from the keyboard, but far smaller than the BBC Micros in the college library, and it had a built-in screen like the ones in calculators. By the looks of it, he'd constructed it himself. Smart kid. Poor bastard.

"You was right!" Goatee squealed. "He's built a fucking bomb!"

The crowd began to bellow. From what Caitlin could hear, some were elaborating on Goatee's accusation. Others just wanted to see Spencer get the crap kicked out of him.

"Defuse the bomb!" Goatee shrieked.

"Don't you dare," Caitlin said. She threw herself at Fucksake at precisely the same moment he started running towards Spencer.

Fucksake pushed her away roughly. She stumbled and fell, grazing her palms on the ground. She mouthed words to herself. *Don't you dare cry.*

Fucksake slapped the computer from Spencer's hands. One of his heavy boots crunched down upon it. He stamped twice more, grinding the LCD screen to shining shards that stuck into the all-weather surface.

This was the way things were.

With a snarl, Caitlin burst upwards from her crouched position. Dimly, she registered the indignant shout of "Students!" which signalled the arrival of a teacher. The crowd of onlookers dissipated quickly, the students shuffling away and gazing elsewhere as if their upcoming lessons, or even the sky, suddenly struck them as more interesting than the fight. Caitlin saw Jane slink away, too, with Evie in tow.

But her momentum was unstoppable. Her left hand

clawed at Fucksake's pockmarked face. As he twisted away her right fist thwacked into the cavity of his eye socket, fitting into it as neatly as an egg into an eggcup.

＊

"'I am in blood stepped in so far that, should I wade no more, returning were as tedious as go o'er,'" Russell said.

Spencer hesitated. "Right."

"So does that mean anything to you?"

Russell noticed a twitch at one corner of Spencer's mouth. The boy's eyes strayed over to the smashed pieces of computer on the kitchen counter.

"Can you repair it, do you think?" Russell said.

Spencer chewed his cheek. He nodded.

"All right then. No point dwelling on it. Those boys will get what's coming to them."

The rust-coloured streaks were still there beneath Spencer's puffy eyes. A sixteen-year-old oughtn't to cry that much. But then sixteen-year-olds oughtn't to be tormented either. Russell squirmed as Spencer gazed at him. Perhaps the kid thought that he, Russell, was going to deal with the bullies. But that was a job for Ellis, not his hired help. Anyway, once Spencer got over the shock of his computer being destroyed, he would probably relish building a new machine. From the little Russell had seen of the kid, he enjoyed a technical challenge. He had talked of little else on the journey to the house, once Russell had coaxed the details of the fight out of him.

Awkwardly, Russell tousled Spencer's hair. Then he pointed

at the battered copy of *Macbeth* splayed open between them on the wooden table. "Come on," he said softly. "Your dad said we had to get through this homework tonight."

Ellis's phone call had come at a point where Russell had begun to tidy up the office for the day. It had occurred to Russell to tell his boss that, no, collecting his son from the sixth-form college was above and beyond his role profile. But he hadn't. In all honesty, he'd felt a pang of curiosity to see Ellis's house, especially without Ellis as a chaperone. Being allowed inside one of these enormous Summertown properties was too tantalising an opportunity to pass up. In contrast to its townhouse exterior, inside it was like a country mansion from another era, a time capsule. The thick velvet curtains hid all evidence of the outside world. The mahogany furniture and mounted animal heads belonged in a museum. And the place was enormous. His own bedsit would have fitted comfortably into one of Ellis's two sitting rooms.

He had hoped to see Ellis's wife, too. He had replayed her encounter with the office security guard over and over in his mind. He had tried to conjure her face. His pulse had quickened as Spencer had led him into the house, but she wasn't here.

"Take it bit by bit," he said. "'I am in blood stepped in so far.'"

"Right."

"Meaning."

Spencer sighed. "Like, um. I've got blood on my feet."

"Yes!"

"Yes?"

"Well, more like, I've walked through a river of blood to get where I am."

"I must have missed a bit then," Spencer said. "I'll read that part tomorrow. Can I go upstairs now? I'm really tired." He looked it, too.

"Tough day."

"Yeah."

"You know…" It wasn't Russell's place to say anything. He considered his words carefully. "You know your dad's going to ask you what happened."

"Right."

"I mean, whether it could have been avoided. What I mean is, he's going to talk to you about taking you out of that college. Putting you somewhere private." Ellis had talked about it many times, often leaving Russell puzzled about how they had reached that topic of conversation.

Spencer fell silent.

"You're not a fighter, are you? Me neither, never was. But your dad feels strongly about that sort of thing. I think he thinks you should stand your ground. Either that, or he thinks you should go somewhere where maybe you'd fit in better."

"I like my college. The teachers are nice. And there's this…" Spencer's face flushed. A girl, maybe? Russell rifled through the pages of *Macbeth*, trying to appear not to have noticed.

"So. I've walked through this river of blood, meaning I've killed people. And should I wade no more, meaning if I give up trying to get across – the blood river, we're still talking about – returning were as tedious as go o'er."

"What does tedious mean?"

"Boring."

Spencer gave him a hard look. "And what about ooh-er? Like ooh-er, missus? Dad watches those *Carry On* films that come out every summer. They say stuff like that all the time."

"It means over."

"Ooh-er."

"It's over."

Spencer flipped the book cover closed. "And about time too. I'm starving."

He hopped off his chair and padded across the kitchen barefoot. He was short for his age, which was strange, considering his breeding. Charmer kids were usually beanpoles, from what Russell had observed. Good genes.

The heavy oak door creaked open. Instinctively, Russell stood upright, as though he were a soldier and Ellis his sergeant.

But it was Nell Blackwood. Her hair was pinned up, but one side had come free of its clips to make a lopsided frame to her oval face. Rather than the suit she had worn at the office, she was now dressed in a grey hooded sweatshirt bunched beneath stained denim dungarees. The curls of wood shavings and the black flecks that clung to her shoulders acted as extensions of the freckled patterns on her cheeks and nose. Russell thought of dust or ashes rising and dissipating.

"I heard voices," she said. "Oh. I recognise you. Cecil, is it?"

Russell found that his mouth had gone dry. Finally, he managed to croak, "Russell. I didn't know you were here." He thought about mentioning the scene outside the office, maybe offering some sort of commiseration. He decided against it.

"Out back. Chipping away."

She moved to the counter where Spencer was preparing a sandwich. She hugged her son from behind. They were the same height, which seemed only right. Spencer was more Nell than Ellis. Perhaps she wasn't a Charmer after all, just Ellis – though it seemed unlikely that the minister would dare invite the criticism and threats of violence often levelled at mixed marriages. Another thought occurred to him: if she was a Charmer, she might not be as young as she looked. Nell reached around her son, took the sandwich and bit off more than half of it.

"Are you early?" she said, still chewing.

Spencer only shrugged, so Russell answered for him. "Minister Blackwood asked me to pick your son up from college. There was a bit of bother."

Nell finally noticed the smashed computer. "Oh, love. More fuss?"

Spencer shrugged again. "The hard drive's knackered, but it was only a half-megabyte drive for the prototype. I'll build another computer, better."

"I know, love." Nell's voice was full of sadness. "I know."

Russell felt awfully out of place, as much as he wished to stay and see more of Nell. He found it impossible to reconcile the strident, confident woman from the office car park with this tender, sad, young person. He took three steps to the door before Nell put her hand on his arm to stop him.

"Why didn't Ellis ring me? When the sixth-form got in touch. I've been home all day."

Presumably, she was preoccupied with the possibility of Ellis being in the midst of an affair. Russell wished suddenly that he was bold enough to embrace her. "I assumed he'd tried. You didn't hear us in here, so maybe you wouldn't have heard the phone? While you were doing your..." He tailed off, realising that he had no idea what had been occupying her.

"Maybe. Yes, maybe it was that. Thank you for doing this, Russell. You shouldn't have to. I'm certain he's not paying you enough."

He was a month's rent late already, but he resisted the temptation to follow up on this line of conversation. He doubted whether Nell held much sway over Ellis's business decisions anyway.

She watched him, unblinking, for several long seconds. "Do you want to see? What I've been doing?"

Russell glanced at Spencer, who was eating his sandwich, still standing at the counter. The boy had his mother's eyes. They both looked wounded, or afraid. Russell nodded and allowed Nell to lead him from the room. Spencer didn't follow.

A trail of footprints haloed with wood shavings led from the kitchen door to a ramshackle lean-to building inaccessible from the main part of the house. Russell guessed that it was originally intended for use as a conservatory. Its windows were grimy with sawdust speckles.

"Your workshop?" Russell said.

Nell flashed a smile and ducked beneath a trailing power cable to enter. He followed.

The wall adjoining the house – or rather, the outside wall of the house – was almost entirely hidden by shelves laden with plastic boxes, tools and tins of paint, piled precariously. Russell smiled despite his discomfort at the disarray. He had always kept his living space immaculate. An ordered mind demonstrated to the world that you were a serious person – though nobody but himself had actually set foot in his bedsit since he had arrived in Oxford three months ago.

At the far end of the lean-to, several clustered workbenches made a small island above the sawdust that carpeted the tiled floor. Russell had skirted all the way around before he noticed the object they supported, as if it were too large for him to process on a first pass. An enormous section of tree trunk lay sideways, resting on three benches and with additional support provided by upturned plastic crates. Ropes tied around four dining-room chairs held the thing in place. The circumference of the trunk was so great that Russell wouldn't have been able to put his arms around it. Its bark was dark, gnarled and knotted.

It was hollow. At least, part of it was, as if Nell had been attempting to fashion a canoe out of the huge trunk, having removed a section of the bark and then worked her way inside. This must be the 'chipping away' she'd referred to.

She had left a thin central spindle of the tree intact, carving her way around and beneath it. The long, slender strand of wood looked like a filament in an old light bulb, or an exposed fuse wire.

He glanced at Nell. She nodded reassurance. He moved forwards and placed his hands lightly upon the dugout inside of the trunk. The wood was rough and splintered. Carefully, he stroked the spindle of exposed wood with his fingertips. It was smooth, as if it had been polished or spun on a lathe. Now that he looked closely, he saw that it wasn't perfectly round. It bent a little in the centre of its length and had its own little knots, though far less grotesque than those on the outside of the trunk. He bent down to look along its length. Its end entered the rings of the main trunk dead centre.

"It's the same tree," he breathed. "But younger."

Nell beamed. "I think of it more as archaeology than sculpture. It's fun."

"It's incredible. Will you end up revealing the entire thing? The sapling that was hidden inside this ugly old tree?"

Her smile disappeared. "I haven't decided. Is it so ugly?"

Russell looked again at the outer part of the huge trunk. It was majestic, certainly, but compared to the slender sapling within, it was a lumpen caricature.

He whirled around at the sound of somebody coughing. Ellis Blackwood stood in the doorway. He was smiling, but without warmth. "Admiring Nell's little art project?"

Russell didn't stop to figure out why he felt so exposed and guilty. He nodded, mute. He sensed Nell's body stiffen beside him. What was their relationship, this husband and wife? He had seen colour-photo magazine lifestyle features that suggested their home life was idyllic. He felt a twinge of guilt for hoping that perhaps it was all a facade.

"I think it's rather good," Ellis said. "All those layers weighing that old tree down. Unnecessary, when you think about it. There was a perfectly good tree right there inside, all along."

It was a closer analysis than Russell would have expected from Ellis. He didn't dare turn to see Nell's reaction.

"Anyway," Ellis continued, "I don't mean to interrupt. In fact, this is a flying visit. I'm afraid I'm off out again. An appointment. Work."

Russell could picture the office diary perfectly. "There was nothing scheduled, sir."

"No. But work it is, nevertheless. And it will take all evening." He turned to his wife. "Which means, dearest, that I shan't be able to take you and our ray of sunshine to the theatre this evening."

Nell spoke for the first time. "Spencer needs a distraction. I'll take him alone, then." She sounded more tired than accusatory.

Ellis nodded, almost a bow. "Of course. But rather less sociable for you." He turned to Russell. "I know I've prevailed upon you already today..."

Russell blinked. "You want me to take your wife and son to the theatre?"

Ellis took two long strides to clap him on the shoulder, then retreated to the doorway. "Excellent. Good man. Right. I'll be off, then. I should think there'll be food provided at the thing." He wavered, perhaps considering whether to make an additional leap forwards to kiss his wife. After a few moments rocking on the spot, he gave an awkward wave, turned and left.

Baffled, Russell continued staring at the empty doorway.

"He's been doing that more and more lately," Nell said quietly. "Sudden, secret meetings with the upper echelons of power. I don't know what it means."

Russell thought of the question marks in the office diary, and the stranger's assertions during the mysterious phone call. What ridiculous name had he used? 'Ixion'. A reference to some character in a science-fiction book, no doubt.

"Upper echelons?" he said. "Are you talking about Adrian Lorde?"

"Would you describe the PM as powerful?" Nell's smirk vanished as quickly as it appeared. "Interesting."

Russell told himself to say no more. As much as he liked this sparky, untidy woman, he still worked for Ellis. And Ellis was a figurehead of the Party, and the Party was Russell's future.

"And for the record," Nell said, her face brightening, "you're not taking us to the theatre. We're taking you." She squeezed his arm and set off back to the house.

Russell glanced again at Nell's sculpture. Something about the tree, its exterior, struck him as significant. Black wood. Blackwood, just like Nell, but only on the outside.

# FOUR

When the house lights came up, Russell felt as though he were waking from a vivid dream. He turned to his left, genuinely surprised to find Nell Blackwood sitting beside him. Tears glistened on her cheeks. Beyond her, Spencer was still staring straight ahead, too. Before the play had started, Russell had imagined that the boy might end up curled in his seat asleep, he looked so worn out. Now he was as alert as anybody else in the audience.

"It was good, wasn't it?" Nell said, without turning.

At first Russell wasn't sure whether he was the one being addressed. When Spencer didn't answer, he said, "It really was. I've never seen *Macbeth* at the theatre before." He paused. "Come to think of it, I don't think I've ever seen a Shakespeare play, full stop."

Nell wrinkled her nose. "And yet you don't appear at all out of place. You're an anomaly, Russell Handler."

Russell grinned. If anyone was the anomaly, it was Nell. How had somebody so pleasant ended up with a Party minister for a husband? Something about this observation struck him as important. Wasn't becoming a high-ranking government official exactly what he hoped to achieve in his own career?

He shrugged. "Sheltered life, I guess." He leant forwards to look past Nell. "At least Spencer's avoided the same dire fate as me."

They all shuffled sideways along the row of seats, slowly following two elderly women blocking the aisle with their coats and shopping bags. Once they had gathered together in the foyer, Russell felt instantly that he was the odd one out. It was plain wrong, adopting this paternal role in their little family. It was wrong to enjoy it so much.

Spencer's forehead creased. "I get it now."

Russell's first instinct was that Spencer had seen through him – that he understood, at that moment, Russell wished Nell and Spencer were his family and not Ellis's. He cleared his throat.

"What Macbeth said, I mean," Spencer continued. "The blood. You know. Stepped in so far. There was no going back, even though he knew he was being a twat. So he just carried on."

Russell glanced at Nell, unsure how to react to the swear word. She beamed at him.

"So you have what you need for the essay, do you think?" she asked. Before her son answered, she added, "But I'm warning you, mister. Don't start with any bollocks about 'It was all Lady Macbeth's fault and Macbeth was only a poor victim'. It's way more complex than that. Right, Russell?"

Russell bowed his head in agreement. In truth, he hadn't

really thought about whether it was any more complex than that. But Nell was probably right. She seemed bookish.

Spencer's fidgeting suggested that their little triangle would soon be broken. Russell realised that he wanted to continue their conversation – any conversation – in order to maintain the illusion.

"How about ice cream?" he said. He grimaced. He couldn't sound more like an interloper father if he tried. Currying favour with the potential stepson. "I'm buying," he added, only making things worse.

Though Spencer looked hopeful, Nell replied, "Sorry. It's been lovely, but we should get back, it being a school night and all. It'll be curfew before long, anyway."

"You both stay here, then," he said, gabbling to mask his disappointment. "I'll whizz round and get the car. See you out front."

Nell smiled. "Another time, though? The ice cream?"

It wasn't much, but it was an offer of more of this. Russell left the foyer feeling stupidly happy.

Gloucester Green was only a few streets away. Russell whistled as he walked. He couldn't remember the last time he had done that.

The path dipped to the entrance to the underground car park and was shadowed by trees. The interior of the building was empty and even more badly lit. It was as if the architects had designed its concrete pillars to block any copper-coloured light from the fizzing wall lamps.

He had no idea where he had parked the car. When they arrived his nervousness had pushed him even further into butler mode, fussing over Nell, helping her out of the car, fetching her coat. She had told him, with great warmth, to piss off.

"Stop," a voice said. It came from somewhere to his left, in the shadows. Deep and menacing. "Turn around."

Russell did as he was told. It would be just his luck to end a pleasant evening with an unceremonious mugging. He laughed to himself as he realised that the worst thing, if he was beaten up and thrown in the gutter, would be leaving Nell and Spencer in the foyer, wondering what had become of him.

A figure stood beneath an illuminated green exit sign. Russell peered into the darkness, but the combination of the backlight and the man's hood made his features invisible. He was tall, though, and well-built. An adult rather than a teenager.

In his pocket Russell gripped the keys to his Vauxhall Nova. He slipped two fingers through the key ring. Perhaps he could use them as a rudimentary knuckleduster? Or perhaps he could simply offer the keys to the stranger, in exchange for being left unharmed. He cursed himself for his cowardice.

"What do you want?" he said. His throat was dry and his voice sounded tiny, lost in the empty ocean of the car park.

The stranger didn't answer.

"I have ten pounds in my wallet," Russell managed to say, finally.

"I don't want your money." The man's voice was quiet and deep enough that Russell had to strain to hear him. It sounded familiar, all the same.

Of course. The crackling sound that he had taken to

be a bad line was actually a feature of the man's voice. It was halting but deep, like the voiceover in a trailer for a Pinewood action film.

"You're Ixion."

"Yes. I don't want to harm you."

"But you're okay with threatening me?"

"I require your cooperation."

Russell noted the evasion of his question. Even the statement 'I don't want to harm you' carried a perverse implication of violence, however undesired. He must escape and speak to Ellis as soon as possible. Tell him everything and plead ignorance of any conspiracy.

They were still two or three paces apart. Russell glanced at the exit. If he abandoned the car, he could make it. He'd always been good at cross-country at school. In fact, as motivation to continue running at full speed, he'd often pretended he was being chased.

He bolted. The man burst into action too, still keeping close to the wall but narrowing the gap to the exit.

Even though Ixion was no closer to him, Russell arced away, putting more distance between them. He realised he was now heading into the depths of the car park, though not the area containing his Nova.

He heard a beeping sound from behind him. He turned. His would-be attacker had slowed to a halt. Russell saw a small blue light flicking on and off. A mobile telephone? Some kind of weapon?

"Stop," Ixion commanded.

Hardly understanding why, Russell did as he was told.

The stranger took a step back. The blue light stopped flashing. When he spoke again, his voice was quiet and calm, though it still carried easily across the space between them. "I beg you: watch Ellis Blackwood. Find out his secrets. Watch him carefully and report to me."

The mixture of pleading and threats baffled Russell. This wasn't how things happened in thriller films.

"If there are rival groups within the government, that's their business," Russell said. "These things happen. I'm just doing my job. Nobody's at risk here – assuming you're really not going to kneecap me or anything like that. You say you're close to the heart of government… It sounds like you're just angling for more power yourself."

Ixion's hood swung from side to side. "No. If Ellis Blackwood's plan comes to fruition, a great many people will be at risk – both Charmers and ordinary citizens."

Russell snorted.

The stranger fell silent. In a much quieter voice, he said slowly, "Specific people, too." He let out a sigh, halting and slightly strangled. "Nell Blackwood, for example."

Russell froze. "What did you say?"

Ixion continued, speaking more quickly, his earlier confidence restored. "The most important thing is to record who Minister Blackwood meets face-to-face. His contacts, his colleagues. And I don't mean those in Westminster. I mean those that work in your building, operating under aliases."

Russell flinched as the man took a step towards him and pressed something into his hand. It was a business card, blank other than a scrawled phone number. Ixion's hood overhung his face almost entirely, casting a visor of shadow.

Then Ixion turned and strode away. Once again, Russell saw a flash of blue light; the man veered to the left. At the exit to the car park he paused, his square shoulders lit by the street lights. Then he disappeared into the shadows.

Russell released his held breath. He stumbled to the car, unlocked the door with shaking hands, then dropped the keys into the footwell before he managed to start the engine.

He pulled up outside the theatre and revved the engine. The foyer was empty other than Nell, Spencer and a few staff filling display stands with leaflets and collecting empty plastic cups. He glanced at the dashboard clock: 22:35. Curfew would start in twenty-five minutes and then the streets would be deserted.

"Everything all right?" Nell asked as she dropped into the passenger seat.

Russell shivered. He stared at Nell, scrutinising her for any suggestion of fear. Then he glanced into the mirror to make sure that Spencer was safely strapped in.

He nodded. "Thank you for a wonderful evening."

*

Gerry gazed down at the tiny village of Ilam, spread beneath her like parts of a model railway set. It had taken her nearly two hours to scale this mountain, and now that she had reached its top she felt nothing but foolish. All she had as a reward was the same pleasant view she'd seen on postcards in the local post office.

'Go back to the source.' The advice sounded grand in theory. But in practice, what did it actually mean? Ilam may have been where it all began – the precise geographical location where a world with Charmers and Snakeskins became a reality – but that didn't mean there was information to be gathered here. So much had been written about the Fall over the last two hundred years. Historians, journalists and novelists had already been here, at this precise location, scouring for clues, searching for any titbits that might warrant a new coffee-table book dedicated to the subject. She had visited Ilam herself at the start of the century, though she hadn't climbed the mountain. Her attention had been focussed on an anti-Charmer protest in the village centre, which ended upon the appearance of several dozen soldiers, along with vehicles with grilles over their blacked-out windows and, mounted on the back of one of them, a water cannon that remained trained on the protesters long after they had abandoned their placards. Gerry had been shocked at the speed of response and the availability of huge numbers of ground troops. She had lobbied for budget to investigate the size of the British Army, but neither *Folk* nor any other newspaper entertained the idea for a moment. It had been soon after this protest, and a spate of larger ones in various cities, all quashed in a similar manner, that an eleven o'clock curfew had been made law.

She stood on a grey rock and shouted, "This was a stupid idea, Drew!"

The wind sped up the mountainside and burrowed beneath her raincoat. Gerry shivered and slumped onto the rock. From her rucksack she retrieved a cling-filmed fist of sandwiches made by the woman who ran the bed and breakfast.

As she munched, she surveyed the miniature houses in the valley. It was difficult to shake the feeling that she ought to have used this 'bonus time', as Drew had put it, quite differently. Even time alone reading or watching films would have been preferable, and better than paying over the odds for a standing-room-only shuddering train journey north, switching carriages regularly to avoid the twin perils of a stag party and a group of wailing toddlers. And now here she was, at the arse-end of the Peak District, freezing to death and eating... what? Fish paste? She rewrapped the sandwiches and dug into the bag for the thickest of the heavy books that she had lugged all the way up here.

The hardback book, pilfered from her local library in Luton, was almost worthless in terms of its informative content. The only reason she had brought it was due to the colour plate on its first page. She held up the book, clamping the pages to stop them whipping in the wind, to compare the image to the real landscape.

She must be close. She turned from side to side before locating another rock outcrop, slightly further east. Grunting, she rose to her feet, clambered over to the outcrop, and settled herself again. Now the view and the illustration matched almost perfectly. The only difference was that, in place of cumulus wisps, the illustrated plate showed a bruise-purple sky, crosshatched with dozens of needle-thin streaks of green.

What would the Fall have looked like, in reality? If she could have sat here on this cold rock on 23 July 1808, what would she have imagined was occurring? Of course, in all likelihood, nobody *had* been in such a position. The artist who painted this picture would have been nestled in bed, as would all the locals. The image was uncredited, but quite possibly the painter had never even set foot in Ilam until after the Fall, when Ilam had already become the go-to destination for aristocrats and rubberneckers.

Still. It would have been fucking terrifying, that's what it would have been.

Like everyone else, she probably would have assumed that the meteor shower was an omen – that the blazing streaks of green light were a hundred malignant signals of doom. She would have pelted back indoors, along with her neighbours – into her hovel, rather than one of the glorified doll's houses now situated in the valley – and shuddered at the window with a rough blanket wrapped around her shoulders. She would have reckoned that her death was imminent. And she would have been as far off the mark as anyone could possibly be.

The owner of the bed and breakfast had talked her through the limited facilities that the village had to offer. They amounted to a public toilet (pristine), the town hall (tiny, abandoned during the mornings, packed with exhausted elderly workers from the local factory in the afternoon) and the visitor centre. The visitor centre had provided barely any information about the Fall, other than a few additional artists' impressions, though none of them any more useful than the illustration in the library book. Donald, the septuagenarian behind the counter, had given a wan smile when Gerry had asked about the meteor shower. "People don't come any more," he had said. "Once, the name Ilam was on everybody's lips. People these days don't concern themselves about where they came from. No sense of history."

*Where they came from.*

Gerry traced the path of an imagined meteor, backwards, upwards, to where the sky shone white. Up there. In a sense, they came from up there.

She tossed the uneaten half of her sandwich over her shoulder and rose to her feet. It was too cold to drag the visit out. She set off southwards, picking her way along the ridge.

Twenty minutes later the rock face rose higher to her right, forming a canopy that blocked the still-rising sun. She shivered and pulled her coat tighter around her body. She hurried to pass its sheer face, eager to reach sunlight again. Then something made her pause.

This was it.

She edged closer to the rock face. Most of its surface was smooth, weathered by the rain. However, above head height, where most of the surface became flatter, it was pockmarked. She wished she remembered what she had been taught in school about rock types. Igneous and sedimentary, but she couldn't recall which was which. The rocks here were the rounded type, that much she knew. Grey-white and smooth, like the bare bones of a dinosaur. She clambered up onto a low ledge, then pushed her fingers into the pockmarked divots. There were over a dozen of them, roughly hemispherical, ranging from the size of a golf ball to a fist. The lips of each indentation were smooth enough, but might once have been sharper. It was hard to shake the feeling that something – or rather, *some things* – had struck the rock, here, long ago. Several of the anti-prosperity newsletters to which she subscribed had referred to these markings, but given their usual conspiracy theories, Gerry had expected them to be less visible, the theory less convincing.

The official histories – in her library book, and every other published account she'd read – stated that none of the meteors had actually landed. But perhaps they had, here, far above the village. Whereas everybody down in the valley saw the green streaks speckle the sky and then vanish, perhaps up here on the ridge lay a dozen, or a hundred, or more, fizzing balls of space rock.

Perhaps.

It wasn't much. She hopped down onto the ground, landing awkwardly and twisting her ankle a little. She crouched like a cat before a bowl of milk, her nose almost touching the ground.

It was only due to this peculiar posture that she noticed the faint marks on the ground. She brushed at the tufts of coarse grass that obscured them. Though the lines disappeared every so often where moss had worked its way across, they described a squarish shape spanning almost the entirety of the flat area below the vertical rock face.

It was the outline of a small building – she was certain of it.

Someone local must know what had once been up here. She stood, wincing slightly at the pain from her ankle, and turned to look down upon Ilam.

A large building squatted halfway up the slopes of the mountain at the end of the valley, as though contemplating passing through. Gerry rifled through the pages of the library book. She'd heard mention of the name Ilam Hall, but the building didn't appear on any of the colour plates. When had it been built? Mid-1800s, judging from the architecture. Well after the Fall. But even so. There might be a library there.

She sighed with relief at this new sense of purpose, then began her stumbling descent.

*

"Rights! For!" Caitlin filled her lungs before bellowing the final word. "Charmers!"

Below her, students milled back and forth in the common area between the classrooms and the canteen. A few of them glanced her way, but only momentarily. Most strode by, smirking. It was as though they had been instructed not to pay her any attention. She wondered whether Jane Rowntree was responsible, or even Evie. The second possibility made her want to pack up and go home immediately.

No. She had to make a stand. She took a deep breath and shouted again, "Rights for Charmers!"

A knot in the tree bark had begun to dig into her spine. She wiggled as best she could, but the rope looped around the tree trunk had no more slack in it. She tried to reach up and scratch the itch but the laminated bike chain jangled as its figure-of-eight coil pulled tight against her wrists. There could be no way of getting relief unless she unlocked the chain. So she would have to distract herself instead.

"Hear me! Hear me!" she shouted. Was that how people started public speeches? "This college is a hotbed of bigots! Who oppress the minorities! Who enslave the weak!" A couple of students turned her way, finally. 'Enslave' was completely the wrong word, and Charmers in general were anything but weak, but at least it had got their attention. "Right here, in this very courtyard, a boy was preyed upon, merely because of his genes. This boy, after being severely beaten and having his property destroyed, was sent home. And his attackers, his cold-blooded assailants, were given one measly detention each. Yes – that's all! And then they were slapped on the back – good job, boys – and everything was forgiven!"

Two boys stopped beneath the tree, gazing up at her perched on two of the boxlike wooden benches that encircled it. She couldn't see their faces. She hadn't counted on the leaves of the lowest branches blocking her vision.

"I ask you, is that justice?" she said in a hoarse stage whisper. Instantly, she felt rather proud of the effect.

"Is that a reef knot?" one of the boys said, peering at where the rope met the bike lock.

The other shook his head. "Reef knot wouldn't work. It'd come loose at the first pull. That's a sheep shank. Right?" He addressed the question to Caitlin, his head tilting to see her beneath her leaf canopy.

"Piss off, guys," Caitlin hissed. If the rope knot was any

type, it was a granny knot. She'd only attended Girl Guides for a single session, and had sat in the corner in a huff, then later declared the whole thing a parental conspiracy to turn kids' brains into mush and to force them to respect authority unthinkingly.

The first boy shrugged and shuffled away. His friend peered at the knot for a few moments longer, then followed without looking up again at Caitlin.

The common area was almost empty now. With difficulty, Caitlin twisted her wrist to see her watch. Break time had officially ended three minutes ago.

Out of the corner of her eye she saw somebody edge out of the shadows beside the bike shed. It was Spencer Blackwood. He glanced from side to side. He looked as though he'd rather be anywhere else in the world.

"Please come down," he said quietly.

"Are you kidding?" Caitlin snorted. "I'm just getting started."

"Nobody's listening."

"Then I'll have to be louder, won't I?" She turned towards the stone arch entrance to the oldest part of the college building, where some late-arriving students were still scurrying to their lessons. She bellowed, "Rights for Charmers!"

"Stop!" Spencer hissed. "I mean, nobody *wants* to listen."

"That doesn't mean we shouldn't say anything. I'm doing this for you, Spencer. I'm doing this because you were victimised. Don't you realise you were the subject of a hate crime?"

He looked as if he might cry. Yesterday, Caitlin had assumed that the dark patches above his cheeks were the beginnings of two black eyes. Had he always looked like that? He was hardly the image of a super-healthy Charmer kid. She wondered whether the dark patches would disappear when he had his first shedding.

Spencer shook his head sadly. "You don't get it. If I wasn't a Charmer – if those guys didn't have that to use against me – they'd find something else. People like them prey on people like me. That's just the way it is."

Poor sod. A lifetime of that sort of crap had left him totally spineless.

Spencer held up a hand to stop her from responding. "It's all right for you. You're stronger. And that's not because you're a Charmer, either. It's because you're you." His face flushed. Caitlin remembered that he had once asked her out on a date, years ago, when they were both in secondary school. It had been during one of her phases of telling everyone that all men were pigs, but she'd still managed to let him down reasonably politely. She'd thought he'd moved on since then.

"Please come down," he said. "You'll only make things worse."

A thought occurred to Caitlin. "Why are you even here at this college? Your dad's in the GBP." Her parents hadn't given her the option of going to a private school – they were well-off, but not wealthy. Her mum had explained how some Charmer dynasties used their extra lifespans and opportunities to gather wealth which accumulated over generations, but that had never been the Hext way.

"My dad doesn't want me to be here," Spencer replied. "He's embarrassed of it. Ashamed. But I begged, Caitlin. I don't want to spend my time with Charmers. At least, not the ones who expect the world to come to them, who already have it made. Knowing that turns them inside out and their insides are rotten. But I was wrong about this place being much better. All I can do is keep my head down."

Caitlin rubbed her wrist as best she could, given the constraints of the bike chain. "You shouldn't have to. You're one of the good guys, Spencer. You deserve better."

"Yeah. Well. I'm smart enough to see how this pans out. I just need to get through college unscathed. My time comes later. A couple of sheddings down the line, Carl and Scotty and all the other idiots will be pot-bellied, middle-aged and washed up, and I'll only be getting started. I understand how lucky we are, you and me, Caitlin. I don't want rid of my gift. I want to be left alone to do my own thing. And, no offence, but this kind of stunt isn't going to help. I know you mean well."

Caitlin smiled sympathetically, but she was no longer giving him her full attention. Two faces had appeared at the window of one of the upstairs classrooms. Jane and Evie, pressed up against the glass while blind old Mr Bowcock pottered around behind them handing out exercise books. Evie's face was hard to read, but Jane's was another matter. She smirked, looking pointedly from Caitlin to Spencer and back again. Then she raised her fist and poked her tongue into her cheek, in and out, miming a blowjob.

Caitlin felt her face redden. She had all the sympathy in the world for Spencer, but the idea of appearing romantically linked to him was distinctly unappealing. This whole thing had been a mistake.

"Get back," she said, glaring at him. "Go on, get lost. This isn't about you."

Spencer obeyed literally, taking steps backwards until he thumped into a wooden post. Then he turned and scurried away.

It was still important to protest. The whole college was corrupt. Even the teachers sniggered about Charmers behind closed doors, probably. Her mum had once described anti-prosperity protests she had witnessed in the centre of town, before the ban. She had waxed lyrical about the protesters' noise and passion, the importance of their continued presence given the lack of any party in opposition to Great British Prosperity. But the target of their protest had left Caitlin feeling conflicted – given the make-up of the GBP, they might as well have been railing against the existence of Charmers. The hate for her kind was everywhere.

She raised her head and shouted as loudly as she could, "Rights for Charmers! Stop oppression! Rights for Charmers!" She repeated the phrases, barely pausing for breath in between. The words were starting to lose meaning; she struggled to recall her initial intentions. She and Spencer had been insulted, sure, but Charmers weren't oppressed, were they? But the distinction between *her* kind of Charmer and the type that ran the country was impossible to articulate.

She saw movement at the fogged window of the staffroom.

After a couple of minutes a teacher emerged. No, worse: the headteacher. Mr Pearl's eyes – piggy behind his too-small glasses at the best of times – narrowed as he approached her. His hands were jammed deep into the pockets of his maroon cardigan. Caitlin shouted louder and louder. Her slogans sounded less meaningful each time she repeated them.

"Miss Hext," he said. His voice was stern.

"Rights!"

"Caitlin."

"For!"

"Stop this. Now."

"CHARMERS!"

Mr Pearl came to a stop a couple of metres from the tree. "It's dangerous to stand on the bench. Among other things, I'm responsible for your health and safety."

Caitlin felt immediately deflated. It didn't feel like oppression, at least not in a satisfying way. Then again, maybe this was how dictatorial regimes worked. Perhaps they came across as efficient and concerned about people's safety, at first.

"I can't come down," she said, willing her voice to sound more indignant than needy. "I'm tied to the tree and I don't know the code to this bike lock."

Mr Pearl leant to one side to look at the chain digging into her wrists. "I expect Mr Beamish will have some cutters to get through that. Don't you worry."

"If you come near me, I'll shout louder." Other students had gathered at the upstairs windows now, alongside Evie and

Jane. Result. "Hey! Watch me being oppressed!" she shouted.

Mr Pearl didn't flinch. "That's a new bike chain, isn't it? Did you buy it through the scheme last week?"

Caitlin didn't reply.

He nodded. "I bet you haven't changed the combination settings yet. Let me guess. One, two, three, four? No. Okay. Four, three, two, one, then. Final offer."

Caitlin pressed her lips tightly together.

"Good," Mr Pearl said. "Right, let's get you down from there. Then you can return to whichever lesson you ought to be attending right now. I know you're not a bad egg, Caitlin. You're a very promising student, your physics grades in particular. I've heard tell that you're considering space science as a field of further study. And you were deputy head girl at secondary school, is that right?" He took a step forwards. "I do understand that things are fraught. I mean, with your—"

"Stop right there," Caitlin said. "Are you going to lecture me about my 'changing body' now?"

"I wouldn't dare to presume." His movements slowed, but he still kept edging towards her with his hand outstretched to the bike chain.

"You know nothing about me," Caitlin spat. "You know I'm a Charmer, but you have no effing clue about what that really means. And—" She watched him carefully, trying to judge whether or not her next words would hurt him. "You're scared. You're scared of me, and Spencer, and the rest of us. Terrified, even. You don't know how to deal with us. Because you know we're stronger than you."

Infuriatingly, Mr Pearl smiled. "You want to know the

truth, Caitlin? I'm scared of all of you students. Charmers and non-Charmers alike. You're all unpredictable. You can all be wonderful when you want to be, but when you sense that things are against you…" His hands reached the bike chain.

Caitlin experienced the attention of the watching students as something physical, a blanket suffocating her and making her insufferably hot. She realised she had to get away. She had made her point. The demonstration had to be abandoned before it fizzled out with her being led away, humiliated, to the staffroom for one of Mr Pearl's heart-to-hearts.

She braced her shoulder blades against the rough bark. Then she bunny-hopped, using the looped rope as leverage, lifting both her feet and planting them squarely into Mr Pearl's solar plexus. His eyes widened with surprise as he staggered back. Caitlin struggled to find her footing again, scrabbling on the smooth wood of the bench. The chain still held her hands tight before her, like a bound Egyptian mummy, and the rope still bound her to the tree. When her feet slipped off the edge off the bench, she bounced awkwardly, painfully, down the length of the tree trunk, an abseiler facing the wrong way. She came to a stop sitting bundled up on the bench, her hands caught under her chin, her hair over her face, and the rope now tugging her breasts upwards through her shirt.

From somewhere beyond the curtain of her tangled ginger hair, she heard Mr Pearl groan. She could also hear the hoots of a dozen or more students.

With great difficulty, she twisted and manipulated the combination lock. Four, three, two, one. She gasped as the chain and rope came free, the sharp end of the lock scraping against her forearm and producing an instant red weal. She pushed her hair from her eyes, then wished she hadn't. The windows of the classrooms all around her were filled with faces. The students' laughter sounded more raucous for being muffled by the glass, like the echoes of a chaotic children's party in a leisure centre swimming pool.

Mr Pearl finally managed to rise to his haunches. He retched and spat onto the gravel.

This was bad.

She ran. The bike chain dangled from her left wrist, jangling as it hit her leg with each stride. She didn't look back.

*

Russell stood on tiptoes, trying to see through the glass door mottled with dirt. He had tried looking into the premises from the outside of the shared office complex, too, but black paint had been applied to the wide window from inside. It made sense. The rusted plaque on the door stated that the business was *Haddo Photography – Portraits and Events*. There was probably a darkroom in there, or a studio requiring full control over the light.

He moved further down the corridor. The next office belonged to the first of the accountants, named Michael Trent, according to the nameplate. Russell had seen Michael before. He always wore a tweed suit and a bow tie, dressing like a relic from the past, despite the fact that he was only in his late thirties. Russell had always avoided him. There was something about his eyes.

The two other accountants' offices were on the opposite side of the wide corridor. Russell paused to listen at each in turn. He heard muffled voices speaking emphatically and with some urgency, as though the accountants were trying to communicate through their shared wall. Russell checked his watch. He had arrived at work even earlier than usual – it wasn't yet half past six.

He could hear more voices behind the door of the historical publisher, Tarragon Books. It sounded as though it was a heated discussion. What on earth could they be arguing about?

At the door to the banner-printers, Russell could only hear a low rumble. That was normal enough, then. He had seen the rollers of the huge printer once or twice in passing. It ran constantly, making this part of the corridor floor shudder like a cross-channel ferry. The door had a thin, vertical window along its outer edge, but louvre blinds fixed to its inside blocked any view. Russell stood on tiptoes again to peer down through the narrow gaps between the panels of the blinds. Several figures were moving about inside, lit by strip lights.

None of this meant anything. Ixion had put an idea into his mind, and of course it affected his perception of ordinary goings-on.

A door closed somewhere behind him. Russell wheeled around.

Ellis Blackwood's head was tilted as he watched Russell. Somehow, Ellis was already halfway down the corridor – Russell must have been so absorbed in his investigation that he had responded slowly to the sound of the closing door, unless Ellis had emerged from one of the other offices.

"Ah. Good morning, Russell." Ellis's eyes flicked briefly from Russell to the door of the banner-printer.

"Minister. Good morning. I was just—"

"Good. Yes. Thank you again for taking Nell and Spencer to the theatre. It does the power of good for a developing boy, I'd think. Once more unto the breach, and all that."

Russell gave a weak smile. His head filled with thoughts of Nell and her wild hair and freckles. It was impossible to believe that she was capable of anything untoward. Generally, Russell had little faith in his instincts, but he was certain of this. If Ellis was up to something, might it really be the case that she was under threat personally?

"Good," Ellis said again. He nodded twice. "Let's treat ourselves, Russell. Coffees from the cafe. If you would be so kind?"

Russell was grateful for the excuse to leave. As he edged past Ellis he avoided looking at the door to the banner-printers. "From the greasy spoon, sir?"

Ellis cleared his throat. "From Silvie's. It's a little further, I suppose, but people do rather recommend it. Thank you so much, Russell. And later on, remind me to speak to you about a particular assignment I have for you. Something rather specialised that I think you'll excel at."

As Russell made his way along the corridor he sensed the minister's gaze upon him. Once outside, he took a deep gulp of cold air. Then, acting on instinct, he jammed his heel into the doorway, stopping the door from reaching the latch. He counted to ten and peeped inside.

Ellis was now standing before the security guard's desk.

"Of course, sir," the guard said.

Ellis fiddled with his cufflinks as he watched the guard operate a wall safe that Russell had never noticed before. From inside it the guard produced a small black box, which he placed carefully upon the desk. Ellis nodded and pressed his thumb firmly onto its lid. It beeped and then sprang open. Ellis plucked out a key, nodded again, and padded along the corridor.

The security guard put the box back into the safe and settled into his chair with his magazine.

Ellis paused outside the door to the banner-printers. Then he unlocked the door and entered.

Russell darted inside, patting his pockets in answer to the security guard's accusing stare. He took long strides, then slid along the wall to reach the door to the banner-printers and its slowly narrowing gap.

Inside the room, Ellis stood with his back to the door. Beyond him Russell saw the long, horizontal rollers of the printer, chugging away.

A tall woman appeared from somewhere to the right. She wore a dark business suit and her hair was pinned up. The severity of the scraped hairstyle tugged at the skin of her forehead. Russell recognised her from TV news reports – what was her name? He chewed a nail while he thought. Angela McKinney. She was a low-ranking minister of something-or-other, but on TV she had always appeared mild enough. Here, in the flesh, she was fearsome.

Angela took Ellis by the arm. She glanced at the door. Russell pressed himself to the wall beside the doorway. He held his breath.

"You're exhausted," he heard Angela say. "Care to explain?"

Ellis's voice was as meek as a scolded child's. "I apologise. It isn't what you think."

Her voice became quieter. The door was now almost fully closed. Russell edged as close to the sliver gap as he dared.

He caught only a few words. "I'm glad to hear it. You know, you really should—"

Then the door snicked shut.

*

Gerry rang the brass bell a second time. Its jangle echoed from the door's stone surround.

She rapped with the iron doorknocker. Nothing. She turned and leant against the door. From here the slope tumbled downwards from Ilam Hall to a lumpy Saxon church that rose from the ground as if it were a naturally occurring rock formation. Its pale surfaces contrasted sharply with the green woodland on each side of the valley and the black of the rushing river in its centre.

She made her way around the hall. A curl of steps led up to a large, square lawn with a perimeter dotted with heavy stone vases, filled with withered and black shrubs. Whoever tended the grounds of Ilam Hall was fighting a losing battle. Even cutting the grass must be a full-time job.

An elderly man was making his way around the lawn,

respectful of the signed instructions to keep off the grass. Gerry watched him for a few moments. Might he be the owner? But he produced a camera from his pocket and turned to take a few snaps of the huge building, then of a single wilted rose in one of the borders. He reached a castellated entrance that led to a spiral staircase to the lower levels, and to the bridge across the river. Gerry wondered whether his knees could take the descent.

She headed in the opposite direction. A sign directed her to *Refreshments*.

The cafe was within a converted barn, separate from the main hall. Inside, salads and crusty pies that appeared homemade, or at least not bought from a supermarket, filled a display counter.

"What'll it be, duck?" The woman behind the counter wiped her hands on her pristine apron. She had wiry, grey hair and her eyes were surrounded by creases and crinkles, like eddies in water. Gerry liked her immediately.

"I was hoping for information," she replied.

"Not before lunch, though?"

Gerry looked at her watch. One o'clock already. Her trek up and down the mountain had taken longer than she had realised.

"Just a coffee for now, thanks," she said. She blushed as her belly gurgled with hunger.

The woman smiled sympathetically. "No need for diets for a stick like you. Here." She pushed a slice of cake onto a plate. "Best Bakewell tart in the area. And yes, that includes Bakewell."

Gerry chose a table close to the counter. There were only two other customers in the cafe, in the far corner. One appeared to have fallen asleep with his newspaper still resting on his chest.

"Have you worked here long?" she said. She held up a piece of crumbling tart. "This is delicious, by the way."

The woman fussed with the coffee machine, wiping its nozzles with a cloth. "A good while."

"Do you know much about the place? Its history?"

"As much as anybody, I'd venture."

"And how about the owners? Do you see them around often?"

"Not them. Her. And yes, she keeps herself busy. An industrious type, she likes to think. Always keen to muck in when things need doing."

Gerry pushed the rest of the cake into her mouth in one go, without meaning to. Journo fail. "I'm so sorry. You're the owner of Ilam Hall?"

The woman grinned. "I am that. Anise Hartwell, and very pleased to meet you. Dad was into herbs, hence the name. That lawn outside was a herb garden, a generation ago. It proved more than I could keep up with."

Hartwell. Gerry remembered the name from her books about the Fall. A Hartwell had been the first Lord of Ilam Hall. If Anise's family went back that far, presumably she was a Charmer. Gerry's eyes darted around the woman's features, reappraising her in light of the new information. The grey hair and wrinkles suggested that she must be well into her seven-year period before her next shedding. Once she produced a new Snakeskin, all those creases would flatten and her hair would gain the colour of her youth.

"I'm Gerry Chafik," she said. "You have a wonderful home."

Anise shrugged. "It could be better. I do my best. The volunteers help. And at least the kids get their money's worth."

"Your children, you mean?" Charmers tended to have lots of them. Spreading the gift, or establishing a foothold in the future of the country, depending on which way you looked at it.

Anise laughed. "Never did have them, no. It rather relies on finding a man first, and I've always scared them off. No, I mean the kids out there, the youths. At the youth hostel. If you came in the front way you won't have seen the entrance. Oh, it's lovely. Just another barn, but the YHA have done it up terrific inside. I get letters sometimes from groups. The loveliest place to stay, they say. They hardly ever trash it. I don't need to deal with the place much at all."

"I'm fascinated by the hall," Gerry said. "I mean, partly because it's so beautiful, and those views... But partly because of the story. The history. The Fall, way back."

"Ah. You have a manner about you. For some reason I didn't take you for a tourist," Anise said. Her posture changed and her tone became more rehearsed. "It's certainly a story, isn't it? Imagine all that time ago, 1808, in the depths of a summer night—"

"Sorry, no, I'm not. A tourist, I mean. I'm interested, but I've already read the books."

Anise looked relieved. "To be honest, folks around here are happy being left alone, left to enjoy their gift." When Gerry held up both her hands in a gesture meaning 'no offence', she hurriedly added, "Not me, though. Don't you worry. I enjoy a chat."

Gerry suddenly realised what Anise had implied. "Are you saying that people around here are all Charmers, still?"

"For the most part. Me too, in case you were wondering. I'm not afraid to own up to it. It's a lovely way to be." She tugged at her hair, as though she had read Gerry's thoughts about her appearance. "I never do dye it. Too much bother, and I'll be shedding in a couple of months. Shame that I've got the type of genes that means I'll be grey again before my next seven years are up, but at least it means I get to change my look every so often. I'm sixty-two, you know."

Gerry's eyes widened.

Anise giggled. She twirled on the spot, flaring out her apron. "You come back in July and see me then. You'd swear I wasn't yet forty." She cleared her throat. "Sorry. I oughtn't to be a show-off about it. If I was, I could hardly blame you folks for carrying a grudge."

Gerry paused at that. Did all non-Charmers 'carry a grudge'? Did she herself?

It was time to move the conversation on, if she was going to take advantage of Anise's talkative nature. "I'm actually hoping to get more information on the Fall. Things that might have been under-reported. It sounds vague now that I say it out loud. I'm a, well, a writer. Do you know if there's anywhere I ought to look?"

"A writer?" Anise pressed both her hands down on the counter, raising herself to look closer at Gerry. "Oh, I see it now. You have that bearing about you. Brains and beauty?" She grinned as Gerry's cheeks flushed. "Good for you. Good for you. And yes. I have just the thing. Wait two ticks and I'll call Rachel up from the kitchens, then we can be off."

A few minutes later, Gerry found herself being led towards the main building of Ilam Hall. Anise gestured at points of interest as they passed, though these amounted to the picnic area and a new water bowl for visiting dogs. Gerry indulged her. Anise had obviously taken a shine to her, so she must milk that as much as possible.

They entered at one of the rear doors to the hall, which was unlocked. The daylight filtering through the grimy windows provided barely enough illumination to make out the interior. Dust danced in the air, parting as Anise and Gerry made their way along the lengths of narrow rugs that formed a path across the stone flagstones. Teetering pyramids of paperback romance novels covered the surfaces of most of the items of furniture.

Anise reached a wide, curved staircase and took the steps two at a time. If Gerry hadn't already known about her being a Charmer, her levels of energy would have been a giveaway. Her bare legs belonged to a woman half her age, too. How long would she live to enjoy her gifts? The Charmer average was an extra thirty years, but the most fortunate could almost double their lifespans. They became less healthy as time went on, of course – the benefits of shedding diminished each time – but even so.

She lost track of their route through a warren of connected rooms. Finally, Anise flung open a door and coughed a "Ta-da!" as dust billowed forth.

It was the library that Gerry had hoped for. She dashed over to one shelf, blinking rapidly to dispel motes of dust. Anise threw open pairs of wide shutters and sunlight turned the air peach-coloured. Gerry traced her fingers along book spines, reading the titles. *A History of Ilam*, and *Ilam Hall: Renovation and Rebirth*, and *The Fall: A People's History*.

"It's perfect," Gerry whispered. "It's everything I need."

Anise stood with her hands on her hips. "What kind of writer are you, by the way? Fiction?"

"Factual," Gerry replied. She felt queasy at the thought of lying to Anise. "I'm a journalist."

Anise hesitated for a moment, then smiled. "It's a noble profession. Good for you, Miss Chafik. But you'll find nothing very topical in here. Nothing salacious."

Gerry shook her head. "That's not what I'm after. I promise. I think there's a story still to be told, about Ilam. I swear I'm not here to dig up dirt."

"Good girl. And speaking of digging up dirt, that's what I ought to be doing myself. Been meaning to plant some peas beside the picnic spot. I get the youth hostellers to shell them. More wholesome than them watching video nasties at home. I'll leave you to it, then?"

Gerry tried to hide her surprise. After only fifteen minutes of conversation, was this woman really going to leave her alone in her library, in her home?

"I'll be as good as gold," she said, then regretted making herself sound so childish.

She remembered another question she had meant to ask. "Anise. Sorry. Do you happen to know about a small building that used to be up on the mountaintop? Up on the western side, beside a rock outcrop shaped like a wave. I think it might have been there at the time of the Fall."

Anise frowned. "Not my area of expertise, I'm afraid. There have been so many changes to the village since then. Not least Ilam Hall itself."

"It was built after the Fall, wasn't it?"

"There was a sixteenth-century building here, back then, though long abandoned. My great-great-great-or-whatever-he-was-grandad only moved in when it was rebuilt, when he was granted the lordship. Eighteen-twenties or thereabouts."

Gerry frowned. "So Hartwell, your ancestor, he wasn't Lord of Ilam at the time of the Fall? In 1808?"

"Goodness, no. I don't suppose Ilam warranted having a lord. Don't get me wrong, my ancestor was important in his way. A mayor, I suppose you'd call him nowadays. But he lived in a house down in the valley, more or less the same as the rest of them."

Gerry hadn't considered that people had benefitted in ways other than receiving their Charmer gifts. "Ilam did well out of the Fall," she said, more a thought out loud than a real observation.

Anise nodded. "For a while, yes. Even the new Charmers saw the opportunity to cash in on the tourists. Before then, people would no doubt have been more interested in Eyam, nearby. Heard of it? It was the site of the plague village, where folks in the sixteenth century quarantined themselves rather than spread the disease. How the people of Eyam must have seethed when Ilam came along and robbed them of all their tourism! And Matlock Bath, of course, the spa town. But even cable cars and amusements only went so far, compared to the chance of visiting Ilam."

"It must have been more than simple tourism. The attention on Ilam must have been feverish at first."

"I'm sure you're right. A visit to Illam would have carried a thrill of excitement that, however faint, there was a chance of it happening again. For decades people held out hope that maybe there'd be another Fall. Taking the spa waters in Matlock Bath doesn't really compare to the possibility of granting the gift of extended life to your kiddies, does it?" Her face fell. "These days people have cottoned on to the fact that there's nothing much here, and that the Fall was a one-off."

"They still come. I've spoken to some of them in the village." But it was true that there had been fewer than she expected. The village was quiet for such a historic location. And, clearly, nobody nowadays believed that Charmer abilities could be gained through anything but hereditary genes.

Anise shrugged. "People will show up anywhere there's a cup of tea to be had. But if we're honest, folks can get all the info they want about Charmers from documentaries on TV, or from photocopied anti-prosperity pamphlets about the prime minister being two hundred years old, or some such nonsense."

She turned before reaching the door. "As for this hilltop house of yours... If you want to do some detective work, that's the bookcase you'll be needing." She pointed at a shelf masked by cobwebs, where a shaft of light made a yellow stripe across the thick spines. The books were rows and rows of bound census records.

Gerry gasped. She was grateful that she hadn't got wind of the existence of this library before she had struck up a conversation with Anise in the first place; her eagerness, or even her desperation, would have been impossible to disguise. "This is beyond perfect. Thank you, Anise. I can't tell you how much this means to me."

Anise appeared a little flustered. With a quick thumbs-up, she ducked out of the room. Gerry listened to her clattering down the stairs.

*

Throughout the morning Caitlin's dad had made offers through her closed bedroom door – food, outings, conversation. Anything to take her mind off her dreadful embarrassment at the sixth-form college. Finally, just before lunchtime, she had heard him leave the house in defeat. He would be wandering the nearby lanes by now, swishing at the long grass with a stick, cursing at the blue tarpaulins in the cordoned-off field behind the house, perhaps wondering again if he ought, at last, to get a dog. He was an open book and Caitlin loved him dearly, but that was the precise reason why she hadn't been able to face him this morning. She had heard the phone ring and could tell from her dad's responses that it was Mr Pearl on the other end of the line.

Ian had made no remarks to Caitlin about the fact that she had been suspended from college. There was nothing to be done. Caitlin had already made it clear that she wouldn't be returning today. Still, she had preferred it when it had appeared to be her own choice.

She had spent most of the morning working on a pencil sketch, another self-portrait. The two angled mirrors fixed to her desk produced an image of a Caitlin that moved in unpredictable directions, so that when she fidgeted it was as though she was watching somebody other than herself. The picture was coming on well. She had reworked it again and again, altering the faint pencil lines, all but restarting when the light from outside the window altered the shadows. She knew it was narcissism.

After another hour of silence she crept out of her bedroom. She patrolled the corridors of the house, a sulking ghost.

The largest sitting room was the coldest room in the house. Caitlin had no memory of a fire ever having been built in the enormous fireplace that funnelled wind from outside. Her dad's old telescope was still fixed on its tripod at the floor-to-ceiling bay window. She bent to squint through it. It was her dad who had got her interested in astronomy in the first place, but it was hard to pin down why she had inherited his passion. He had never once claimed to have seen anything interesting. Caitlin sighed and pushed at the telescope, but it didn't budge. She flicked the tightening handle on its base and pushed again. The telescope squeaked as it swung around and around. When it came to rest she peered through it. Her vision was filled with an image of Uncle Tobe.

He was pottering around outside his wooden shed at the foot of the garden, laying out wet clothes on the backs of plastic chairs. He insisted on doing his own laundry these days. Perhaps he wanted to avoid bumping into Ian, or perhaps he was ashamed of all the semen stains.

Caitlin wrestled with the rusted lock of the door in the bay window.

Her uncle didn't hear her coming. He jumped in fright as she called out his name.

"How's it going?" She slumped down on the only plastic chair that wasn't draped with an item of his clothing. Tobe watched her. He held a sodden pair of jeans in his hands.

"Okay," he replied uncertainly.

"I could fix you up with a washing line."

"Okay. Thanks."

"I'll do it later. Hey, Tobe? Can I talk to you?"

Tobe looked around as if hoping for a distraction. "What about?"

"Sit down, why don't you."

Tobe gazed at each of the chairs in turn, at the clothes hanging over them. Then he sat cross-legged on the floor with the wet pair of jeans draped over one knee. A dark puddle began to spread on his tracksuit.

"My shedding's in just over a week."

Tobe nodded slowly. He'd probably forgotten.

"What's it like?"

"I already told your friend. It's tickly."

"I don't mean the physical feeling. If it hurt, I guess I'd have heard about that already. I mean afterwards. Do you feel weird about it?"

"Nope."

"But there was another you! Just for a moment. He was there – he was exactly like you in every way – and then he was gone. Dead."

"Nah. Dead people don't turn into dust. Least, not in only a few seconds."

"Even so. Your Skin was afraid, Tobe. Don't you think?"

Tobe coughed and glanced inside the shed. The bulky TV showed the pause screen of some Commodore computer game. She wouldn't have long before he succumbed to the urge to return to whatever digital war he was waging.

"I always thought of it as a sort of trick," he said. "You know them mirrors at the funfair?" He paused, appearing to struggle to collect his thoughts. "No. Not that. But I saw this magic trick once. A man in a box. My mate Mousey went in – you know, as a willing volunteer from the crowd. And he disappeared, fair and square. But it was mirrors, see? He was deep in there, in the box, and it was only his reflection that disappeared. I nearly shit myself when he was gone, just for that second, but then there he was all happy and fine. Then his mum bought us both a lolly. We was only seven or eight at the time."

He gazed at the birch trees that marked the end of the garden and the beginning of the fields, where blue tarpaulins fluttered like flags from builders' scaffolding.

Caitlin had never heard Tobe speak so much in one go. "So you think it's an illusion and nothing more? That the shedding is really about the rejuvenation, that it's all about *us*, and that the Snakeskins are only some kind of by-product?"

"I know it's not so simple. Nothing is. But yeah. That Skin, he weren't me. And he weren't someone totally new either. And then he just *went*, didn't he? So the way I see it, it don't matter all that much. If each Skin only hangs around for half a minute, who cares if they can think for themselves or not?"

"Yeah." She was far from certain that she agreed. "Anyway. I should let you get back to your thing."

Tobe's knees clicked as he rose to his feet. When Caitlin vacated her chair he tossed the wet jeans onto it.

"One thing, though," he said as she turned to leave. "I heard you and that fit friend of yours talking. About your shedding. And it ain't right, what you're planning."

"Evie's not my friend," Caitlin said. Saying it out loud, she felt she might cry.

Tobe shrugged, oblivious. "It's private, see."

"Shedding?"

"Them government types shouldn't stick their noses in. And if you ask me, normal people shouldn't be watching either."

Caitlin felt the now-familiar righteous rage bubbling up within her. Nobody understood. "But they need to see that we're not afraid. That we're proud."

"Whatever." Tobe plodded onto the decking. "But being proud is something inside you, isn't it? It's not about shouting stuff out to the world, especially when the world doesn't give two shits about you and your extra-long life and your magicky healing and your freaky Skins. That's just what I think. I'm not so thick as all that, you know."

He ducked into the shed. The sagging armchair positioned too close to the TV swallowed him up.

Caitlin didn't move.

He was right. As difficult as it was to believe, her uncle was actually right. Rather than making a big scene, displaying her shedding in public, she ought to be dignified. That would show Evie and the others, far more than making a circus of the whole thing. It's what her mum would have done, too.

Yes.

When she shed, when she produced her first ever Snakeskin, she would do it without a crowd, without Evie. And she would be silent. It would be beautiful.

# FIVE

Caitlin sat cross-legged on the grass, facing away from Ivy Cottage. Her left hand rested on one knee. The other stroked a faint red scar on her forearm. The cut, made by the bike chain as she had wrestled to free herself three days ago, had healed almost entirely but the red line remained. Every time she saw it, she winced at the memory of her stupidity.

She hadn't returned to college. Mr Pearl had taken to ringing Caitlin's dad mid-morning each day, insisting that her suspension had now been lifted. Ian had passed the messages on to Caitlin, but he hadn't pressed the point. There was an unspoken agreement – that there could be no changes to the way things were until after the shedding.

And now the day had finally arrived. Her seventeenth birthday. Ian and Tobe had been ready with the cake as soon as she emerged from her bedroom just before lunchtime. She had felt a little overwhelmed about the idea of the two men doing anything as a team, but she'd told them not to make a fuss. A shedding easily outweighed the importance of a birthday. If there was going to be a celebration, it could wait until after the Skin had been and gone.

She shivered and hoicked her scarf to cover her bare shoulders. Wearing her mum's ceremonial gown was a fashion error, but it was important. She watched the lowering sun and imagined that its descent was controlled by the strokes of her finger upon the scar. The shedding ought to occur soon after the sun had fully set. It wouldn't be long now. The foot of the garden had already dipped into darkness, the trees lit more by the glow from the house than by sunlight.

She heard voices behind her. She didn't turn around.

"—marvellous cup of tea," a woman's voice said. "Thank you, Mr Hext. Not everyone is so cordial, I can tell you."

"It's the least we can do," Ian replied. "Careful where you step. The garden slopes away from this point on."

Caitlin leapt to her feet and spun around. "No!"

Her dad's face crumpled, expressing a mixture of apology and what-could-I-have-possibly-done? attitude.

Caitlin almost spat at the government woman as she emerged from Ivy Cottage, edging carefully down the shallow slope. "Not her. Dad! Seriously. Anyone but her."

The woman – Ms Blaine, that was her name – extended a hand. It wavered when Caitlin didn't take it. "It's good to see you again, young lady. You must be thrilled that it's your turn at last!"

Caitlin pursed her lips. She stared at Ms Blaine until the woman turned away in embarrassment.

"I'm not doing it," she said sullenly. "Not with her around."

Clumsily, Ian attempted to take her by the shoulders but

she shrugged him off. He thrust his hands into the pockets of his cardigan. "It's not exactly something you have control over at this stage." He lowered his voice to a whisper. "I swear, I won't let her call the shots. This is your night. But the government were never going to let you do this without supervision, were they? It's the law."

Caitlin glared at Ms Blaine, who was standing on tiptoes and craning her neck to see the glittering blue tarpaulins in the field beyond the end of the garden. It occurred to Caitlin to wonder why the scaffolding and tarpaulins had been in place for so many months, without any signs of construction beginning.

The presence of another woman made Caitlin's mum feel even more missing, as though Ms Blaine was an unconvincing stunt double. It felt like the final straw. She could hardly remember which aspects of the shedding ceremony had once struck her as romantic.

She just wanted it over and done with.

Her dad and Ms Blaine set off towards Tobe's shed. Ian gave a quick, hopeful thumbs-up. Caitlin scowled but plodded after him.

"Tobe!" Ian called out. "It's nearly time. Up you get."

The door to the shed opened and Tobe emerged. To Caitlin's surprise, he was not only dressed, he was wearing a suit and tie. His hair glistened with whatever product kept it from springing upwards as it usually did. Caitlin stifled a laugh. This was a gesture for her benefit, after all. Her uncle was softer than she had suspected.

Tobe ducked back inside, fumbling with something.

Caitlin gasped as dozens of white fairy lights appeared along the lip of the roof of the shed, turning this corner of the garden into a vision of festive cheer.

Abruptly, Caitlin began to sob.

This wasn't right. She didn't want this. It wasn't anything to do with being watched by the government. If anything, it was this unconditional support from her dad and Tobe that was pushing her over the edge. They were acting as though being a Charmer was something wonderful, and yet all it had done for her was make her bitter and lose all her friends. If she'd had a choice, she'd choose to be normal.

Through her tears she saw her dad gesture to Tobe and Ms Blaine: *Keep quiet*. He scurried up the hillside and crouched beside her.

"Tobe was determined to do something," he said. "He means well."

Caitlin shook her head. "It's beautiful. It's perfect. It's just—"

Ian put his arm around her. "I know, love." He glanced up at the sky, as though he could tell the time by looking at the stars – perhaps he could? "It's almost time. There's no way to really be ready, I know. But are you ready?"

Caitlin bobbed her head, more from her continued sobbing rather than a nod. She hefted herself up. The grassy incline made her even more unbalanced on her weak and wobbly legs. She allowed her dad to lead her to the shed. He stopped beside Tobe and Ms Blaine, who stared at her clipboard rather than meet Caitlin's eye. Ian ushered Caitlin onto the decking. Caitlin looked up at the fairy lights. Her tears transformed each one into a streaked star.

"No," she mumbled. "This doesn't feel right."

She saw Tobe's shoulders slump.

"Uncle Tobe, no. I don't mean that. It's wonderful. You're wonderful. But bear with me. Could the three of you stand up here instead of me?"

Confused, Ian, Tobe and Ms Blaine stepped onto the decking. Ms Blaine appeared suspicious. She was probably worried that Caitlin might make a run for it.

Caitlin took three steps up the slope. The three of them were framed by the fairy lights, like Mary, Joseph and Jesus in a primary-school nativity.

"I want her to see you all properly, when she arrives," she said. If she were the Snakeskin, she'd want to see her family, not her originator. Even more, she would want to experience this view of the reddening sky and the black towers of the trees. It was the least Caitlin could offer during her few moments of life.

Her new-found sense of calm was shattered by the slam of a gate. She whirled around.

Evie was stumbling across the hillocks, the heels of her boots digging into the grass. Caitlin's cry of relief came out as a croak.

"Tell me I didn't miss it?" Evie panted. "The taxi got a flat tyre, would you believe that?"

She tripped and fell into Caitlin's arms, then planted a kiss on her cheek as though the entire action were intentional. "You look ace," she said. "Very ethereal, a touch goth. Love it."

Caitlin held her at arm's length. Perhaps she oughtn't to accept Evie again so quickly. Wasn't her pride at stake? "I thought you hated me."

"Well you're a twat, then. Didn't bring you a birthday present though, so *ha*."

"I said you shouldn't come."

Evie stuck out her tongue. "When have you ever known me to listen to you? I figured you'd keep saying so, if I asked. So I didn't ask. And today's about more than you properly joining the Charmer club. Today's the day you can get over yourself and all this bullshit and then come back to college and, you know, hang out again. Right?"

Caitlin considered possible responses: anger, accusations, insults. But what was the point? Evie was her best friend. So instead she said simply, "Right."

"Miss Hext." From the tone of Ms Blaine's voice, Caitlin knew it was time. She pushed Evie gently towards the decking. Evie took her place beside the others. She made a cross with her index fingers. It was the sign they had invented when they were kids. Star-crossed lovers, together forever.

Ian cleared his throat. "We're over-running already, I'm afraid. But it's fine. You know the drill, Cait. And you know that—" his voice cracked a little "—your mum's proud of you. Okay?"

He tossed a bundle of cloth towards her. She caught it and draped the blanket around her shoulders.

"Okay," she replied.

The sun was a narrow strip of gold punctured by the arrows of the treetops.

"I love you," she said. She didn't direct the words to anyone in particular.

The light became less gold and more purple, then finally green. The fairy lights turned grass-green too. Without a particular sense of surprise, Caitlin realised that the colour change was due to the green aura that now surrounded her.

A tickling sensation began at her toes, then crept upwards, as though she was being immersed slowly into a warm bath. The tickliness soothed her skin and somehow supported her, making her body feel lighter and her limbs floaty and difficult to locate. She felt a glimmer of panic, too, as the green light threatened to eclipse her view of Evie and her family, but it was as though the fear were something small and hard and unthreatening, buried beneath the pleasant sensations.

There was beauty in this. She felt a flush of pride. She thought of her mum, watching. Her mouth opened.

The feeling disappeared.

She looked to her right.

There she was.

The first thing that struck her about the Snakeskin was her nakedness. Rather than feel prudish on behalf of the other girl, Caitlin had the sudden notion that her own clothes must make her look ridiculous. The Snakeskin's body was stunning. Not because of its shape – though seeing her own body from this angle was both alarming and oddly gratifying; she realised that she was more curvy and less gangly than she had always imagined – but more because the Skin held herself in such a way as to appear unashamed of herself.

Even so, Caitlin swung the blanket off her shoulders and offered it to the other girl. As she did so, she noticed that the red scar on her own arm had disappeared entirely. Her body had been healed, rejuvenated. She really was a Charmer, now. During each successive shedding, the changes would be more pronounced. She would continue to reap the benefits long after her Skin became ash.

The Skin took the blanket, careful not to let her fingers touch Caitlin's. Only now did she start shivering.

Caitlin heard her dad speak, somewhere far away. His voice sounded small and dry.

Out of the corner of her eye, Caitlin saw Tobe reach over to take the crimson notebook from her dad. He read haltingly. "We honour you. And with your arrival we acknowledge this important milestone in the life of Caitlin Usborne Hext. With your passing, she will learn and grow. You are the instrument of her maturation. We thank you."

Caitlin kept her eyes on the Snakeskin. The girl blinked and her teeth chattered. Her eyes glistened with tears. She was gazing upwards, as Caitlin had intended, at the last pinks of daylight. It suddenly struck Caitlin that the Skin wasn't allowing herself to look at Evie or Ian. Perhaps it was too painful.

"Can you remember?" Caitlin whispered. "Everything?"

The Snakeskin turned. She didn't respond, but Caitlin knew the answer. That crumpled look was exactly the expression she herself would make, if she found herself in her situation. She had read all the science books about Snakeskins. She understood the phrase 'trace memory'. But that didn't cover it. The Skin had Caitlin's memories, her character, maybe even her soul, whatever that might be. The only difference was that the Skin was the one wearing the blanket. She must know that she was the copy. And she must know she had only moments before she would be gone forever.

Recently, Caitlin had spent all her time thinking about unfairness. But she had only been thinking about herself.

Before she even realised she was going to do it, she rushed forwards. She flung her arms around the shoulders of the Snakeskin. The Skin gasped and cried out.

The four onlookers erupted into confusion and chaos, leaping off the decking and struggling up the slope.

Evie reached her first. Caitlin pulled her close, hugging both Evie and the Skin.

"Cait!" Ian cried. He held back until Evie edged to one side and let him into the little huddle. Tobe appeared at his side. Caitlin stretched her arm to pull them both in tighter. All of their foreheads met in the centre of the throng, making a wheel with their necks as spokes.

Ms Blaine started saying something. Evie bared her teeth at her. Caitlin grinned. Ms Blaine retreated, tapping her fingernails on her clipboard in anxiety.

This was what it was all about. Family. The Skin was one of them, for these brief moments.

The Snakeskin seemed unable to catch her breath. She shivered uncontrollably. Soon everybody in the huddle was shuddering too.

"It's okay," Caitlin whispered, only partly for the Skin's

benefit. "You're safe. Right at this moment, you're safe. We love you."

They stayed like that. With each moment that passed, Caitlin expected the Skin to disappear – for one of the spokes of the wheel to suddenly be absent and for the group to become unbalanced.

But the Skin didn't ash.

After several minutes, Caitlin extricated herself from the group. She took a step back and Evie, Tobe and Ian did too.

The fairy lights reflected in the Snakeskin's shining eyes, making constellations of stars.

"I don't understand," the Skin said. Caitlin realised that it was the first time she had spoken. Her voice sounded strange, as though she was listening to a recording of herself – a little more nasal than she would have expected, the accent a little more Yorkshire, like her mum.

Caitlin looked at her dad. He would know what to do. But Ian only gave a little shrug.

"I really do think—" Ms Blaine began. Then she stopped dead.

Caitlin spun to see what had shocked her.

The Snakeskin was running barefoot up the slope.

After a moment's hesitation, Ms Blaine charged after her, followed by Ian. The Snakeskin's progress was quicker, though – her bare feet had better purchase on the slippery grass – and she reached the doors of the sitting-room bay with seconds to spare. She fumbled with the handle, then she was inside.

Caitlin released her held breath and gulped air.

This shouldn't be happening.

She flinched as Evie slipped an arm around her waist. Tobe put a hand on her shoulder, kneading it. Were they trying to prevent her from following? Caitlin ducked free and took a couple of strides towards the house. But even without any physical restraint, she found she couldn't make herself go any further.

Shouts came from inside the building. Ms Blaine's voice, demanding something. Then Ian's muffled voice, calmer, trying to reassure. And then the Snakeskin's shriek. A sound brought up from deep within the belly.

At first Caitlin thought that this was the moment, that the Skin was disappearing – would her dust be left on the walls in there, as a gruesome reminder? – but then three silhouettes appeared at the hallway window. Two were upright and the other flailed and struggled between them. The shapes became smaller. They must be dragging the girl to the front door.

Caitlin's knees buckled. She would have fallen to the floor if Evie hadn't held her up.

"I'll go," Evie said.

"No. No. Stay here. Please."

Tobe was making his way up to the side door of the cottage, as if it would be distasteful to take the same route as the fleeing Skin. Caitlin pressed her forehead to Evie's neck and concentrated on breathing, breathing, breathing. She had no tears left.

A few minutes later, Tobe returned. Ian followed. He looked tiny, his body narrowed by the glare of the lights of the house. His mouth was a tight line.

"What happened?" Caitlin managed to ask. "Has she gone?"

Ian hesitated. "Not in the way you mean. A few others came, or they were already waiting out the front, I don't know. She didn't fight them once they arrived. There was a van."

"Where will they take her?" Caitlin asked, though she realised that she didn't want to know.

"There are rules. They'll do what's right."

Nobody said anything for more than a minute.

"She shouldn't have run, should she?" Caitlin said, finally. "They won't be happy about it."

Ian was about to say something, but he only puffed out his cheeks. Caitlin wondered if he was thinking what she was thinking. *She's exactly the same as me. Of course she made a run for it.*

Another thought struck her. "Dad? What would have been the point of running? Where did she think she was going?"

Ian rubbed at his eyes with his thumb and index finger. "Upstairs. She wasn't trying to escape, exactly. She was trying to get into your bedroom."

# SIX

Russell pushed the oak door to the drawing room, gritting his teeth with the effort of keeping the silver tray level. The two brandy bottles on one side were far heavier than the stack of glasses on the other, threatening to tip the tray. To make matters worse, the route from Ellis's kitchen to the drawing room was cluttered with antique tables, umbrella stands and cabinets designed to trip him up.

The hubbub of the guests paused as he entered the room. A few of them – there must have been twenty in all, with more arriving all the time – looked his way. They saw his grey waiter's uniform and resumed their conversations.

"Good man, Russell," Ellis said, clapping him on the back and almost upsetting the tray entirely. "Pop it down there."

Russell deposited the tray upon a cabinet that surely would have been the sensible place to store brandy in the first place. Ellis was still watching him. Over the course of the evening, Russell had become convinced that Ellis's insistence that Russell should give up his time to help at his 'soirée' was some kind of test. Perhaps he already knew about Russell snooping around at the office. Perhaps he knew about Russell speaking to the shadowy stranger in the Gloucester Green car park.

A man poked his head around the door. Ellis was upon him in seconds to shake him by the hand.

Russell recognised the newcomer. He was unmistakable, in his tweed suit and bow tie, his goatee beard. It was Michael Trent, one of the accountants from the office complex. He bent his head to listen to Ellis amid the din of the other guests. Something about the body language of the two men surprised Russell. From their postures, anyone might have thought that Michael Trent was the one with power and influence, not Ellis.

Ellis turned and beckoned to Russell. His face appeared slightly flushed.

Russell retrieved one of the bottles of brandy and two glasses.

"I wanted to introduce you, not summon the help," Ellis said. Even so, he watched on as Russell unstoppered the bottle. To Michael he said, "May I introduce Russell Handler, my right-hand fellow. Handler by name, and all that."

Michael smoothed his beard. "So that's how you get anything done, Blackwood!"

"I'd be nothing without him." Ellis said, looking suddenly mournful.

"You do look bloody tired. You might want to see what can be done about that," Michael replied. He clucked his tongue. "So. Going up in the world, Russell Handler, aren't you? Play your cards right and soon enough you'll be personal assistant to His Lordship!"

Russell took a moment to get the reference, though he understood he was being mocked. He had heard people refer to the Prime Minister, Adrian Lorde, as His Lordship a couple of times before. The term was otherwise redundant since the abandonment of the House of Lords more than seventy-five years ago, when Charmers finally absorbed the old Tory party, rebranded themselves as the Great British Prosperity Party and announced the reformation of government. He remembered Nell Blackwood's undisguised scorn for Lorde. Perhaps it was a standard joke, that Lorde held no real power. But then who did? Some of the people in this room?

Russell hadn't realised that Ellis knew any of the other occupants of the offices socially. Then again, judging from the way he treated the accountant, perhaps 'socially' wasn't quite the right word.

"Very glad to meet you," Russell said, squirming under the accountant's continued scrutiny. He poured the drinks. "I should offer the brandy to the other guests."

"Glad to meet you too," Michael murmured, "in the flesh."

From the little that Ellis had told him, Russell guessed the guests were all dignitaries of various sorts. They conducted themselves in a way that suggested that they knew their own importance. It made a certain amount of sense that Ellis might need to schmooze them. His government department was Redevelopment and Funding, after all, and these people looked as though they might have the means to fund an awful lot, if the mood took them. Russell recognised a couple as MPs that he had seen on news broadcasts – presumably invited to lay on the charm, along with Ellis. Others were familiar, but Russell struggled to pin down where he'd seen them. They all appeared more or less the same – both the men and the women – in their dark suits. Business leaders of some sort, perhaps? There was only one thing he was sure about. They were all Charmers. Their cheeks and hair shone with health.

Russell picked his way among the guests, pouring drinks. A pink-cheeked man in his sixties downed his glass immediately and held it out again. Then he turned to the three guests who had crowded around him. "Bit of a blunt instrument, I'll admit. It wasn't me who came up with the format, or the name, but I sure as hell took the credit! 'Champions of Eternity' sounded pretty ridiculous at first."

Russell remembered the cartoon, from the late eighties. Even after people saw it for the Charmer propaganda it was, it was still remembered with affection.

"Still, it worked a treat," the man continued, swaying slightly as he slurped his drink. "The kiddies lapped it up – lunch boxes, sticker collections, cereal, the whole lot. Bloody shame when the policy changed and we had to wrap it all up. Not much artistry in the sweeping-it-under-the-carpet approach, if you ask me. The fools at Pinewood, Shepperton and Rank are all talking about audience approval ratings and review scores now, rather than support for Party messaging." A woman nudged him in the ribs. He looked at Russell and coughed.

Russell sloped away but then almost bumped into two

men huddled at one side of the enormous fireplace. They both glared at him until he retreated, then returned to their conversation.

"You don't understand," the younger of the two said in a low voice. "Their broadcast capabilities are improving all the time. If France, say, became determined to make contact – or even America, come to that – then increasingly we're going to have a hard time preventing it."

His elderly companion waved a hand. "We have a programme in place. Shifting broadcast frequencies, all that."

"But you – all of you – are still talking about radio and TV, and you're entirely missing the point," the first man insisted. "The technology out there is beyond anything we understand. Wireless communication far beyond the scale of the new cellular phones. Messaging between computers. Adrian Lorde can decree that development is slowed as much as possible, sure, but you must understand that devices get smuggled in occasionally, despite the restrictions. And if anybody were to—"

The man looked up. Russell realised he was still hovering before them, having backed away only a few steps. His head dropped and he made a show of restacking the glasses on his tray. Without looking up, he spun and marched away.

He kept to one side of the room. He was intent on watching Ellis through the crowd.

The woman he had seen inside the banner-printers – Angela McKinney – approached Ellis silently, a predator sizing up its prey. Her dark hair had been straightened to make sheer walls on either side of her face. Once again, her body language suggested that she was his superior. Russell had done a bit of research in the file of GBP staff profiles that he had found on a shelf in the office. Angela McKinney's official role was as Minister for Progression – a title no more prestigious or meaningful than Ellis's. Russell edged around the crowd to get within earshot.

Angela was looking around the room even as she spoke to Ellis in an offhand tone. "—and at short notice too. Did you furnish it yourself?"

"It was Nell," Ellis replied. His brow furrowed as he gazed around at the mahogany side tables and deep leather sofas. "It's all her. She has an eye for that sort of thing. History. What fits."

"Ah." Angela's eyes flickered over Ellis's features. Russell wondered whether she had feelings for him. "And she isn't..."

Ellis cleared his throat. He said in a firm voice, "No."

Russell thought again about the scene Nell Blackwood had made outside the office. It now seemed conceivable that Ellis was having an affair with this severe woman. Her being here might explain why Nell had stubbornly remained in the kitchen with Spencer, nursing a cup of tea and barely acknowledging Russell as he came and went with the trays. At one point, while Russell was refilling his tray, Ellis had been pleading with Nell to say hello to the guests. Her only response had been a steady glare. If she was at risk, as the stranger Ixion had asserted, perhaps it was the risk of adultery or her loss of self-respect.

However, the more he watched Ellis and Angela together,

the less plausible it was that they were romantically involved. From the way she was looking at him, what she had in mind seemed more in the vein of acquisition.

"I see," Angela said. "Still. She's done wonderful work here."

Russell noticed the door to the room open. Nell appeared. Russell winced at the thought of the altercation that might soon play out. But instead of approaching Ellis and Angela, Nell snuck over to Russell and plucked the half-full brandy bottle from the tray. Her conspiratorial grin made his stomach leap. Seconds later, she had left the room again.

Ellis drew Angela further into the corner of the room. Russell edged along the mahogany-panelled wall to stand closer.

"While I have you here," Ellis said in a low voice. "I wanted to offer reassurance."

"Are you mixing business and pleasure?"

"Perhaps. Sorry. But after yesterday, I wanted to make it clear that we're back on track."

"You've solved the issue?"

Ellis fiddled with a shirt cuff. "Yes, solved. Or rather, it sorted itself out. It's the nature of projected locations, ma'am. With anything of this nature, the target does tend to shift, rather."

A projected location? A target? Russell leant in closer to listen.

Angela's expression hardened. "Not an exact science, is it?"

"That's not what I meant. The data—"

"Data be damned. This is your job, Blackwood. If you're

not up to it, perhaps you should scurry back to the PM and leave us to the real work. It was your lobbying of Lorde that brought you to my attention in the first place – you were right about the need for automation in factories, for example, though if Lorde has his way we'll never see it happen. But the game has changed profoundly. If we're to establish the UK on the world stage we'll need to work with what we've got. And your being a progressive is worth nothing if you're a damned fool when it comes to practicalities."

"Ma'am. I really do think—" Ellis scanned the room. When he saw Russell he blanched. "Thank you, Russell. I think we can manage from here on in." He waved a hand in the manner of a king dismissing a serf. His fingers were trembling.

Other guests had noticed the dispute between Ellis and Angela. Russell heard the same word – 'target' – muttered several times. Even though Ellis was still watching, Russell slowed his movements as he deposited the tray and walked to the door, still trying to listen in.

Finally, he could delay no more. He closed the oak door behind him as he left. It must be immensely thick – he could hear nothing from inside except a low murmur.

How had Ixion phrased it when he had accosted Russell in the underground car park? *The Party is on the verge of disintegration, and Ellis Blackwood will play a key role.* Certainly it seemed clear that a great number of Party members found Adrian Lorde contemptible, and if their plotting related only to ousting him, Russell would have found it easy to turn a blind eye. But some of the things he had overheard tonight…

He shook his head. He could blame Ixion for so much of what he had seen and heard sounding sinister. Conspiracy theories were always intentionally vague, so that credulous people could fill in the gaps for themselves.

Yes. It was only the power of suggestion that was responsible for Russell's heart beating so rapidly. The word 'target' could be perfectly benign, after all. Angela McKinney was Ellis's superior, clearly, and every employee had targets. Targets for improvement. Targets for revenue. But part of the problem was that even after three months, Russell still wasn't sure quite what the remit of the department was, even in broad terms. *Redevelopment and Funding.* A meaningless description. From Russell's limited point of view, Ellis's job was to meet with wealthy clients over afternoon tea at the Randolph or the Old Parsonage. What was discussed in those meetings, he had no idea.

He plodded away from the drawing room. The kitchen was dark now – Nell must have taken the brandy upstairs. He imagined sharing the drink with her, tucked up in bed.

The sound of his footsteps was amplified by the darkness of the house. His limbs were heavy with exhaustion. The catering company were scheduled to arrive soon, ready to serve the main meal – but as far as Russell was concerned, somebody else could let them in. He'd be at home on the sofa with his duvet and some mindless Pinewood action film or a Shepperton comedy, and if Ellis complained in the morning, Russell would give him what for. He smiled at his capacity for self-denial. Sure he would.

As he neared the front door, he jumped at a sharp beeping

sound from his right. A thick curtain hung behind the door. He pushed it aside and peered into the darkness. It was difficult to make out, but there was a narrow corridor that would normally be obscured by the bulk of the curtain. Given the age of the house, he supposed it might once have led to the servants' quarters. Perhaps the caterers had already arrived? Grudgingly, he supposed he would have to point them towards the dining room after all. No doubt he'd get embroiled in serving the dinner, too.

The beep sounded again. Dim light leaked from somewhere along the narrow corridor.

He yelped in fright as somebody appeared at the end of the corridor. His feet skidded on the polished floor. He fell backwards through the curtains and then to the ground, his shoulder blades striking the wall.

"Russell?"

He shielded his eyes. "Nell? Mrs Blackwood?"

She reached out a hand to help him up. For a fleeting moment, Russell imagined she was going to draw him towards her for a kiss.

"You shouldn't be here," she said softly.

Russell winced at the throbbing in his shoulders. "I was going to say the same to you. I thought you were in bed." Suddenly, he found that he didn't know where to look.

"Well, in that case we'd both better say nothing about this encounter, then."

Whatever marital issues Nell and Ellis had, there was no reason he ought to get involved. Ixion's reference to Nell being at risk was a calculated strategy to prod at Russell's chivalry. Even so, a small part of his mind was already processing the implications, the prospect of Nell being freed from Ellis's influence. If she were his wife, Russell would encourage her sculpture work. She would thrive. And perhaps Nell would rub his shoulders, which ached terribly.

"Mrs Blackwood. I don't know how to put this. Are you... safe?"

She tilted her head. "In what respect?"

"I don't know. I just want to know that you're okay. Here in this house. I had an impression..." He peered around Nell. The curtain was still drawn to one side. Light still leaked around the corner of the narrow corridor.

All traces of good humour left Nell's face. "This is not your concern."

He gaped up at her.

"I mean to say," she continued, "there's nothing for you to worry about. I'm just fine. All right?" She drew in a deep breath. "So. Are you all finished kowtowing to the muckety-mucks?"

Russell's throat was dry. What he had witnessed in Nell's behaviour was a glimpse of the reality of her situation. She may not appear afraid exactly, but he was convinced that she was grappling with something awful.

"I'll be off in a minute," he managed to say in a croaky voice. "The catering people will—"

The chime of the doorbell cut him off.

Nell laughed. "I suppose that'll be them. But you go now. I'll deal with the caterers, then I'll nip upstairs before Ellis can collar me for a meet and greet."

Russell began to protest but Nell opened the front door and ushered him out, past the black-uniformed caterer and the two other staff already beginning to unload trays from a small van.

Dejectedly, he crunched along the gravel driveway. It was cold. He jammed his hands into the pockets of his jacket.

He turned at the end of the driveway to look at the house. The only light visible was from the drawing room. He wondered if the guests were still talking about targets. It was a vague term, certainly, but it didn't sound good. He understood that what was really bothering him, deep down, was Nell Blackwood. His desire to act as a white knight, rescuing her somehow.

His fingers brushed against something in his pocket. He pulled out a business card with numbers written in spidery handwriting.

A red public phone box stood at one side of the Blackwoods' driveway. On an impulse, Russell dived inside and dialled the number on the card. It rang six times – almost enough time for Russell to consider hanging up – before a man answered.

"Russell." Ixion's voice was as low as before. Now there was a tinny ring to it as well, as though he too were in a phone box.

"I'll do it," Russell said, breathless with his sense of recklessness. He watched Nell on the doorstep of her house, still letting catering staff in and out of the building. She was smiling, as though this were her own party, as if she were excited about the evening to come. Her easy attitude was excruciating to watch and, perversely, seemed only to confirm that she was in great peril. Russell felt a sudden conviction that only he could help her.

"There's definitely something strange going on," he said slowly. "I'll find out, and I'll tell you what I know."

The call ended with a click.

＊

A knock came from the bedroom door. Caitlin tried to ignore it. She put down the pencil and leant back in her chair to better see the portrait. She had done a good job of capturing the light reflected in her eyes. In the drawing she appeared pensive, world-weary, like a queen or a heroine from ancient myth. She glanced into the fixed, angled mirrors: her real face told a different story. The irony was that she felt healthier, more vital, than she could remember ever having been. The shedding had worked perfectly in that sense. Her skin was soft and elastic, her guts free of even the smallest of complaints. Her eyes shone. But the physical state of her body was only partly dictated by her health. The skin around her eyes was puffy and her red hair was matted where she had slept on it.

Another knock. Then, "Caitlin?"

She understood that she was in denial about what had happened. She didn't care.

"It's lunchtime, Cait," her dad said through the door. "I had a go at shepherd's pie. Didn't turn out as bad as you'd think."

"Good work, Dad."

She waited for his footsteps to pad away. They didn't.

"Could you bring it up and leave it outside my room?"

"I just want to see your face. Is that okay?" His voice sounded shaky.

She picked up the pencil, then dropped it again. It rattled on the desk and fell to the floor. With a sigh, she got up and unlocked the door. Her father stood uncertainly on the threshold of the room.

"I'm all right," she said.

"Sure."

She didn't like the doubt in his voice. It was up to her to decide whether she was coping or not. She turned away from him and pretended to look at the posters on the walls. It had been years since she had replaced any of them, and now she was too old for the kiddie films, and most of the singers had long since retired. The only picture she really liked was a framed photograph she'd taken herself on a walk with her mum. It showed three trees, side by side. They had been up at Shotover Hill, just off the path where locals paraded their dogs. The leftmost tree was no more than a sapling, the second one larger with blossom beginning to emerge on its branches. The third was wider, with a cracked trunk and two branches that drooped down, as though they had become too heavy to be supported.

"Tobe's locked himself away in his shed," Ian said.

"Nothing strange about that." She whirled around. "Hey. Are you trying to say something about Charmers in general? Are you saying we can't cope?"

Ian held up his hands. "I'm just saying I've got two people

to worry about. Three, if you count Evie. She keeps calling, you know."

"So it's all about you, then, is it? Your responsibilities?"

He looked hurt. Caitlin's hands bunched into fists. "Sorry."

"You can't stay in here, you know."

"Why not? It's obviously the place to be. *She* wanted to be in here, didn't she?"

"Oh, Cait. You can't let yourself think like this."

But she couldn't help it. The Snakeskin had tried to get upstairs. She had had a chance to escape – not a strong one, but a chance all the same – and instead she had tried to get into Caitlin's bedroom.

When she had excused herself after dinner yesterday, Caitlin had experienced a renewed sense of shock when she entered her bedroom. It had suddenly become alien. She hadn't really looked at it, properly, for as long as she could remember. The piles of clothes, the holiday keepsakes, the art materials on the desk – layers and layers of evidence of the life she had lived. A plush orangutan peering out from behind the laundry basket, a hand puppet that hadn't been worn for maybe a decade. A wooden wall-rack holding a collection of porcelain thimbles inherited from her gran, who had died in a factory fire before Caitlin was born – even at the time the newspaper reports had noted the peculiarity of a Charmer choosing to take on menial work.

If the Snakeskin had managed to make it up here to the bedroom, what would she have thought about all of these things? From her second-hand memories she would have known the stories and significance of every last item. But there would have been a difference, all the same. Caitlin thought of it in these terms: if she were diagnosed with a terminal illness, and then she stood here in this room, she would certainly see all these objects in a new light. Knowing that she had limited time would mean that she could take nothing for granted. Everything would be painfully poignant.

She felt utterly miserable.

She realised that her dad was crying.

Of course he was suffering, too. That whole scene yesterday must have been almost as traumatic for him as it had been for her. She remembered the scuffle in the hallway. Ian and the government woman, wrestling with the Snakeskin. How much had that hurt him? The girl looked exactly like Caitlin. It might as well have been her. And he had helped bundle her into a van to be taken away to who knew where.

"Dad."

Ian nodded several times, but then his head didn't lift up.

"Come here." Caitlin put her arms around him. His body trembled. "I'm okay, Dad."

He shuddered, wave after wave. Over his shoulder, out of the window, Caitlin saw Tobe emerge from his shed. He wore a thick coat and carried a heavy-looking hiking rucksack. She couldn't blame her uncle for abandoning them.

Ian Hext was all but alone. She wished she knew how to reassure him. She wished he hadn't had to touch the Snakeskin. This was why it was against the rules. It was too upsetting.

The word 'everyone' made her pause. Again, guilt grew within her. This wasn't only about the Hext family. There was another person involved.

The Snakeskin.

"She's okay," she said.

"Yes," Ian said in a strangled voice. "I think she's okay."

"It's trace memories, that's all. Dead skin plus an illusion. It's convincing, but it's not real. She's not real. And they don't last long. She's probably already gone, overnight."

Ian's shuddering stopped.

She froze, too, then pushed him away gently. "Dad. Do you know something?"

He didn't raise his eyes. He rubbed at one cheek.

"Dad. Is she gone?"

Their eyes met, only for a second. "No."

She watched his crumpling face. There was something else going on here. Some other reason for him being guilty and upset.

Of course.

"Dad. Have you been—"

"I had to go. She's okay. Safe."

While Caitlin had been prowling around in her bedroom all morning she had found a small sense of reassurance in the fact that her dad had been downstairs, ready to console her when she needed it. Instead, he had been racing off around the country.

"What the hell, Dad? So you're more concerned about a Snakeskin, rather than your own daughter?"

"I'm sorry. I know it looks bad."

"I'm the one who's flesh and blood, Dad. That thing, it's a waste product. A trick."

"Her," Ian said, frowning. "Not it. Her."

Caitlin tried to push him out of the door, but her dad held firm.

"I'm sorry," he said. "I understand that it's strange. But I couldn't not go. I'm certain you understand, deep down."

Caitlin clasped her hands together; they were shaking badly. "*I'm* your daughter. She – it – isn't even a person, let alone a member of the family."

Ian sighed. "I understand. I know all the arguments. All I can say is, she looked like a person. She seemed like one, in every way that matters. She seemed like you."

"Right. Fine. So here I was, crying to myself. And you just thought to yourself, 'I know what I can do to help. I'll abandon my daughter and go and see some stranger – some alien-meteor-shower freak of nature – who reminds me of her, instead.' Is that it?"

Ian's shoulders slumped. "You wouldn't even let me in the room."

"Oh, fine! So you went to see someone who would? I bet that bitch welcomed you with open arms."

"Stop that. But of course she was glad to see me. I'm not trying to hurt you, Cait. I still think it was the right thing to do."

Rather than look him in the eyes, Caitlin concentrated on the tuft of hair in the centre of his forehead. Her dad wasn't a bad man. He wouldn't know how to be bad. And he hadn't betrayed her, exactly. She forced herself to take deep breaths.

"Tell me about this place, where she is," she said.

"A home. A care home, sort of. North of Reading, out of town. There are others like her there."

"Is it nice?"

"It's big. Impressive." He chewed his cheek. "Yes, nice, I suppose. They'll take care of her."

"How long does she have left?" Caitlin couldn't imagine what might be a reassuring answer.

"They don't know." Now it was Ian's turn to examine the posters on the walls.

"There's something else you're not telling me."

Her dad shuffled past her and into the room. He sat heavily at the foot of Caitlin's bed. "Your mum. The same thing happened with hers."

A chill ran through Caitlin's body. "Her Skins?"

He nodded. "They didn't ash, not straight away. They always lasted longer than most. We – I – thought she was a one-off, a fluke. When Tobe's first two Skins stuck around for only a handful of seconds, it seemed reasonable enough to assume—"

Caitlin found that she couldn't stop shivering. "How long did they last?"

"It varied."

"How long?"

Ian placed his hands on his knees and straightened his posture. "The shortest was about a day. They didn't have government people witnessing each shedding back then, so the Skin was held in the local magistrate's court until the government came and got her. They said she ashed on the way to the care home."

"And the longest?"

"It's so unlikely that it would be repeated. There must have been something particular—"

"Dad. Just tell me."

He took a deep breath. "Five months."

She stared at him. Her hands covered her mouth. She gazed out of the window, at the open door of Tobe's shed. Below the windowsill, her self-portrait sketch rested on its easel, staring at her blankly.

"Five months," she repeated. "Five months, in one of these care homes? When?"

"It was your mum's final one. I'm not sure there's a pattern. The Skin before that one lasted only a few days, the one before that, weeks."

"So this happened when I was—" she frowned, trying to do the calculations "—fourteen? And you didn't think I ought to be told?"

Ian gazed up at the ceiling. His face was sickly pale. "More like fifteen, I think."

But Caitlin had been fifteen when her mum had died, when the truck had blindsided her Astra and crushed it against the brick wall of a newsagent. Her mum's last shedding had been only shortly before that. Caitlin hadn't been allowed to the shedding but they all went out for pizzas afterward. To celebrate.

A realisation hit her like a slap. "Mum's shedding was two months before the accident."

Ian nodded slowly.

"And her Snakeskin lasted for five months."

This time there was no nod.

"So the Skin kept on living for three months after Mum died."

"If you can call it living."

She looked around for something to hold onto, to keep her steady. "And you visited her – the Skin – afterwards."

It wasn't a question. She thought of the time directly after her mum's death. Caitlin had shut herself away, just as she was doing now. Her dad's response had been to take an extended leave from his teaching position at the local sixth-form college, which had eventually turned into early retirement. He had kept himself to himself, too. He'd often left the house for whole days, saying that he'd discovered a passion for long walks. But even then Caitlin had understood that he was telling lies. He'd always taken the car.

She tried to imagine him, back then. Visiting the Skin in the care home, after his wife Janet was dead and buried. How had he described Caitlin's Skin? *She seemed like you.*

The thought filled her with revulsion. Without speaking, she opened her wardrobe. Tobe had the right idea, heading off with his rucksack, getting away from this sick house. She found an old sports bag and began stuffing clothes into it.

Her dad didn't say anything. He was probably being swallowed up by his guilt.

Would her mum's Skin have been similar enough for Ian to treat her as his wife? Perhaps. He would have been grieving, after all. Desperate to gain more time with the woman he loved.

And there were the trace memories, of course. Janet Hext's

memories. The Skin could have indulged Ian's nostalgia, contributing Janet's recollection of each of his cherished memories. Solidifying them in his mind, ready for when she, too, left him.

It might have been more than that. There must have been a temptation. A woman so much like his wife. Caitlin tried not to imagine them hugging. Kissing. It would have been a betrayal.

Her dad looked tiny, crouched on the bed. Caitlin didn't dare ask him any more questions. She wasn't sure she could bear to see him try to lie – or even worse, try to tell the truth.

She had no idea whether the clothes she had shoved into the bag were enough.

"I'm going away," she said. "For a while. Don't try to follow me."

With his legs hanging loosely over the edge of the bed, it was as if Ian were the child, not her. His face was grey, though. Old.

Caitlin slung the bag over her shoulder and left, hurrying in case she lost her courage.

# SEVEN

Ixion had arrived before Russell. He was sitting on a bench in the centre of the children's playground, as though he had sat down when it was daylight and hadn't noticed that it was now night.

Russell pushed open the yellow gate. Already, he felt as though he were committing a crime, or at least something morally wrong. On the phone, Ixion had been insistent. Eleven o'clock – coinciding with the start of the curfew, though being out on the streets after that time was hardly the most significant of their misdemeanours – and at this precise location. During his walk across town, Russell had tried to ease his anxiety by conjuring up ridiculous visions: finding the stranger on a swing, or at the top of the helter-skelter slide. The small playground was unlit – the lamps on the tarmac path alongside didn't penetrate through the trees – and silent as a graveyard. There were houses nearby, but none of their windows overlooked the playground.

The man's hood was pulled up. He wore a thick overcoat despite the lack of chill in the air. A beer can rested on one knee. Russell could smell it, too, but he couldn't tell whether it was from the can or from the man's breath.

"Drowning your sorrows?" Russell said.

"Anyone passing would assume that I am a drunk."

"Or a psycho. I looked up your name, by the way. Ixion, the Greek king who slept with Zeus's wife and then got himself imprisoned in Tartarus. Aspirational stuff."

The man's only response was to pat the bench. Russell sat. Even sitting here beside him, Ixion was only a shadow, a void against the grey leaves of the trees. Was he wearing a balaclava, or a scarf covering his mouth? It was impossible to tell. There might as well have been no face there.

"You have information?" The man's voice was halting, almost machinelike, and peculiarly deep.

"How do I know it's safe to tell you anything?"

"You don't. But you want to tell somebody, and you have nobody else."

It felt like a personal insult rather than a comment about his status at work. But either way, it was true. Only Ixion, who had put the conspiratorial ideas into his head in the first place, would give his stories any credence.

Russell noticed the flash of a blue light, somewhere low down. Ixion changed his sitting position. The light disappeared.

"I need you to tell me something first," Russell said. "What's kind of trouble is Nell Blackwood in?"

After a pause, Ixion replied, "I shouldn't have mentioned her. It wasn't my intention."

"But you did. And I need to know."

The man let out a sound somewhere between a hum and a growl. "I wish I knew. I have no desire to lie to you about this. I'm convinced that she's under threat, but without your help I have no information to give you about Mrs Blackwood."

Russell contemplated this. Ixion would refuse to volunteer information without Russell demonstrating his intention to collaborate. It was equally deluded to imagine that he would explain about Nell once Russell provided him with the details he had overhead at Ellis's party. But he could think of no other options.

"Fine," he said. "I'll tell you."

The man sipped his beer. Then he bowed his head like a priest waiting to hear a confession.

"I think you were right about Minister Blackwood having colleagues nearby. I don't know how you knew, but you were right. There's something fishy about the whole office complex. People coming and going that just don't fit, and it all involves Ellis. I swear I'm surrounded by people who are in on the joke. I think I may be the only one who doesn't know what's going on. Perhaps you should ask one of *them* to give you information."

The hooded head turned towards him. Though Russell couldn't see any glimpse of Ixion's features, he imagined a hard stare.

"Okay. It was only a joke. But the more I think about it, the more I see it. Rivals struggling for power, beneath the apparently calm surface of the GBP. You mentioned the Party being at risk of being broken apart, and I don't know if you know this, but Adrian Lorde doesn't exactly command

respect, whereas this woman, Angela McKinney..."
Russell had hoped that his conclusions might sound more
revelatory. Ixion's silence suggested that this was all old
news. "I'd be surprised if she wasn't pitching herself as a
rival to Lorde. You can't blame her for wondering whether
forty-odd years as PM might be plenty, I suppose. And
there have always been those rumours about our country's
missed opportunities – till now I'd dismissed them as
urban myths, but who knows? About Americans travelling
to the Moon, about wild inventions and alternative forms of
government. The way some of those guests at Ellis's party
were talking... I mean, they seemed to be taking all that
sort of thing seriously, and I got the impression they were
blaming Lorde for the UK being left behind.

"Anyway... the other thing is that there's been talk – this is
amongst a wider group, politicians and bigwigs and the like,
milling around at Ellis's house. You should see the place.
You'd think the house would sink into its foundations, the
amount of mahogany and antiques they've got in there."
He sensed the invisible eyes upon him again. "Sorry. I go
on when I'm nervous. They were talking about targets,
or maybe only one target. I heard Ellis say it again, this
afternoon on the phone. 'The target is widening,' he said,
and he sounded pretty upset about it. He used the word
'triangulation', too. I don't want to jump to conclusions, but
the first thing I think about when I hear the word 'target' is
weapons. Do you think I'm being crazy?"

Ixion gave no response.

"Minister Blackwood is acting weird too."

"Weird?"

"Maybe he always has, maybe I'm only now beginning to notice it. But he looks absolutely exhausted. I guess that's not odd in itself – I mean, he's a Party official and even in the normal course of things he has a lot on his plate, probably. But what's strange is that he keeps denying it. This woman he keeps talking to, in the banner-printers and at the party – he seems desperate not to let on how tired he is."

To Russell's surprise, the man released a deep chuckle. Was this all a game to him? Russell was suddenly outraged.

"Look, this isn't right. Me telling you all this, and nothing in return. And now I'm suddenly getting wind of some kind of attack… and you're just going to let me stew?"

Ixion composed himself. "It rarely pays to make assumptions."

"Well. That's as maybe. But it turns out I can't help it. Do you know what my assumptions are about you, for example? I think this talk about being at the heart of government is rubbish. I assume that you're a disgruntled ex-Party worker of some sort, or just an anti-prosperity protester with a personal grudge. That maybe you hate Ellis Blackwood personally for whatever reason…" He paused. The man had flinched, he was sure of it. "Right. So that's it. And you know what? It doesn't matter. I think you're on to something, and I think you're right about Nell being in trouble, and I think that whatever is going on may mean that my rock-solid government job might actually be a sham. But I'll tell you what does matter: this has to be a two-way process. I tell you what I know, and you give me something in return."

The man cleared his throat. Now his deep voice was less grating. "There is plenty that I don't yet know. I see only the peripheral details."

Russell bit his tongue. Let him continue.

"I do know something," the man continued. "It's not much. Tell me, does Blackwood have a series of several appointments over a two-day period, beginning the day after tomorrow?"

"That's a question, not information." When the man didn't speak, Russell relented. He could picture the cluster of bookings Ellis had instructed him to add to the diary, all scheduled for the end of the week. Each of them tagged with a question mark. "Yes. He said they'll keep him so busy that he won't be in the office. He didn't want my help making any of the arrangements."

Ixion nodded, holding onto the rim of the hood to prevent it from slipping back. "As I thought. It's actually only a single appointment, though. And he will be away from the office because he will be away from his home, for two nights minimum. The reason, I believe, is that he fears that somebody may follow him, and that making the journey only once would be pragmatic."

"And you want me to find out where he's going."

"Where, and why."

"Why?"

"As I said."

Russell shook his head. "No, I mean: why do you want to know? Isn't it about time you told me... No, I know you're not going to tell me who you are, otherwise it'd make all this cloak-and-dagger furtiveness awfully silly. But isn't it about time you gave me a hint why this is important to you?"

The man paused before replying. "I think it may be important to everybody."

"That's too vague. Come on. You have to give me something. Explain to me why you think this is the crucial detail. Why Ellis travelling somewhere – if, indeed, he will be – for a two-night stay is the one thing you so desperately need to understand."

The head turned towards him. Russell shielded his eyes but the man's street light halo made his face utterly blank.

"Because—" The deep voice faltered a touch. "Because he doesn't want us to know."

Ixion rose from the bench. Russell barely noticed. The reply echoed again and again inside his head. There had been something strange about the intonation. A peculiar stress on the word 'us'. What did it mean?

Ixion had already crossed to the yellow gate, moving with surprising grace across the uneven ground, leaving Russell alone and facing an empty sandpit. He shivered, suddenly feeling the cold. Ixion closed the gate gently behind him and strode along the tarmac path. A pinprick of blue light flashed at his feet.

Russell gave him a couple of seconds' head start, long enough for him to reach the line of trees. Then he leapt from the bench and followed. He bent over the yellow gate to see along the path. He saw the dark figure walking away, his dark coat absorbing the orange light of the street lights.

He eased the gate closed silently, took a few strides after

the receding figure, then snuck into an alley. He counted to ten, then popped his head out. He continued in this way for several minutes, feeling increasingly proud of his ability to stay hidden. Then, with a start, he realised that the silhouette was no longer getting smaller. Ixion had stopped. Russell pressed himself into a mass of ivy that clung to a tall brick wall. The leaves tickled his neck. He forced himself to take shallow breaths, despite the distance still between him and his quarry. He leant out far enough to look along the path.

Ixion was standing in the same spot. As far as Russell could tell, he hadn't turned to look back. He was staring down at the tarmac path.

Russell waited and Ixion waited too. The ivy began to itch.

This was ridiculous. He had been talking to Ixion only minutes ago, so why should he be scared of him now? And he hadn't even instructed him not to follow.

With a sudden impulse, Russell pushed himself away from the wall. He walked towards Ixion, attempting a stroll but managing only a stiff-legged strut. When he reached him, he would wish him a cheerful 'Good night', then walk past and immediately turn on the spot. The nearby street light would surely illuminate the stranger's face.

He rubbed his itching neck as he walked.

He reached Ixion.

He almost fell forwards onto his face. He had tripped on a rope that ran from the man's hand and across the path.

"Sorry, fella," the man said. "Didn't see you coming."

He wasn't wearing a hood, after all, and his face was lined

– he must be in his seventies. No, that couldn't be right. This couldn't be—

At the other end of the rope, a dachshund squatted at the side of the path. It finished defecating and then trotted onto the tarmac.

Mumbling apologies, Russell extricated himself from the tangled dog lead and hurried away in the other direction.

*

Caitlin's head bumped against the inside of the train window. She pulled a jumper from her bag and rolled it up to make a pillow. An armed train attendant interrupted her rest, insisting on seeing her ID card as well as her ticket, tutting as she fished it out and reminding her that identity papers must be carried at all times. Then, just as she settled down, her pager buzzed: it was another message from Evie. *CALL ME.* She jammed the pager into her pocket, closed her eyes and listened to the clatter of the wheels and the rain drumming on the window.

Train journeys always reminded her of holidays. She tried to latch onto memories in the hope of calming the churning sensation in her stomach.

It was a miniature train that transported her family to the Museum of Automata, holiday after holiday, year after year. It was barely wide enough for two people to sit side by side, and it was roofless and its walls came only to the height of the passengers' knees. The chill air would become a sideways blast of icy wind as the train trundled along the coastal track. The many visits merged in Caitlin's memories, only differentiated by annual changes to the landscape: the appearance of the Sea Life Centre, the council's abandonment of the cable cars, the opening of a pirate-themed golf course which was in bad repair even when it was new.

The only visit she remembered in absolute clarity was the first one. She had been seven years old.

*

Caitlin padded along the narrow aisles. Her parents were in the main part of the museum, with its metal roof that amplified the rain. When she left them they had been trying to convince Tobe that the waltzers he'd strapped himself into weren't operational. Tobe's voice was beginning to break and his complaining alternated between childish squeaky and bellowing.

She pressed herself up against one glass frontage after another, gazing at the mechanical dioramas within, dropping in ten-pence pieces from the clear plastic sack her dad had given her. One showed a pair of peasant boys playing a game of bowls, the pins dropping even before the ball bearing hit them, then leaping up again as the mechanism reset. Another showed a baby suckling at his mother's breast, watched by a peeping tom who emerged from the bushes. The third scene showed a burning building, into which a fireman slid up a ladder and slid back down carrying a blanketed child.

She had enjoyed it all immensely. After viewing all of the automata she emerged, blinking and confused in the daylight, as though the miniature scenes had been windows into the real world, and as though the world outside was the unnatural one, huge and populated by giants and waves that bore down upon the beach with mechanical regularity.

Tobe tried to drag her dad away along the jetty, muttering about some shop in town that traded second-hand computer games.

"Where's your mum?" Caitlin's dad asked her.

He ushered the two of them to a bench to wait. Janet must have left the museum already to stroll along the concrete coastal path and back. Surely she'd return to where they'd last been together. After waiting twenty-five minutes, he asked the woman at the ice cream booth whether she'd seen anybody. He returned shaking his head, but holding two ice creams. After another ten minutes, he checked the nearby shops.

After another half an hour he paid for Caitlin to go into the museum to search. She peered into every room twice before she finally found her mum.

Janet was tucked into a booth only a handful of metres beyond the foyer. She had been hidden by a velour curtain that produced a puff of dust as Caitlin pushed it aside. In her mum's cupped hand was a stack of ten-pence pieces. She grinned at Caitlin and shuffled along a hard bench to let her in. The curtain dropped. The booth was so dark that Caitlin's eyes took a while to adjust.

The glass window lit. Caitlin glanced at her mum, who was staring straight ahead. The booth was still so dim that the scene was difficult to make out. Perhaps some of the bulbs had blown. Caitlin leant forwards so that her nose almost touched the glass.

Inside the box was a painted wooden figure. A man, four or five inches tall. He sat at the foot of his bed wearing a white nightgown that reached almost to his feet. His bare wooden toes protruded from beneath it. He turned to look up at the window above the bed, from which shone simulated moonlight. It shimmered, and when Caitlin bent to one side she could see a partly-painted, translucent disc spinning, casting shadows of gnarled trees into the room. The man watched the moonlight and his body shook, his wooden joints rattling audibly.

He stood and took a couple of paces away from the bed, centre stage. Another bulb lit, somewhere to his right, illuminating him and making the rest of the room dark in contrast. His neck clicked as he peered into the gloom.

Then something appeared in the empty space before him, becoming more and more visible. A dark-haired man in a white nightgown. But it wasn't a solid image. It shimmered and shuddered. Even though Caitlin had seen the effect in some of the other dioramas, she was still taken aback. The figure hung in the air. She gasped as the wooden man in the scene gasped, his jaw clacking open abruptly.

"Don't fret, love," her mum whispered. "It's just a trick. They call it Pepper's ghost. There's a mirror somewhere back there, in the dark."

Caitlin couldn't see a mirror. It was magical. It was magic.

The man on the stage staggered backwards. He raised his spindly arms and the nightgown dropped down to his elbows, revealing tiny joints.

Then the ghostly image before him warped, as though

it were a reflection in water and somebody had dropped a stone in. The tiny man bumped against the bed. He watched, and Caitlin watched, as the hanging figure became as speckled and insubstantial as an image on an old-fashioned TV. Then it began to rise. No, that wasn't quite right. Not all of it, only the top, stretching and then dissipating before vanishing entirely. Within a few seconds the entire reflected person appeared to have drifted away like dust.

And then another person appeared. Directly behind the man, looming out of the darkness, from a space that had contained nothing beforehand.

"I've been trying to work it out," her mum said. "The man's nightgown is solid, so I'm thinking there must be a hinged compartment. Or perhaps there's a hidden hatch in the surface of the stage. But no matter how many times I watch it, I fall for the trick. I get so distracted by the ghost that I forget to watch for the mechanism behind him."

The man gave no impression of having noticed the newcomer. His shoulders slumped and his miniature hands went to his face. Relief. Joy, maybe.

The person that had appeared was his exact twin. The same man, the same dark hair and stern mouth, though lacking the nightgown. Unlike the spectral vision moments before, he was wooden, solid, real. His limbs were skeletal, all pin-joints and thin struts. His crotch was a flat, blank space. He raised his arms high above the first man's head. Some subtle mechanism turned his tight mouth into a smile.

The first man spun around. His hands clattered against his body. He looked up at the newcomer and his jaw dropped.

The naked wooden figure lunged forward.

Then the lights cut out.

Caitlin continued staring at the dark window. She could see nothing inside, no hint of movement. She crossed her arms tightly across her chest.

She jumped when her mum spoke. She had almost forgotten that she wasn't alone. "Are you okay, Kit? Not scared?"

"Dad and Tobe are waiting outside."

"Kit. This is important. A piece of history. This is how people used to feel about Charmers – that we were monsters, or cursed. This machine was made to warn the public about us. But the people who made this, they were wrong."

The ice cream wasn't sitting well in Caitlin's stomach.

"I want to go."

✳

Caitlin's forehead knocked against the train window again.

Something rose up in her belly.

The teenage boy sitting opposite her swooped to gather his books and magazines. He watched her, wide-eyed.

Puke burst from Caitlin's mouth, splattering on the surface of the table.

✳

Gerry glanced in both directions along the dark street, then awkwardly nudged the car boot closed with a buttock. She paused for a moment on the kerb, regaining her balance as the pile of hardback books teetered and threatened to topple from her outstretched arms.

The journey from Ilam had been fraught, and the second half had been in rain-streaked darkness. There had been roadworks most of the way along the M1, and then, as the road cones had petered out, Gerry found herself in the immediate aftermath of a three-car pileup that had blocked the width of the road. She, along with the rest of the returning weekend tourists, had been caught there, static, waiting for the ambulances and fire engines to squeeze through the throng.

The holdall containing her clothes and toiletries was still on the back seat of the car. She ignored it and set off along the road. The books were more important.

Anise Hartwell had been equally helpful when Gerry had returned to Ilam Hall on the second day, after spending the entire previous day holed up in the library. They had dined together on the first night, too – trout, wonderfully prepared by some unseen member of staff. After the meal, Gerry had excused herself after the second bottle of wine, when she noticed Anise draw closer along the sofa. Though she was attractive enough, and her warmth was inviting, Gerry was wary of complicating their agreement with anything that might make either of them jumpy. And that was even without considering the fact that Anise was almost double her age, despite not looking it. What had shocked Gerry, though, was how flattered she felt. A Charmer was interested in her. All her life, she had seen Charmers as remote and almost godlike. The idea that she might hold sway over one of this elite class was intoxicating.

Even so, she worried a little that she had exploited Anise's friendliness. Using the library had been one thing, but taking this stack of books with her when she left had been an unreasonable request. Anise had agreed immediately.

Anise hadn't allowed Gerry to take the census books, though. She had talked about her civic duty, and the function of Ilam Hall as a repository of local knowledge, regardless of whether any locals actually used it. Gerry admired her steadfastness, but the decision still rankled. She had pored over the heavy, bound census documents for hours, without revealing any scraps of new information.

Until the late 1820s, the census reports didn't refer to specific buildings, listing only families and occupations. The census for 1813, the first one conducted after the Fall, was far thicker than the previous ones. By that point, more people had been attracted to the area by recent events, and Ilam had already grown in population and had become a tourist trap. Gerry had spent most of her time leafing through the 1807 census. Judging by scribbled notes she had found on one or two of the documents, it had been conducted around nine months before the meteor shower. Whoever had lived in that tiny building up on the mountainside, where the meteor appeared to have actually struck the ground, must be included in the book.

But she hadn't been able to make any headway. Part of the trouble was that the 1807 census covered a far wider area than just Ilam itself, including vast parts of the countryside straddling the borders of modern-day Staffordshire and Derbyshire. The other issue was that the reports were written in slanting, cursive handwriting that was, at times, close to illegible. Given time and resources, Gerry would have cross-referenced the 1807 census with the enormous 1813 one, to check for any commonalities, but she had found the task impossible to even begin and her head had throbbed with the effort of reading.

So what was required was more research into the area itself, to determine who might have lived in that tiny building. The majority of the books she had taken from the library at Ilam Hall were about the village and the hall itself, as opposed to history books about the Fall. Gerry's instinct was that, by the time accounts of the Fall had been written down, the event had already passed into folklore. Whatever she was searching for was far from clear, and would involve a slog, but it was like Drew had said: *Go back to the source*.

She veered from side to side along the pavement, blind behind the tower of books. The drive had exhausted her, and this final act of coordination was almost more than she could manage. Her flat seemed further away than usual, though it was only around the corner, where parking permits were allocated only to people prepared to pay through the nose for the luxury of parking outside their own building.

She paused to renew her grip. A sound of footsteps continued for a few seconds, then stopped.

Some instinct made her turn.

She saw the figure for a moment before it melted into the darkness at the side of the street. She waited. Perhaps it was one of her neighbours, taking out the bins or chasing in a cat. She saw no movement.

She set off again, straining to listen.

There, again. Soft footsteps from behind. When she sped up slightly, the footsteps did too.

It took all her willpower to stop herself from turning around again. The windows she passed were all curtained. If she picked a door at random, would anybody answer? It wasn't worth the risk. The best thing she could do was to get into her flat, only a hundred metres away.

It suddenly struck her how comical the situation was. If she dumped the books, she could sprint to the door of her building in seconds. But there was no way she was going to abandon them now. She hoped that Drew, at least, would see the funny side if things went really bad. Gerry Chafik, journalist through and through. Chasing the story to the very end.

When she turned the corner, the footsteps lessened in volume only for a moment. Whoever it was, they were right behind her.

Abruptly, she turned around.

There. The figure had been visible, for a second, behind the privet that surrounded her neighbour's garden. Male, almost certainly. Adult. A hood pulled up over his head.

She forced herself to take a breath before speaking. "Hey. Mister."

Nobody appeared.

"I saw you there. Give me a hand, would you? Please? These books are heavy as hell."

After a pause, the man emerged from behind the tall bush.

*Don't move*, Gerry told herself. *Not yet.*

The nearest street light was behind him. His face was invisible inside his hood.

Gerry tilted the books, making the pile wobble. "Quick, take these top ones before they fall. They're worth a mint."

The man moved agonisingly slowly and it was all Gerry could do to stop the books from actually slipping. He reached up to the topmost books.

There was something in his hand. Its flat surface shone white. A knife?

She had taken self-defence classes, long ago. She tried to remember the three steps of avoiding an assailant. Had there been a helpful acronym or a slogan? But the only advice in the world she could remember was something from her childhood. *Clunk, click, every trip.* Useless.

So, as the man steadied the pile, she kicked out her right leg with all her strength. Her foot made a sickening impact with his crotch.

He crumpled immediately, his fingers scrabbling against the heavy books and then at Gerry's legs as he slid to the ground. He made a peculiarly low grunting sound, like someone at the bottom of a well.

Incredibly, Gerry managed to avoid dropping any of the books. She swung around and took long strides to the door to her building. She rested the teetering pile of books against her hip, fumbled in the pocket of her jeans for the keys, grunted to heft the books into both hands, then staggered forwards into the lobby.

A slapping sound echoed up the stairwell. Gerry whirled around, expecting to find the man following her inside.

She exhaled in relief. One of the books had dropped to the concrete floor; that was all.

She hurried up the stairs and along the corridor, faster and faster as the leaning pile of books pulled her forwards with unstoppable momentum. After a fumble with another lock, and with a sigh of relief, she dropped the enormous tower of books onto her coffee table.

She dashed to the window. The street outside was empty. She was safe.

The sagging sofa groaned under her weight. She flung her feet onto the table. The toe of her left boot tapped the lowest books in the pile. The pile shuddered and then collapsed, landing on the lino with a dozen loud *cracks* like rifle fire.

Something was still falling, though. The white oblong fluttered and wafted to rest on a book. It was an envelope, marked with the name *GERRY CHAFIK* in shaky block capitals, as though the author had written it using whichever of their hands was unaccustomed to holding a pen.

She lifted it. A message from Anise, perhaps?

Or.

The stranger outside. This must have been the white object she had seen in his hand, when he had reached out.

She ripped open the envelope, before remembering that she should have taken more care. It might be needed as evidence.

Inside was a single, folded sheet of A4 paper. The text and the lines of the table were faint – a photocopy of a photocopy. She raised it close to her face to read it. Her eyes widened.

# EIGHT

The taxi deposited Caitlin at a broad, paved area dotted with wooden picnic benches and clusters of palm trees. Until the final turn to the roundabout that led from the road, the taxi had passed only industrial parks and shopping complexes, their uniformity interrupted only by GBP campaign hoardings scrawled with anti-prosperity graffiti. Here, Caitlin could no longer hear the hum of the ring road that had foiled her attempts to sleep at the hotel. This place was an oasis of calm.

As she stepped lightly from the taxi, Caitlin noticed once again how in shape she felt. Absently, she rubbed her forearm where her scar had been. It occurred to her again that in each of her successive ceremonies, the rejuvenating benefits of shedding would be more and more significant as her body dialled back the effects of the passing years.

The front of the building was tall and wide and was made entirely of glass panels. It looked more like a modern leisure centre, or an architect's vision of the train stations of the future, than any kind of medical establishment –

though the pair of armed police officers standing outside contrasted with the otherwise welcoming appearance of the entrance. Beside a revolving door that swung slowly was a sign: *JANUARY CARE HOME* and, in smaller text, *By appointment of Her Majesty The Queen*. That must have been Queen Victoria, the last monarch of England. Presumably the care home had been very different then.

Inside, there was even less evidence of the building's purpose. Against the glass wall was a collection of plush red sofas interspersed with magazine racks and tall bookcases. It looked more like a library than a traditional waiting room. Daylight turned the air golden. The people sitting on the sofas were relaxed, as though they had come here to read rather than for any more serious purpose. Caitlin smelt coffee. There was a drinks stand behind the seating area. *Help yourself*, a sign read. *Freshly brewed.*

The centre of the vast area was empty apart from a metal sculpture. At first, Caitlin couldn't make it out – the two bronze figures were intertwined and confused the eye. Then she saw the young boy at the bottom. His arms were outstretched and he gazed upwards at the second figure. No, not quite a figure. Now that Caitlin examined it more closely, she saw that it was only the boy's jacket that rose above him. Its hollow arms were stretched out like wings. She understood the sense of it: Snakeskins were angelic. Not *people*, mind you: the coat-figure had no head, hands or feet. Then there was the name of the care home: *JANUARY*. As a kid, Caitlin had been obsessed with Greek and Roman myths. The month of January was named after Janus, who was usually shown with two faces, one looking back, one looking forward. Janus was the god of time, transitions, beginnings. The founders of the care home had nailed their colours to the mast. To them, Skins were symbols of good, not evil.

She wished she felt the same.

It hadn't only been the noise of the road that had stopped her from sleeping. She had thought of nothing but her Snakeskin. The knowledge that her Snakeskin was still out there, somewhere, was immensely unsettling.

All that talk with Evie about how Skins should be treated with humanity and kindness. All that talk about showing 'normal' people how beautiful sheddings and Charmers and Skins were. But when it came to it, Caitlin wanted her Snakeskin gone. The thought of her mum's Skins lasting days, weeks or months revolted her. It wasn't right. It wasn't fair. *She* was Caitlin Hext. The thought of somebody else having the chance to play-act at being her made her feel sick. What if her Snakeskin was a better Caitlin Hext than she was?

She hadn't reached any conclusions. She was far from certain that she should be here. An image kept popping into her mind, of her mum at the Museum of Automata, years ago. She longed to hide away like that.

To the right of the statue, a long, patterned carpet indicated a route that led further into the depths of the building. The path was blocked by a metal-detector gate, like the ones in airports. Security was evidently an issue here.

Before Caitlin left Ivy Cottage, after the argument with

her dad, she had stopped off in the kitchen. Inside her sports bag she now carried a sharp kitchen knife. Overnight, she had wondered again and again whether she would use it – whether she could plunge it into somebody who looked just like her, whether ridding herself of her Skin was important enough. Skins didn't have rights like people. There would be a scene with the care home staff, and the police standing outside would get involved, but maybe she wouldn't even go to prison for it.

She felt a swell of relief at seeing the metal detector. Now that the decision had been made for her, she realised that she never could have gone through with it anyway.

A hatch revealing a single reception desk was situated close to the front facade of the building but tucked behind the revolving door itself, so that this most functional aspect of the lobby was all but hidden to a first-time visitor. Next to the hatch stood a potted yucca plant. Caitlin bent beside it as though tying a shoelace. She slipped the knife out of her bag and pushed it deep into the soil in the pot.

The young, dark-haired receptionist looked up and smiled as Caitlin approached. His teeth and uniform shone white in the bright daylight.

"I'm here to visit a patient," Caitlin said.

"We don't have patients here." The smile widened. "Only residents. What is the name of your loved one?" Despite his confidence, he must have been only a few years older than Caitlin.

"Seriously? 'Loved one'?" Caitlin replied. "Is that how most people describe the Skin they're visiting?"

The man spread his arms wide. "They are loved, by all of us. We cherish their time here."

Caitlin realised what the vast, bright lobby reminded her of. Not an airport. A cathedral.

There was no point arguing with the receptionist. He was only doing his job, however creepily. "I don't know her name. Are they supposed to have names?"

"Our residents retain the same name as their originator."

"Meaning the Charmer? Caitlin Hext."

The receptionist nodded. He leant forwards to peer at a screen embedded into the counter, tapping with an index finger. "Ah yes – newly arrived. And your association with the loved one is…?"

"Charmer. Originator. Whatever. I'm Caitlin Hext. The real one."

For the first time, the receptionist's professional manner slipped. Red blotches appeared on his cheeks. "I'm sorry. You're Caitlin Hext? To visit Caitlin Hext?"

She shuddered and wished he would stop calling the Skin that. "Is that so strange?"

The receptionist's blinking and his sudden stammer suggested that it was. "Please do take a seat," he said, pointing to the red sofas. "I'll call somebody to escort you inside. It may take— I'll fetch them as quickly as I possibly can."

Caitlin frowned. Fetch who? The receptionist appeared far younger now. She felt sorry for him. She nodded and moved away.

"I couldn't help but overhear," someone said as Caitlin sat down. A woman was sitting on the sofa opposite. A tweed hat like the ones worn by duck hunters hid most of her hair, but grey wisps floated free at the sides. Her face was lined, and the deepest folds were at the corners of her eyes, suggesting a life of smiling. Upon the lap of her ankle-length skirt was a cling-filmed sandwich. She unwrapped the sandwich as she talked, with careful movements as though it were an anticipated birthday gift. "Good for you, visiting your Skin. Good for you."

Caitlin gave a tight smile.

The woman grinned. "I'm Dodie." She gestured to the precariously balanced sandwich, then waved instead of offering her hand to shake.

"Caitlin. As you heard."

"I am sorry. I'm not in the business of eavesdropping. I noticed you because you're young. It tends to be fogeys like me visiting this place."

With a glance around, Caitlin could see that that wasn't true. Several of the other visitors reading magazines were far younger than Dodie, though all were adult. "Is it just Charmers that come here?"

Dodie shrugged. "Almost certainly. Why would anyone else? But the receptionist was right. It's rarely the originators themselves who show up."

"I don't understand that," Caitlin said, although in truth she felt more and more sympathy for Charmers who wanted nothing to do with their Skins.

"I can understand your being surprised. This must be your first shedding?"

Caitlin nodded.

"Of course it is, look at your beautiful skin – you're little more than a baby. It's not my place to pry, but I can imagine you have all sorts of thoughts in your head, and it's those thoughts that brought you here all on your own."

"I don't know what brought me here. Curiosity, I guess?"

"I doubt that goes halfway to explaining it," Dodie replied gently. "But that'll do for now."

Caitlin hesitated. "Then what do other people hope to get from visiting Skins?"

Dodie pursed her lips. "I suppose some hope to learn something. Speaking with a Snakeskin can be enlightening. Speaking to your *own* Skin doubly so, I'd have thought. But people's reasons for visiting might not always be positive. I've chatted to enough visitors over the years to pick out a few themes. Guilt, that's the big one."

Caitlin blinked. She had no idea how to respond, or which category of visitor she would fall into.

"Goodness. Listen to me," Dodie said. She nibbled at a corner of a sandwich. "Sorry. I'm known to go on a bit."

Caitlin hesitated before speaking. "Do you have—"

Dodie shook her head. "I'm a Charmer, but only in theory. It's a fairly rare condition that I have. I haven't shed since I was in my teens."

"And yet you visit the Skins here in the care home."

Dodie pressed her lips tightly together. "I visit the Skins because I'm fascinated by them. I worry for them, too, even in a place as well-equipped as this. But I believe that many of them feel desperately *unsafe*, all the same. At any moment they might simply disappear. And many of them are, effectively, abandoned by the very people who ought to welcome them the most. This idea that people have, that Snakeskins are a by-product, mere waste material... It makes me very angry and sad." She pointed at a well-dressed man and woman who sat side by side, poring over their respective magazines. "It's the parents who visit. But from what I've observed, they tend not to be very parental towards the Skins. It's a duty, that's all. And then it's a relief when there's only dust."

Caitlin flinched as a slim hand entered her field of vision.

"Dr Scaife," the owner of the hand said. "And you must be Caitlin Hext."

The doctor turned and started to walk away as soon as Caitlin was on her feet. She was tall, with long, striding legs. The skin on the back of her neck, below her frizzy bob, appeared chafed and sore. Caitlin turned to look at Dodie.

Dodie waved half a sandwich. "See you on the inside, probably."

Caitlin hurried to keep up with Dr Scaife. The doctor ushered Caitlin towards the gate. Her dark eyes looked Caitlin up and down.

A uniformed security guard pointed at Caitlin's rucksack. "You'll have to empty that, miss."

Caitlin wondered when they would find the kitchen knife hidden in the pot plant. How would they have reacted if she had left it in the bag? She tipped the bag upside down and the guard and Dr Scaife peered down as her clothes, toiletries and underwear spilled out into a plastic tray. The guard leafed through Caitlin's dog-eared copy of

*The War of the Worlds.* Then he transferred the toiletries to a transparent plastic bag and sealed it. "These will be confiscated. Apologies, miss."

Caitlin shrugged and stuffed the rest of her things into the bag. At the guard's gesture, she stepped through the gate. No beep.

Beyond the gate, the corridor was glass-walled along its left-hand side. Through it, Caitlin could see annexes and extensions to what must have been the original brick building. She walked slowly, trying to test the patience of Dr Scaife, who seemed determined to hurry. Caitlin had already decided she didn't like her.

"What's your job here?" she asked in a conversational tone.

"I'm the managing director."

"Not a real doctor?"

Dr Scaife didn't flinch. "None of us are, at least in the sense you mean. This isn't a hospital."

"Of course. More like a hotel. Residents, and all that."

"No. It would be facetious to say that. This is a care home."

"So your job is to care?"

The doctor didn't respond. She strode in silence along the bright corridor.

"So why am I getting the VIP treatment?" Caitlin said. Her dad would say that she was in one of her 'frames of mind', when all she wanted to do was piss people off. "I'm guessing you don't have to give the tour to every single visitor?"

"You're an originator. Visits by originators are a rarity. This is a courtesy."

Something about Dr Scaife's tone suggested that she regarded Caitlin with some degree of awe. She mustn't be a Charmer.

"Because without me, you'd be out of a job," Caitlin said.

"Partly that."

Caitlin waited for the second half of Dr Scaife's observation, but it didn't come. The featureless corridor made it hard to judge how far they had walked. They hadn't passed a single door. "Where are you taking me?"

"You're a visitor. I'm taking you to the visitors' lounge."

"Not a ward?"

"I told you, this isn't a hospital."

A shudder ran through Caitlin's body. She had no real idea what to expect. She wanted to run back the way she had come, through the security gate and the revolving door, and gulp lungfuls of air. Whatever was in store was something that normal people would never have to experience.

"Here we are," Dr Scaife announced. The parquet flooring ended at a door. Beyond, the corridor continued white-floored, then stretched away in two directions from a junction.

The glass surface of the door to the visitors' lounge was engraved with etchings of curled leaves, though for a moment Caitlin thought they looked like paper or even peeling skin.

"Your duplicate has been made ready for you," Dr Scaife said as she pushed open the door. "There's no need to be afraid."

Caitlin shielded her eyes against dazzlingly bright light. An enormous, arched window took up most of the opposite wall. Through it, Caitlin could see a lawn encircled by drooping willows. Birds hopped around a stone birdbath in its centre. She could see no doors leading from the building into the garden.

Her eyes adjusted to the light. Against a wall, between two large vases bursting with flowers of all colours, was a large, crimson armchair. And sitting in the chair, dwarfed by its high back, was Caitlin's Skin.

A smaller chair had been pulled up to face the Skin, a few metres away from her. Caitlin edged towards it at the speed of a sleepwalker. The effect of seeing her twin was disorientating – a mirror image that refused to mirror her actions. The girl was sitting very still. She was pale and the air around her seemed to shimmer and sparkle. Was she about to ash, right here, right now?

Then Caitlin saw what was creating the light effect. A curved wall of transparent plastic formed a barrier between the two chairs. It made a semicircle around the Skin.

The building was full of invisible walls. Was this one designed to keep the Skin in, or Caitlin out?

Caitlin glanced at Dr Scaife, who nodded. When Caitlin sat in the chair her knees touched the clear barrier. As well as being smaller than the Skin's chair, it was lower. The Skin sat on a raised dais, so that Caitlin had to tilt her head up to make eye contact. Perhaps whoever designed this setup wanted visitors to feel that Skins were higher in status, like royalty in the old days. Or perhaps they wanted to make visitors feel uncomfortable so they wouldn't stay long.

The Skin watched her wordlessly.

"Can you hear me?" Caitlin said in a small voice.

"Yes." In contrast, the Skin's voice was clear, though a little higher than Caitlin had expected. She reminded herself that that was natural enough. Her own voice would probably sound higher-pitched without the bass rumble she experienced in her chest when she spoke.

The Skin was dressed in a pale-blue smock, halfway between a summer dress and a hospital gown. Her red hair was loose around her shoulders; Caitlin never wore her hair that way in public.

They sat in silence. Caitlin examined her twin, still uncertain whether it felt like appraising her reflection or a stranger. The girl's freckles spilled from her face and onto her shoulders. Her legs were pale and too thin for her body. Caitlin noticed things other than physical characteristics, too, things she couldn't be certain she shared. A blink that was fractionally too slow. A mouth that was never quite still. One hand gripping the wrist of the other.

Caitlin looked down at her own hands. They were held in exactly the same way.

She had no idea what to say.

"Could you come closer to the wall?" she said at last. "Your chair is so far away."

"I'm fine here. Thanks." The Skin glanced downwards momentarily. Caitlin saw a thin strap threaded across the Skin's waist, like a car seat belt.

"Have they told you anything?" Caitlin said. She hoped she wouldn't be forced to complete the sentence. *About how long you have left?*

The Skin shook her head. "I don't think they know. It's a waiting game."

"I spoke to Dad," Caitlin said.

The Skin's mouth twitched.

"It's okay," Caitlin said. "I know he's been here to visit you."

The thought that only hours ago she had seriously considered killing her Skin filled Caitlin with revulsion. The girl was calm, on the outside, but Caitlin knew enough about herself to see that she was terrified. And Caitlin was certain that she wasn't only terrified of ashing, either. The Skin was scared of Caitlin.

She took a breath. "Dad told me about Mum's Skins. Some of them lasted. You might too."

"He mentioned it. I couldn't decide whether it was a good or a bad thing."

"Are you kidding me?"

The Skin's eyes became darker, or at least more piercing. "So is that what you think? That me living for a month would be good?"

"Of course." But Caitlin could see that the Skin had noticed her hesitation.

"For you?"

"For you. And that's what matters."

"Because why?"

"Because that's how people are."

"I'm not a person. I'm a Skin. I could pretend that I thought I wasn't, that I was you. But I know what I am. These memories in here—" she tapped the side of her head

"—have a certain... I don't know... *flavour*. They're mine but not mine."

Caitlin sensed that she was being tested. Given how much the Skin was able to anticipate her thoughts, had she also guessed that Caitlin had considered murder?

"But you can think, can't you?" Caitlin said. "You can feel?"

"You ask that as if you're not sure yourself." The Skin's hands were digging deep into the arms of the chair.

It really was like arguing with herself. An internal argument, going around and around. Was she always this hot-headed?

"So put me right," Caitlin said. "Tell me whether you think and feel."

The Skin turned to the enormous window. Outside, the breeze pushed one of the willows to brush against the glass. "I feel. At least, it *feels* that way." She laughed hollowly. "Now, there's a philosophical conundrum. How can you decide whether you feel, if your only evidence is a feeling?"

"Stop it."

"Sorry." For the first time, the Skin's facade fell away. "But I don't know how else to put it. I can remember things. And I make sense of the world by comparing what I see to the things I remember."

Caitlin's throat was suddenly dry. "Everything? You remember everything?"

"Who can tell? I think so."

"Prove it."

Was this what she wanted? To prove that the Skin was

just like her – that there was no appreciable difference? She would be happier not knowing. But Caitlin kept prodding, the way she would play with a scab or a loose tooth.

"You want to set me an exam?" the Skin said. She sounded genuinely angry now. Angry and tired. "I know you're watching me, sizing me up. But you haven't for a second considered that I'm doing exactly the same thing. I'm as curious about you as you are about me. And you know what? We're equally horrified."

"I want to understand. I didn't have to come here."

The Skin's eyes glistened. She wriggled, fidgeting against the restraining belt. "No. And you shouldn't have come. None of the others do. And we understand it, us Skins. We know we're abandoned. And you know what? It turns out that you being here doesn't make me feel one tiny bit better. *Now* do you understand?"

"Stop," Caitlin said, her voice little more than a whimper. "Stop."

"You bloody well stop." The Skin leant forwards in her seat. Despite the distance between them and the barrier, Caitlin recoiled.

"You want to know if we have the same memories? Let's see now." The Skin's voice became a staccato rattle. "Getting stuck up the oak tree in the garden, then cracking an ankle on the way down. Pushing Mum into the swimming pool in Dorset, while she was still wearing her dress. Losing Little Doggy in that hotel in Blackpool. Dad setting up the old reel-to-reel to record our own version of *Alice in Wonderland*, with me as Alice and him doing the voices of all the animals. Me and Evie cutting our thumbs and pressing them together, saying we were 'blood sisters' at that caravan park in Thirsk. Doing a poo in the bath because I was so scared of Tobe's wolfman costume at Halloween." She sat back. "Yeah, I think it's all there."

Caitlin's chest pounded. She felt utterly defeated.

"You're panicking," the Skin said. There was a cruel tinge to her voice. "You're not up to this."

"I'm not. I—"

"Go. Don't come back. Piss off home to your family." The Skin choked slightly on the world 'your'.

Caitlin jerked up from her chair. Suddenly, the Skin appeared dreadfully ugly, sneering with triumph. Nobody should have to see themselves like this. It felt like a nightmare.

She tried to recapture the sense of what she had lectured Evie about, again and again until Evie rolled her eyes and told her to shut the hell up. Charmers and Skins were as similar to one another as anyone could be. More similar than sisters. More similar than twins. It ought to mean something.

She took a step closer to the barrier. She forced herself to smile.

"Don't you fucking dare," the Skin said. Her voice trembled with rage.

Caitlin refused to move away. She watched the girl, her wild red hair, the swollen patches under her eyes. She was almost unrecognisable now.

The girl writhed against the seat belt. Her fingernails looked as though they might tear through the fabric of the chair. She spluttered and sobbed.

"I said go," she croaked. Then, in a sudden roar that shook the barrier and make sparkles dance before Caitlin's eyes, "GO!"

Caitlin staggered backwards as if the Skin had shoved her. Her hands clamped over her mouth in a muddled instinctive attempt to stop the other girl from shouting.

The Skin continued to scream as Caitlin pushed past Dr Scaife, then fumbled at the door and dropped to her knees in the corridor outside.

# NINE

Ellis Blackwood was one of the few people that Russell knew who possessed a mobile telephone. It wasn't even one of the ridiculous models with enormous battery packs that he had seen London businessmen lugging around. Ellis's handset was compact enough for him to slip into a briefcase – something he always did whenever Russell entered the corner office.

The thing was temperamental, though. Russell listened to the sounds of Ellis's halting voice ("Can you hear me now?"), then his wrestling with the swivel chair as he tried to find a region with better reception ("And how about now?"), then his tapping of its buttons, before he hung up with a sigh of exasperation.

Then Russell heard the dial tone hum of the main phone line. He picked up the handset of his extension phone and heard a sequence of beeps – only four of them, which indicated an internal call. Ellis cleared his throat noisily before the call was answered.

"Yes?" a female voice said.

"You can hear me now? I have a status update, ma'am." Ellis sounded like a schoolchild forced to speak to the head teacher.

"Naturally. That's essentially all that is required of you." Russell recognised the voice as Angela McKinney's. "Go on."

Ellis cleared his throat again. "The target radius has widened, ma'am."

"I'm aware of that."

"Yes. But more than before. Substantially more."

"Greater than the agreed tolerance levels?"

"Many miles, ma'am. Yes, much greater."

"How many miles?"

Russell heard a faint tapping sound. Recently, Ellis had developed the bad habit of chewing his fingernails. "A little over one hundred miles, ma'am."

Silence. For a moment, Russell wondered if the line had cut out. Then Angela spoke again. "That is unacceptable."

"I understand."

"You understand?" More silence. Then, "There's something else you intend to tell me. I can tell. Is it conceivable that you have still more bad news?"

Ellis's voice was now so quiet that Russell had to strain to hear him. "It's moved, as well. The centre has shifted."

"To where?"

"Are you sitting down, ma'am?"

"Spit it out, Blackwood, you fool."

"The centre of the target area is now identified as the western outer edge of the capital, ma'am. Close to the M25 at West Drayton, to be specific."

A chill passed through Russell's body. Until now, he had suspected that if the secret related to the prospect of a GBP attack, it must be on some far-away country – something covert, possibly illegal, but relating to the maintenance of world peace. But now the mention of West Drayton, which suggested an external threat that Russell had never in his life considered, and Ellis's uncertainty about the target... This changed everything.

The line buzzed. Russell imagined it as the sound of Angela's impatience.

"It hasn't settled, quite," Ellis continued, gabbling in his haste. "There's every chance that it will shift again, before—"

"Then you must track it. And I would advise that all of you get some sleep before you leave, because you sound moronic when you're tired. You have a little over a week." Incredibly, Angela's voice had become even colder.

"I'll do everything I—"

"I don't care what you do. Solve this."

The line cut out. It was several seconds before Russell heard another click as Ellis hung up his phone. Russell replaced his handset carefully. He kneaded his hands and watched the door to Ellis's office.

So he had been half-right. It must be an attack – but not one that Ellis, or the government, could control. An attack on Britain by some foreign country that was supposedly docile and yielding to British supremacy. And somehow, the Party possessed intelligence that proved that it would be soon. Should he warn his parents to leave London immediately, or wait until he had more concrete information?

The study door opened. Russell stood up.

Ellis appeared even more defeated than usual. His hair stuck out at the sides in two triangular tufts. Russell imagined him sitting at his desk with his head in his hands.

"The car is on its way," Ellis said in a faraway voice.

Russell glanced down at the desk diary. "I haven't called the driver, sir. Would you like me to?"

"Different driver. Jeremy is indisposed. I should expect I'll be away for a while."

Russell's cheeks flushed. His knee-jerk reaction was to think of Nell and the chance of approaching her – rescuing her – in Ellis's absence. But there would be no chance of meeting with her while Ellis was away. He had mentioned earlier that Nell and Spencer would be visiting her parents for the half-term holiday.

"And your other appointments, sir – shall I reschedule?"

Ellis shook his head. "I'll take care of it. Time I took a bit of responsibility for myself, yes?" He wavered visibly, on the cusp of saying something else. He shook his head. "Well then. Goodbye, Russell. Please do field calls as best you can. I ought to be back by Friday. Or thereabouts."

Before Russell could reply, Ellis had edged out of the office, leaving the door slightly ajar. Russell crept to it. He watched Ellis's mournful shamble along the corridor to the plate-glass door. Ellis made a slight deviation, tracing an arc around the door to the banner-printers.

As soon as Ellis had left the building, Russell jogged after him. He jammed his foot to stop the outer door from closing. The security guard frowned and then returned to his magazine.

A black saloon car was waiting outside with its engine running. Ellis slumped into its rear seat without speaking to the driver, who was hidden behind smoked glass. The car began to move away as soon as the door closed and barely paused at the car park exit. Its wheels spun as it accelerated along Marston Street.

Russell glanced at his battered old bike, chained to railings at the side of the building. He had intended to follow Ellis, whenever he left, as far as he possibly could. He laughed at the thought of pedalling alongside the car, tapping on the window.

\*

"No, please don't," Gerry said. "I've already been on hold for the twenty minutes since I last spoke to you."

The other end of the phone line went silent. Then, the scratchy voice said, "It's not our department. You need Health." The line clicked and the voice was replaced with tinny muzak.

Gerry squinted up at the window. Daylight pierced the gap between the heavy curtains – it was nearly midday. She had started researching contact details for government departments when it was still dark, and had made her first phone call at nine. She realised that she was humming one of the inane hold-music melodies.

Last night, she had stared for hours at the faded photocopy, willing it to make sense. The variety of line items in the table was baffling. Third-party cleaning and maintenance services. Infrastructure and admin. Lighting. But it was the numerical values beside each item that had caught her interest. Hundreds of thousands of pounds spent in a single month. Many of the largest figures were tagged against unexpected items that made the least sense to her. Location services. Refuse and collection. Public relations.

It was a leaked government document, that was clear enough. The digital watermark included the initials *GBP* several times – Great British Prosperity. But why had the hooded stranger given it to her?

Then it hit her.

The financial data wasn't for a single month. That wasn't what the all-caps word at the top of the document meant.

*JANUARY.*

The Snakeskin care home. It wasn't something the Party tended to talk about much, nor anything related to Snakeskins, these days.

The realisation had galvanised her for the first handful of hours that morning. However, her conviction had faded with each new obstructive person she spoke to on the phone. Perhaps it was wrong to dedicate so much time to a vague tip-off from an unknown source. The amounts of money listed in the spreadsheet were pretty obscene, but she had no idea how much it might cost to run such a large institution. Even if her following up on the tip could be defended from a journalistic point of view, her being so eager showed that she was desperate for a lead. She wished she had something more important to do.

"Can I help you?" a buzzing voice said.

Gerry fumbled with the phone. "My name's Gerry

Chafik. I don't think we've spoken before, although I've had conversations with your colleagues in other departments."

"They said you're a reporter?"

"Yes. Sort of. Yes, I am a reporter. I'm looking for information about the January care home in Reading."

"What kind of information?" It was only now that Gerry decided that it was a male voice, made squeakier by the bad line.

"Specifically, about their funding. There doesn't seem to be any mention of January in the budget information available to the public. Even a rough figure would be a start, some kind of overview. Do you think you might be able to help me?"

The man coughed. "Yes. One minute."

Gerry exhaled and stretched in her chair. *Finally.*

"Right. I'm putting you through to Budgetary Affairs."

"No, don't, please. I've already—"

The line clicked. A synthesiser waltz started midway through a song. Gerry watched a sliver of sun creep past the gap in the curtains. The track looped three times before a voice said, "Budgetary Affairs. How can I help?"

Gerry recognised the voice – she had spoken to the woman half a dozen times already. "Sylvia? It's Gerry Chafik again." A pause followed. "Yeah, sorry. No offence, but I didn't ask to be put through to you. I know I'm ruining your morning. Could you put me through to Health again, please?"

She increased the phone volume and, without thinking, began to hum along to the reedy rendition of a song half-remembered from her childhood. In the kitchen she pulled cereal boxes from the cupboard, shaking each in turn. All were empty.

"I'm afraid I'm going to have to ask you to stop."

Gerry grimaced and nodded. Then, realising the voice hadn't actually been merely her own thoughts, she dashed to the phone. "Hi. Look, don't worry. I know you'll have been told to get rid of me. But I have a different question now, an easy one. Could you point me towards the overall budget for the Department of Health, please? Maybe with a breakdown of the other normal services – as in, not specifically for Charmers."

It wouldn't be much, but at least if she could compare January's costs to the costs of running a standard commercial hospital, she might be able to gauge if there was anything amiss in the levels of spending. It was possible that the shadowy stranger had been trying to alert her to overspending for exclusive services. Charmers were only a tiny fraction of the population, after all. Given the lack of any nationalised health provision, any public spending on Snakeskins was dubious and a source of ire from the general public, who were overtaxed and yet were forced to spend a high proportion of their meagre salaries on their own healthcare.

The line clicked several times. Gerry held the phone away from her ear. Then she recognised the sound as the man clucking his tongue.

"Yes," he said. "I can do that. Do you have a postal address related to an authenticated establishment?"

Gerry groaned. The chances of Zemma Finch allowing

her onto the premises at *Folk* were low. She gave the address anyway.

"You'll receive it within the next ten working days," the man said with a note of triumph in his voice. "Goodbye now."

Gerry threw down the phone in disgust. The handset skidded across the coffee table, coming to rest against the stack of books from Ilam Hall.

She flipped through the phone directory, called British Rail, and ordered return train tickets to Reading.

\*

Caitlin made a wide berth around three protesters with placards outside the January care home. Their signs read, *CARE FOR US, NOT SNAKESKIN HUSKS* and *GREAT BRITISH PROSPERITY PARTY*, with *PROSPERITY* crossed out and *DISPARITY* scrawled above. Two police officers with truncheons and pistols conspicuously visible watched in silence. One had her head cocked, perhaps listening to an earpiece. Legally, it took four or more protesters to constitute a mass outdoor assembly which could be stopped by any means necessary, but Caitlin was certain the officers would receive orders that this protest could be curtailed, too. One of the scruffy protesters was in discussion with one of the January staff who had emerged from a side door, who seemed intent on getting rid of them before the police could intervene. Caitlin overheard the woman saying, "I assure you that there are no Skins belonging to Party members in residence. You'd be far better addressing..."

Caitlin slipped through the revolving doors and plodded over to the red sofas. She wished she were somewhere else. She also wished that whoever was brewing coffee would knock it off. The smell permeated every part of the enormous lobby of the care home and it was beginning to make her retch.

She had spent another night in the hotel on the outskirts of Reading. Her back ached from the too-soft bed.

It had been Evie who had convinced her to return to the care home, though Evie herself didn't know it. *Hey, u OK hun?* her pager message had read, yesterday afternoon. Caitlin hadn't called her. Her normal, everyday life was too far away for her to summon the energy to get involved. A few hours later, Evie had sent another message: *Forget Caitlin Mk II. U R the real deal. Love you.*

The trouble was, Caitlin was less and less sure that she *was* the real deal. At least the Skin knew her own mind – she was angry and scared and full of resentment about the hand she'd been dealt. Caitlin, on the other hand, felt only a creeping numbness about the whole situation. She couldn't remember having been apathetic about anything in her life. Her mum was the one who had taught her to be opinionated, and political, and proud of her heritage. This passivity was unbearable.

So she returned to January. If her Skin was going to be a contrary prick, then she was too.

"They're making you wait, then?" a voice said.

It was the old woman, Dodie. She dropped heavily onto the sofa.

Caitlin managed a smile. "You too?"

"I've already been in and out," Dodie replied, waving a hand airily. "Visiting a few friends, making new ones. Now it's time for a sandwich before the drive home, even though it's only a hop. Something about this place makes me ravenous." She reached into her large handbag and pulled out a cling-filmed package, then placed it on her knees. Her grey hair flopped and covered her face as she bent to unwrap the sandwich. "You know, if they make you wait then that shows you're important. They let me in lickety-split, every day."

"You really come here every day?"

"I see it as a duty of sorts." Dodie munched her sandwich. "So, what kind of VIP are you, my love?"

Caitlin frowned. The bright sunlight made it hard to read the woman's expression. "Other than being what they call the 'originator', you mean?"

Dodie puffed out her cheeks. "My goodness. Now I see why you're being made to wait. They'll be rolling out the red carpet, no doubt. You're a rare breed."

"Yeah." Caitlin watched her carefully. Dodie gave no sign of recognition. "You told me more or less the same thing when we met yesterday."

Dodie's expression clouded. She put down the sandwich. "Oh. I see."

It might have been a trick of the light, but Caitlin thought she saw the glistening of tears.

"I'm sorry," Caitlin said. "I didn't mean—"

"I'm a little forgetful."

"Right. But please don't be upset. Maybe I have the sort of face that doesn't stick in people's minds."

Dodie's eyes shone. "No, my love. You're positively beautiful. You may have told me this yesterday, too, but what's your name?"

"Caitlin Hext."

"Caitlin. Hext." Dodie repeated it to herself, twice, under her breath. "I have it this time."

Dodie glanced up. Out of the corner of her eye, Caitlin saw somebody approaching them from the direction of the metal detector. She tried to gather herself. She wasn't in the mood to take any of Dr Scaife's passive-aggressive crap.

But it was her dad.

"Cait!" His voice was hoarse. When he reached her he looked as though he might try and hug her, but then crossed his arms over his chest. His shirt was crumpled and he hadn't shaved.

Their argument at Ivy Cottage now seemed ridiculous. Caitlin couldn't recall seeing anybody look quite so crushed as her dad did right now. She was hugging him tight before she knew it. He felt small in her arms.

After a while Ian extricated himself. He glanced at the gate that led to the visitors' lounge. He must have been with her Skin moments ago. "I've been so worried. Are you okay? Sorry. Of course you're okay. Where have you been? Here, I suppose. I don't know what I want to say to you, now that I've found you."

"Stop, Dad. I'm fine," Caitlin replied. "I'm really sorry I didn't call."

She felt awkward and exposed, even though the other people in the lobby were paying them no attention. She turned. Tactfully, Dodie had already left. Caitlin saw her making her way through the revolving door.

Ian cleared his throat. "So, you decided to come after all."

"It's my second time. If she'll let me back in."

His eyes widened. "You were here yesterday? In the morning? She didn't mention it."

"Yeah. She's sort of a bitch, isn't she?"

Ian's response was half laugh and half cough. "That's a dreadful thing to say."

"I figure I'm allowed to, of all people. So, anyway. You came back too."

"It's not what it looks like. I wasn't trying to—"

"Replace me?" Caitlin took his hands in hers. She had been an idiot, before. "Don't be stupid, Dad. Me and her look the same, but we're different. Or we *mean* different things, at least. You can visit my Skin all you like. I won't be angry with you. Okay?"

He sniffed. "Okay. You won't want to hear this, Cait... but maybe it's true about sheddings being a milestone. You've changed." He must have noticed her grip tighten. "No, no. I mean you're growing up. You're becoming a woman."

"Oh God. Dad, really? Because if you're going to start explaining to me about the birds and the bees..."

He shook his head. "Sorry. I'll leave it there. Just... I'm proud of you, Cait. For everything. For coming here, especially." He rubbed his eyes. "Hey, is your uncle here too?"

She frowned. "Why would he be? I mean, why on earth

would I know, and you wouldn't?"

"Tobe hasn't been with you, these last couple of days?"

She shook her head. "No offence, but I don't think he'd be much of a travelling companion."

"No. No. Okay."

Caitlin remembered seeing Tobe leave his shed with his rucksack slung over his shoulder. "There's been no word from him at all since he left?"

"No. It's no big deal. I think I remember him talking about seeing some friends, playing cards. You know what he's like. He probably didn't think to tell us. He gets like that."

"When he's upset, he does." Caitlin remembered the fairy lights that Tobe had strung up for her shedding. She'd never known him to go to any trouble for anything. Maybe sheddings were more important to him than he let on. Or maybe she was.

Caitlin saw Dr Scaife approach. "Urgh. Looks as though I'm about to be summoned."

Ian glanced around and scowled. "That old battleaxe. Do you want me to come back in with you?"

Caitlin imagined how awkward he would feel, stuck in a room with his daughter and her identical twin. "Thanks. No, you head home. I've got a return ticket and I think I might prefer a bit of time on my own, after the visit. But I promise I'll be home later and I promise I'll perk up. Sound good?"

He beamed and planted a stubbly kiss on her cheek. He nodded curtly at Dr Scaife and then scurried away.

"Miss Hext. Your loved one is ready to meet you," Dr Scaife announced.

Caitlin glared at her. Loved ones didn't usually have to be

restrained with belts to stop them from leaving their seats.

Once they had passed through the security gate, Caitlin hurried along the glass-walled corridor, more to annoy Dr Scaife than from any sense of urgency. By the time she reached the door to the visitors' lounge, the doctor had to sprint to prevent her from walking further along the corridor. Caitlin noticed a plainer door on the same side as the door to the visitors' lounge. That must be the one that led to the Skins' annex within its transparent barrier.

"What's down there?" Caitlin said, pointing towards the junction where the parquet flooring ended and the sterile white flooring began.

"That leads to the living quarters and leisure areas," Dr Scaife replied, panting slightly. "But they're only for staff and patients."

"You mean residents."

The doctor's face darkened. "Yes. Residents, of course."

Caitlin smiled. Then, without warning, she dashed to the junction. Dr Scaife made a strangled blurting noise behind her.

Caitlin skidded to a halt at the junction. The passages in either direction were more like those in a standard hospital and were interspersed with plain, windowless doors. At one end of the left-hand corridor were the steel double doors of a lift beside a fire exit. She was almost disappointed at how ordinary it all looked.

When Dr Scaife caught up, Caitlin allowed herself to be led back. "Sorry. I got mixed up for a second. I could get lost anywhere."

"Then we will make sure that you are not left alone."

"Right then. In we go?" Caitlin pushed open the door to the visitors' lounge before the doctor could reply. Dr Scaife remained in the corridor.

Caitlin strode to the transparent wall. She didn't sit down.

This time, the Skin was sitting less upright. The seat belt restraint dug into her belly. She reminded Caitlin of a rag doll that had lost most of its stuffing. Did Skins decline physically before they disappeared? Most ashed so quickly after they appeared that there could be no telling.

Beside the Skin's chair, within the semicircular barrier, stood a man wearing a white nurse's uniform. Caitlin noticed immediately that he appeared more human, more *alive*, than most of the staff she had encountered. His eyes were alert and his black skin shone with health. He watched Caitlin silently as she paced up and down before the wall.

The Skin spoke first, as if there had been no interruption to their conversation the day before. "I do know that those aren't my memories, not really. They're yours. Because no matter how much I feel like you, I know that's not the case. I'm not you. But I'm hardly me, either. There is no me."

There was no anger in her voice. Her speech was slower and a little slurred.

Caitlin had no idea her features could crumple like that. "That's not what it looks like. You look like a real person. And you talk like one. If you have my memories of my life, then you have my memories of other people's opinions about Skins, too?"

A nod.

"Then you know how the argument goes. Nature versus nurture. So what if you arrived fully-formed instead of as a baby? Good for you for missing out the grossness of childbirth. The point is this – the exact second you arrived, your experience of the world was different to mine. You knew you were a Snakeskin. And that means that everything you saw and felt from that moment on was affected by that knowledge."

The girl shrugged. She looked utterly exhausted. "What does it matter?"

With a new sense of conviction Caitlin gazed around the room, the daylight, the patterned walls, the glistening window. "It means we're not the same. You may only have been around for a couple of days, but you're already a different person. Sod the fact that we look alike and that our minds sort of work the same – if we were sisters, that might have been the case anyway. You've only had a short life so far, but it's your life. We've separated, which means that you're a person in your own right. And that means that you should *have* rights. Right?"

"Yeah. Whatever." The Skin looked down at the restraints that held her in place.

Caitlin's mouth was dry. "I'm sorry."

The Skin was silent for a while, then said softly, "What is it you want to talk about?"

"I don't know. I want to know who you are."

"You already know that."

"There's no point in thinking of you as me. You're a three-day-old new person. What should I even call you?"

"That's a stupid question."

"It isn't. And I know for sure you've thought about it."

The Skin rubbed a thumb along her bottom lip, back and forth. Caitlin imagined she could feel the touch of it on her own lips. She'd never thought about it before, but it was the same action she did when she was lost in thought.

Finally, the Skin said, "Kit."

Caitlin smiled. When she was six or seven, she had tried to get the children at school to call her by that name. It hadn't stuck and only her mum had used it for a few weeks. Eventually, Caitlin had begged her to stop.

"It suits you," she said. She reached out so that her fingertips touched the clear barrier. She mimed shaking hands. "I'm very pleased to meet you, Kit. I like your dress."

The Skin – Kit – looked down at her plain blue smock. She snorted a laugh, then mimed shaking Caitlin's hand in return. She arched her back, then shook her head as if to clear it. She rubbed her eyes. The skin all around them was cracked and dry.

"You look like hell, Kit," Caitlin said.

"It's this place. It's not easy to feel rested."

"I thought it was quite plush, all things considered."

"This room, yeah. The 'residential areas', as they call them, not so much. You know what they say about removing all distractions in order to have space to think? Well, I can do plenty of thinking in my room."

"So it's just for show? All this luxury?" Caitlin pointed at the garden courtyard through the window. "I'm guessing you wouldn't be saying that if Dr Stoneface was still here. What about—" She nodded at the nurse standing beside Kit's chair. He gazed straight ahead, looking increasingly uncomfortable.

"Don't worry about Ayo. He's a love."

*He's a love.* That sounded more like Janet Hext than Caitlin. It was as though Kit was trying out other peoples' characteristics, remembered quirks and oddities. Trying to find a new template for herself. It's what Caitlin would do.

Ayo appeared as though he didn't know where to look.

Kit shrugged. She bent forwards in her chair as much as the restraints allowed. "He brought me a banana when I cried because they'd all been taken by other people. And he even—"

Gently, Ayo placed a hand on her arm. Kit clammed up.

Caitlin looked from one to the other. What kind of a relationship did they have? Then, suddenly, the thought of Kit having her own life – her own secrets – made her feel immensely grateful. "Are they leaving you alone, though? Letting you do your own thing?"

"There's nothing here. Each day's the same as the last, apart from visits, which they prefer kept as short as possible. There's nothing to do and nothing to be done." She wiped at her eyes, which had begun to tear up. There was a slight tremor to her movements. "Sorry. Tired. It's tough getting any sleep, for whatever reason."

Caitlin frowned. "What do you mean? Do they stop you sleeping?"

Kit shrugged. "We all look like this. Knackered. Can you blame us? We Skins aren't in the best place, geographically or, you know, emotionally."

"Seriously. Kit. Answer the question. Do they stop you sleeping?"

Kit's head bobbed. When she raised it again, she appeared years older. The dry skin around her eyes looked terribly painful. Her bottom lip wouldn't stay still. When she spoke, her voice cracked.

"I don't know."

# TEN

Russell rang the doorbell three times. Nobody answered.

He skirted around the Blackwood house, taking care to tread lightly on the gravel of the driveway. Ellis was away on his mysterious trip, and Nell had taken Spencer to her parents' house for the weekend, but North Oxford was full of busybodies who might inform the Blackwoods about somebody sneaking around.

Of course, there might be CCTV cameras, too. But surely nobody would check the footage, without a particular reason to do so? As he pulled up the hood of his dark coat he thought of Ixion dressed in the same way, and experienced an odd pang of satisfaction. He was determined to find something in the house that might incriminate Ellis and reveal what the GBP was really up to. Whether it would satisfy Ixion or not, it was his only route towards understanding how to help Nell.

The house was far larger than the Blackwood family needed. It would have taken half a dozen more children to warrant its size, with its vast garden crammed with hedged enclosures and outdoor dining areas.

He breathed more easily once he passed from gravel to grass. A strip of lawn led to Nell's lean-to workshop. The outer wall was mottled plastic that was only semi-translucent. Russell kept low to the ground and every few metres he peered through the plastic, trying to see inside. There was no sign of movement.

The workshop door was slightly ajar. Despite his hurry, Russell felt a sudden impulse to enter. Inside, the thick tree trunk, Nell's work in progress, seemed to glow as though from some natural phosphorescence. It appeared brighter than the daylight that seeped through the filthy plastic windows.

Nell had been working hard. The tree that lay lengthwise on its struts was now almost entirely hollow. The hole in its side was a couple of feet wide and five or six long, rounded at the corners. Russell frowned. The hole had the dimensions of a body, or at least an abstraction of one, like the shape of a coffin. The insides of the tree trunk were rough and splintered. Running through its precise centre was the sapling Nell had revealed. It looked absurdly fragile. Instinctively, Russell kept his distance. His anxiety that he might snap the slim tree within the hulking, fossil-like exterior had nothing to do with concerns about his break-in being discovered. It was something more unconscious. It was real fear.

He backed away and found himself outside in the bright daylight. He must get into the house. The longer he stayed out here, the greater the chances of being spotted.

The kitchen door was overlooked by the top floor of a

neighbouring bank of executive apartments. All of their balconies were empty. Likely, the apartments were second homes, pieds-à-terre for city bankers, and most would be unoccupied for months on end. Even so, he jogged the remaining distance. For a moment he thought he had forgotten to bring the keys, which he had kept after his stint as a waiter at Ellis's party. Finally, having located them in his jacket pocket, he fumbled with the lock and then he was in.

He stifled his instinct to turn on the light. Though the kitchen window was half obscured by vines, the natural light was enough to allow him to see. One half of the wooden farmhouse table was strewn with debris, all of which he attributed to Nell and Spencer – two hardened half-crescents of croissant, a packet of jeweller's screwdrivers upon a demolished computer motherboard, an array of chisels and other woodworking tools apparently abandoned part way through cleaning, judging by the sawdust sprinkled all around. Only one corner of the kitchen was immaculate, with packets of cereal aligned in order of size, and a stacked coffee cup and plate arranged on a crumbless chopping board. Russell pictured Ellis hunched over the counter beside the window, intently preparing his breakfast. There were a couple of small, cuboid paper packets, too. Medication. Perhaps Ellis was not a well man.

He made his way deeper into the house. It was darker here – the kitchen must have been a later extension to the main building, which had far smaller windows, some with stained-glass elements that made the light duller and sadder. The oak door to the drawing room was open. Russell pictured the Party officials and their guests milling around on the night of Ellis's 'soirée'. It occurred to him just how dramatically his opinion of them had changed. Once he had been impressed at powerful Charmers' confidence, their decadence. Now he felt only suspicion and resentment.

The walls of the drawing room were lined with antique curios. A glass dome covered a tiny bonsai tree. A pair of crossed swords hung on the wall opposite the large fireplace. Russell flinched as a carriage clock on the mantelpiece rang the hour. A tiny figure emerged from the lower part of the clock. Its loose arms shook as it juddered along its semicircular path. It was little more than a skeleton, its limbs joined with pins. He held his breath until it re-entered its housing.

With a renewed sense of urgency, he hurried along the corridor. The window at the half-landing of the staircase was laced with lead strips which cast a cross-hatched pattern onto the hallway tiles and onto Russell. He wondered what he might discover if he went upstairs. Did Ellis and Nell sleep in the same bedroom, or separate ones? It was difficult to imagine them spending any amount of time close together, even unconscious. He thought of his theatre outing with Nell and Spencer. He would give anything to have the two of them as his family.

He passed further into the dark depths of the house, past a dining room and into Ellis's study. It was small, and a mahogany desk took up almost half of it. The shelves behind the desk held only a few books. Russell plucked one out to read the title. *Herding Cats: Overcoming Stubborn Behaviour.* Ellis must be having problems with those hidden-away colleagues in the office complex. Next to the photos were framed photographs of Nell and Spencer, alongside a few monochrome images of a boy who must be Ellis himself.

Beside the desk was a cabinet. Each of the three drawers was locked.

Russell discovered two additional drawers beneath the surface of the desk. Both were locked, too. He suddenly felt an idiot for expecting anything else. He spun on the spot, hunting for anything that might hold a key. On instinct, he groped around underneath the surface of the desk, then felt even more foolish – the locks were clear to see, so they couldn't be operated remotely.

He froze. Perhaps he was simply in the wrong room. Locks or no locks, this study was in the centre of the house, visible and vulnerable. If Ellis had secrets, surely he would keep them better hidden away.

And he had already seen a likely route to such a place, when Nell had emerged from the servants' corridor on the night of the party. Perhaps she had been snooping around, as he was now. But then, what if Nell hadn't been investigating, that night? What if her dazed reaction hadn't been fear of some physical threat, but instead fear of Russell learning something he oughtn't to know? But he simply didn't want to consider that she might be an insider to Ellis's secret. His need to characterise her as an innocent victim was overwhelming.

He crept in darkness towards the front of the house.

He pushed the heavy curtain aside and found the narrow corridor more by feel than by sight.

A glow greeted him at the corner of the passage. Light leaked from the edges of a white door. It appeared new, in contrast to the original oak doors elsewhere in the house. It had no window and instead of a normal lock, there was a brushed-steel keypad fixed to the wall beside it.

Russell told himself that a light didn't mean that anybody was in there. He listened for sounds from the door, but heard nothing. He examined its edges closely, but all he could make out in the gaps was yellowish light. He dropped to his knees, awkwardly bunching his body to fit sideways within the corridor. If he pressed his cheek hard against the floor, he could see through the slit beneath the door.

The room appeared no wider than the corridor. His view was limited, but he could see low shelves to either side. On the left-hand side were coloured boxes that might be cereal packets. These weren't the box files and folders full of secret plans that he had hoped to find. The items on the opposite shelf were easier to make out. Tins of food, stacked three deep. Baked beans, tomatoes, sweetcorn, potatoes.

He sat up. It was a dead end. It was just a larder.

But then, what could possibly be the need for a keypad-operated lock? There must be something in there that required being locked away.

He bent to look again. The wall directly opposite him, only a few feet away, appeared blank, but something about it confused the eye. Light reflected oddly on its surface – the narrow slice of wall gradated from dark to light.

He stared at the keypad. Ellis wasn't an imaginative man. The code might well be something straightforward, to ensure that he remembered it. His birth date? No. Nell's, perhaps, or Spencer's? Not that it mattered. Russell had no idea what any of those dates might be.

With a start, he realised he could hear a noise, a regular thudding. He dropped down again to look beneath the door. The tiny room was still empty. The thudding continued. What could be making the noise? It was possible that he had triggered some security system, but surely the result would be a siren.

The thuds sounded tinnier now. Russell realised what they were.

Footsteps.

Specifically, shoes clanging on metal.

The opposite wall transformed with this realisation. The light appeared gradated because the wall was sloped. And the wall was sloped because—

The top of a head appeared at Russell's eye level. Somebody was climbing a staircase that must lead downwards from the tiny room behind this door.

The head had wild, curly black hair and the hint of a widow's peak. A face followed.

It was Ellis.

He was more ruddy-cheeked than normal, his eyes less sore and tired, even though he was unkempt and stubbly.

And he kept climbing.

Before Russell bolted backwards he noticed that Ellis was wearing a loose grey tracksuit. He had never seen Ellis wear anything but a business suit.

He clambered away from the door, willing his shoes to squeak less upon the shiny floor.

The footsteps stopped.

Five beeps sounded from the keypad. Russell turned and sprinted away around the corner of the corridor.

He stumbled through the dark house and burst out through the kitchen door.

The daylight stung his eyes. He spun around wildly. He couldn't risk retracing his route to the front of the house.

He scrambled up the tall fence and dropped down on the other side. Pain shot up his thighs upon landing. Limping, he navigated the low hedges of a well-tended garden and slipped along the side of Ellis's neighbour's house, muttering thanks to some nameless deity for its windows remaining dark and no neighbour appearing. Then he sprinted away along the street.

\*

Caitlin let herself into Ivy Cottage. Even after only a couple of days, its proportions were as unfamiliar as a home remembered from childhood.

"Dad!"

There was no answer.

The journey from Reading had taken far longer than it ought. The train driver had announced a temporary halt just before they arrived at Didcot station. Forty minutes later, he had revealed that the reason for the delay was a suspected suicide. An hour later, one of the carriage staff had admitted to Caitlin that the body was still trapped under the wheels.

Along with all the other passengers, Caitlin had watched the fire engine arrive and the men set to work. She had winced as the train eased backwards a few metres to reveal whoever was beneath. It was another ten minutes before the train driver explained, breathlessly, that the 'suicide' had been a dog. When the train finally arrived at Woodstock, the taxi queue was immense. Caitlin had walked to Ivy Cottage in the dark.

Her dad wasn't in the kitchen. Perhaps he was already in bed. She hoped he hadn't been worrying too much. On the train, her pager battery had died before the dog had.

Upstairs, she eased open the door to her dad's bedroom. "Dad? Sorry, I wanted to—"

The curtains were wide open. The bed sheets were in a tangle.

She padded downstairs. Perhaps her dad had gone looking for her. Perhaps, when she hadn't returned, he had taken the train back to the care home. Perhaps he was there now, speaking to the Skin, Kit.

The front room was empty, the kitchen too. She was pulling on her boots when she heard someone cough.

The sitting room in the eastern wing of the house was lit only by moonlight. Ian stood facing the bay window. His shoulders were hunched. Caitlin sighed with relief when she realised that he was stooping only because he was looking through the telescope on its fixed stand.

"I'm so glad you're home," Ian said. He didn't turn.

"Sorry I'm so late. There was an accident. The train stopped dead."

Ian exhaled noisily.

"Are you all right?" Caitlin said.

Her dad said nothing for a long time. Finally, he said, "Saturn's bright as anything tonight. I keep thinking I can see the rings, but I haven't used the telescope for so long. It took me ages to realise I was staring at a hair on the lens."

"You used to look up at the stars every night."

One of Ian's hands reached out blindly to fiddle with the focus. "I did. It felt important."

"Because of the Fall?" She resisted the temptation to add, *Because of Mum and me?*

"I was trying not to think about anything, Cait. I suppose this is my calm place." Seconds passed. "Yes. Because of the Fall."

"She's not okay, is she? I mean Kit." She wondered whether the Skin had told Ian her name.

Again, Ian drew a deep breath. "She'll be gone soon. And then it won't matter."

"You went through this before, with Mum's Skins. Is there really no other way?"

"The government people are insistent. They have to keep Snakeskins apart from the rest of society, they say. Issues about ID, country of residence, all that. It makes a kind of sense."

"Except when you talk to them."

"Yes."

"Because they're people."

"I believe that, Cait. Yes." Ian fussed around the telescope, checking the settings. He was still facing away from her. "But it's not because I think she's you. You do know that, don't you?"

Caitlin tried to judge her real feelings, about Kit, and about her dad spending time with her mum's remaining Snakeskin, after Janet had died. She accepted that he hadn't believed they were one and the same person. But it was impossible to imagine that he hadn't treated the Skin like Janet, a little. "I think so. And it's your business, Dad. Like you say, she'll be gone soon. And then you'll be stuck with just me again."

Ian laughed softly. "That'll do me fine. You're all I—"

His shoulders hunched even more. He had stopped looking into the eyepiece of the telescope. His body shook.

"Dad?"

He turned. Now Caitlin saw the tears shining on his cheeks.

"Cait. There's been some bad news."

Caitlin didn't know how to respond. Something in his manner told her that this wasn't about her.

"It's your uncle. It's Tobe. He's dead."

Instinctively, Caitlin glanced through the bay window to the dark area of the garden where Tobe's shed was. He ought to be in there, snoring loudly, or pulling an all-nighter playing some computer game.

"No," she said.

Ian nodded slowly. "It happened the day before yesterday, but they only rang today. They couldn't figure out who he was at first, so it took a while before they knew to get hold of me."

Something bitter rose up in Caitlin's throat. She didn't want to ask the question, but finally she said, "Why couldn't they figure out who he was?"

"Oh God. No, Caitlin, no. Nothing so gruesome as that. He didn't have any identification on him, that was all. He was— Well, he was naked. In the swimming pool, at some hotel over Ilford way."

Caitlin thought of the dog beneath the train. "Was it suicide?"

Ian paused. "They don't know. There'll be an autopsy, they think. It hardly matters, Cait."

Caitlin waited for a wave of grief to hit her. She felt worse for its absence. Uncle Tobe was gone and yet her only response was confusion. That, and a trace of anger about Tobe providing a final frustrating distraction when she already had enough to deal with. She hated herself for her coldness.

"What was he even doing there?" she said.

Ian waved a hand. "They told me, but I didn't really take it in. He was there for a game of some sort. Computer games, maybe?"

Caitlin half-remembered Tobe talking about something coming up, in one of his rare moments discussing the future. "No. You were right before. It was a card-game tournament. It was a big deal. To him."

Ian nodded. "Well, he won it. I don't think there was any prize money. But that's how they identified him in the end. Eventually, they found something—" he choked back a shuddering sob "—lodged in the filter of the swimming pool. A trophy."

He wiped his eyes, then reached out to her with fingers that glistened with wetness. "He wasn't a happy man, Cait.

I mean, I don't know that for sure, but— You know what he was like."

Caitlin nodded. And though she'd seen him for hardly any time since her first shedding, Tobe had been even more dejected after what had happened. It was hard to avoid the conclusion that his death might have been partly her fault.

"They couldn't tell me when we'd be allowed to have the funeral. I mean, when they'd give us back his body." Ian shuddered again.

He must be thinking of her mum's funeral. His wife's.

Three years ago, Caitlin had made a fuss about having to wear black. Her mum would have hated everybody looking so gloomy. She had been painfully red-eyed before they even reached the crematorium, and then she had run out in the middle of the service, stumbling along the aisles of her mum's grieving friends, sobbing and coughing. Evie had followed her outside. Caitlin had no idea what her dad had said in the speech he'd prepared for the service. She'd been sitting in the lobby of the crematorium, crying and, when the attendant wasn't looking, taking swigs from the hip flask Evie had snuck in under her dress.

She couldn't bear the thought of going to another funeral. Her relationship with Tobe might have been barely communicative at times, but he was family and she preferred the idea of sorting through her memories on her own, rather than in public.

Her dad was watching her closely. He held her at arm's length, still studying her face. She wondered whether he was expecting her to break down in tears. Why wasn't the news about Tobe's death hitting her harder? It felt like information about somebody else's family. Sad, but not really her business.

"So, you were right saying I've been thinking about the Fall," Ian said. "But not necessarily in the way you mean. I've been thinking about your mum, and about you. About what this means."

Even though she hadn't cried yet, Caitlin's eyes were sore. "What?"

"You're the last of a line of Charmers, a direct line from the Fall. Your mum was sure that you three were the last, after all her research into family ancestry. There are no cousins, no other branches in the family tree. It was only her and you and Tobe left. So it's just you, now. I may have taken your mum's surname when we married, but that hardly counts. Cait – you're the last of the Hexts."

Caitlin's throat was suddenly dry. She shook her head. No.

Her dad was wrong. She wasn't the last Hext, not quite. There was another.

*

Gerry tried to appear patient as the kid behind the reception desk whispered to a male nurse. They both looked anxious. The boy was trying to hide his mouth as he talked and the nurse glanced up at Gerry as he listened. He patted the receptionist on the shoulder, then moved to the counter.

"It's not possible to show you around at this time," he said.

It was a formal response, carefully worded, but she detected a note of genuine apology.

Gerry smiled. "I don't need a grand tour or anything. Just a bit of detail, so that I don't misrepresent anything that's going on here."

The nurse hesitated. "This novel – what is it about? Charmers?"

When she had been speaking to the kid, Gerry had used the word 'book', keeping it as vague as possible. Several times over the years she had tried to access the January care home, but she had never made it beyond the lobby, resorting to interviewing any visitors in the lobby who would speak to her, then being chased out once the police were called. She ought to have considered subterfuge sooner.

"Not really," she replied. "They're in the background. Like they are in everyday life, I guess. But I'm a stickler. My readers expect all of the details in my books to be accurate."

The man frowned. His long lashes and gleaming black skin made him appear full of life, despite the sterility of his surroundings. It occurred to Gerry that he was the healthiest-looking person she had seen for a long time. Did that mean he was a Charmer? Either way, she found him enormously attractive. It had been almost a year since her last romantic encounter, and two since her last proper relationship had ended. She felt a sudden surge of loneliness.

"Perhaps you could arrange a formal visit," the nurse said. "You'd need to speak to the Department of Health, I should think."

"No."

His eyes widened with amusement. "No?"

"Sorry. I mean, I've already spoken to them. In fact, they're the ones who sent me here in person. It was a long journey, and I'm very tired…" She craned her neck to read his name tag. "Ayo."

"I'm sorry, too." It was clear that he meant it. His easy smile made Gerry dizzy.

Ayo leant over the counter to look over at the security gate, where a guard was in the process of emptying somebody's bag. "Look, give me a second, okay? I'll have to run it by my manager. She might want to speak to you in person. Actually, it might be more than a second. Take a seat?"

Gerry beamed. She resisted the urge to take his hand. She headed to the red sofas in the waiting area, concentrating on keeping her walk steady.

"Making you wait, are they?"

The woman perched on a nearby sofa had to be in her sixties. She wore a tweed hunting hat and a coat too thick for the season.

"I'm used to it," Gerry replied. She watched the reception counter until Ayo disappeared from sight, then she turned her attention to the security gate. A teen girl stood on its far side, speaking to a woman wearing a doctor's white coat. Ayo reappeared from some hidden door and spoke to the doctor, who responded with an expression of resigned frustration. After a few more exchanged words, she left. Ayo accompanied the girl away from the lobby and out of sight.

Gerry realised that the tweed-hatted woman was watching

her intently. Her wrinkled nose suggested suspicion. Perhaps the girl was a relation of hers.

"We haven't met before, have we?" the woman said.

"I doubt it. And people tend to remember me pretty well. That kind of a face."

The woman nodded. "I can imagine. Though I find faces tend to merge no matter how striking they may be. I'm here every day – if you're back tomorrow, you do the introductions, okay? I'm scatty enough that I might not remember you."

Gerry forced a smile. Perhaps lonely people particularly liked hanging out with Snakeskins, who were the lowest of the low in the hierarchy of society. The fact that Skins at the January care home were a captive audience might be part of it. Then again, Gerry was the one who had been obsessed with Charmers her entire life. Momentarily, it struck her as odd that she found Snakeskins less fascinating than their originators. The difference between them was like the difference between members of a fairy-tale royal family and their subjects.

The woman pointed. "Less of a wait than you expected."

The doctor was striding towards them. She stopped a few metres from the seating area. After a few seconds Gerry took the hint and walked to meet her, out of earshot of the other visitors.

"Gerry Chafik?"

"That's right. And you are Dr Scaife, I presume?"

The doctor looked flustered, then she glanced down at the name tag pinned to her white jacket. "My name is neither here nor there, young woman. Yours, on the other hand— You'll be pleased to know that your reputation precedes you."

"So you know I was a journalist. I didn't lie to your colleagues, I promise."

"It's a gross misrepresentation, passing yourself off as a harmless novelist."

Interesting. Gerry raised an eyebrow. "So novelists are harmless, whereas journalists are—"

"Unwelcome. An unannounced journalist would be unwelcome at any official place of business, if they arrived under false pretences."

This line of conversation wasn't going to get her any further. "Anyway. You may remember I said 'was'. I'm a journalist no more. So it's not a lie. I intend to write a book, and I'm not certain yet what it's about. Maybe it will be a novel, who knows."

"This establishment is full of busy people doing their jobs. We have no time to indulge your whims." Dr Scaife pointed at the revolving door. "I'm certain you're aware that there are police officers outside the building, who can be summoned at any moment. Please leave."

Gerry nodded. She took a few steps, then swung around. "Except that's not quite right, about my not knowing what will be in the book. One thing I do know is that it's related to the funding arrangements for this place. Some people might think of finance as a dull subject, but me, I think it's fascinating."

Dr Scaife's lips pressed together, turning white.

"You see," Gerry continued, raising her voice. The tweed-hatted woman and a few other visitors turned to look. The more people that witnessed her bluff, the better. "The Department of Health were good enough to send me a finance breakdown. There was more detail than I expected. It's encouraging to see the enormous amounts of citizens' taxes the Party dedicates to keeping the population of 'spontaneous duplicates' fit and happy. That's a heart-warming bestseller right there."

The doctor folded her arms across her chest. From the look in her eyes, anybody might think she was trying to bore into Gerry's forehead through willpower alone.

It was shocking, but it wasn't enough. Perhaps Gerry had been following the wrong train of investigation about the finances. She looked around at the glistening windows, the shining surfaces, the obvious wealth.

She projected her voice across the still air of the lobby. "But still, you can't blame me for being a little baffled about the discrepancy. A big hole in the budget is one thing – goodness knows we all make mistakes when it comes to submitting our tax forms – but the weird fact is that there's so much detail about outgoings and none at all about any sources of income... Well, it's a puzzle."

The people around were still watching but, other than the tweed-hatted woman, they now displayed annoyance at the volume of Gerry's voice rather than fascination with her words. If there was a tabloid story here, it was related to the unfairness of public spending on Snakeskins who would soon turn to ash anyway. But Gerry sensed a new line of investigation which, though potentially less scandalous in the eyes of the public, might lead her closer to the truth.

Her broadcast had an immediate effect on Dr Scaife. "Perhaps we can accommodate you better in my office," she said. "For a few moments, and no more."

As the doctor led the way, the tweed-hatted woman gave Gerry a wink.

\*

"Please don't disturb anything while you're here," Dr Scaife said.

With exaggerated care, Gerry replaced the snow globe on the doctor's desk. The artificial snow whirled and then settled on a grand house and in the prongs of miniature evergreens.

It was a surprise that Dr Scaife's office was so small, as if it had been designed to a different scale than the rest of the building. As the doctor had led her along the glass-walled corridor to her office and Gerry had recovered from her euphoria at passing the guarded checkpoint, she had been amazed at how far the rearmost segments of the complex extended beyond the facade. Despite Dr Scaife's annoyance and hurry, Gerry had stopped to peep through a glass door labelled *Visitors Lounge* to see a vast room with a cathedral window. Inside, she saw the girl she had noticed at the security gate. On the other side of a transparent barrier sat her exact double. Gerry had shivered at the sight. Part of it was envy, she realised. She had always dreamed of what it might be like to shed, to suddenly possess a double of yourself, somebody so similar but subordinate. Even so, seeing such a young Charmer and her Skin was unnerving. She remembered her own awkwardness at that age, her inability to self-analyse and her obsession with trying to do so. She wondered what the two of them might find to talk about.

Dr Scaife exhaled impatiently. Gerry tried to clear her thoughts. She was here to learn something about the care home. She'd clearly hit a nerve when she questioned the funding sources.

"So, Miss Chafik," Dr Scaife said, "explain to me why you're here."

From experience, Gerry knew to begin broadly and then home in on the real subject. "I don't think the subject of Snakeskins is treated seriously in the press. The subject has become a fairground attraction at best, ignored at worst."

"I agree. Did you expect that I wouldn't?"

"What do you think should be done about it?"

A mix of expressions passed over the doctor's face. "I think that the public ought to bear in mind that spontaneous duplicates – Snakeskins, if you prefer the popular term – are enough like us that they should be given our respect."

"See, that's an interesting view, right there," Gerry said with an encouraging smile. "Although there's a philosophical angle. Are you saying they warrant respect *only* because they look like their originators, like humans? So that if instead of duplicates, Charmers' sheddings produced cats, for example, then the rules would change?"

Dr Scaife scowled. "I'm not a cat lover, myself. I'm not a philosopher either. But it's clear to me that duplicates are rather more complex than cats. More to the point, they can speak to us. That makes them worthy of…" She hesitated.

"Of what?"

"Of our care. Now, what is it that you actually want to ask me about?"

Gerry leant against the desk. She hadn't been offered a seat. "Like I say, I'm only looking for some background. So, the question that interests me is how much care Skins deserve. Keeping them comfortable until they blow away on the wind, that much I understand. But this place?" She gestured towards the corridor. "It's lavish."

"I'm wary of expressing my response in these terms… but I only work here." There seemed other implications to her statement: *I'm not GBP. I'm not a Charmer.*

"Oh, come. You run this place. Even if I hadn't been told as much, it'd have been obvious. You're monitoring everything. And that's admirable. But I suspect that it also means that you have visibility of all the processes that keep January ticking over. Just how much money is funnelled into it?"

Dr Scaife's lips tightened. "I'm sure you appreciate that I'm not about to discuss financial matters with you, Miss Chafik."

Gerry chewed her cheek. She wasn't sure how far she could progress with so little concrete information. The bluffs were beginning to pile up. "All right. I'll put it in a different way. Given the huge amounts of money flooding into this place—" she held up a hand to prevent the doctor from interrupting "—and for argument's sake, let's assume that's the case. So, given that amount of money, can you give me any clue what it's actually being used for?"

"This is childish, Miss Chafik. From what I've read in *Folk*, I thought you were a serious journalist."

Gerry grinned. "From what I've read in *Folk*, I think there are no serious journalists left. But do go on."

"The money goes towards providing an appropriate end of life for Snakeskins, some of whom may remain with us for substantial periods. All that care costs money, Miss Chafik. And I think it's admirable that the Party is prepared to foot part of the bill. Don't you?"

Gerry chose not to point out that Party members *were* Charmers, for the most part. "Of course. Like all journalists, I prefer to assume that the government is doing the very best it can."

"Be sure not to rely on sarcasm in your articles. It isn't your forte."

Gerry had stopped listening. She replayed Dr Scaife's earlier words: *The Party is prepared to foot part of the bill.* There, that was something. But Dr Scaife had mentioned it casually, and it wouldn't help to draw too much attention to it. Another bluff was required. "The Department of Health sent me their budgets. Only top-level, with no breakdown, obviously, but it was interesting all the same." Her mind raced. She must guess at a conclusion, based on only her hunch. "Now, comparing the overall budget against the care home's spending might make any lesser journalist jump to conclusions." As she had hoped, Dr Scaife bristled. She must be on the right track. "But I can read between the lines. It doesn't imply that there ought to be money available for health provision for non-Charmers, because only a fraction of January's costs are funded by the government. The majority comes from private donors."

Dr Scaife's eyes rose to the ceiling. Which direction did people look when they were about to lie?

Gerry continued in a casual tone. "It's okay. That much was already in the public record. *Folk* covered it years ago. You're unlikely to have seen it, because it hardly made a ripple." She grasped for another on-the-fly deduction. "If anything, readers were grateful that Charmers were prepared to pay up, to look after their Skins. It made them seem more sympathetic."

The stiffness in the doctor's shoulders disappeared. Gerry had guessed correctly. Still, she mustn't congratulate herself. There was something else.

She pushed herself away from the desk and strolled towards the row of filing cabinets that lined one wall of the office. "Look, we could dance around like this all day, but the fact that you haven't chucked me out yet shows that you're sizing me up as much as I am you. And that tells me that there's something here worth looking into. So, why don't you tell me one thing I actually want to know, and then I'll leave? I appreciate you're not going to show me your receipts – fine. But tell me, what's going on in the rest of those buildings I saw out of the corridor window? Because I'd put money on *them* being the reason for needing so much cash."

"Kitchens and a laundry," Dr Scaife replied, too fast. "And

no, I'm not going to give you a tour, if that's what you're angling for."

"Wouldn't dream of it. But you do understand that not doing so only looks more suspicious?"

Dr Scaife shrugged. The motion was awkward, as though it was a gesture she had only recently learnt.

"And the thing about journalists," Gerry continued, "is that obstacles only make us more dogged. I could go through other channels, over your head."

"You can try. There's nothing to hide, but I'll make certain that you won't be allowed entry."

It was time for the blunt approach. "What happens when the Skins ash?"

"There is a modest commemorative service among the other residents and the staff."

Gerry tried to recall the line items in the photocopied spreadsheet. "And is there enough ash to warrant disposing of the remains in some manner?"

"Hardly. You know as well as I do that it simply mixes with the atmosphere. There's a beauty to it. And rest assured that the premises are thoroughly cleaned afterwards. We pride ourselves on sterility."

Gerry stifled a laugh. "Naturally. But it might be traumatic. What happens if a Skin ashes while they're in the visitors' lounge, for example?"

"It has never happened yet, I'm happy to say."

Gerry nodded. Once again, she sensed a point at which she ought to drop her current line of questioning. As she stretched and yawned she scanned the notes pinned to the noticeboard, the stacks of paper on the desk. She tried to commit everything to memory. There was no chance she'd get in here again.

Her gaze settled again on the snow globe on the desk. Something about the shape of the house inside struck her as familiar. One end of it was arched and the other ended in a blunt, square tower.

It was Ilam Hall.

Ilam and the Fall were inextricably linked, of course. It might simply be a nod to Charmers' heritage.

"Miss Chafik," Dr Scaife said sternly. "You've occupied enough of my time. Please leave."

Gerry's mind raced. Perhaps these new revelations about funding could be linked to Ilam Hall. She remembered the faded magnificence of the building. Perhaps the Hartwell family were donors to the January care home, along with other wealthy Charmers?

Dr Scaife lifted the phone handset and said hurriedly, "Please come to my office. Immediately."

Gerry realised she might have only seconds remaining.

"Tell me about Hartwell," she said.

Dr Scaife replaced the receiver. Her hands shook slightly. Gerry couldn't tell whether it was from anger or panic.

"Is Anise Hartwell responsible for the funding?"

Now the doctor appeared confused. She recovered herself quickly and glanced at the door. No, this was nothing to do with Anise Hartwell. It was impossible to believe that she might be supplying money and leaving herself in poverty, despite the grand shell of Ilam Hall.

Her ancestor, Lord Hartwell, on the other hand…

No. That couldn't be right. Ilam Hall was built years after the Fall. Hartwell had only been a small-town mayor at the time, and had been made a lord much later. But Gerry realised that the fact had always troubled her, deep down. Rubbernecking tourists couldn't explain Hartwell's promotion and sudden wealth.

"No, not funding," Gerry said, speaking more to herself than to Dr Scaife. "The money went *to* Lord Hartwell, not *from* him. He was involved, wasn't he? In setting up the care home. And he was rewarded for it."

Dr Scaife was making an effort to let no particular expression settle upon her features.

The door opened. Two burly men in grey uniforms entered. They had batons fixed to their belts and pouches that might hold pistols.

Gerry smiled, then shook the snow globe once more and replaced it on the desk. She held up both hands.

"I'll come quietly."

\*

Caitlin watched Kit's face carefully, noting the fractional changes in her expression as she processed the news. Surprise became shock, shock became grief, and grief became something altogether more complicated.

"Was it suicide?" Kit said, finally.

"We don't know. The autopsy came in this morning, but it wasn't conclusive. He didn't drink and we both know he wouldn't have a clue where to find drugs, or even what to do with them. Those are pretty much the only other reasons I can think of to end up floating face-down in a hotel swimming pool at three in the morning."

Kit began to cry softly. Caitlin experienced a sudden surge of anger. Since receiving the news about Tobe she herself hadn't cried once. Seeing Kit's reaction made her feel like an emotionless monster.

Ayo, the nurse, stood beside Kit. He shifted his weight from foot to foot uneasily and looked at the door. Dr Scaife hadn't accompanied Caitlin to the visitors' lounge, but she or another member of staff might appear at any moment.

Kit bent almost double, still sobbing. The restraints dug into her belly.

"Nurse," Caitlin said. "Ayo. Please. Let her breathe."

Ayo was clearly startled; this was the first time Caitlin had addressed him directly. He nodded. Moving cautiously, as though he had previously believed himself to be invisible and now felt suddenly exposed, he bent down to unclip the restraints. The moment she was free, Kit turned and pressed her face into his shoulder, holding on to him so that he couldn't straighten up. Finally, she patted his arm and turned.

As Caitlin stared at the girl's face, crumpled and blotched with red, her only thought was: *Am I really capable of looking as ugly as that?* She hated herself for her shallowness.

Of course it made sense that Tobe's death meant something different to the Skin than to her. Death, in general terms, meant something different. Part of Caitlin's cool response to the news of Tobe's death was because it would have no practical impact on the course of her life. For Kit, it was a reminder that she, too, would be gone very soon.

Perhaps Kit prized life more than she did. Even though she was only days old as an independent being, perhaps she was already diverged enough from Caitlin that she felt differently about her uncle. Perhaps Kit loved Tobe in a way that Caitlin could never have.

She had been wrestling with a decision all morning. With a jolt she realised that she had suddenly reached a conclusion. The fact that it made her feel a martyr was part of its appeal.

"I can't go," Caitlin said.

Kit wiped her nose, leaving a glistening snail trail on her wrist. "Go where?"

"To the funeral. It's tomorrow. Everyone wants it over and done with."

"Why are you telling me?"

Caitlin shrugged.

Kit chewed her cheek, watching her. "Because you can't tell Dad. Sorry. I mean *your* dad."

Caitlin nodded. She glanced at Ayo, who seemed to be making a deliberate show of not paying them any attention. She was certain that he genuinely liked Kit. He hadn't even glanced at the mucus stain that Kit had left on his otherwise pristine white uniform. He would help them if he could. Still, the security in the care home meant that Caitlin couldn't appeal to him directly. Instead, she would have to trick him and take advantage of his good nature.

"I know I'd regret it if I didn't go, though," Caitlin said. "Remember how awful it was, missing Aaron Henson's funeral?"

Kit's head jerked up.

Aaron Henson was alive and well. Now that he had been diagnosed, he no longer suffered from the fits he used to have at secondary school.

Caitlin prayed that Kit had got the message. Her plan was the only way she could think of assuaging her guilt about Tobe, about her dad, about Kit.

"I assume you *do* remember him?" Caitlin said. "And how he died?" She widened her eyes.

Evidently, Kit understood. Her eyes widened, too. A slight tilt of the head: *Are you certain?*

Caitlin nodded slowly and deliberately.

Instantly, Kit burst into tears again. She began to wail. Her body bucked and spasmed.

"Nurse!" Caitlin yelled. "It's a seizure. I've had them since I was tiny. She's the same as me."

Ayo looked panic-stricken. Clumsily, he bent to hold Kit in his arms. "What should I do?"

It was quite possible that January nurses had no real medical training. Ayo stared down at Kit, who shuddered and jerked, mimicking Aaron Henson perfectly.

"I've got pills," Caitlin said. "Here, in my pocket. Let me in there, quick!"

"Throw them over the barrier!"

Caitlin ignored him. She dashed to the door and into the corridor.

The next door along the corridor – the door to the Skins' annex of the visitors' lounge – was locked. Its cold surface suggested that it was made of steel. Caitlin hammered at it and after a few seconds she heard scrabbling from the other side. It opened. Ayo was utterly distraught.

The room was small and dark. It reminded Caitlin of working backstage at a performance of *The Canterbury Tales* at school, scurrying about behind the painted backdrops. Ayo stood to one side to let her pass through a low door. She emerged within the clear-walled annex and immediately experienced a strange sense of vertigo. For a moment she half-expected to see herself still out there, looking through the transparent barrier. The effect was made worse by the sight of Kit slumped on the floor, one arm over her chest and the other pressed against the barrier, her fingers making streaks on its polished surface.

Caitlin bent beside her, positioning herself carefully so that she blocked Ayo's view.

"Here," she said loudly. "Take this, quick."

She pushed Kit's lank red hair aside. Kit winked at her and opened her mouth to receive the peppermint that Caitlin offered.

Caitlin made a show of helping Kit sit up.

"She'll be all right," Caitlin said to Ayo, who hovered awkwardly behind her.

Kit made a hoarse, croaking sound.

"What's she saying?" Ayo asked.

"She's exhausted. The after-effects are sort of like a hangover. She'll need rest."

Ayo stepped forwards but Caitlin shook her head. "You have to let me take her."

"I can't do that. I'm sorry." He tried to take Kit by the

arm. She pushed him away roughly, then corkscrewed with the momentum, ending up crumpled in a heap on the floor. She sobbed and sobbed. Ayo tried again to help her, but she spasmed and crawled away.

"Can't you see that she's in shock?" Caitlin said, introducing a note of pleading into her voice.

"Even so, I'm not allowed to—"

Caitlin scrunched up her face. She thought of Tobe, but still felt no grief. Instead, she thought of her mum and of her unfair suspension from college. She dug her fingernails into her palms. The tears came.

Ayo looked less and less certain of himself. The sight of two identical girls weeping pushed him over the edge.

"We have to be quick," he said.

Kit rose to her feet. Her hair was plastered to her cheeks. Caitlin supported her weight, trying not to flinch at the strangeness of being in contact with her duplicate.

They made their way through the antechamber and out into the corridor. Ayo darted ahead to the junction. Once he was out of earshot, Kit whispered, "You're sure about this?"

Caitlin squeezed Kit's waist in reply. "When we get to your room, you'll have to put up a fuss, okay?"

"You don't need to worry."

Caitlin wondered whether their imaginations were enough alike that this entire plan had occurred to Kit, too. "Shush, now," she said.

Ayo beckoned them towards the junction. They increased their pace. Being spotted by Dr Scaife would end the whole charade.

Ayo turned left at the junction and scuttled along the passageway, casting nervous glances over his shoulder. Kit moaned every so often to dissuade him from offering to support her. They passed door after featureless door before Ayo came to a stop before one of them.

"That's me," Kit whispered. "Home sweet home."

"Time to ramp it up, then."

Kit grew heavy and loose in Caitlin's arms. She began to sob and wail again.

"Please, stop shouting," Ayo hissed. He wrung his hands.

"I'm not going in there!" Kit cried.

Caitlin held up a hand to Ayo. "It's all right. I can deal with this." She bent to Kit's ear and made nonsense whispering noises, pretending to be talking her around. At the end of the string of nonsense, she whispered real words. "I trust you."

Kit whimpered. Her weeping was convincing even up close.

"I can get her to go inside," Caitlin said to Ayo. "Give me a couple of minutes to settle her. Don't worry."

Ayo hesitated, then fumbled with a pass card that hung on a lanyard around his neck. When he pressed it against a black panel on the wall, the door emitted a click and swung open. Caitlin guided Kit inside and yanked the door shut.

The room was tiny. The bed wasn't large, but it still filled more than half of the space. Instead of a proper window, a thin rectangular panel let in dull light but no view. The walls were bare plaster.

"Quickly," Caitlin said.

Kit had already begun pulling off her clothes. It didn't take her long, given that she was wearing only the blue smock and leggings over her underwear. Caitlin pulled her jumper over her head, snagging her hair. She tripped on one leg of the bed as she wriggled out of her skinny jeans.

For a moment they stared at each other. Now that they were each wearing only underwear, Kit was far more Caitlin's mirror image than before.

A knock on the door shook them from their trance. Caitlin whirled around, expecting Ayo to enter. The door remained closed.

"It's all right," Kit cried out. Now her voice sounded clear and controlled. She smiled at Caitlin. "It's all right."

Caitlin felt a sudden compulsion to back out of the whole thing. But she knew it was too late. Kit held up the blue smock.

In a flurry of limbs and fabric, they pulled on each other's outfits. The creases of the blue smock settled on precisely the same contours they had covered on a different body only seconds earlier. Caitlin pulled on the leggings and black slippers. When she raised her head she saw Kit dressed in the clothes she had picked out for herself that morning. Kit fished around in her back pocket to retrieve the slim wallet that contained Caitlin's rail tickets, a couple of notes and her ID card – without it she wouldn't get far. She nodded and avoided meeting Caitlin's eyes as she slid it back into her pocket. Caitlin felt she might burst into tears any second.

Kit smoothed her jumper and ruffled her hair so that it looked less obviously unwashed.

She was about to say something when the door opened.

Immediately, Kit adopted Caitlin's former role. She gripped Caitlin's bare arms and bent to look into her eyes. She mouthed the words, "Thank you." Then she glanced over Caitlin's shoulder. "It's fine, Ayo. She's okay now. She'll be fine, I think."

"You'd better get out of there quick," Ayo said. He let Kit pass, then his eyes flicked to Caitlin. He gave no sign of suspicion. His expression was one of warmth and sympathy. Caitlin wasn't sure whether it was relief that she felt, or terror.

The door closed with a dull thud, followed by the click of the automatic lock. Caitlin heard Ayo's and Kit's muffled voices as they walked away.

She slumped onto the bed. Her fingers tugged at the itchy fabric of the leggings, then her hand fell to the slick, wipe-clean bed sheet.

This was a mistake.

# ELEVEN

When Caitlin woke she felt as though she were bobbing and swaying in her bed, like a body-memory of a sea journey or a rollercoaster ride.

Her throat was dry. She reached around for the glass of water that she always kept on the floor, despite her dad's warnings that it would one day spill onto the hair straighteners and hairdryer that she left littered around.

The glass wasn't there. Her fingers grazed cold flooring, not the thick carpet of her bedroom.

She opened her eyes. A neon strip light fizzed above her. The ceiling was plain beige and the pale expanse of the opposite wall was interrupted only by a skylight. She couldn't make out any difference between its top and bottom halves that might indicate land and sky. The room might as well be floating in a white void.

She rolled off the bed, landing heavily. Her bare feet stung with the cold of the polished floor. As she ducked under the bed for her slippers, her legs wobbled. Her head ached terribly. She had only experienced hangovers a handful of times – she had avoided heavy drinking since one evening last year which had resulted in her spitting at Evie and then snogging Evie's man of the moment, Paul Farrier, even though he wore too much Lynx and quoted Shepperton teen comedies incessantly – but this certainly felt like one.

Was it possible that dehydration alone could leave her feeling this way? It didn't explain the shuddering, which continued even once her feet were protected from the cold by the slippers. She touched her neck gingerly, then her cheeks. Her skin was hot. She put her palm flat on her forehead. A throbbing sensation passed through her in a sickly wave. Gagging, she slumped onto the bed.

She remembered what she had asked Kit on her second visit to the care home: "Do they stop you sleeping?" and Kit's answer in a shaking voice: "I don't know."

What had they done to her? To them both?

There was a knock at the door. Instinctively, she pulled her legs up onto the bed. She was genuinely afraid. The worst part was that it was nothing to do with being here on false pretences. Kit didn't know what was happening to her in the care home either. She had been afraid, too.

The door opened. It was Ayo.

Questions crowded her mind. What was happening to her? What was really going on? Instead, she said, weakly, "I'm so thirsty."

"I know," Ayo said. His wide, kind eyes made her feel a little better already. "I know. I'll bring you some water when you're in there. I'm sorry – that's all I can do for you, right now."

Caitlin gripped the steel rail of the bed. "I'm not going anywhere."

Ayo frowned. "You don't want to see her?"

"Her?"

"You have a visitor."

The surge of relief, or adrenaline, made Caitlin want to puke. Kit. Kit had come back, after all. She leapt off the bed, gritting her teeth to make her body cooperate. She pushed past the nurse and into the corridor.

"You have to walk," Ayo hissed. "They're watching us."

Caitlin brushed off the strangeness of the comment. Why would anyone be watching him, as well as her?

"I know where I'm going." She set off at a jog.

She reached the visitors' lounge, but before she could see through the glass, Ayo pulled her away. "Wrong door. That one's for visitors."

Caitlin allowed herself to be led to the unmarked, painted metal door. Ayo accompanied her through the dark antechamber. Caitlin rushed towards the visitors' lounge annex. Intensely bright daylight from the cathedral window stung her eyes, intensified and doubled by the reflections of the transparent barrier. She shielded her eyes to make out the girl on the other side of the wall.

No. Not a girl.

Not Kit.

Not even Evie.

The sunlight accentuated the creases in the woman's face, which were vertical around her mouth and in fans at the corners of her eyes. She wore a tweed hunting hat and a thick coat. At first, Caitlin struggled to remember where they had met before.

"It's good to see you." the woman said. She frowned, perhaps noticing Caitlin's confusion. "It's Dodie."

Once again, Caitlin felt that her body was swaying, even though she wasn't actually moving. She dropped onto the cushioned chair. Out of the corner of her eye she saw Ayo take his position at her side. He placed a glass of water on the table beside her chair.

"Of course," she said in a faint voice. "Thank you for visiting, Dodie. It's lovely to see you again."

She felt no sense of pleasure. If anything, the visit was a turning point, making Caitlin more permanently a resident at the care home.

Dodie's mournful eyes shifted around slowly, looking first at Caitlin, then at Ayo.

"Did you get a good night's sleep?" she said quietly.

Caitlin's mouth was awfully dry. She glugged from the glass of water. "I had strange dreams."

The woman exhaled and looked down at her clasped hands. She nodded. "Would you like to tell me about your dreams?"

Caitlin couldn't think how to reply. Maybe Dodie was a religious nut. She probably thought that interpreting a Skin's dreams might give some insight into her soul, or whether she actually had one.

She shook her head. The last time she remembered dreaming had been before her shedding, before all of this.

"It's the funeral today," she said, hardly noticing that she said it out loud. She felt a wave of guilt – this was the first she had thought about it since she had awoken. "Uncle Tobe."

Dodie's expression was difficult to read. "I heard about what happened. I'm sorry. I really am."

"They'll all be there."

"And not you."

"And not me."

Silence fell again. Dodie sighed, then fished under her chair and retrieved a newspaper. "Shall I read to you?"

Without thinking, Caitlin blurted out, "Why?"

Dodie shrugged, calmer now. "To find out what's happening outside these four walls. Or rather, three and a window, but you know what I mean."

"Why?" Caitlin said again. Anger flared up inside her. Even though she knew it was wrong to direct it at this innocent woman, she snapped, "What good would it do me to know about the outside world? I'm never going to leave this place until I die."

A sour taste filled her mouth. She was no longer sure whether she was acting the part of a Snakeskin or not. It might be true. If Kit never returned, she might not be released. She wouldn't ash, of course. At least she would never disappear in a puff of smoke. But that didn't mean she wouldn't remain imprisoned here, at least until she surprised everyone by shedding for a second time.

Dodie's head tilted. "Before, you seemed interested. You wanted to glimpse the world. At least I thought so. Or have things changed?"

Caitlin felt intensely aware of the nurse standing at her side. She desperately wanted to shout out, "I'm not a Skin!

I'm a human!" But Ayo had already warned her that they were being watched – and it wasn't as though she could be certain of his help anyway. The only option was to give Kit a chance to make good on her word. If Caitlin revealed what had happened, and she was believed, that might get her out of this awful situation, but what would it mean for Kit? She would be hounded and captured. Being brought back here would be the best-case scenario for her. The worst-case scenario didn't bear thinking about.

"It's not fair," Caitlin said. Her voice shook and she couldn't bear to look at Dodie's concerned face. Dodie wasn't evangelical, or morbid. She was a kind woman, trying to make things better for the Skins in the care home. It was unbearable.

"It isn't fair!" Caitlin wailed. "I'm so thirsty, no matter how much of this I drink. I can't even—" Abruptly, she began to sob.

Her head bobbed loosely and heavily, making her feel even more seasick. When she finally managed to raise her head, she saw that Dodie was now standing up against the barrier with her palms pressed flat against it.

"Hush, child," she whispered. "Hush. I'm here. I understand. I understand."

*

A pager message had woken Russell that morning. *Come to my house, NOT office*, it read. It was from Ellis.

He had dressed in a hurry, had stubbed his toe on two different items of furniture, and had burned his toast to an inedible crisp before stumbling out of the house. The Summertown bus had dallied for long periods at each stop along Woodstock Road, and each time Russell had been tempted to plunge out of the open doors and run far away. Now he stood at the foot of the driveway to the Blackwood house. He found himself unable to set foot on its gravel.

Ellis must know. What other reason could there be for summoning him here?

And if Ellis's reaction to Russell breaking into his house was not to call the police but to deal with matters himself, then there could be no telling what else might be involved. Among those covert Party officials there might easily be someone responsible for punishing or torturing dissidents. There had always been rumours about the GBP's treatment of anti-prosperity campaigners who made themselves more than a mere nuisance.

He must escape while he still could.

As he was turning to leave, a voice rang out. "Ho, daydreamer!"

He turned from side to side. He could see nobody, either on the street or in the windows of Ellis's house.

"Up here!"

Ellis was edging along a shallow sloped roof adjoining the arched porch of the house. His boiler suit reminded Russell of the tracksuit he had worn when he saw him climbing the stairs to the hidden door in the servants' passageway. Perhaps Ellis always dressed casually in his free time.

Ellis's arms shot out in the manner of a tightrope walker. His knees bent. "Lost my footing for a second there. Stand

245

over here, would you? If I slip you can break my fall."

This didn't seem the attitude of somebody who intended to conduct any form of torture. Gingerly, Russell crunched up the driveway.

"What are you actually doing up there, sir?"

"I believe it's called abseiling, isn't it?"

"Sir?"

"It was a bloody joke, Russell. Here, toss up that cable, would you? Bugger slipped out of my grasp and I'm damned if I'm scrambling through that window any more times than I absolutely have to. The ladder's gone walkabout somewhere. Wouldn't put it past Nell to have taken it to her parents' house with her. She has a head full of daft ideas."

Bewildered, Russell scanned the ground. Sure enough, a thin black cord lay in a snakelike pile to one side of the porch. One end threaded into the house. He threw the loose end up onto the sloped roof. Ellis almost slipped again as he grabbed at it.

He watched on as Ellis scrambled on his hands and knees to the porch roof, dragging the cable behind him like a serpent's tail. With a grunt of triumph, he attached the cable to something fixed to the top of the arch, an object Russell hadn't noticed until now. It was a CCTV camera.

"That'll do it," Ellis said, clapping his hands together and nearly slipping off the roof. "Meet me inside. Door's open."

Russell entered. At the foot of the stairs he listened to Ellis's distant grunts as he struggled through the window. When he appeared on the landing, Ellis's hair was in disarray and one arm of his boiler suit was torn. He clapped Russell on the shoulder. "Cuppa before we begin?"

"Thank you, sir."

They stood looking at each other for several seconds before it dawned on Russell that he would be the one making the tea. Ellis followed him into the kitchen, fussing over his torn sleeve, then stood directly behind Russell as he filled the kettle.

"You said 'begin', sir," Russell said, not daring to turn around. "Begin what?"

"Well, I've already begun, I suppose. But you can take the baton now you're here. I've bought four cameras in all. Then there are the door sensors with something called intrared – or infra? – and remote locks, and the instruction manuals for those are as thick as my arm. You'll need all your technical knowhow to get the buggers installed."

"Are you having security issues, sir?"

Ellis quietened. "There was an incident, yes. Nothing taken though. But you can't be too careful. We can't let these types of characters have unrestricted freedom, isn't that right?"

"Somebody broke into your house?" Russell cursed his voice for cracking at the wrong moment.

"That's right. Some anti-prosperity vigilante, in my estimation."

"But nobody saw anything?" Russell stared at the kettle, willing it to boil. "And you didn't have CCTV before now?"

"Goodness, yes," Ellis replied. "This place has them dotting the walls like barnacles. Caught the whole thing on video."

The kettle clicked. Russell lunged for it, missed the handle and scalded his thumb. He swallowed his cry and started filling the two mugs even as his eyes began to tear up. Ellis's arm snaked past him to retrieve his mug as soon as Russell had poured the milk.

"And—" Russell cleared his throat and started again. "And what did he look like, this intruder? If it was a he."

Ellis waved a hand. "The usual sort. A man in black. Hooded top." He slurped at his tea and finally moved away to sit at the table. "Could've been anyone."

For the first time, Russell dared to believe that Ellis hadn't summoned him here for punishment. He genuinely didn't suspect that it was Russell who had broken into his house. Emboldened and giddy with relief, he said, "I forgot to ask, sir. How was your trip?"

Ellis frowned into his mug. "You know. Business trips aren't meant to be jolly."

Russell wished he had the courage to ask more probing questions. What would it take to make Ellis confess that he had been in the house all along? And what further revelations would that admission lead to? He reminded himself that only ten minutes ago he had been convinced that his life was in danger, or at least his career. It was best not to push his luck.

Ellis had entered a gloomy reverie. They drank their tea in silence. Finally, Ellis heaved himself to his feet, disappeared through the door to the house, and returned with several opened boxes with electrical cables spilling out.

"I'll survey the site with you," Ellis said, "and then I'll leave you to it. A quick catnap will do me the power of good."

Installing the remaining three cameras was straightforward enough, once Russell located the missing ladder in Nell's workshop. He considered the resulting trail of wires throughout the house to be somebody else's problem. After browsing the manual for the remote door locks he quickly came to the conclusion that, in fact, the doors would have to be replaced along with the locks, so he put those packages to one side. The infrared door sensors were fiddly and oversensitive. He set off the alarm twice while attempting to install one on the kitchen door, each time summoning a bewildered and unkempt Ellis from upstairs. It was after lunchtime when he finished.

"Not much of a technical whizz, are you?" Ellis said, not unkindly, as he prodded at the boxes containing the uninstalled items. "Never mind. I'll summon a tradesman to deal with the rest. But now you have one final task and then it's back to the office with you."

He led Russell through the house. "Can't be too careful. If there's prowlers around, there's certain information that'd be better kept elsewhere. A very pleasant fellow installed a safe in my bedroom wardrobe only this morning. Damned if I'm going to haul everything up there myself, though."

Russell gawped at Ellis's back as he followed. After all his efforts to find something incriminating, risking breaking into the Blackwood house in the process, was Ellis now about to lead him directly to his prize?

He was so convinced that Ellis was heading to the hidden servants' passage that he kept on walking even after his boss had halted outside his study. Ellis produced a key from his pocket and bent to open the bottom desk drawer. He produced five cuboid box files, placed them on the desk, and opened the uppermost one. He rifled through a dozen or more stiff envelopes, numbered consecutively in thick marker-pen ink. Russell saw that each was sealed with tamper-proof tape.

"Let me help you with that, sir," Russell said, reaching out.

There were still some other items in the drawer. Before Ellis could bend to close it, Russell tipped the open box file upside down. Several of the stiff envelopes dropped noisily onto the desk and one fell onto the floor.

He made a show of cursing his clumsiness. As he retrieved the envelopes from the desk, he kicked at the one on the floor. It slid beneath the desk and he dived after it.

"One more. Very sorry about this, sir. I promise I'll be more careful." From beneath the desk he could see spilling from the envelope some loose sheaves of paper, pens, what appeared to be an old porn magazine and a three-and-a-half-inch computer disk. There could be no way of tucking any of the papers away without them being noticed. Instead, he made for the smallest item that appeared at all valuable – the floppy disk. He shoved it into his pocket, rescued the dropped envelope, and rose to his feet.

"Never mind about the butterfingers," Ellis said. "Right, onwards and upwards."

Russell staggered up the stairs, holding the heavy pile of box files steady with his chin. He cursed Ellis for climbing the stairs so slowly. The man appeared utterly exhausted, moving in slow motion.

In contrast to the rest of the house, Ellis's bedroom was sparsely furnished. A bed and a white set of a chest of drawers, a matching wardrobe and a bedside table were the only items of furniture. Russell noted with satisfaction that a political memoir and a pair of glasses lay on the bedside table, and a collection of aftershaves on the chest of drawers, but there was no evidence suggesting that Nell shared the bedroom.

The newly-installed safe was bolted to the floor of the wardrobe. Russell failed to see the digits on the combination wheel as Ellis spun it. He passed the box files to Ellis one at a time, who then eased the heavy door closed, sighed with satisfaction and sat on the bed.

"Good lad," Ellis muttered. For a moment, Russell wondered if his boss was sleepy enough to have mistaken him for his son. "Now, you'd better get to the office. As for me, I'll clamber into bed for an afternoon's sleepy slumber. I believe I've earned it." He slumped onto the bed and pulled the duvet around himself, a boiler-suited caterpillar.

It was only once he was safely on the bus that Russell dared to take the floppy disk from his pocket. He turned it over to see its scrawled label: *CLIENTS.*

When the bus deposited him on St Giles he headed west through town, rather than east towards his flat. If he was quick, he would reach the electrical shop before it closed.

*

Caitlin watched the door of her room, willing it to open.

She hugged her knees and squeezed herself into a tight ball on the bed. It was the only thing she could think of that made her a little less claustrophobic. The smaller she made herself, the more space there was in the rest of the room.

Footsteps in the corridor outside grew in volume but then quietened again. Whoever it was must have passed by. Perhaps one of the other residents had a visitor.

*One of the other residents.* It was amazing how quickly she had accepted her new role. Kit had left only yesterday afternoon. Today had been endless. The mottled skylight had now turned rust-coloured.

Perhaps another meal would be delivered to her room. The first had come soon after Dodie's visit, delivered on a tray by a starched-uniformed female nurse. The nurse hadn't spoken as she pressed the tray into Caitlin's hands. Miniature microwaved vegetables, mashed potato with the consistency of broth, a palm-sized piece of pale meat that could have been either beef or chicken. She hadn't eaten much of it. When the same nurse returned for the tray, Caitlin had asked when she would be allowed to go for a walk. The nurse had replied, "This afternoon, as usual."

Well, it was afternoon now, wasn't it? And it wasn't only that she wanted out. Her belly ached from hunger. When she was a kid, she had read somewhere that hunger was the sensation of your stomach walls rubbing together when there was nothing inside. The thought had always revolted her. Her own flesh, deep down inside, pressing and squeezing and chafing.

She shuffled backwards and pulled the thin bed sheet over her legs. What was Kit doing now? The funeral must have ended. Caitlin imagined Kit and her dad preparing dinner together in the kitchen. Would he notice any difference in his daughter? Some deep-down sense of pride made Caitlin feel that he ought to. Then again, Kit would have returned wearing the clothes Caitlin had dressed in that morning. She would move in the exact same way. She even carried the same memories in her head. So what differences might her dad notice? The funeral would have left him at a low ebb. He would just be pleased that his daughter was there with him.

The thought chilled Caitlin. Perhaps the only thing, really, that distinguished her from Kit was that Kit might turn to dust at any moment. It was a matter of their prospects in life, rather than any measure of innate superiority. Until Kit ashed, they were interchangeable. Caitlin savoured this new sense of shock. It was made worse by the knowledge that her mum's Skins had outlasted those produced by other Charmers.

There was another concern, a bigger one. What if Kit refused to return to the January care home? She might flee and hide away in some remote part of the country. Or, even worse, she might decide to stay put at Ivy Cottage. Caitlin would have no proof that she was the human originator and Kit the Snakeskin.

She was utterly trapped, and it was all her own doing. She had left herself at the mercy of somebody who might hate her, for all she knew; might want Caitlin's life for herself.

She shivered. The room would get even colder overnight. The word 'resident' seemed more and more absurd. She had been locked in this tiny, bare box of a room for half the day. She had seen only two people. She had been given barely edible food and she had been ignored. In what sense was she *not* a prisoner?

She gasped at a clunking sound from the doorway.

The door swung open. Nobody entered.

Caitlin slipped off the bed. Her slippers squeaked on the polished floor.

The female nurse who had brought the food was standing a foot away from the doorway. She carried no tray but held up her ID card. Caitlin turned to see a device attached to the wall, with a single green light. It must be some hi-tech replacement for a standard lock.

"This way," the nurse said.

"Will there be food?" Caitlin said. She hated herself for caring more about food than freedom. She hated her body for needing anything.

The nurse didn't reply and led the way in silence. At the corridor junction, Caitlin turned to her right to see two people standing outside the visitors' lounge – Dodie and Ayo, deep in conversation. As if sensing her presence, Ayo turned to look at her. At this distance, she couldn't make out his expression.

The silent nurse ushered her away from the junction to continue along the sterile white corridor. She stopped outside a smoked-glass door with a nameplate that read *Dr Victoria Scaife*. She pushed the door open and stood to one side.

"Come in."

Caitlin glanced at the nurse, who stared back at her impassively.

She took a breath and went inside.

Dr Scaife was sitting at a desk with her elbows upon it and her fingers intertwined, perhaps a rehearsed pose intended to make her appear formidable and in control. Mr Pearl, the head teacher at Caitlin's college, adopted it whenever she was called to his office.

"Stop there," Dr Scaife said.

For several seconds neither of them spoke. Another head teacher trick. Caitlin took the opportunity to look around the small room. The walls were covered with charts and tables of spidery handwriting. Dozens of blue card folders made stacks on shelves that sagged under the weight. In contrast, Dr Scaife's desk was entirely free of clutter. The only objects on it were a single opened folder – information about Kit, presumably – along with a snow globe and a phone with a rotary dial. The receiver lay on its side on the desk. Dr Scaife must have been midway through a call.

The doctor stood and moved around the desk. She watched Caitlin in silence. The thought entered Caitlin's mind that she should remember to act like Kit, before she realised that no play-acting was required. Kit would be equally terrified.

Instead of speaking to her, Dr Scaife turned to pick up the phone receiver.

"Your information is incorrect," she said.

Caitlin chewed her lip. What information? While she had spotted CCTV cameras interspersed along the corridors, she hadn't seen a camera in her room. Anyway, if there existed security-camera footage of her and Kit switching outfits, or any other concrete evidence, there could be no doubt about her guilt and her real identity. Perhaps Kit had done something stupid once she had left January, drawing attention to herself. She might have told Evie. There was no telling who could be trusted with the secret.

Dr Scaife frowned as she listened to the person on the phone. "You're certain about this decision?" She nodded and her eyes flicked to Caitlin. "Yes, ma'am. I understand."

She hung up. Her expression hardened. Caitlin felt a sudden certainty that she was in real trouble.

"Are you comfortable here?" Dr Scaife said.

Caitlin resisted the urge to laugh. Instead, she nodded. It was better to appear to have accepted her fate. Dr Scaife might worry less about a Skin that appeared meek.

The doctor bent to open a cabinet. Her body blocked Caitlin's view.

"Good," Dr Scaife said. "I care for all of you, you know."

When she stood, she held something in her hand. It was a one-inch-square patch. Sickly yellow liquid swilled inside. In the centre of one surface was a single short point. Caitlin edged away instinctively.

"It's nothing to fear," Dr Scaife said. "A blood sample is required, that's all." She raised both arms as though she were about to embrace Caitlin. But she still held the patch in her right hand.

Caitlin heard a scuffling sound, then raised voices. Before she had time to react, the door thumped painfully into her spine, knocking her to the ground. Someone pushed at the door again, forcing it open and sending loose papers sailing through the air.

It was Ayo. He was panting. His wide eyes darted around

the room, looking first at Caitlin, then at Dr Scaife and the needle patch in her hand.

"No," he muttered.

Dr Scaife took a moment to recover herself. "What's the meaning of this?"

"Leave her alone."

Caitlin struggled to her feet.

Ayo wiped a hand over his face, which shone with sweat. Out of the corner of her eye, Caitlin saw the silent female nurse dart past the doorway, no doubt to fetch backup.

"Pardon me, Doctor," Ayo said. Despite his formality, his voice shook with constrained anger. "This young lady has a visitor waiting. An elderly woman."

Dr Scaife chewed her lip. "Then you can simply tell this woman—"

"No."

"No?"

"There are others. Several visitors. The young lady's father, and a friend. Her originator, too. They're waiting in the lobby."

Caitlin was sure he was lying. Her dad and Kit would be unlikely to make the journey to Reading so soon after the funeral. And Dodie had already visited earlier today.

"I see no reason to change any course of action." But uncertainty had crept into the doctor's voice.

"Let me make this clear," Ayo said. "There are four separate visitors who would all be disappointed not to be able to meet with our resident. Once they have left, all will be calm again. The night-time will be calmer still."

Dr Scaife seemed to be weighing up the possibilities. Finally, she nodded.

Two security guards and the silent female nurse appeared at the doorway. Dr Scaife surveyed them with disdain. She placed the needle patch into a desk drawer.

"Please escort our resident to her room," she said. "She will be called when the first visitor is ready."

The female nurse took Caitlin by the arm and pulled her roughly into the corridor.

Caitlin watched the two security guards enter Dr Scaife's office. When they emerged moments later, they were flanking Ayo, who walked with his head hanging. In his plain uniform he looked as much a prisoner as any of the Skins. He would be punished.

The female nurse paused at a wall hatch. An unseen member of staff passed her a tray of food and the nurse in turn passed it to Caitlin. On it was a single bread bun with dry, minced contents, a packet of crisps and a bruised apple.

Caitlin had already eaten the bun and crisps by the time she was pushed back into her room.

*

As Gerry entered the cafe, Anise's face reddened and she brushed her hands on her apron, producing a cloud of flour.

"I've got into the habit of making myself useful during the off hours," Anise said, pointing at the disc of dough on the counter.

Gerry smiled. "Me too."

"Except I end up with a few more cakes, whereas you…"

Her voice tailed off. "It's good to see you, Gerry Chafik. I didn't think you'd be back." Her face flushed again.

On the long drive up to Ilam, Gerry had given a lot of thought to whether Anise really had feelings for her. She had hoped her fears would be dispelled quickly.

"Well, your Bakewell tarts are pretty special." She groaned inwardly. Everything she said, every mannerism, came across as blatant encouragement. Gerry had always harboured a certain amount of pride at never having been *that* sort of journalist. "Look, could we talk in private?"

Anise chuckled. "Here's private enough, wouldn't you say?" The only customer was the same elderly man who had been sitting in the corner of the cafe during Gerry's previous visit. Now he was accompanied by a Basset hound who licked at his fingers as he dozed.

"One sec," Anise said. She turned her back, retrieved some kind of device – a mobile telephone? – from her apron pocket, and fiddled with it for a while. She finished up and gave an apologetic smile. "Delivery coming in. If I left them to their own devices they'd dump it at the gatehouse. It'd be muggins who'd have to cart it up the hill."

She pushed a slice of Bakewell tart onto a plate and motioned to a table away from the others. She took her seat, pulling one foot up beneath her buttocks. Her body language was more like a teenager than a sixty-two-year-old. Gerry felt a familiar ache of envy for Charmers' longevity and agility. Her neck was as rigid as a pole after hours of staring at the motorway.

Anise took a small bite from the tart, then pushed the

plate across the table. Gerry hesitated. It would send a bad signal, sharing bites of a cake. She was hungry, though, so she ate a mouthful. It really was good.

Anise stared out of the window. Droplets of water ran along the streaked tracks left by earlier rainfall. "Sometimes crappy weather helps bring people into the cafe, sometimes it doesn't. If the rain kicks in once people have arrived, then we have a bumper day. Too soon in the day, and people head to Buxton Odeon instead. It's all a matter of timing." She made eye contact, investing her observation with extra meaning.

Gerry flashed a nervous smile. "Look, Anise, I—"

Anise cleared her throat noisily. Her voice became cracked and croakier. "Phillip, our curator, thinks the key is to open up the hall itself. Make it an outing for all weathers. He keeps muttering about a proper museum, or at least an exhibit, or something. About the Fall, I mean, and the meteors and all that. But then I imagine the red ropes cordoning off parts of the house. Once or twice I've woken up convinced that someone's peering down at me while I sleep. I shudder at the thought of tourists creeping around the hall, taking pictures and looking inside my laundry bin. It's silly, I know. I'm too long in the tooth to change things now. Or I'm too afraid."

This seemed a different Anise to the person Gerry had met before. Perhaps she didn't revel in the extra years granted to her by being a Charmer, the ability to cram more into her life. A Charmer's loneliness would last longer than other people's.

Gerry took another mouthful of Bakewell tart, then realised she had finished it off. "I think I'm homing in on something, Anise. There's a story here, I'm certain of it. And I think that Ilam Hall is the key."

Anise nodded. "What do you think it's all about, Gerry Chafik?" Her voice sounded far away, as though she were dreaming.

"I'm sorry," Gerry said with a frown. "What are we talking about here?"

"My father always told me we were privileged. And we are. I mean, look at this view from the grounds of my ancestral home, for crying out loud. But whatever we got from the Fall was a fluke – a fluke that then echoed down through the generations. Some people would tell you that Charmers are superhuman, but to me that implies some kind of inner strength in addition to our gifts. It's not true. We're as flawed as anyone." She blinked rapidly. "Look at me. A mad old biddy, feeling sorry for herself."

Gerry reached out and took her hand. Her skin was warm and soft. "I want to know the truth."

Anise choked a little. She checked her watch. "So. Ilam Hall. Why do you think it's so significant? Other than Ilam being the site of the Fall."

"Because of what came afterwards. Anise, how much do you know about your ancestor, Lord Hartwell?"

"Only what I told you, and what's in the books. He was the mayor, and then a lord much later."

"But why?"

Anise shrugged. "Because Ilam became popular. I bet

people visited even in the rain, back then."

"Sure. It makes sense, up to a point. But think about it. Why would the mayor of a town be made a lord, solely because of increased tourism? Ilam Hall wasn't made for people occupying a new role in the town. It was built specifically for Lord Hartwell. For your family."

Anise chewed her cheek. "You know, I've never thought of it in those terms. I'm— Well, I'm embarrassed."

"Don't be. I didn't question it myself, no matter how many times I saw the same conclusion repeated in account after account of the Fall. And I should be more embarrassed, anyway. Spotting discrepancies is pretty much my entire job."

"It's sweet of you to try to make me feel better. I do feel awfully blind, though. But what are you actually telling me? What does it mean?"

"I'm trying not to come to any conclusions. There's always a risk of trying to make facts fit a certain expected outcome."

One of Anise's eyebrows raised. "That's a lie. You have a theory, and you're wondering whether I'm complicit in something. I've been around longer than you, Gerry Chafik. I've been fibbed to and fobbed off before."

Gerry saw there was no point in keeping things from Anise. "All right. I'll start at the beginning. Hartwell was mayor, fine. And he was made a lord in 1822."

"Is the year significant somehow?"

"It is. Let me finish. The Fall was in 1808, but of course nothing happened immediately, other than the meteor shower and the public interest that it inspired. The sheddings occurred later that year, which is when we get the first frantic accounts of Skins appearing in the village. But here's the thing that most of the history books gloss over, due to our hindsight. After that first spate of sheddings, after another year passed without incident, there was no reason to think that there'd be any more Snakeskins."

"Until seven years after the first sheddings."

"Exactly. Which brings us to 1815. And what happened in 1815?"

Anise held up both hands, flummoxed.

"Ilam Hall may have been completed in 1821, but work began in 1815. They started with the wings to extend the main building, with the facade left until the end. But I've checked and rechecked, and it's true."

"Before my ancestor was made a lord. But what does that mean?"

"It means that a larger building was required, at the very moment the second batch of Snakeskins made an appearance. Your family had no particular wealth then, which means that it was paid for by someone other than Hartwell. And what's more, I think it also means that his reward, his being made a lord, was linked to the construction of the new hall, too."

"Oh God."

"I may still be wrong, Anise. But I think that Hartwell was bought off by the government of the time."

"And you said this is about the truth. So he was paid off in exchange for hiding the truth about something?"

Gerry nodded. "In exchange for hiding the truth, and in exchange for hiding the people that could *demonstrate* the truth. Anise, here's the thing. I'm pretty sure I've read all the historical accounts of that first year of sheddings. There are dozens of them, all slightly different in their own way. But only four of them mention the Snakeskin turning to ash."

Anise's face had turned pale. "And the rest…"

"My money is on the fact that the rest *didn't* ash. At least, not at first."

With a shaking hand, Anise rubbed at the condensation on the windowpane. Ilam Hall appeared through the streaks. "And instead, they were in there."

Anise gripped both of Gerry's hands. "You have to leave."

"Look, I'm sorry. I know this must come as a shock—"

"No. That's not it. You have to leave *right now*."

"Why? What's happened?"

Anise kicked her chair away, waking the sleeping man in the corner of the cafe. "I've been a fool. I thought he was a friend of yours at first, seeing as he was asking the same questions."

"Who? Who are you talking about?"

"Terry? Todd? Trent? It started with a T. Dark little beard, like the Sheriff of Nottingham in films. Smart tweed suit and bow tie."

A shiver ran along Gerry's spine. "What did he want?"

"Why, the books."

"The census records? But you told me that they couldn't leave the building. All that talk about 'civic duty'. They're what I trekked all the way back here for!"

Anise wrung her hands. "But then you didn't talk about

all the legal stuff. Warrants and national security. And when I finally mentioned your name, he was less than complimentary about you."

"National security? Anise, are you telling me that you believed this guy was a crappy tabloid hack? He was a government employee – anyone could see that."

But why? Gerry's mind reeled at the implications of the Party's concern about the historical population of Ilam. And an equally important question: Why now?

"I never was one for all that Party conspiracy nonsense. I'm a doddery old woman, all right? But this man, whatever his name is, made me promise to let him know if you ever showed up again. He even lent me a fancy phone." She pulled the mobile telephone out of her apron pocket and brandished it.

Gerry's eyes widened. "So—"

"He's been staying down there in the village. He's on his way right now."

So she had been sending a text message when Gerry arrived. It took all Gerry's willpower not to lash out.

"Is there another way out of here?" she said.

"Through the kitchens – they're shared with the youth hostel. But then don't go out of the main exit, you'll be too visible. Take the— Look, I'll just take you. Come on."

With the speed of a much younger woman, Anise darted behind the counter and into the kitchens. Gerry followed, bumping from cabinet to cabinet, then burst out into a dark corridor that smelled of sweat and bleach. The heels of Anise's shoes clattered on the bare wood of the stairs.

"This way," she hissed, yanking Gerry away from the

glass-panelled front door of the youth hostel and into a featureless corridor. At first it appeared to be a dead end, but then Anise heaved downwards on the bar of a fire exit door.

They emerged into a muddy clearing roofed by dripping foliage. Anise pointed along a pathway barely visible through the trees. "Keep going until you pass the giant squirrel sculptures, then there's a sharp bend to the right. You'll get to the car park the back way. With any luck, that fellow will already be much further up the drive."

Gerry nodded, breathless. "Anise—"

"You don't have to say anything nice, and for Christ's sake don't make me feel any more guilty than I do already. But there's one more thing. I'm pretty sure I know what you came here for and, as luck would have it, I haven't had a chance to pass this nugget of info to our government friend yet."

Gerry was too out of breath to question her.

"I mentioned the place you were asking about," Anise continued hurriedly. "But he was all focussed on the census books, and then on finding out what I knew about you. But once he got his hands on the books he was out again in a flurry."

"What place? What did you mention?"

"Up on the western hillside of the valley. Beside that wonderful outcrop, the one shaped like a cresting wave. You can see that outcrop from my bedroom window. I can't tell you how many times—"

"Anise," Gerry interrupted. "Please. What about it?"

"Well, I had a brainwave, soon after you left. I'd have phoned you, but I couldn't summon the courage. I thought you'd finished with me. And then, when your friend didn't seem interested, I suppose it dropped out of my mind."

Gerry's hands clenched. Her fingernails dug into her palms.

"My dad was a bit of a heritage nut, you see. But when he talked about all the old occupations in the village, I never made the connection to that building up there on the hill." She looked up, then blinked several times, as though only now realising the urgency of the situation. "A shepherd's hut. That's what it was, the ruins you wanted to know about. Well, probably a little bigger than that sounds, but not much. But it turns out that there was a whole family in there."

Gerry's hands went to her mouth. "At the time of the Fall? You're certain?"

"I did a bit of detective work myself. I'm not sure I'd ever actually *read* those books in the library before. There was never any need to look anything up. It took a bit of cross-referencing, but what I realised was that all the other people with 'shepherd' listed as their occupation were tenant farmers, not landowners. So there was actually only one family that fit the bill."

"And you got the name? Please tell me you got the name."

"I did, I did. An odd name, though. Creepy." Anise pulled a notepad from the pocket of her apron and began leafing through its pages. "Unlucky, I thought at the time, though I'm the superstitious type anyway."

Gerry looked up at the ceiling. Any attempt to hurry Anise would only slow her down.

"Here," Anise said. "Like I said. Unlucky."

She turned the notepad so that Gerry could read the four letters in shaky handwriting.

*HEXT.*

# TWELVE

"You're late," Russell said.

Ixion approached slowly. The shadows of the underground car park made his hooded face a blank, but his body language was quite different. Instead of the usual confident stride, his walk was hesitant and his paces shorter.

He stopped several feet from Russell and they faced each other in silence. A faulty exit sign blinked on and off behind the man's head. It was hard to believe that outside it was still daytime. Russell felt a fool for agreeing to meet here again. He ought to be setting the agenda. He was the one in possession of evidence. Then again, like the fool he was, he had already described the contents of the floppy disk over the phone.

"So what does it mean?" he said.

Ixion didn't reply. His head tilted slightly.

"I'm not going to hand it over without an explanation."

Tracking down one of the new three-and-a-half-inch disk drives had been tricky. At the first computer shop, the staff member who tried to help him was in his early twenties and had no idea what Russell wanted. At a larger chain store further along Botley Road, a series of assistants had been summoned before a senior manager had finally, proudly, produced a box from some back room. "Not yet available to the mass market," he had said, and the thing had accordingly cost a small fortune. When Russell had finally arrived home and hooked up the disk drive to his Acorn computer, he had discovered that the disk contained a single file also labelled *Clients*, a spreadsheet with fields in only three columns. The first two were both unhelpfully labelled 'Name', and the third simply '#'.

The names listed in the second column had caught his eye first. He recognised many of them from his own work diary. These were the people that Ellis had been meeting, at the Randolph, the Old Parsonage and various other upmarket locations in the centre of Oxford. At first the strings of digits in the column headed '#' baffled him, until he recognised some as phone numbers.

Then he had turned his attention to the names in the first column. A few of their surnames nagged at him. Hadn't he shopped at a department store of that name? Hadn't he seen those names on the list of benefactors at the Ashmolean and at the Natural History Museum? Further down the list, he discovered names that he recognised immediately. Nathan Fix, the CEO of Cormorant Media. Oma Williams, an up-and-coming Pinewood star who specialised in villainous roles requiring an affected American accent. Maxine Kemper, the inner-city property investor he had read a puff piece about in the *Daily Counsel* only last week, focussing on the assertion that non-Charmers were perfectly capable of making a fortune from the ground up.

Some of the names featured umlauts and strings of consonants; this peculiarity triggered something in his mind. He looked again at the strings of digits in the '#' column. Perhaps they were all phone numbers, but the unusual ones represented contacts in other countries – assuming foreigners *had* phones. The immensity of this breach of the law actually made him shudder. He searched for some of the British names in the phone book, to no avail. He had leafed through all of the reference books in the office and managed to locate several names in lists of board members of influential companies. One thing was clear. The people listed in the spreadsheet were stupidly wealthy.

"What do *you* think it means?" the man said after a long pause. His tone of genuine uncertainty contrasted oddly with his too-loud, deep voice.

Russell sensed that he was falling into the trap of giving information and receiving none, but he couldn't think how to avoid a direct reply. "I think it means that there's funny business going on. Money changing hands. I think it shows that whatever Ellis Blackwood – whatever the *government* – is up to goes beyond local funding and development, and beyond national security, even."

"Because."

"Is that supposed to be a question? You really need to work on your conversation skills. Because... Because the contents of this disk—" He patted his right jacket pocket, then wished he hadn't. His intention had been to pretend he hadn't brought it with him, if Ixion refused to answer his questions. "—show that the people involved are *outside* of the government. These 'clients' aren't Party members, and they aren't even Charmers as far as I can make out. Most of them aren't even British, for goodness' sake."

Ixion's low sigh was wheezy, like radio static. He nodded.

"Do *you* know what it means?" Russell said.

Once again, Ixion seemed reluctant to speak. Several seconds passed in silence before he replied, haltingly, "It means we have a lead."

Interesting. *We*, as opposed to *I*. Several times, Russell had wondered whether Ixion was operating alone. Would that have made the handing over of data more or less rash? Or more or less illegal?

"What will you do?" he said. "And I insist that you tell me something about Nell Blackwood's part in all of this."

Ixion's silence might have indicated stubbornness or uncertainty. Russell imagined throttling the man, forcing him to speak. Perhaps it was down to the fact that this was their third meeting, but Ixion no longer seemed nearly so imposing. Russell realised that he was actually the slightly taller of the two of them.

A small, gloved hand stretched out. "The disk, please."

In the weeks before all this intrigue had begun, Russell had spent his evenings working through a VHS box set of wildlife documentaries. Suddenly, he could think of nothing more pleasurable than locking the door to his flat, fetching his duvet and falling asleep to footage of tottering newborn foals. He pulled out the disk from his pocket and held it up.

"Have you taken a copy?" the man said. His voice cracked slightly. Despite his deep pitch, he sounded anxious, or even afraid, or... young.

"Of course not," Russell replied. In fact, he had made two copies, after a great deal of fiddling with the computer. One of the disks was on top of his boiler, the other wedged into a hole behind his sofa where the skirting board had come away.

Ixion gave a hollow chuckle. "Don't let anybody find it." His thin outstretched fingers twitched, beckoning.

As Russell stepped forwards to offer the disk, with his other hand he pulled an object from his back pocket. The electrical-shop manager had nodded conspiratorially when Russell had described the other item he wanted to buy. "The old marital disharmony, am I right?" the manager had said with a smirk. "This is what you need, trust me. It'll clip onto any item of clothing, light as a feather. She won't feel the weight of it, no matter what she's wearing."

The tracking device clipped onto Ixion's jacket without a sound. Russell stepped away and tried to calm his breathing. Ixion gave no suggestion of having noticed.

"Will you keep me updated?" Russell said.

Ixion slipped the disk into his pocket. He shuffled backwards into the shadows, so that his diminutive outline became as difficult to make out as his face.

"Thank you, Russell."

\*

Russell's hand darted out to steady the tracking unit on the car dashboard. He looked up just in time to see the zebra crossing and the yellow-jacketed traffic warden striding to its centre. He slammed both feet onto the brake pedal. The car swerved from side to side and lurched to a stop. The engine stalled. The traffic warden glared at him and mouthed something indecipherable.

Once a parade of toddlers had weaved its way across the road, Russell edged the car away, avoiding eye contact with the traffic warden and keeping the engine sawing away in first gear. He ignored the backed-up stream of cars behind him and fished beneath his seat for the tracking unit.

The device was simple, with four bulbs at the ends of a cross printed onto its black surface. After he had set off in pursuit he had driven for five minutes, trying to orient himself north, before realising that the uppermost light represented a direction of travel – *straight ahead* – rather than a compass direction. After that, he'd broken the speed limit several times in his attempt to close the gap. Each bulb lit intermittently and there was no indication of distance. He was breathless from panic.

Now the uppermost bulb was flashing on and off steadily. He guessed that meant he was close. He would have to proceed carefully. When he had left the underground car park he hadn't seen which vehicle Ixion had taken.

The car behind him sounded its horn. Russell accelerated away. In the rear-view mirror, the other driver showed him her middle finger.

The bulb flickered faster and faster.

He parked in a lay-by around the corner and hopped out of the car. The air was cool and refreshing. Each of the four bulbs began to light in turn, then all of them at once. The clipped tracking device must be very close.

Half a dozen cars were parked in a row on the grass verge. All appeared empty. On the opposite side of the road was a wide, low building. A sixth-form college. Russell realised that he had been here before.

It was Spencer Blackwood's college.

His stomach lurched. He thought again of Ixion's slight figure, the uncertainty of his movements. The voice was harder to explain, but it was conceivable that it had been altered by some kind of mouthpiece.

Was it really possible? Had he been meeting with his boss's teenage son, all this time? All of this conspiratorial behaviour for the benefit of a shy, spotty kid.

The next course of action was clear. He would call Spencer out on his pretence. Then, if there was anything to the conspiracy, they would discuss it as adults. He'd be damned if he was going to continue with the cloak-and-dagger game any more.

An intercom was fixed beside the tall metal gates. Russell pushed the button and the intercom crackled.

"Yes?"

"This is Russell Handler. I've been sent by Ellis Blackwood, the MP. We've met before. Am I speaking to Freya?" When he had picked Spencer up from college before, the maternal receptionist had seemed quite taken with him.

"No." The voice fizzed with static. "Freya's off ill. Got diarrhoea, she said."

"Minister Blackwood sent me here to collect his son. Spencer."

"Final bell isn't for another half an hour."

"Well, not collect. I need to speak to him." Russell winced. "To give him something."

The intercom went silent. "What is it, then?"

"It's private."

"Sounds weird."

"Look, the minister sent me. Ellis Blackwood. He's quite an important man. I don't know if you're filling in for Freya while she's suffering with – while she's off ill – but I'd suggest that it's probably not a good idea to—"

"All right."

"Oh. Is it?"

"I'll send him out. I'm only here today, then I'm off to Butlins. Who gives a crap. I'll bring him out."

Russell backed away from the intercom, baffled by his success. He began to pace up and down. What attitude should he take with Spencer? Paternal? Man-to-man? Or should he treat the boy totally seriously? Spencer wasn't like other kids. Russell had always liked him. What if he had hidden his identity because he genuinely feared his father and whatever he was doing? Perhaps Russell was about to make a terrible mistake, outing Spencer in public.

He bit his thumbnail. By now, the receptionist would have located Spencer, spoken to his teacher, and might at this moment be leading him to the gates. Russell peered through the gap in the metal bars but couldn't see anybody.

He should leave. The receptionist would shrug and take the boy back inside. Russell could go home and consider what to do more carefully. The concrete playground was still empty. There was still time to call this off. Yes, that—

Something struck him on the back of his head.

His cheek smacked into the metal gates, which made a dull ringing sound like a cloister bell. Then his forehead thumped onto the pavement and then there was nothing at all.

\*

Gerry rang the doorbell a second time. She rechecked the scrawled writing on her notepad. Ivy Cottage: a ridiculous name. Not only was the building far too large to be classed as a cottage, she could see no evidence of ivy either.

The door opened to reveal a man in a shabby black suit. His hair was ruffled, revealing two deep widow's peaks. His black tie had been loosened and the top button of his white shirt was undone. He stank of whisky.

"Mr Hext?"

The man eyed her suspiciously. "You a journalist?"

Gerry had already jammed her notepad into her coat pocket. "Yes, actually. How did you know?"

He waved a hand. It was difficult to tell how drunk he might be. "Figured we'd lost you, that's all."

"Lost me?"

"Yup. All of you."

"I was hoping to talk to you."

"It can't hurt now, I suppose. We're all done and dusted. So to speak."

Gerry tried to see past him. The interior of the house was dark. "Do you think I might come in for a moment, Mr Hext?"

He folded his arms, then unfolded them, then folded them again. "You know what— What's your name?"

"Gerry Chafik."

He nodded, as if that explained everything. "You know what, Miss Traffic? I'd like that very much indeed." He sidestepped to allow her to enter, bumping against an umbrella stand as he did so.

Gerry made her way along the passage, aiming for a sliver of light. She pushed open a door to reveal a large farmhouse kitchen, lit only by the lamp of an extractor fan above an electric oven and a portable TV showing grainy footage of Adrian Lorde at Number 10, looking imperious and ancient, propped up behind his desk. She flicked on the main lights.

There was a half-full bottle of whisky on the table. The man noticed her looking at it. "I'm never much of a drinker normally. It's a replacement for people. I prefer people, all things considered."

There was something about his shabbiness that was instantly appealing, as though she had known him for years, as though he were a favourite uncle.

"Just back from work?" she said, indicating his crumpled suit.

He looked down at himself. A crease appeared on his forehead. "No."

"May I sit down?"

"Course. Sit down. Cuppa? Bugger, no teabags." He glanced at the whisky bottle. "Water?"

"Water would be fine. Thanks."

His hands shook as he passed her a glass. A spilled pool of water spread in a growing halo.

"You haven't asked what I was hoping to talk about," Gerry said.

"No. Seems obvious, though."

"It does?"

"Doesn't it?"

"Sorry. I'm confused." She glanced again at his suit, suddenly unsure of herself. "I wondered if you knew much about your family history, Mr Hext. Actually, can I call you Toby?"

This produced a strange reaction. The man blundered backwards, halfway through the process of sitting down. He missed the seat and fell to the floor, then leapt up immediately. Even though he was groaning with pain, the accident appeared to have woken him up.

"Why in God's name would you want to do that?" he said.

"I'm sorry. I'll call you Mr Hext, then. Is that okay?"

"No! I mean, why would you want to call me Toby? I'm Ian. I'm not that drunk."

Instinctively, Gerry pulled out her notepad. She ran her finger down the list of Hext family members that she had copied from library records. The names on the final line were Janet, Toby and Caitlin.

She clapped a hand to her forehead. "I'd completely forgotten. Charmers lend their names to their spouses, not the other way around. So you're…"

"Ian Hext. Né Usborne. Janet Hext's husband. I was proud to take her name. I don't care about the Charmer rules, I'd have done it anyway." His face crumpled.

"I'm so sorry, Mr Hext." From the records, Gerry had learnt that Janet Hext had died a few years ago in a car crash. "You must still be feeling her loss very badly."

"You're commiserating me about Janet... So you really don't know, then?"

"It seems I don't know much about much."

Ian grunted. "Toby Hext is dead too. He... well, he died. And today I went to his—"

Now it was Gerry's turn to groan. The shabby suit. The black tie. The drinking. "Oh shit. Mr Hext. Ian. I'm so sorry. If I'd known..."

Ian pulled himself out of his chair awkwardly. He shambled over to the window. His shoulders shook.

Gerry stood, too. After a few seconds of hesitation, she placed her hands on his shoulders. Instantly, Ian turned on the spot and hugged her, pressing his face into her neck. His wet cheeks skidded against her skin.

A minute passed, or more. The shudders subsided. Ian pushed Gerry away gently. "I needed that. Sorry, though. Your top's wet."

"It's fine. I should go."

"No. Please. Stay. I'm rather—" Only the word 'lonely' could fill the pause that followed. "It's good to speak to someone." He sat down. "So. I'll fill you in, and then your turn. Toby Hext – we always called him Tobe – died last week. They're calling it suicide." Another phrase with implications. "There weren't many people at the funeral. A couple of his friends who played cards together. One of his old teachers. Me. My daughter and her best friend Evie. There were more, but nobody that he knew."

"What do you mean by that?"

"We all arrived together, in two cars. When we got to the cemetery there were all these cars waiting. Journalists, we figured. Cait couldn't bear the thought of being photographed."

Gerry thought of Zemma Finch's attitude to news stories about sheddings. Toby Hext wasn't a celebrity, and she doubted that journalists really had shown up to the funeral. But if those suspicious cars didn't belong to journalists and photographers, then who did they belong to?

Ian continued, interrupting her line of thought. "So we all headed off and left them to it. A body's a body. We preferred to mark the occasion on our own, elsewhere, at this spot where we used to picnic. Tobe would have hated it, mind you. Hardly a word was said, and no fuss. We spent longer in the pub than up on the hill. Right, now your turn."

"It seems trivial now," Gerry said, though in fact her mind was racing as she tried to process the implications of Toby Hext's death. "I'm from *Folk* and I was hoping to do a piece about Charmer families. Nothing sensational. I'm thinking it should be the story of real families who happen to be a little different to— well, not 'normal' families, but you know."

"I know. Sounds like a nice piece."

"Except now—"

"Except now we're not much of a family. Two dead in three years. And I'm not a Charmer, just a hanger-on."

"That's not what I was going to say."

"I know. But it's still the case. It's okay, and I'm still happy to help, if you want?"

Gerry saw the pleading in his expression. She understood his craving for distraction.

She nodded. "If you're sure. Perhaps you can tell me a little about your wife, first. Her family." It seemed best to avoid referring to Toby Hext directly. She wasn't sure she could bear to see Ian cry again.

He drew himself upright. "They were a fine family. They went back all the way to the Fall. Well, that's obvious, isn't it, but I mean there were none of the confusions in their family tree that other Charmer families might have had. The Hext name was solid, and the Hexts tended not to marry into other Charmer dynasties, which I suppose was the usual way of things. After a bit of research, Janet was sure that ours was the only branch of the tree left. More of a twig, now, I suppose."

Gerry pretended to refer to her notebook. "I did a bit of preliminary research, about all of the families I was hoping to speak to. Do you know if I'm right in thinking that the Ilam Hexts – or the father of the family, at least – were shepherds? At the key moment, at the time of the Fall, I mean."

Ian nodded. "You've certainly done your homework. Janet was always proud of that. She once said that that's the profession she ought to have taken up. As it was, she was in HR. Maybe it's not so different. Herding sheep, herding people. I don't know. She would've liked us to have more of a flock of our own. We never got around to it, but maybe we would have, in time. We only had the one child, in the end."

282

"And her name is Caitlin?"

After a pause that Gerry found difficult to decipher, Ian gave a slight nod.

It dawned on Gerry that Caitlin Hext was the only remaining Charmer in the Hext family. The list of names on her notepad was a list of the dead.

"Would you like to see a photo of Janet?" Ian said in a cracked voice. "She was beautiful."

Gerry smiled. "I really would. Thank you."

"I don't keep them out on display. That might seem strange. I found I couldn't see her, not every day. Hang on."

He left the room and Gerry heard him bumping his way up the stairs. She couldn't hear any other sounds from within the house. Was Caitlin here in the building?

Ian returned a couple of minutes later, carrying three heavy-looking ring-bound photo albums. He gave a sheepish grin. "I couldn't decide which one to bring."

He dropped them onto the table with a slam that echoed around the kitchen. Gerry's smile was more forced now, but she told herself to indulge him. The Hext family was her only lead.

She opened the first photo album. Janet really was beautiful. Her eyes sparkled with intelligence. Even in the faded photos, with their colours bleeding to sepia at their centres, the redness of her hair was exceptional. Her face was lean, her cheekbones high. In every photo she was either laughing or smiling. Ian was, too. His young face was suited to happiness. Gerry glanced up to see those same features creased in an altogether different way.

She leafed through the pages, images of the young couple at parties, camping, sharing food, splashing in the sea. If she really had been intending to write an article about Charmer families, any one of these images would be a wonderful inclusion.

Another man appeared often in the pictures. "Is this Toby?"

"He might not have been one for socialising with others, but we had fun. Janet was the glue between us, of course. It was always a bit strained after she passed, even when Tobe moved in here. My fault, not his."

One photo was dark and difficult to make out. Gerry peered at it and made out Janet's face, lit from one side. The photo must have been taken in a theatre. On the stage Gerry could see a figure sitting at the foot of a bed.

"They're puppets," Ian said. He pointed at tiny figures on the right-hand side of the photo. Now Gerry realised that they were miniature rather than on a stage in the distance. "This was one of Janet's favourite spots – the Museum of Automata on the Scarborough seafront. There's a bit of a family history, I suppose. This photo was taken donkey's years ago, but we went there most summers. One time, we lost Janet in there for hours and it turned out she'd been watching this little diorama again and again on a loop, burning through ten-pence coins. She was fascinated by portrayals of Charmers, especially from times gone by. Caitlin was only a little kid, though, and she was pretty shaken up by the whole thing."

"By Janet being missing, you mean? Because she thought her mum was gone?"

"Yes, but only afterwards. By which I mean that it took us ages to convince her that the woman we found *was* her mum. She had a young, impressionable mind, I suppose, and she was coming to terms with being a Charmer and all that entailed, and then this episode at the museum… I think Cait ended up all muddled. She was convinced that the Janet we brought home was a Snakeskin. She had nightmares for weeks."

Gerry realised it was the last page in the album. She reached for the next one. On its first page was a single photo.

In the picture Ian appeared more exhausted than Janet, as close to tears as he was right now. Sweat glistened on Janet's brow, but she looked utterly at ease. She held up the newborn child in her arms, proud and content.

Gerry noticed Ian turn towards the kitchen doorway, through which the stairs were visible. Caitlin was all he had left. She must be in the house.

She flipped through the pages quickly. Baby Caitlin became a toddler. The toddler became a girl with red pigtails and the same proud expression as her mother. Her hair lengthened, so that she looked more and more like her mother when she was younger. And she looked increasingly familiar.

Gerry leapt up from her chair. Standing, she continued rifling through the pages. Caitlin grew older, and now Gerry was certain.

"I've seen her," she said, breathlessly. "I've seen your daughter before."

"Where? The sixth-form? I assumed you weren't local."

"I saw her at the care home. Has she shed?"

Ian nodded. "Her first. Last week. Just before Tobe died. I keep worrying that it affected him somehow. He—"

"Is she here? In the house?" she said breathlessly. She thought again of Ian's mention of mysterious cars at the funeral. A thought chilled her: Perhaps the Great British Prosperity Party had followed *exactly* the same thread of logic as she had in her investigation. Perhaps their interest wasn't only Ilam, but the Hext family. "Can I speak to her?"

"What's the urgency?"

"I'm sorry, I really am. Please. I'd really like to speak to her."

Ian watched her for a few moments, perhaps trying to decide whether she was trustworthy. Finally, he nodded. "I'll fetch her. Stay here. She might not be up to it, given the circumstances."

Gerry listened to the thuds and creaks of the stairs. At least now Ian was moving quickly – if nothing else, she'd managed to sober him up. She stood at the sink and peered out of the window. Outside, her car was parked badly, partly overlapping a circular patch of grass which acted as a roundabout in the centre of the wide driveway.

Where the driveway dipped down to meet the main road, the nose of another car protruded from behind the bushes. Gerry shielded her eyes. The driver's window was tinted so that it was impossible to see inside. The car pulled away smoothly. Its engine must already have been running.

That was no journalist, and neither were the mysterious cars at the funeral. Representatives of the Party had been close behind her in Ilam. It was perfectly possible that they could have found the same links to the Hext family that she had. She had no idea why they were searching for the family members at this point in time, but this very urgency – and Toby Hext's untimely death – spelled trouble. Getting Caitlin to somewhere safe was the most important thing now.

A knock came from upstairs, and Ian's voice called softly, "Cait?"

Silence.

She hovered at the kitchen door, then moved to the foot of the stairs.

Ian appeared at the top of the staircase.

"She's gone," he said, flatly.

Gerry was determined not to reveal her panic. "Is that so surprising?"

Ian plodded down the stairs, deep in thought. "No, I suppose not. She's been acting... I mean, who wouldn't, though. It's been a tough day. A tough time." He turned to look up the staircase. "Sorry. I got distracted. I can see the garage from up in my daughter's room."

"I don't understand. Why would that be distracting?"

"Don't know. I'll go and check." He pushed past into the kitchen. Gerry followed him, and then through another door into a scullery. Ian fiddled with a latch that led to a back garden. Badly laid crazy paving gave way to a lawn with a large shed and tall trees. To the left-hand side of the paved area stood a brick garage. Its double doors were wide open.

Ian stood before the doors, looking from one wall to the

other. Spades, rakes, saws and other tools hung from pegs on both sides.

"No ladder," Ian said softly. He turned to face Gerry. "It's the strangest coincidence. I think I've been robbed."

＊

Caitlin understood that she was dreaming.

Even so, she was horrified to see the skin of her chest begin to peel away to reveal raw, red flesh beneath. The thin surface curled like burnt paper, rolling up on itself. She clawed at her breasts and belly, trying to press the papyrus-like, brittle skin back into place. Her exposed flesh stung. She screamed an undulating, two-tone shriek.

She woke up, panting. Her fingernails were nipping into her chest. Her hair was damp with sweat and strands criss-crossed her vision, turning the ceiling into a hazy web.

The shrieking sound continued.

It wasn't coming from her. It was an alarm.

She could hear other sounds, too. Hurried footsteps in the corridor outside. Scuffles. Bickering, strangled voices, though she couldn't make out the words. This wasn't a drill.

Then someone shouted outside her door. It wasn't directed at her. "Central controls are down. The doors aren't opening!" Another voice, further away, bellowed, "Some bastard's stolen my ID!"

Caitlin jumped out of bed and pressed herself up against the door.

Another shout came from the direction of Dr Scaife's office. Caitlin squeezed her eyes shut, trying to concentrate on making out the words, which were repeated several times in a voice almost as shrill as the alarm. Something about 'evil'? No. 'Level'?

Then she understood.

"Leave them! Leave them all!"

Caitlin had an almost hysterical compulsion to laugh. With each hour that passed in the care home she had become more convinced that she would be trapped here for the foreseeable future. Instead, she was going to die today, surrounded by Snakeskins trapped in their poky cells. And nobody but Kit would ever know that Caitlin had been different to the others.

More heavy footsteps; then the voices stopped.

She thumped on the door with her fists. The metal barely budged. It was heavy, secure. There was no physical lock and not even a handle on the inside. She thumped again. Her elbow caught on the steel head of the bed, leaving a graze, reminding Caitlin of the flayed skin in her dream. She slumped down to the floor.

Perhaps the fire might be elsewhere in the building. Dr Scaife's abandonment could be a calculated decision. Maybe she was confident that this part of the care home didn't need to be evacuated. Caitlin wished she could summon any amount of faith in the doctor's moral code.

She realised she could smell smoke. It was leaking through the narrow gap beneath the door.

She was going to die alone. Just like Uncle Tobe had done, face down in a swimming pool at night.

"Hey!" she shouted. "In here! Hey! Hey!"

"Hey," she said again, in a quieter, muffled voice.

It took her a moment to register that she hadn't spoken, this last time.

The door lock bleeped. Caitlin edged backwards along the slippery floor.

The door crunched open. Caitlin saw herself, wreathed in smoke.

"Hey," the girl said again.

Caitlin sobbed with relief. "Kit!"

The Snakeskin held a finger to her lips. "Keep your voice down. A few members of staff are still pelting around out here. We'll have to move fast."

Kit bent down to yank Caitlin up and pulled her roughly from the room.

The corridor was thick with smoke, but it appeared deserted. The smoke grew thicker further along the residents' corridor, the very direction Kit was leading them in.

Caitlin held back. "But the fire!"

"It's contained," Kit replied, shouting to make herself audible over the noise of the alarm. "It's in a bin, jamming the lift doors open. All smoke and no fire! Thank me later."

The alarm wasn't the only sound Caitlin could hear. Thuds came from each of the metal doors that they passed, and shouts from inside. The Skins were trapped and afraid.

Kit had noticed too. "There's a different pass card for each door. I've only got yours. There's nothing I can do for them." She dragged Caitlin along, waving her arm to clear the smoke.

Then Kit breathed, "Bollocks."

Caitlin rubbed her stinging eyes, trying to identify the problem. Now she could make out the double doors of the lift, beside a staircase. The interior of the lift flickered red, a metallic vision of hell. Below, Caitlin saw a waste bin lying on its side with its burning contents spread over the floor. Parts of corridor lino had set alight.

"Doesn't matter," Kit shouted. "We can still get to the stairs. We'll be up there before the fire spreads too much."

They waded through the thickening smoke. Caitlin looked back. The metal cell doors were impossible to see now, but the thudding and screaming sounds were louder.

"I'm not going," she said. She wriggled free of Kit's grasp.

"What are you talking about?"

"I'm not leaving them! They'll die."

She had already set off the way they had come before Kit responded. "But they're Skins!" she shouted after Caitlin. "Dying is what they do!"

Caitlin bent her head down and charged through the noxious smoke. She turned right at the junction and gulped in air that tasted sweet in contrast. The passage to the visitors' lounge was empty too. She burst through the plain door to the annex. As she had hoped, in below the shelves of supplies was a large fire extinguisher. The staff here might not care much about Skins, but the general public was another matter.

She raced back to Kit with the fire extinguisher held over her head. She had no idea where she found the strength. When she pulled its trigger, the force almost knocked her off her feet. The jet of foam made streamer spirals in the air. Kit's arms snaked around her, reinforcing her grip on the extinguisher and directing the foam to the burning bin.

The fires on the lino were extinguished instantly. The waste bin hissed as its burning contents became saturated.

When the last lick of flame disappeared, Caitlin dropped the fire extinguisher to the floor with a clang. All strength left her body.

Kit whooped. "You know what?" she said, barely audible beneath the shrill siren. "You're all right, you are."

Panting heavily, Caitlin grinned at her.

"That dress you're wearing," she said. "I remember."

Kit glanced down at herself and her face flushed. Over black leggings she wore a green-and-white dress patterned with images of ivy. It had belonged to Caitlin's mum. She had loved ivy, hence the name of their house, Ivy Cottage, despite the fact that she had never successfully trained the plant along its north-facing front wall.

"For strength," Kit said. "I hoped you'd be okay with it."

She didn't wait for an answer but instead charged towards the flight of stairs. Caitlin followed her up, barely able to run fast enough to keep sight of her.

On the first floor Caitlin saw the chrome counters of a kitchen, as well as a lounge area where shabby, low armchairs had been arranged in a horseshoe formation around a bulky TV.

"Ayo let me out of my room one night and snuck me up here," Kit said from behind her. "We ate fruit cake and watched a wildlife documentary together. Baby birds tumbling down a cliff. It was heavenly. But we're not going that way." She dashed to the winding stairs. "Next floor."

Caitlin stumbled up the stairs. Kit stood at the top,

holding open an unmarked door to let Caitlin pass through. Caitlin's slippered feet sunk into thick carpet. There was a wide bed covered with a plush quilt. Through a side door she saw a pristine bathroom suite. It looked for all the world like an upmarket hotel room.

"You'll never guess whose room this is," Kit said, but didn't wait for a reply. "Dr Vicky Scaife. I figured it was appropriate." She plucked something from the pillow – a soft-toy puppy – and scowled at it.

Caitlin rubbed her forehead. The two-tone shriek of the alarm was beginning to make her head swim. "What are we doing here? What does Dr Scaife have that we need?"

Kit grinned. "We just came here for the view."

"Are you serious? Have you actually gone crazy?"

Kit ignored her and moved to the window. From here Caitlin could see the other buildings of the January complex and, in the distance, fields of bright yellow rapeseed and the motorway.

Kit heaved against the window. It opened. She turned and smiled.

Then she stepped backwards.

Acting on instinct, Caitlin darted after her with both arms outstretched. Her palms jolted against the wooden windowsill. She gazed down.

Kit was directly below the sill, beaming up at her. A steel ladder stretched away to the ground, two storeys below.

"Fast as you like," she said.

The wind whipped at Caitlin's smock as she edged out of the window. Her hands shook, threatening to release their grip on the rungs of the ladder, which reverberated with every step. Rather than look up or down, she stared only at her hands. Her knuckles turned white, followed by her fingers, then the backs of her hands lost colour too.

The ladder stopped rocking. Caitlin froze, terrified that it had slipped away from the sill and that she was gradually tipping backwards. She looked down. She saw her own face – no, Kit's face – peering up at her from the ground with one hand shielding her eyes. Now the bounce of the ladder with each step became much less pronounced. Finally, Caitlin's feet met flat concrete. Breeze from an enormous ventilation fan at the rear of the building flung her hair around as though she were still high up in the air.

"You made a meal of that," Kit said scornfully. "I thought we were identical."

Caitlin bent double to try and regain her breath. There was a fundamental difference between the two of them, of course. Kit had nothing to lose.

"Still, what you did in there was pretty great," Kit continued. "Putting out the fire. You made me feel like an utter shit for being ready to abandon them."

"Girls!" a voice hissed.

Caitlin jerked her head up, expecting to see Dr Scaife or one of the nurses. Instead, she recognised the thick coat and hunting cap of her visitor from yesterday, Dodie.

"There's no time for hanging around," Dodie said. "Hop in, would you?" She pointed at a car parked at the corner of the building, a blue Morris Minor with three white daisies painted on its rounded boot.

Caitlin had so many questions she didn't know where to begin. So, instead, she did as she was told.

Kit blocked her from getting into the passenger seat. "Not dressed like that, you don't."

"But I'll still be visible anyway. Oh. You don't mean the back seat, do you?"

Dodie had already clicked open the boot. It appeared barely large enough to hold a suitcase. As she clambered in, Caitlin studied the woman's face, hoping to see something there that proved that she was trustworthy. But Dodie was looking elsewhere.

"We must get going," she whispered. Her hand clutched the rim of the car boot. "They'll figure it out soon enough."

Caitlin's view of the sky narrowed to a line, then was eclipsed entirely. She tried to stretch out her limbs to test the available space. It wasn't much at all. Her spine was awkwardly curled and something was jabbing into her shoulder blades. But that wasn't the worst of it. She couldn't remember ever being somewhere so profoundly dark. She realised that she was as much at other people's mercy, trapped in here, as she had been in her locked cell.

Two dull thuds signalled that Dodie and Kit had taken their seats. An engine rumble made the walls of Caitlin's tiny prison buzz against her shoulders and her tucked-up knees. When the car began to move, the judder made her bite her tongue. She pressed her elbows out against the walls to brace herself.

After less than a minute, the car slowed to a halt. Caitlin heard a faint squeak and guessed that Dodie was winding down the window. She held her breath. She couldn't make out what she said, but Dodie's muffled voice rose and fell melodically, sounding unconcerned. She must be putting on a show, acting the doddery old woman for the benefit of whoever was guarding the gate to the January complex. Caitlin tried to imagine what she might be saying. *Good grief, that alarm was loud! I do hope everybody in there is safe. I must dash – the hanging baskets need watering.*

The car spasmed and began to move. Caitlin counted to five before allowing herself to breathe again. Her body rocked violently from side to side: the car was accelerating. She thought about thumping on the backs of the car seats – had they forgotten she was in here, getting bashed around? But she didn't know either of these people, not really. Her instinct was to bide her time.

Soon, she heard muffled voices again. Kit and Dodie's conversation began in low tones but became more animated. She couldn't hear their words. Dodie's voice was slow and sounded tired, and Kit's often rose to a high, emphatic note. Was that what Caitlin herself sounded like, when she was emotional? The fact that Kit sounded upset robbed her of a little more of her dwindling confidence.

Her experience during the journey was reduced to patterns – the regular rocking of her right thigh against the floor of the boot, the musical stop-start of Kit's voice, the pauses in conversation during which time Caitlin tried to guess which of them would speak next. She lost all sense of time and had no idea how far they might have travelled. She was too alert and afraid to succumb to sleep, but in the blackness she felt as though she were floating in space.

She barely registered that the car had stopped. When the boot was thrown open she yelped in alarm.

Dodie held out a mass of cloth. The gesture reminded Caitlin of the cape she offered to Kit on the night of the shedding.

"Kit's already inside," Dodie said. "Quick, put this on, and out you get. We don't want anybody clocking the two of you appearing in quick succession. The neighbourhood's full of curtain-twitchers."

Now Caitlin filled the tiny boot entirely, like dough risen in a too-small oven. With difficulty, and with her elbows knocking painfully on the walls of the boot, Caitlin struggled free and shrugged on the thick duffel coat. Dodie pulled the hood over her head.

The car was parked half on and half off the pavement of a residential cul-de-sac ringed by a dozen semi-detached houses. Their identical keystoned driveways appeared like the supporting strands of a spiderweb, with the single tree on a tiny roundabout at its centre. Caitlin saw no evidence of curtains twitching, but in the beige depths of each house she imagined neighbours watching with curiosity.

Gently, Dodie spun her around. The house before which the car was parked was similar to all of the others, though Caitlin guessed it may have been a little older. The only clear difference was that this house was double the size of the others and detached.

"No dallying, now," Dodie said. "In you go. Your Skin is waiting."

Caitlin walked ahead of Dodie. The fur-lined coat hood obscured everything but the door to the house. She pushed at it. It was unlocked.

Inside, the soft interior lighting made her feel instantly warmer. She recognised the flower-patterned wallpaper as that which hung in the rarely-used second lounge in Ivy Cottage.

"Second door on the left," Dodie said.

Caitlin glanced inside the first door as she passed it. The sofas were covered with plastic sheeting. A side table held a single lace doily. She remembered learning about Victorian homes and the convention of reserving the front room for use on Sundays and on special occasions, despite the small size of the houses. It occurred to her that this would be the only downstairs room visible from the street outside.

The next door opened before Caitlin reached it. Kit smiled and stood aside to let her enter.

"Welcome to our home," Dodie said. She was standing in the centre of the large room.

Instantly, Caitlin spun around. Dodie – *a* Dodie – was still behind her in the doorway.

"What?" Caitlin said. She couldn't think how to articulate any other question.

"Welcome," the Dodie in the doorway said.

"Welcome," Dodie said again, her voice now coming from elsewhere.

"Welcome."

Prickles of light appeared at the corners of Caitlin's vision. She felt suddenly hot and faint. She pulled down the hood of the duffel coat.

More people – eight of them in all – lined the edges of the room. In her dizzy state, they reminded Caitlin of the houses of the cul-de-sac, arranged to watch each other.

But instead they were all watching Caitlin.

They were all Dodie.

# THIRTEEN

"But I visited just the other day," Gerry said.

"Doesn't matter," the security guard replied, cosy and warm within his tiny cabin beside the front gate of the January complex. "I'm not letting you in and that's the end of it."

Gerry gripped the steering wheel. Would her car survive if she tried to bash through the red-and-white striped barrier? It would wipe the smug look off the guard's face, at least.

"Let me speak to Doctor Scaife," she said. "I can square things with her. We got off on the wrong foot, that's all. I'm sure she didn't intend to blacklist me."

If only she hadn't blustered her way into the care home, broadcasting her real intentions, she might have stood a chance of getting in there today. If Caitlin Hext wasn't at home, she must surely be inside visiting her Snakeskin. From what Ian had told her, Caitlin had spent much of her time here recently.

A flurry of movement in the distance caught her eye. The car park was vast and the care home entrance was partially hidden behind a row of palm trees, but she could still make out the people rushing in and out of the glass-walled lobby. Another group wearing white staff uniforms stood in a huddle to one side. She wound down the car window fully and stuck out her head. Now she could hear a faint sound. It rose and fell as the breeze changed direction. A siren.

"This pig-headedness of yours isn't about Doctor Scaife, is it?"

The guard's mouth tightened. It might have been unconscious agreement, or confusion.

Gerry peered at the care home again. Until now she had taken the grey mass in the sky behind the building to be a low cloud. "Is that smoke? Has there been a fire?"

The guard unfolded an edition of *Folk*. With exaggerated concentration, he began to read.

It was clear she wasn't going to get any more information out of him. She revved her engine as a childish protest, then backed up between the concrete pillars, weaving as she tried to navigate in reverse. Finally, she swung the car backwards around the corner and pulled up at the edge of the country road.

She had no idea what to do next. So much for going back to the source. She'd been travelling for days and had got nowhere.

She thought of the shepherd's hut on the mountainside at Ilam. Artists' impressions always depicted the Fall as a widespread shower of meteors – but perhaps that hadn't been the case. They had certainly affected the Ilam villagers, of course, that much was beyond doubt. But none of the history books had mentioned fragments of the meteors actually reaching the earth. Historians agreed that they had broken far up in the atmosphere, and that it was their dispersal that ensured that so many people in the valley were granted the inexplicable gifts of sheddings and Snakeskins. But those indentations on the crest of rock beside the shepherd's hut were a contradiction. And if one or more of the meteors had actually landed up on the mountainside above the village, what did that mean for the occupants of the shepherd's hut? Whatever the answer was, Caitlin was its embodiment – the last member of the Hext family line.

Gerry returned to reality with a start.

A face appeared in the bushes at the roadside. It took her a moment to recognise him as Ayo, the nurse she had spoken to at the January reception desk.

She leapt from the car. "What the hell are you doing?" she hissed.

"Will you help me?" he said in a strained voice.

"Of course. Come out of there."

As he emerged, Gerry saw that he was injured. His left eye was swollen shut, and when she reached out to support him he shook his head vigorously and clutched at his ribs.

"Who did this?"

"A colleague of mine started the job, but then a couple of gents in black suits finished up. Friendly types, but a bit clumsy. One of them hit me with a chair, the daft thing."

"Seriously? Were they GBP?"

Ayo shrugged.

302

She guided him carefully to the passenger seat. "For what?"

"I picked a side, I guess. And it wasn't theirs."

"Whose side did you pick?"

He eyed her with suspicion as he eased himself into the seat. "I appreciate the help. But how do I know I can trust you?"

Gerry dashed around and hopped into the driver's seat. "I can save you the trouble. This is about Caitlin Hext, isn't it? I came here to help her."

His look of immense relief was followed by a wince of pain. "Her Skin. Yes. I wanted to help her too. She's gone."

"She ashed? Turned to dust?"

"No. *Gone* gone. Got away. The senior staff are furious, and the Party emissaries even more so. And not just furious. Panicked. Terrified."

"And do you know where the Skin might have gone?"

After a pause, he nodded.

Gerry jammed her foot down. She flicked two fingers in the direction of the security guard as she accelerated away.

✳

Russell opened his eyes then shut them again, fast. The sting of daylight was unbearable.

He focussed on how his body felt. His arms and legs were bare and covered with a soft sheet. As he moved his head a pillow remoulded to accommodate him, tickling his cheeks. The back of his skull throbbed dreadfully at the point—

—where he had been hit.

He sat up sharply.

Blackness pressed in from the corners of his vision. He sank into the bulky pillows. He squeezed his eyes tight, breathed deeply and prayed not to be sick.

Tentatively, he opened his eyes. He bunched the covers in his fists and waited for the nausea to pass. He felt his pupils contracting against the golden glow from the curtains.

The room was plain but decorated tastefully in shades of peach and white. A hotel?

On a chest of drawers beyond the foot of the bed stood an ugly statue. The carved wooden figure was squat, with a bulbous head and large concave eyes like two dishes sunk into its face.

Another odd aspect of the room took him a while to register. Hotels always had the artificial smell of cleaning products and the chemical sweetness of perfume to mask them. Here, the scents of bread and coffee mixed with the smell of people, a particular mix of bath products, deodorant and sweat. It was oddly calming.

Familiar, too.

He recognised this decor. It was the same as in another room that surely must be within the same house. A similarly plain room containing only a bed, side table, a chest of drawers and a wardrobe hiding a cast-iron safe.

This was Ellis Blackwood's house.

Which made sense, of course, because—

Pain bloomed at the back of his head, then enveloped him, smothering like a tight bandage.

"Jesus fuck!" he bellowed.

The door opened soundlessly. He tried to blink away the

tears that had formed in his eyes.

"Spencer," he moaned. "Don't."

He flinched as something cool touched his forehead. A hand. Small. The fingers of another hand danced around his jawline and his neck.

"Don't," Russell said again.

"I won't," a voice replied. "Yikes. There's a bump right here. It's a whopper."

Russell blinked rapidly, desperate to clear his vision.

That voice.

He wiped at his eyes to clear the tears. A face hung over him. Freckles and dark, wild hair.

It didn't make sense.

"Nell?" he managed to croak.

"It's all right. Don't make any sudden moves. I mean, you've hurt your head. I'm not trying to threaten you."

Her fingers walked carefully along his skull. His teeth clenched, though he noticed that the stroke of her fingertips actually lessened the discomfort.

Why was Nell covering for Spencer? Did she know what he was capable of?

"I'm afraid for your safety," he said. "Is he here?"

"No. Don't worry." Her face showed only kind concern. Where her cheeks creased, the bands of freckles touched.

"Don't worry?" he repeated. "You've seen what he did to me. Why are you—" He winced again, more from confusion than pain. There were all sorts of ways he could complete the question: —*defending him?* —*here?* —*so absurdly wonderful?*

"I don't love him, you know," Nell said.

"Your own son?"

Nell frowned, then clapped a hand to her forehead. "I was talking about Ellis."

Of all the implications that occurred to Russell at that instant, the foremost was, *Whatever trouble she's in, she's free of her husband.* But not far behind this was, *I've got every single thing wrong, somehow.*

He drew himself deeper into the nest of pillows in order to look Nell over. Her slight frame, her rounded shoulders. He tried to recall her body language as she walked.

"You," he whispered. "It was you."

Nell smirked.

"It was you that I met you in the underground car park. I noticed you were small."

"Hey!" Nell exclaimed. She straightened. "I'm a tough customer, I'll have you know. Sculpting's physical work. Here, feel this bicep." She leant forwards with her arm outstretched.

Russell touched it. It was true – beneath the skin he could feel a tight knot of muscle. He tried to suppress a shudder of delight. As a distraction, he groaned and pulled his hand away to rub at his neck even though, suddenly, it didn't hurt a bit.

"You have to tell me what's going on," he said.

Nell chewed her cheek.

"Nell," Russell said. He reached out again but missed another chance for contact when she folded her arms. "All this time. You could have just spoken to me."

"If it had been up to me, perhaps I would have."

Russell sighed. "So I was right. You and Spencer are in this together."

Nell hopped off the bed. "Can you walk?"

"It hurts a bit."

"I'm sorry, all right? I didn't know what else to do."

He gaped at her. "It was you? You hit me?"

"I couldn't have you blurting out what you knew – or what you thought you knew – in public. There was a *Guinness Book of Records* in the car, wrapped up for Spencer's birthday. It's what I had to hand. It's kind of hefty. Seriously, though. Can you walk?"

Russell shuffled to the edge of the bed. "Probably. Let's go and chat to Spencer, then. Enough of the secrecy."

Nell looked as though she might say something, but then she only smiled. She took his hand. "This way."

The house was still and silent. Russell noted the twin guilty pleasures of being barefoot in Nell's home and of her warm hand in his. Her skin was smooth. Perhaps all that woodworking had rubbed away at it, eradicating her fingerprints.

He wondered again how he ought to treat Spencer. Despite everything, he was an insecure teenager. Russell ought to let the boy speak before accusing him, otherwise he might clam up.

Nell turned right at the foot of the stairs. Russell glanced into the kitchen to see Spencer bent over a collection of circuit boards arranged on the farmhouse table. The boy raised his head and gave a wistful smile, then frowned again at his computer project.

To his surprise, Nell led Russell away, past the dark doorway of Ellis's study and towards the front door.

Russell glanced down at himself. He didn't recognise the

shorts and T-shirt he was wearing – they must belong to Ellis. He shuddered at the thought of his boss's body in these same clothes. The unpleasant idea occurred to him that the outfit was a shed skin that Russell had wriggled his way into.

"I can't go outside like this," he said.

Nell didn't turn. "You won't need to."

She started along the narrow servants' passageway, her slim arm trailing behind her to pull Russell along. She tapped on the keypad on the wall. Five beeps and the metal door swung open.

Russell craned his neck to see over Nell's shoulder. He had been right in his earlier deduction – a flight of steps led down from the small store cupboard.

Nell squeezed his hand. He squeezed back. Any further questions were pointless. Despite all this mystery, he trusted her.

The steps were carpeted. The staircase ended at another heavy door that took all of Nell's weight to push open. Above the door was a handwritten sign that read, *Welcome to Tartarus*.

Inside, wall-mounted lamps marked the perimeter of a large lounge dotted with leather sofas, tables and chairs. The low ceiling gave the room the atmosphere of a gentleman's club or a den. The man-cave effect was heightened by the presence of five men assembled in a horseshoe shape around the entrance.

"Guys," Nell said. Her tone was both mocking and scolding. "You could have gone easy on him and shown up one at a time."

She stepped aside.

One of the men sniggered. Russell blinked in the dim light.

Moving as one, each of the men held out his right hand.

Russell stared at the collection of podgy hands. Then his gaze travelled slowly upwards, to the five Ellis Blackwoods standing in a semicircle around him.

*

Caitlin allowed herself to be guided by Kit towards an armchair in the bay window. White, veil-like curtains obscured the view. She sat down heavily. Dodie – the Dodie who had brought her here – perched on a stool to remove her shoes. She had already taken off her tweed coat and hat. If Caitlin looked away for too long, she might easily lose track of which person had rescued her from the care home.

The other women took their seats. Caitlin realised that the Dodies weren't identical. For a start, they all wore different outfits. The woman to her immediate left wore a dark trouser-suit; her neighbour a long plaid skirt and white blouse. Another wore tatty denim overalls spattered with paint, and one wore a pale green dressing gown, beneath which Caitlin could see cotton pyjamas.

At first Caitlin thought their physical differences might be an effect of their having arranged their hair in different styles. But no, the faces weren't identical, either. She turned to the Dodie she knew, studying her features as a method of calibration. A Dodie to her right had a face that appeared far more lined. The crow's feet at the corners of her eyes met the vertical creases either side of her mouth. In contrast, the Dodie closest to Caitlin had a face that was relatively smooth. Her cheeks shone like polished marble.

There was one thing they all had in common, though. All of the women were smiling.

＊

Russell's knees buckled. Nell darted forwards to hold his arm.

"I don't understand," he said. He looked around at the pack of Ellis Blackwoods, trying to determine which one was his boss. "Sir."

One of the Skins stepped forwards and took Russell by both shoulders. Russell batted him away weakly but the man renewed his grip. Reeling from claustrophobia, Russell managed to push him away, but then fell to the floor on his backside. His palms hit the lino with twin slaps.

"It's okay, Russell," Nell said quietly.

He gazed up at her, then at the semicircle of Ellis Blackwoods. All of their faces held the same expression – concern, with a hint of amusement.

"It's not okay," he murmured. "It's not bloody okay." What did it all mean? Nell, working with Ellis, in order to spy on Ellis... None of it made sense.

"He isn't here," Nell said.

It took Russell a moment to realise who she was talking about. "Ellis. My boss."

She nodded.

All of the men were dressed identically in black pinstripe

trousers and white shirts. The top button of each of their shirts was undone.

"None of you are the originator?" Russell said. "You're all Snakeskins?"

"And proud of it," one of the Skins replied. His voice sounded a little different to the Ellis that Russell knew. Stronger.

"Do take a seat," another of the Skins said, gesturing at one of the black leather armchairs.

"No. Thanks all the same. I prefer to stand."

One Skin turned to his neighbour. "He prefers to keep near to the exit, more like."

The other man snorted with laughter.

*

Kit knelt beside Caitlin's armchair. "Now would be a good time to say something, I reckon," she whispered.

Caitlin took a breath. Some of the Dodies leant forwards expectantly.

"Hi," she said. She glanced at the Dodie who had driven her here. "Thank you for getting me out of there."

All of the women spoke in sync. "It's a pleasure."

The Dodie wearing the plaid skirt laughed at Caitlin's startled response. "All right girls, knock it off."

At this, all of the women appeared to relax. They fidgeted, played with their sleeves, chewed their nails. Caitlin immediately felt calmer.

"You're hiding," she said. "But why here and not somewhere more remote?"

"In this cul-de-sac, you mean? It does feel rather that we're being watched by our neighbours, doesn't it?" The plaid-skirt Dodie smiled. "There's method in our madness. We chose this place precisely because it means we can never afford to lower our guards. If we can manage to avoid alerting our neighbours, we can rest easier in the hope that our subterfuge is convincing enough to fool anybody else who might pry into our affairs."

"How long have you been hiding here?"

The plaid-skirt Dodie replied. "Sixteen years."

The Dodie in the trouser-suit said, "Twenty-three years."

Someone at the other side of the room said, "Forty-four years."

Plaid-skirt snorted. "What nonsense. We only bought this place twenty-five years ago."

"That's splitting hairs." The Dodie who spoke wore a lilac dress of a style that Caitlin had only ever seen in old Pinewood or Elstree films. She was one of the few women wearing lipstick and would have been at home at a cocktail party. "What the girl wants to know is how old we are. Am I correct?"

Caitlin wilted under her gaze. "I don't know. Yes, probably."

"Well," cocktail-party Dodie continued, "let me give you the broad-brush overview, then." She stood up and moved to the centre of the circle. She pointed at each of the women in turn. The motion made her dress flare out at the knees, as though she were dancing. "Two years old. Nine years old. Sixteen. Twenty-three. Thirty – you met her today, of course.

Thirty-seven. And I'm forty-four, as I say. Fifty-one." Then she turned to the Dodie with the polished-marble cheeks. "Sixty-seven."

"You're the originator?" Caitlin said, addressing the final woman. "The human?"

The woman's marble cheeks turned pink. "That's a loaded term. Furthermore, we don't care to make any distinction. But yes."

*

"You have to explain what's happening," Russell said. He addressed Nell. The shifting collection of Ellis Blackwoods was beginning to make him feel queasy.

Nell laughed. The sound eased Russell's mind a little.

"Of course," she said. "You think I'm going to bring you down here to see the singular occupants of this room – handsome though they are – and then send you away again without an explanation? Do you really think I'm that kind of a tease?"

Russell felt his cheeks glow. He shook his head.

"So. Where would you like us to start?"

Russell struggled to his feet, then wished he'd stayed on the floor. Suddenly, all he wanted was to go back to sleep. "I've been speaking to one of you, all this time? The hooded stranger. Ixion. It wasn't you, Nell, was it?"

She smiled. "Today, it was. I was very much the understudy, a part forced upon me by recent developments. Ellis – my husband – ramped up the house security. There are cameras and sensors everywhere. I think you might have

313

been involved in installing them? Thanks a bunch, Russell."

A thought struck Russell. He looked down at the Skins' feet. A couple of them noticed and lifted their trouser legs to reveal thick black bands around their ankles. Blue lights flashed – the same blue lights Russell had noticed on more than one of the occasions they had met in secret.

"Radio-frequency tags, steel-reinforced and permanently attached," one of the Skins explained. "You can trust the Party to import technology in areas that suit them. One step outside our allocated zone and Ellis knows about it instantly."

Of course. That would explain why they could only meet in certain locations. If their rendezvous points were plotted on a map, Russell expected they would describe a circle around the Blackwood house.

From her pocket, Nell retrieved a small, black object. She raised it to her mouth and spoke into it. "I'm not sure my performance was a patch on the original." Her voice came through the mouthpiece at a lower pitch, crackling a little.

One of the Skins raised his hand. "You spoke to me."

Another did too. "And me."

"Me too."

"And me, but only on the phone."

The final Skin said, "I didn't get my turn yet."

Russell remembered his first encounter with Ixion – his sense that the man's movements were familiar. It seemed absurd now, that he'd come directly from the real Ellis Blackwood's office to meet his facsimile, and yet he still hadn't managed to pin down the reason for the familiarity.

He said in a weak voice, "So Spencer wasn't involved at all? He isn't involved?"

"No, thank goodness," Nell said. "He knows about these handsome fellas, of course, but he doesn't know a thing about all this other hoo-hah, the angel."

"But nobody else knows about this underground lair? All of you—" Russell pointed at the Skins "—you live here, presumably?"

"We keep a low profile," the Skin closest to him said.

Russell glared at him. "I still don't understand. What are you even doing here? Skins are supposed to turn to dust. Aren't they?"

"Some do."

Another Skin added, "But some don't."

Russell felt anger suddenly bubble up. "And that's it? You consider that a full and frank explanation?"

"In a moment, I suspect you'll feel two things in quick succession."

Instinctively, Russell backed away. "Are you going to hit me? Is that the joke? I'm going to feel your fist in my face, then the floor?"

"No, Russell. I'm going to tell you the truth about the people in power."

Russell gazed at the man's face, so familiar and yet so strange. He had never seen his boss look this determined.

\*

It seemed wrong that the youngest-looking Dodie should actually be the oldest, but it made perfect sense. If one of the Skins was only two years old, then that meant that this Dodie had shed only two years ago. Her rejuvenated skin was the happy side-product of shedding.

"But you all look different. I mean, if the rest of you are Snakeskins, then why—"

It was Kit who answered. Caitlin flinched, having almost forgotten that her own Skin was kneeling beside her chair. Seeing the top of her head produced a slight sense of vertigo when Caitlin realised she might as well be looking at the top of her *own* head. "There's nothing odd about that," Kit said. "I've been around less than a week, and we're already different enough. Can you imagine how much we'd grow apart from each other if we spent our whole time doing different things? You gadding about outside in the sunshine, me stuck inside with my nose in a book? Or whatever."

Cocktail-party Dodie turned to face her. "True enough, but that's only half of it. Each of us begins life as a snapshot of our dear host, at the precise moment she sheds." Her voice lowered to a conspiratorial whisper. "I'm not saying she lets herself go, exactly, but you should see her at the tail-end of a seven-year stint. Each time she's a little more ragged around the edges than the time before."

"I heard that!" the marble-cheeked Dodie exclaimed. Caitlin was relieved to see her eyes twinkling. She was obviously used to this kind of teasing. "Please don't get the wrong impression about us, my dear. We're very much a happy family. Unless I'm wrong about that, girls?"

Once again, the Dodies all spoke together, though this time they were all saying different things. The room was filled with a cacophony of voices, all with the same vocal patterns. Caitlin couldn't make out a word.

The marble-cheeked Dodie continued, "We've found an acceptable arrangement. Only one of us can leave the house at a time, of course, and I pride myself in taking only as much leave as anybody else. But being stuck in the house doesn't mean the rest of us must be idle. We each have our specialisms – though I suppose if you were unkind, you might call them hobbies – and our minds are similar enough that we're all able to pitch in when necessary. We have devoted ourselves to the visual arts, the study of history, writing. We have a cookery column in a national magazine. One benefit of having multiple versions of oneself is that sleep doesn't tend to get in the way. Once a project begins, there's no need for a single moment of let-up before it is completed. Also, having all of us involved tends to temper egos."

Caitlin smiled and nodded, though she wasn't paying full attention. While the originator had been speaking, she had finally honed in on the most important question.

"But," she began, hesitantly, "you're all *here*. All the Skins that you ever shed…"

Several of the Dodies gave encouraging smiles.

"Why didn't you all evaporate? Turn to dust?"

Slowly, cocktail-party Dodie took her seat again. Without prompting, the marble-cheeked Dodie took her place in the centre of the circle.

"My dear girl," she said. Her voice was steady and slow, but tinged with sadness. "That is very much the question."

＊

"Perhaps you've reached the conclusion already. But to be clear, Russell..." The Skin took a deep breath. "A great number of the people who hold a great deal of the power in this country are Charmers. That, you knew. A great number of those Charmers have retained all of the Skins produced during their lifetime. That fact may be a surprise. Working together, Charmer originators and their Skins are able to operate far more effectively than an ordinary person could possibly function... though one could argue that many of them squander that opportunity by devoting themselves to maintaining power rather than doing anything truly useful. When I think about all the scientific developments that ought to be made possible due to increased focus and accumulated expertise, the medical breakthroughs, all the novels that ought to have been written..." He coughed and shook his head sadly. "It's a matter of sleep, predominantly. By working in shifts, Charmers and Skins are able to offer a round-the-clock service, so to speak."

Russell thought he might topple over again. "But... but not you. Not Ellis Blackwood and his Skins."

"That's right, Russell. We have refused. We are conscientious objectors. We refuse to support Ellis's agenda – in his government role and otherwise. If we had the capacity to play-act at being faithful Snakeskins, pretending to support him, undermining his progress every day whilst sitting behind his desk... It would have been better for everybody. But we are no actors, and the truth is that from the earliest moments of our respective existences Ellis has been aware that each of us loathes him. And so we are locked away down here."

Between the lounge area and a small galley kitchen was a bookcase so full that books had been squeezed in sideways, some protruding precariously from the stack. On the edge of one sofa Russell saw a neatly folded pile of woollen blankets. This basement apartment was a den all right, but now he realised that it also functioned as a prison.

"But it's so dark down here," he said, without meaning to say the thought out loud.

One of the Skins placed a hand on his arm. Russell stared at the hand. He couldn't remember Ellis ever having made physical contact with him. "We get outside. One by one, when he's not here. Even with the added security and without ID cards of our own – which Charmers in power would ordinarily arrange for their Skins – we can get out to the grounds. But our physical imprisonment is the lesser part of the punishment anyway. The lack of access to resources is far worse. Our potential is being wasted every day."

"Does he know? Do you even have any dealings with him? Your originator?"

"There are some unspoken rules. We don't venture up into the house when he's around. He leaves us be. He knows that we could cause him more bother if we were disgruntled, and he's too cowardly to do away with us. So he attempts to hide the fact that he's operating alone."

In the conversations Russell had overheard between Ellis and Angela McKinney, Ellis had always been intent on hiding his exhaustion. It made sense now. Being tired showed that he wasn't working in tandem with his Snakeskins – that he was one man, not many, and that his Charmer status gave him no benefits or added stamina. It showed that he was weak.

"While the cat's away," Russell murmured.

"Well. Except we don't do an awful lot of playing. A potter in the garden, get ourselves a bit of vitamin D, pop in at the lean-to to see how Nell's wonderful projects are getting on. That sort of thing."

Russell's eyes flicked to Nell. He understood her poor relationship with her husband now, but this new revelation raised all sorts of other questions.

Nell raised her eyebrows in response. "I know what you're thinking. You're thinking, 'This is none of my business.' But it is now. You're part of this. I hope you're okay with that."

Russell wanted to tell her that, yes, it was okay, that no matter the peculiarity of the situation, he would be willing to follow her anywhere. Instead, he replied, "I suppose."

He was still unsure which of the Skins to address. "Why do you all wear the same clothes as Ellis, if you never take his place at work?"

A couple of the Skins grinned.

"We wouldn't normally," one of them said. "Nell borrowed them from upstairs. It was just for your benefit, to make more of an impact. We couldn't resist."

Nell chuckled. "Christopher's got a wicked sense of humour."

"Christopher?"

She indicated the Skin who had spoken. "Sorry. How rude of me." She pointed at each of the Skins in turn. "Jules, Peter,

Lewis, Christopher and Clive."

"To be clear," Clive said, "we don't consider ourselves to be Ellis Blackwood. None of us are him and he's not one of us."

"He's a jumped-up little prick," the leftmost Skin – Jules – said.

Russell cleared his throat. "Do you know what? I think I will have that sit down, after all."

He shuffled over to the black sofas, his sense of balance still a little off. Nell and the Skins followed. After a small amount of disagreement about positions, everyone found a seat.

"All this is fascinating," Russell said. "But if I'm really part of this, you need to explain. Not about your living arrangements, not about whether Ellis Blackwood is a jumped-up little prick—" he flushed, feeling self-conscious about repeating the words to Ellis's own duplicated face "— but about the cloak-and-dagger stuff. This thing that Ellis and the government have been so intent on hiding."

Several of the Skins exchanged looks. Now that they had changed positions, Russell had no hope of using their given names.

"If we knew," one of them said, "we wouldn't have had to resort to using you to supply information as we did."

"So all that subterfuge, and you're still no closer to the truth?"

"No. We still have no idea. But we know Ellis well, as you can imagine. What's clear is that whatever he's involved in is dangerous. And it's coming to a head. Ellis has been energised in recent days. We're convinced that something is due to happen soon. We must act quickly."

Russell felt a stab of frustration. "Act quickly to do what? This whole thing is ridiculous. The conspiracy theory seemed wild before, but now…" He gestured at them all, unsure how to finish his point.

Nell spoke up. "Now that you understand the complexity of Ellis's private life, you're wondering whether this may be simply our vendetta against him."

Russell sighed. "I don't know, Nell. You can't blame me for considering it. Ellis is in the awkward position of having to hide the fact that he has a small army of Skins hidden away, refusing to cooperate." He thought of Ellis's clumsiness, his exhausted absentmindedness. "Isn't it possible that he's just a government lackey? He seems so… ordinary." He glanced at the Skins, unsure whether this comment was an insult to them.

But it was Nell who appeared offended. Her back arched. "He's far from it, Russell, I promise you that. When you learn what he's really capable of, you'll understand why we're certain we must stop whatever he's doing. You've heard of the January care home, where Skins are taken after their sheddings if they fail to ash immediately?"

Russell nodded. He didn't relish where this explanation might be leading.

"And now you know that many senior Party officials retained their Skins – that they *didn't* ash. What does that imply to you?"

Russell swallowed noisily. "That lots of Snakeskins wouldn't turn to dust, if they were left to their own devices."

"So…"

"So Charmers within the government don't want the public to know that Skins can live on. And…" He closed his eyes, trying to follow the logic. "And the Skins of less influential Charmers are being locked up, in the care homes."

"At first, yes. In a place called Ilam Hall, at the location of the Fall. Yes, they were locked up there, out of sight, while the government tried to come to terms with the implications – in both practical and societal terms – of waves of additional sheddings every seven years. But that all changed when January was constructed, a generation ago."

"They're not simply being hidden away in the January care home?"

Nell raised an eyebrow. He understood the meaning of her expression: *No. Try again.*

"Oh no," he whispered.

"Yes."

"The care home isn't for locking Skins up. It's for—"

"Yes."

"—killing them."

Dizziness engulfed him. The faces of Ellis Blackwood spun before his eyes.

"No," he managed to say. "I won't believe it. Nobody could— What proof do you have? From all you've said about your relationship with Ellis, I can't believe you'd even be allowed to come close enough to know whether this is true."

Nell's voice softened. "Russell. I promise you that I know."

"How?" He didn't want to know, not really, but there was nothing else to say.

"Ellis is ashamed at his lack of control over his Skins, but he daren't ship them off to January. He's terrified of his colleagues finding out if he ever registered his Skins in the system. A GBP Charmer without an attendant team of Skins would be seen as weak, a failure. He could dispose of them himself, of course, but he's far too squeamish for that. But you haven't asked about me yet, Russell. You know I'm a Charmer too."

It was true. Faced with the collection of Ellis's Skins, he hadn't thought to wonder about Nell's.

"Your Skins aren't here," he said. "Oh God. And they didn't turn to dust either, did they?"

"It was the project that made Ellis's name in government circles," Nell replied. "Streamlining, they called it. Greater efficiency in the care home, with all that that entailed." Tears welled at the corners of her eyes.

Russell experienced an overwhelming desire to embrace her, but found that he couldn't raise himself from his chair. Weakly, he said, "He killed your Skins."

"He conducted the process personally," Nell said. Her voice sounded as if it was coming from very far away. "And he enjoyed it."

# FOURTEEN

Gerry glanced sideways at Ayo in the passenger seat. The muscles in his jaw were working as he stared out through the windscreen. Both of his hands were pressed on the dashboard. She was grateful that his swollen left eye was out of sight.

"Could you watch the road?" Ayo said quietly.

Gerry wrenched the steering wheel to avoid careering into the gulley at one side of the country lane. "Sorry. I'm not used to having passengers." She slowed the car and stole only quick glances at him. Ayo's arms relaxed a little, no longer bracing against the lurches of the car.

"Where are we even going?" she said.

He retrieved the map from the door pocket. "A residential area. Abingdon, south of the town centre."

"And you're certain that's where Caitlin Hext's Skin was taken?"

"As certain as I can be. The house belongs to Dodie Hope. We didn't talk at length – just long enough to agree that we were both concerned, and for me to hand over my ID card, which is preloaded with access to all the residential cells. It was the right call. Security would have removed my access privileges less than ten minutes later, once I intervened in Scaife's office." He twisted to watch the traffic behind them.

Gerry frowned. "You haven't actually told me what you were intervening in."

"No, I haven't."

"So?"

"What's your interest in all this? Please be honest."

Gerry found it difficult to answer the question. It seemed ridiculous that he might even ask it. "I want to know the truth."

Ayo grunted in response. "Perhaps we shouldn't be going to Dodie Hope's house. I'm not at all sure it's what she would want. I only wish we could have spoken more freely, before."

He had refused to say Dodie's address out loud, insisting on reading the map and providing directions instead. If he changed his mind now, Gerry would have no clue where to go.

"You helped a Snakeskin escape from a government-sponsored care home," she said softly. "You broke the law, you no longer have an ID card, and you *will* be tracked down."

"She's not just a Snakeskin, she's a person. She's called Kit. And I can look after myself."

"Let me finish. You helped Kit escape and now you don't know whether or not she's safe. You have a duty of care, Ayo. You need to know that she's okay."

The silence that followed was punctuated only by the click of indicators and the hiss of passing cars.

"And you need to know, too."

"I'm your ride. But yes. I need to know, too."

He nodded slowly. "Okay."

"So tell me. What's going on behind closed doors at January?"

"At first I only had suspicions. Miss Chafik – Gerry. You have to believe me. I was only a nurse. I provided care. What I did was far from enough, but my interest was in making the Skins' remaining days as comfortable as they could be. But I wasn't doing anything *to* them."

Gerry gripped the wheel. "And who was?"

"Scaife. Senior staff. They were classed as nurses, same as me, but the difference had always been clear. Different meetings, different treatment by the management, different pay. You can imagine that was a sore point for most of us low-levels. Until we started to suspect. People didn't ask so many questions after that. I didn't either."

His long fingers rubbed the bridge of his nose. "They were taken at night," he continued, speaking more slowly. "For years, that was as much as I knew. The Skins knew nothing about it, either. I was able to speak to them individually in the course of my duties, and it was clear they were oblivious. But in journalistic terms, I'm a bad source, Gerry. I still don't know what was done."

"But what do you suspect?"

"Tests. I heard the word used by the senior nurses. Night after night. I think that the Skins are being studied. I think that's partly what January is for."

It began to rain. Gerry flicked on the wipers. "Ayo,

Snakeskins are the most amazing phenomena. Isn't it only natural... I mean, if that's all that was happening..."

"You have to remember that these tests were a secret. And the mood amongst senior staff became more desperate. Whenever Scaife took calls from GBP top brass, she came out of her office looking pale as anything."

"The Party ordered the tests." Gerry thought of Zemma Finch, begging her to return to *Folk*. Paying through the nose for a scoop about the workings of government.

Ayo shrugged. "Anyway. You misunderstand me. The nightly tests were only the first indication that something was wrong. If that aspect of the care home went unreported in official updates, I figured there might be more. I started looking out for clues."

*Tink-thunk. Tink-thunk.* Gerry watched the windscreen wipers. She stayed silent to give him time to find the right words.

"It seems obvious, with hindsight," Ayo said. "A building full of Skins, all waiting for the end. And none of us nurses ever witnessed them ash."

Gerry swerved the car and swore. "Never? What are you telling me?"

"I'm telling you what I know. I'm trying not to add anything that I'm not certain about. The Skins were taken away from their rooms, every night, for tests. And then, at different times, each of them was taken away at night, but didn't return. And that's why I interrupted what was about to happen in Scaife's office."

"They were murdered." She had meant it to be a

question, but it didn't sound or feel like one.

"Like I say. I'm telling you what I know, not the conclusion. Their rooms were empty in the morning, and we junior staff were informed that the Skin ashed in the night, of course. I never searched for traces of ash. Maybe, deep down, I wanted to believe Scaife and the others. I couldn't let myself believe that somebody might do what I thought they'd done, just to save money. But if I'm right, then I've got blood on my hands."

Gerry tried to disguise her breathlessness. "That's some story."

Ayo didn't reply. He appeared lost in his thoughts and gave only perfunctory instructions as they neared Abingdon. Gerry slowed the car to a crawl as they entered the cul-de-sac where Dodie Hope lived. She pulled up to the kerb and the two of them walked in silence towards the ring of semi-detached houses.

*

Caitlin thanked Dodie again as she took the offered carrier bag. Inside were packets of crisps, bottles of water and a clear plastic box crammed with sandwiches.

"You're certain you'll be all right?" Dodie said.

Caitlin turned to Kit. "What do you think? Will we be all right?"

"More than." Kit took Caitlin's arm and Caitlin barely shuddered at her touch.

Dodie pointed at the timetable that hung beneath the Radley station sign. "Change at Oxford, then take any train heading north. Manchester, Glasgow, wherever. The world's your oyster, as long as it's an oyster far away from here. It's for the best if you don't tell me where you're thinking of going."

Caitlin tried not to think through the implications of Dodie's words. Would anybody really threaten this old woman, just to get their hands on Kit? Of course, she understood that the escape would be an embarrassment to the January care home. But they treated Snakeskins with such disdain that it was difficult to imagine them mounting a search party.

She and Kit had been inside Dodie's house for only a couple of hours. As promised, Caitlin had been shown the studio and gallery upstairs. She had been overwhelmed by the sheer quantity of artworks Dodie and her Skins had completed together: paintings in a range of styles from pointillist landscapes to portraits in hard, black lines; enormous tureens and vases adorned with sculpted flowers; carved, hollow wooden balls that contained other balls in concentric puzzles; dioramas of dolls, driftwood and flotsam in wooden boxes fixed to the walls. She wondered if she might ever be nearly as productive, even if she had twice the number of Skins to work alongside her. Dodie's Skins gave no impression of feeling trapped. They seemed content living their peculiar lives.

Dodie – or rather, *one* of the Dodies – had given Caitlin a change of clothes to replace her blue smock. As they had left the house Caitlin had pulled the hood of her blue tracksuit top over her head. Kit had offered to take her turn in the boot of the car.

Dodie turned to leave.

"You won't wave us off?" Kit said.

"Best if you work on looking as normal as possible." She tapped her hunting hat. "Some might say I'm memorable. You girls may be as cute as buttons, but you'll pass as sisters as long as you avoid drawing attention. Good luck, girls." Her gaze settled on Kit. "Look after her, won't you?"

"I'm the originator," Caitlin said, frowning. "She's the Skin."

Dodie smiled. "I know."

She turned and strolled along the platform.

The lack of Dodie's presence made Caitlin feel instantly adrift. Having Kit beside her only made her feel more alone.

Kit took her hand. She still wore Janet Hext's ivy-patterned dress, although she had twice offered to switch and wear the tracksuit instead. Caitlin had refused, but she regretted it now.

"So," Kit said. "Do we need to figure out where we're going?"

Caitlin stared into Kit's eyes. Did her own shine so much?

"I think we both know where we're going."

*

When Ellis's Skins had talked about the necessity for sacrifice, Russell had assumed correctly that they were trying to talk him into something. But it was soon clear that his wouldn't be the only sacrifice. After explaining the nature of Russell's first duty, Nell had retreated to grip the hand of one of the Skins – Peter? Another of them, Clive, had stepped forwards to accompany Russell. It was Clive, not Russell, whose shoulders were patted and who received sympathetic looks from the other Skins and a teary blotch on his white shirt from Nell.

The door of the den closed behind them. Russell walked ahead and Clive plodded behind, ascending the stairs as slowly as somebody condemned to be hanged. As the Skin followed Russell through the outer door of the kitchen he shivered, even though the air outside wasn't cold. He padded onto the lawn and gazed up at the stars for several minutes. Russell shivered too.

Russell hesitated at the threshold of the lean-to workshop until Clive pushed him gently inside. They stood together before the charred-black tree sculpture. The sapling that Nell had revealed within the trunk looked like a tendon, taut and fragile. Bile rose in Russell's throat.

Clive stood beside the rack of hanging tools and waited in silence as Russell retrieved the saw.

"Why you?" Russell said.

Clive shrugged.

"There must be a reason." Russell realised that he was playing for time, delaying the inevitable. "Were you his first?"

"His second. I understand your logic. The first would be next in line to take the blame for Ellis's actions. Peter volunteered but I wouldn't let him. Please, Russell, we must hurry."

"There must be another way." Russell bounced the saw, getting the measure of its weight.

Clive didn't reply. Despite Clive appearing identical to Ellis Blackwood, a man he now despised, Russell wished he had the courage to embrace him.

The Skin shook his head. He deposited a set of keys into Russell's palm. "Nell's car," he said. "In the circumstances, you'd better drive."

It was a joke, but it made Russell feel physically sick. He looked down at the saw and then at Clive's left leg.

"Do it now," Clive said. "And do it quickly."

*

Gerry slumped into the driver's seat. When Ayo didn't enter the car, she rapped on the window. He got in.

"What the hell was that about?" she said.

While it had been clear that Dodie had recognised Ayo, she had given no suggestion of having remembered meeting Gerry at the care home. Her expression had been one of horror and the only thing she had said was, "They're not here. Leave them be." Then she had closed the door firmly.

"We shouldn't have come," Ayo said forlornly.

"But it was our only chance of finding out where Caitlin and Kit are."

His swollen eye made his glare even more accusatory. "We could be endangering them both. Dodie Hope, too."

"Nobody knows we're here."

"You don't know that. We should go."

"Not yet. Let me think."

From the look in Dodie Hope's eyes, Gerry was convinced she was telling the truth. Caitlin Hext and her Skin weren't in the house. Gerry didn't hold out any hope that she would reveal their destination under any amount of questioning.

Ayo's clenching and unclenching hands distracted her from her thoughts. "I need to think out loud," she said. "Okay?"

"Whatever it takes to make you agree to move this car."

"Let's start with January and your suspicions, which I happen to believe are well-founded."

Ayo closed his eyes. Clearly, he still suffered from an enormous amount of guilt. For how many years had he had these concerns about what happened to the Skins each night, without taking action?

"These tests. What were they actually for?"

"To find out what makes a duplicate different from humans. I guess."

Gerry nodded. "That, yes. But track back a bit."

"They've been trying to learn what makes originators produce a duplicate in the first place."

"Good. Hold that thought. Back to the killings. Sorry – the *alleged* killings." There were implications that even Ayo hadn't considered. "Here's the thing. Let's assume that you're right – that Scaife and her staff have been in the habit of killing Skins. But you said that you never saw a Skin turn to ash. Which suggests that…"

There could be little point in going to the trouble of euthanising somebody who was only hours or days away from disappearing spontaneously in a cloud of dust.

"Christ. I hadn't even thought about it. It suggests that they wouldn't have dispersed. At least, not nearly as quickly."

"Exactly. Charmers are even more charmed than we suspected. Everything we thought we knew about Skins is unravelling. For now, I'm going with the alarming possibility that Skins – or, at least, some proportion of them – don't ash spontaneously. Or, if they do, it takes longer than advertised. So the January staff give them a bit of a nudge to pass over to the other side. It's a good story."

"A good story? That's it? Listen, I made a judgement about you when we first met. That you weren't a hack."

Gerry waved a hand, trying to concentrate. "There's more. It doesn't make sense, you see. So Scaife, or rather the Great British Prosperity Party, decides to bump off Skins because they're taking too long to die. There are a handful of motives. The simplest one is your conclusion – money. Upkeep of Skins costs money. Killing them, particularly the ones who don't have families and whose deaths won't even be reported, saves money."

"No."

"No. It's not enough. For one thing, January's rolling in cash. My mysterious source tipped me off about that."

Ayo's eyes narrowed.

"Never mind. So what's the alternative explanation for curtailing Skins' lifespans?"

Ayo chewed on a thumbnail. "There's only one answer. To keep up the pretence."

"Of?"

"Of the idea that spontaneous duplicates expire soon after a shedding. Because that makes them less threatening to the public. It makes Snakeskins only sideshow oddities. People that don't need to be considered as people."

"Bingo. You have the makings of a decent journalist."

"Thanks. Now, please – will you drive this car? I just want to go home."

Gerry couldn't understand how anybody could pass up the chance to follow a mystery like this. "Fine. Home it is."

She circled the car around, taking a last look at Dodie's house before they left the cul-de-sac.

Ayo turned in his seat to look through the rear window. "Oh Christ."

Gerry twisted to see. A black Bentley pulled out of the driveway of one of the houses at the mouth of the cul-de-sac. It was the same car that she had seen at the Hext house.

Immediately, she jammed her foot onto the accelerator. Ayo yelped as his head was thrown back. The houses became a blur. Gerry yanked the steering wheel and the car tipped violently as she took a right turn onto the main road.

The Bentley in the rear-view mirror only grew in size.

"We have to get out of these empty streets," she muttered. "Get us somewhere where there'll be more traffic."

Ayo fumbled with the folded map. "Go right, then right again. Almost doubling back behind the cul-de-sac. There's a crossroads."

Without warning, Gerry swung the car into a residential street that ran parallel to the main road, separated only by a bank of grass. The pursuing car responded immediately to follow them. She willed somebody to emerge from one of the houses on the street, pulling out in a car or taking out a bin. The thought surprised her. Would she really be happy to endanger innocent people?

The side street curled to join the main road, like a tributary flowing into a river. Ayo clung onto the handle above the passenger door with both hands. It was clear that he was utterly terrified.

In contrast, Gerry felt a strange sense of calm. Adrenalin had always helped her think clearly. The only times she ever made use of her expensive gym membership was when she was in the midst of a complex investigation. Unlike most workaholic journalists that she knew, following a story that consumed her had the result of making her fitter and healthier.

"They're going to kill her," she muttered. The road ahead was straight, but she weaved the car from one side of the lane to the other, hoping to at least confuse their pursuers.

"Yes, they are," Ayo replied.

"Don't talk. They're going to kill the Skin, but not because of the embarrassment. You said it yourself – Kit didn't know about the tests or how close she came to death."

Ayo only gulped noisily as Gerry swerved the car right at the junction, narrowly missing a postbox on the corner.

"The Party ordered her death, ahead of schedule. And that's because—" She grunted as she overtook a slow-moving delivery van with a driver whose head was bent low to examine the house numbers. She checked the rear-view mirror. The black Bentley traced a smooth arc around the van, too. "Because the Hext family is special, for some reason."

Despite his panic, Ayo said, "Special in what way?"

"Don't know. I think at least one of their ancestors got

a bigger dose from the Fall than any of the Ilam villagers. Who knows what that might mean."

Ayo winced as the car swerved to avoid a pedestrian. "And Caitlin?"

"Whatever it is, I don't think Caitlin herself knows. All I know is she's the last of the Hext line. At least, she will be once her Skin's dispatched."

She sensed Ayo staring at her. She didn't dare look away from the road.

The car bucked suddenly. The Bentley loomed large in the mirror – it had rammed the rear bumper.

"Where's this crossroads of yours?" she said.

"Up ahead. You're not going to do anything stupid?"

"Quite the opposite. I'm going to do something immensely stupid."

The road widened. The Bentley accelerated, pulling into the opposite lane of traffic and drawing almost level with Gerry's car. Though its windows were tinted, she could see the outlines of two people up front and another in the back seat.

"This bugger won't go any faster," she muttered.

The crossroads appeared up ahead. Twin traffic lights shone red.

"Hold on tight."

The tall bushes outside the houses on the junction blocked her view of the perpendicular traffic. Never mind – it was better to work blind, to stop her having second thoughts.

The car burst onto the crossroads. Immediately, horns blared and Gerry heard the squeals of tyres as other cars swerved out of the way. At first, the sounds were the only evidence of the havoc she was causing. It was only when she checked the rear-view mirror that she saw two vehicles tear diagonally across her wake, like splinters in the aftermath of a bullet fired through a plank of wood.

The Bentley missed the first of the obstacles, but its bumper tipped the wing of the second car. To Gerry's relief, it spun off at an angle rather than colliding full-on. Two more vehicles came to a sudden halt, preventing the black saloon from finding a route through the melee. The Bentley weaved madly through this newly formed maze, hurtled across the remaining distance to the opposite side of the crossroads. Then it collided with a tree.

Gerry's eyes flicked to the road ahead: It was clear. In the rear-view mirror she saw smoke pluming from the bonnet of the Bentley.

"Pull over," Ayo said. To her surprise, his voice was unwavering.

"Are you kidding?"

"Pull over right now. I'm medically trained. I'm not going to leave them."

"They were trying to kill us."

"They won't do it with everybody watching."

It was true. There must be thirty people watching open-mouthed from the cars still backed up at the lights. Gerry cursed inwardly and pulled the car onto the grass verge. Ayo leapt out as soon as it stopped.

Her legs shook a little as she jogged to catch up. The air was bitingly cold; steam rose from the bonnet of the black

Bentley, along with smoke. One of its front wheels had found its way into a ditch so that the vehicle tipped to one side. Some onlookers exited their cars to watch, but nobody approached the crashed car.

As they neared it, one of the back doors cracked open, then swung out fully due to the downwards angle.

A man emerged. He wore a tweed suit and bow tie and his dark hair was cropped short. He crawled free of the wreckage but then slid slowly into the ditch, out of sight. Ayo accelerated to a run.

Gerry was more hesitant. Through the tinted windscreen she could still see the two other occupants. They weren't moving. She moved to the passenger door and eased it open gingerly.

Both men had slumped sideways so that their heads met, making a triangle of their bodies. The driver's face was streaked with blood and they both appeared unconscious. She noted that neither man wore his seat belt.

It took her a few moments before she noticed.

They were identical to one another, and identical to the man she had seen crawl into the ditch. The same tweed suits and bow ties, the same goatee beards, the same faces.

A shadow fell across them. Gerry spun around. It was Ayo.

"He's gone," he said. "The one who crawled out of the car. He must have been able to run."

If Ayo noticed that the men were identical, he didn't show it. "It's the same guy who questioned me at the care home."

"Do you think they're dead?"

Ayo bent into the car, peering at each man without touching them. "No. I found someone with a mobile telephone – they've already called an ambulance. Best not to move these two until the paramedics arrive."

"We have to get away from here."

Now that the initial shock had passed, Gerry experienced an adrenalin burst again. Something sparked in her mind, which must still be processing the puzzle unconsciously. What had she said to Ayo, before the collision? *I don't think Caitlin knows herself.* Caitlin had no concept that she, too, was being hunted by the Party. She and her Skin were fleeing in order to ensure Kit's freedom until she ashed.

And where might a panicked seventeen-year-old, possibly suffering an identity crisis, hide out? Somewhere that reinforced her sense of belonging to something. Somewhere that resonated with her current dilemma.

"I think I know the answer," she murmured.

Ayo either didn't hear or he ignored her. "We can cut straight through that street over there on foot. It'll be faster than trying to drive. The crossroads is a mess."

Gerry frowned. "On foot? To where?"

"Dodie's house, of course."

"Why on earth—"

Ayo interrupted, speaking slowly as though she were a child. "These men saw us go into her house, Gerry. And one of them's conscious and on the move. My money's on him heading directly back to Dodie."

Gerry gritted her teeth. "But I think I know where Caitlin Hext is heading."

Ayo slammed the car door. Gerry peered through the window, terrified that he might have woken the concussed men, but there were no signs of movement.

"I understand," Ayo said. His voice was little more than a hiss. "I understand now. To you, this whole thing is still about getting a story. That, and some childhood wish-fulfilment. I get that you worship Charmers. I get that you don't give a damn about Skins – do you think I didn't see how little you care about the prospect of them being murdered at January? But I never should have let you talk me into coming to Dodie's house. And I'll be damned if I'm going to hare off after Caitlin Hext, leaving that poor woman at the mercy of who-knows-what. Caitlin and Kit are safe. You following them can only endanger them, just as you endangered Dodie."

Gerry's mouth opened and closed. Her muted reaction about the extermination of Skins, following her initial adrenalin rush of deduction, was in part related to her assumption that the response of the general public would be similarly conflicted, if the policy were announced. The argument would be that Snakeskins were unnatural; that it was a relief that they quickly turned to ash; that if they didn't, their demise ought to be hastened. But none of this could possibly defend her actions to Ayo.

"Fine," Ayo said. "Get in your car. Good luck with the story."

With a final hard look, he turned and sprinted away, picking his way through the cars and towards the cul-de-sac.

When she climbed into her car, Gerry tried and failed

twice to start the engine. There was nothing wrong with the car – it was only that her hands were shaking uncontrollably. She had no idea whether it was from shock or excitement.

The wheels spewed up mud from the verge as she wrestled the car onto the road and away.

*

The Doppler effect of the sirens of two fire engines that hurtled along Cowley Road disoriented Russell momentarily. This confusion, combined with Clive's leaden weight, almost made him topple to one side. Clive grunted and clung on to Russell's arm tighter.

"Nearly there," Russell whispered.

Clive only nodded. Or perhaps he was about to pass out.

Russell looked down at the Skin's left foot – or rather, the space where his left foot had been only forty-five minutes before. It had taken Russell a long time to bind the wound after he had finished sawing through Clive's ankle and he was far from certain that the tourniquet would staunch the blood. He glanced behind them. It was too dark to see whether or not the pavement was stained.

Every few minutes, an image reappeared in Russell's mind's eye: Clive's sawn-off foot balanced on top of a workbench. Still in its shoe, its radio tag still blinking blue.

Nobody on the street paid either of them any notice. Darkness had fallen and the drunks were out in force, wheedling money out of passers-by and trying to force their way into the pubs that once would have been full of students, when Oxford had been a university town. Russell wondered if there were any Party members in there, relishing a taste of the seedier side of Oxford, as opposed to the rooftop bars and converted churches in the city centre.

Clive was becoming heavier with each minute that passed.

"Can you go faster?" Russell whispered. He wished he could have parked closer, but the office car park was always locked after dark.

The Skin didn't answer, but he lolloped faster on his single foot, leaning forwards so that his momentum forced a quicker pace. He would certainly collapse soon.

The security guard did a double-take as Russell and Clive entered. He scrambled to his feet.

"Sir? I don't understand."

Clive waved a hand. His teeth were gritted tight. He jerked his head to indicate the corridor. "Key."

"Oh. You need yours now? Absolutely, sir." The guard fumbled with the wall safe, getting the code wrong twice before hauling the door open.

A black puddle was spreading on the carpet beneath Clive's stump. The desk creaked as Clive put his full weight onto it. His face was white.

The guard placed a black box on the counter.

With difficulty, Clive lifted his right hand. His thumb hovered over the fingerprint scanner on the top of the box. Russell could barely watch. How would the guard react if Russell helped Clive move his hand? Seconds passed.

The Skin breathed deeply. Then, with surprising accuracy, he pressed his thumb onto the scanner. It beeped and the lid of the box flicked open. Clive's body slumped and Russell darted forwards to support him. With his free hand he plucked the silver key from the box.

Russell didn't allow himself to look back as they staggered together along the hallway. He didn't know if the guard saw the smear of blood.

He saw no sign of light or movement within the banner-printers. Clive continued hobbling along the corridor towards Ellis's office, using the wall for support.

"I'll come and find you as soon as I get out," Russell whispered.

Clive didn't turn but raised a hand. He was barely able to keep his injured leg above the floor. Every couple of steps the stump grazed the carpet, leaving a black comma.

"I promise I will," Russell said to himself.

He waited until Clive had stumbled into the Redevelopment and Funding office before he unlocked the door to the banner-printers.

Thin strip lights cast a yellow pall over the enormous printer in the centre. Russell edged around it with his arms spread out to prevent him from knocking into the printer or the surrounding cabinets. It had begun to rain outside; droplets hitting the windows made a drumbeat, underscoring more fire-engine sirens. Three or four of them must have passed along Cowley Road now.

As Nell had instructed, Russell ignored the banner-printer itself. He headed to a featureless door on its far side.

The room within was crammed with desks and a dozen or more computer terminals. There were no windows and Russell realised he couldn't hear the rain or sirens any more.

In its place was the low hum of technology on standby.

He approached the nearest terminal and pushed at its tracker ball. A bright white icon appeared onscreen – a padlock against a crimson background. He tried others, all with the same result.

On some of the desks were piles of printouts. Russell flicked on the torch Clive had given him and leafed through the papers. Calculations and jargon.

As he moved further into the room he kept glancing at the door through which he had entered. If anyone followed him in, his only chance would be to dive beneath one of the desks. None of the printouts contained any information he understood. Perhaps he should just take whatever he could carry. Perhaps Ellis's Skins, or Nell, could make sense of it all? But whatever their suspicions about Ellis and the Party, none of them were experts. They were operating as much in the dark as Russell was right now.

Two things made him stop in his tracks.

One was a pinboard at the shadowed end of the room. Upon it were large, square images. Maps.

The second was the doorway beside it. It was only visible due to the hairline of light at its edges.

He held his breath. He heard the hum of voices.

He crept closer. The door must be thick. It sounded as though there were at least three people speaking. The volume suggested that they were close to the other side of the door, but none of the words were audible.

He ought to run. Whoever was in there might come out at any moment.

He held up his torch to light the pinboard.

The first map showed Oxford and its surrounding towns and villages. A red outline, a polygon with many sides, formed a rough ring around one particular area. Woodstock, to the north-west of the city.

The 'target', as they had called it at Ellis's house party. It must be.

The second map showed the entirety of the British Isles. The same polygon had been redrawn on this map, correspondingly smaller. The only difference was that on this map it was labelled *APR*.

There were other rings. The one marked *05JUN* was far larger. It encompassed an area that spanned from Coventry to the south coast vertically, and from the west to the east coast horizontally. Russell tried to judge its centre. He remembered what Ellis had told Angela McKinney over the phone. *The centre of the target area is now identified as the western outer edge of the capital. Close to the M25 at West Drayton.* It fit.

Another ring was far closer in size and location to the first one. It was drawn in blue pen and labelled *14JUN*.

Affixed to the map with small pins was a transparent plastic sheet. A shape had been drawn on it, freehand and ragged at the edges. Instead of a ring it made a sausage shape, rounded at its lower end which coincided with the first outline, and open-ended at its upper end. Placed as it was, it described a sort of corridor leading north from Woodstock. Its label read *16JUN*. Yesterday.

Suddenly, light flooded from the doorway, making Russell wince.

"Oh, Russell," a familiar voice said.

Ellis Blackwood stood in the doorway, framed by Angela McKinney and Michael Trent.

"Sir—"

It was impossible to make out the expression on Ellis's face. "I rather thought something of this nature might happen. What a shame."

"What are you going to do with me?" Russell felt a flush of shame that his first instinct was for his own safety.

"Do?" Ellis said in a mocking tone. "You believe we're monsters, don't you?"

Russell had no idea how to reply.

"You're human, Russell," Angela McKinney said. "You have no reason to be afraid."

"That sounds like a confession," Russell managed to say. "So you mean if I was a Skin, I ought to be afraid?"

She shrugged. "Depends on whose Skin you were. I'm a Skin myself, as is my colleague Mr Trent here. And, to be frank, we haven't a care in the world."

The thought that Snakeskins might be complicit in the killing of others like them, those who belonged to less valuable humans, made Russell's skin crawl.

"But he's an originator, not a Skin!" Russell said, jabbing his finger at Ellis. "Ellis Blackwood is just like any normal person, coming to work each day, knackered. His Skins hate his guts."

Angela smiled. "Yes, they did."

"It's all out in the open now," Ellis said. He placed a hand on Russell's arm.

Russell shrugged him off. "What do you mean, *did*?" he said to Angela.

Ellis moved into the light. His expression was a mixture of menace and avuncular good humour. "You're all mixed up. But don't worry. For a time we considered it prudent to rely on somebody unencumbered by Charmer abilities – somebody who might actually consider themselves *unworthy* of such power – for fear of the risk of duplicity by somebody possessing more guile. Now that you've come this far, I think we'll be obliged to take you into our confidence after all."

Russell shuddered. At least he might learn the truth. Escape was unlikely, but the Party seemed in no mood to kill him. If he ever made it back to Nell, he was determined he would have something to tell her.

He pointed at the map. "All right. Take me into your confidence, then. You can start with this target of yours. What is it?"

"A good question," Ellis replied. "As you can see, its location has changed over time – a mystery that has been exercising our minds a great deal, but which has now been cleared up thanks to Mr Trent's sterling detective work. Anyway, the fact that it is now 'on the move', so to speak, rather accelerates our plans. Having you on board may have been necessary even if you hadn't made this transgression."

"What plans?"

"The plans to reach the target at the appropriate moment, of course. Along with our close friends. I believe you may know some of their names? They're noted down on a disk, about so big." Ellis held up his thumb and forefinger. "It's quite all right, Russell. I know you won't have been a tittle-tattle and confided in anybody. I trust you."

Russell shuddered. "If I'm going to help you, you'll have to give me more to go on."

A phone rang. Ellis frowned and rummaged in his jacket pocket. "Excuse me for a moment, please." He turned away from Russell to speak into the mobile phone. Russell eyed the door, but Michael Trent stepped forwards to block his escape.

"Yes, it is," Ellis said into the phone. "This morning, after breakfast. Yes. Oh. Good lord. Good grief." His face displayed no particular signs of concern.

"Thank you for calling me," he said. "You must excuse me. I must be alone with my thoughts. Yes, I will. Thank you again." He hung up, then held the bulky phone against his chest. He turned, looking first at his two colleagues, then at Russell.

"I'm afraid to report," Ellis said, his face still expressionless, "that there's been a fire at my house."

Russell remembered hearing the fire engine sirens. And there was another thing. When he had inexpertly accelerated Nell's car away from the Blackwood house, he had had to swerve to avoid somebody struggling to carry what had appeared to be a heavy-looking suitcase. He realised now that it had been a fuel canister.

Ellis continued in a quiet voice, "And I've also been informed that my wife has been found dead."

Slowly, a smile spread across his face.

# FIFTEEN

Caitlin followed Kit along the rocking train carriage. Their change at Oxford had been delayed by a broken-down engine blocking the track, and so they had had to sprint along the platforms at Manchester Piccadilly to make the north-east-bound train. Once aboard, Kit had huddled beside a luggage rack while the attendant checked Caitlin's ticket at the other end of the carriage. He hadn't asked to see her ID, but on her way past Caitlin slipped the card to Kit before the attendant reached her; then she disappeared into the next carriage to avoid the attendant having a chance to compare their faces.

A line of sweat tickled her back under her T-shirt and thick tracksuit. The weather was too warm for her outfit, but she didn't dare remove her jumper for fear of exposing any more of her skin than she needed to.

Caitlin dropped into one of a pair of seats with a table. The two seats opposite were empty. Before long, Kit joined her.

"Perhaps we should sit apart from each other this time?" Caitlin whispered.

Kit shrugged. "You can if you want to. I'm all right here."

Caitlin glanced around the carriage. A few passengers glanced her way and one or two smiled. She deposited herself on the seat opposite her Skin. Even now it was difficult to overcome the sense of sitting before a mirror. Kit fished in her rucksack and pulled out the publications they had bought at Oxford station: *Folk* for her and *Astronomy Tonight* for Caitlin. Caitlin smiled her thanks but left her magazine lying flat on the table.

While she read, Kit fiddled with something at her neck. Caitlin saw a leather cord tied there. It was familiar.

"Was Evie there?" she said.

Kit blinked and pulled her hand away from the cord. "At the funeral? Of course."

"You asked her to come?"

"She's our best friend."

Abruptly, Caitlin leant forwards and tugged the cord free. She recognised the ugly elliptical pendant immediately. Evie had worn that necklace every day for a couple of years. It had been given to her by Paul Farrier, who had promptly cheated on her by kissing Caitlin at the school prom. Evie had dumped Paul and forgiven Caitlin immediately, but she had kept the necklace. She said it reminded her that she already had everybody she needed. There was no need to replace the people she loved the most.

"I wouldn't have asked her," Caitlin murmured.

It occurred to her that by switching places with Kit, she had made a more profound choice than she had realised. Deep down, she had known that Evie would accept Kit. The fact that she had given Kit the precious necklace indicated an even stronger bond than she shared with Caitlin.

Perhaps, unconsciously, Caitlin had made a decision to move on. She thought of her other friends at college, but struggled to name a single one that she needed to have in her life. She thought of her dad, gazing through his telescope at the stars. It was easy to imagine herself becoming dreamy, like him.

"I've been thinking," she said. "We should call home. Dad'll be getting worried."

Kit chewed a cereal bar. "Remember what Dodie said. January will do anything to hide what's happened from the public. It's too embarrassing. They'll make some excuse to your dad. Anyway, he was already talking about cutting down on his visits, or even stopping. You can't blame him. He did his bit."

If it was true, then Kit was taking it well. She would effectively have been abandoned by the closest thing she had to family. Then again, Ian had said all this to Kit, after the switch. He hadn't known it, but it was Caitlin that he was threatening to abandon, not the Skin.

"I didn't mean he'd be worried about us escaping from the care home," Caitlin said. "You've been gone more than a day now, without any explanation. And so soon after the funeral. His daughter's missing."

"Oh. Yeah. You're right. You should call." Caitlin could imagine her thought process and how painful it must feel. *Ian Hext isn't my dad.* Her cheeks were hot with shame.

Caitlin watched Kit's smooth, bare shoulders rub against the coarse fabric of the chair. The Skin's eyes fluttered for a moment as she found a comfortable divot, pressed into the armrest with her knees slightly drawn up.

If Kit hadn't broken her out of the care home, Ian Hext wouldn't be Caitlin's dad any more either. What could she say to him, now? She shook her head. "There's a payphone next to the loos. Can you call him? You spent the last couple of days with him. I could easily end up dropping a clanger. All you need to do is tell him you're taking a breather, and you're fine."

"You're sure?"

"Please."

Kit pulled herself out of her concertina position. Before she could shuffle across to the aisle seat, an enormous holdall was deposited onto it.

"This seat taken?" The man must have been in his twenties. His short, fair hair was so fine that it rose upwards where it wasn't collected in clumps. His face was friendly enough.

Kit grinned at him. "Let me out and then you can sprawl wherever you like." She hopped over the armrest and into the aisle. "I'll leave you to get acquainted, sis."

Caitlin leafed through *Astronomy Tonight*, trying to avoid making eye contact with the newcomer. The young man huffed as he struggled with the holdall, first trying to jam it into the luggage rack close to the ceiling, then finally cramming it into a space beside a bin.

He dropped into his seat. "I'm Florian. My parents thought giving me a French name meant they were giving the middle finger to the UK's isolationist policies, or some misguided shit like that. All it did was give me grief at every checkpoint in the country."

Caitlin managed a smile. She raised her magazine higher. "You two twins?"

Caitlin scowled. "No. Just sisters. We're not all that alike, when you get to know us."

Florian patted his pockets and pulled out a dog-eared Jane Austen novel. Caitlin suspected it was a prop. His eyes kept straying above the pages.

A few minutes later, Kit reappeared. She made her way along the aisle, chuckling as she weaved from side to side with the motion of the train. Janet Hext's dress fitted her perfectly. The cotton clung to her narrow waist and the skirt flared just above the knee. Caitlin ought to have tried it on sooner.

She was wearing lipstick. Caitlin had always hated the greasy feel of it.

Kit must have noticed her stare. "A nice lady outside the loo gave me it. And then I found these when I went in." She put on a pair of sunglasses. They were large with dark pink lenses, like a Pinewood star might wear to go out in public incognito. Caitlin would never have chosen them, but somehow Kit carried off the look.

The Skin wiggled into the seat beside Caitlin. "All fine," she whispered.

"He sounded okay?"

"He's fine. Don't you worry."

Caitlin bit her lip. Somehow, her dad being unaware of all that had happened made the situation worse. If this escape went wrong, perhaps Ian Hext would never know the truth. Perhaps he'd end up at another funeral, for the wrong daughter.

Kit was looking at Florian. His eyes were fixed on hers.

Caitlin pulled her hair over her eyes, sank further into her too-warm tracksuit top, and watched the prickles of light that had appeared in the sky.

*

Gerry cursed as she tried to overtake a lorry and narrowly avoided hitting a transit van in the fast lane. Something was preventing her from thinking straight.

Ayo.

It wasn't only that she was attracted to him and that she was unlikely to see him ever again. To her shame, it wasn't even that he might currently be in danger while he attempted to protect Dodie Hope.

She had always hated being called out on her errors. Then, following her apprenticeship at her local paper instead of attending university, she had developed a thin skin about her motivations for following a story. Only Drew had ever been permitted to point out that her tendency to prioritise stories about Charmers stemmed from a childhood wish-fulfilment.

But Ayo had seen through her. He had been horrified at her reaction to the news about what went on behind January's doors. Skins were being killed systematically and Gerry's first consideration had been about the scale of the conspiracy, the size of the journalistic scoop. She hadn't expressed any particular concern for the Skins themselves, because she hadn't felt it. It was as Ayo had said: *A building full of Skins, all waiting for the end.* Ayo's reaction was to treat Skins as humanely as he would anybody who was suffering, whereas Gerry's instinct was to dismiss them. Not only had she never considered Snakeskins as human, she had never considered them as people. They were a commodity, a gift granted to Charmers to be used as they saw fit.

All of this cast doubt on her reasons for racing off into the night after Caitlin Hext. But no matter how monstrous her opinions may be, Gerry had to believe that she was still needed – that the truth still had to come out, and she was best placed to make it happen. The Great British Prosperity Party was determined to trace Caitlin and her Snakeskin, but it was also still covering up for the destruction of a sizeable proportion of Skins who might otherwise have lived full lives.

She must put Ayo out of her mind. She was a professional and she was on the trail of the most important story of her career.

Now she swung the car from lane to lane with greater confidence, finding the optimum path. She was prepared to drive through the night.

The key to Caitlin's destination had been given to her by Ian Hext, in his story about the event that had lodged firmly in Caitlin's mind as a child. Janet Hext was still the most significant person in Caitlin's life. Ian's story resonated with Gerry – it was great fodder for an article – and she was convinced that it would be foremost in Caitlin's mind at this moment. The museum. The puppet diorama. The missing mother. The fear that Janet had shed and had been replaced.

In the distance, specks appeared in the northern sky.

# SIXTEEN

Caitlin covered her eyes with an arm as harsh daylight flooded into the room.

"What the hell?" It was her own voice, but it didn't come from her own throat.

She groaned. "I was just about to say the same thing. Close the curtains, Kit."

She rolled over in bed, but Kit jostled her awake.

"You need to see this," Kit said.

Grumbling, Caitlin struggled out of bed and pulled on her jeans. Kit was dressed already, her hair was brushed and her cheeks shone with cleanliness, making Caitlin feel even more slovenly.

She slouched to the window, squinting against the light. Their room was on the second floor of the hotel. Last night the owner had been apologetic that all of the rooms overlooking the sea had been taken. Their only view was of the car park.

"Not down there," Kit said. "Up there."

The sky was the colour of steel. It was cloudless.

But it wasn't empty.

There were a dozen or more narrow streaks, high in the sky, claw-mark slashes. At first Caitlin took them to be vapour trails. The lowest end of each streak was slightly bulbous and a greenish shade.

"You know what that is," Kit said.

"Is that a question?"

"No."

Caitlin found it hard to look away from the sky.

"After all this time," she murmured. "Why now? And why here?"

*

Russell's eyes flicked left as Ellis's mobile phone chimed. Ellis grunted as he read the text message.

"Everything all right, sir?" Russell said. Since he had been caught in the banner-printers office yesterday, he had adopted a subservient tone, and hated himself for it. It was a shameful method of self-preservation. His cheeks flushed and he turned to face the motorway. The only other vehicles that had ventured onto the A64 this early were haulage trucks. The dawn light reflecting from the tarmac was almost blinding.

Ellis ignored him. He tapped buttons and raised the phone to his ear. Though Russell couldn't hear the words of the person on the end of the line, he recognised the strident, accusatory tone of Angela McKinney.

Ellis had been complicit in the burning of his own house, and therefore the deaths of Nell and, presumably, all five of his Snakeskins. His demeanour had changed entirely, with no sign of his previous clumsiness or uncertainty. Russell wondered whether revealing to Angela his shameful secret about the hidden Snakeskins had lessened his mental burden, or whether it was simply that the death of his wife and Skins signified a point of no return.

Either way, he was clearly a far more dangerous character than Russell had understood, and yet still Russell suppressed any outward indication of his outrage. He was a coward and a fool. He had served Ellis faithfully, then had served Ixion due to some half-baked hope that he might help, or at least impress, Nell Blackwood and that she had romantic feelings for him. Following the shock of her death, Russell now recognised something he had previously denied. Nell had never had any interest in him. She had remained married to Ellis Blackwood for one reason – or rather, five reasons. She loved Ellis's Snakeskins. When Russell had last seen her, in the underground den, she had been clutching the hand of one of them. Theirs was a strange relationship, certainly, but a relationship that would have left no room for Russell.

Now they were all dead – all but Clive, though Russell felt less and less sure that he might have survived the loss of blood after the clumsy removal of his foot. It was impossible to believe that Russell might not have prevented the murders if he had done things differently; if he had stepped up. And yet here he was, acting as bus driver for his murderous employer and his cronies. What was the quotation? *I am in blood stepped in so far that, should I wade no more, returning were as tedious as go o'er.*

361

"All settling down nicely, ma'am," Ellis said into the phone. He unfolded a sheet of paper and read out a string of numbers that meant nothing to Russell. "There was no change for around six hours overnight, following a consistent north-easterly vector, and only very minor fluctuations in the last hour. Yes, the tech experts are positive. I know I've said that before. But there's no time left for substantive variation. I'll pass the coordinates on to the others."

The others.

Russell peered into the rear-view mirror. The fifteen seats of the minibus were all filled. As they had filed on board a couple of hours ago, Russell had recognised many of the faces, despite the people trying to hide their identities with sunglasses and headscarves. Almost all of them had been at Ellis's 'soirée' in North Oxford, and Russell was certain he had seen a couple of them at the office complex on Marston Street.

Several times, he had considered yanking the steering wheel and sending them all into the oncoming traffic. Whatever these people were up to, he was in a position to stop them, temporarily. As it was, he checked his mirrors diligently and kept both hands on the wheel.

"There are more minibuses, sir?" he said.

Ellis put his phone away. "No. You have the honour of being our sole bus driver. Our other guests will be arriving in dribs and drabs. They prefer the comfort of travelling in their own vehicles, though I've made clear that limousines would be far from appropriate, given the subterfuge required."

Russell made the connection. "The names listed on the floppy disk. The people who arranged all those mysterious meetings."

"That's right."

"The millionaires."

"Mostly. Some aren't millionaires quite yet, but if I were a betting man I'd say they may be soon. Wealth may be common amongst them, but that isn't their common denominator, Russell."

"Then what?"

Ellis's smile struck Russell as almost demonic in its zeal. "Their usefulness. Watch the road, Russell. You have precious cargo."

Russell yanked the steering wheel to overtake an army truck. The road ahead was clear. "Useful to you? Or to that insane woman who orders you around?"

"Watch yourself. That's your future prime minister you're talking about. And it's your future deputy prime minister you're talking *to*."

Russell digested the statement. Ixion had been right from the start. "So all of this, whatever we're doing, is in the name of a political coup? You're aiming to topple Adrian Lorde and the Party administration, then take over?"

"You make it sound prosaic. And I would like to make it clear that this 'coup' has been a long time in its gestation. Even before recent developments, our faction represented the progressives within government. I have been among the loudest voices demanding changes that would have benefitted our economy. Developments that would allow our nation to thrive once again. Automation in factories, for example. Your own father performs menial work, does he not? Then you ought to approve. My lobbying would have resulted in faster, safer, more effective work."

Russell refused to allow himself to engage in the details, though he wanted to ask whether the changes would result in his father being paid more, or being allowed to retire, finally.

"You said 'would have'. Something's changed, then?"

Ellis gazed out of the window. "Our ambitions have been adjusted. The ending of Lorde's premiership and the installation in power of those sympathetic to our cause are now only consequences of a greater good."

Russell twisted, trying to look Ellis in the eye. "But what I don't understand is why dozens of millionaires would help fund all of this. What's in it for them?"

"Eyes to the front, Russell."

Russell did as he was told. He could now see the sea. At a gesture from Ellis, he took the next turn. A sign at the roadside read: *Welcome to Scarborough*.

He braked. A barrier blocked the road ahead. A man and woman wearing army uniforms stood before it. Russell heard the passengers of the bus, who had been silent until now, mutter excitedly.

"One moment," Ellis said. When the bus came to a stop he reached for the door release, then hopped out onto the road. Ellis produced something from his pocket and showed it to them, and the army officers began to shift the barrier aside. Russell squinted to see more barriers further along the road. What on earth was happening here?

He heard the thrum of helicopters. He pushed the sun visor away to see them.

The helicopters were far less arresting than the other sight that greeted him. High up above the ground, the sky was laced with green-tinged diagonal lines.

He had seen the pictures in books. He had watched all the Elstree heritage films about it.

The Fall.

A second Fall.

Ellis grinned as he clambered on board the bus.

"And to think," he said with a smirk, "that all our friends have paid so handsomely for a chance to be here at the right moment. And you've hitched a ride for free."

\*

Caitlin ducked into the empty ticket office of the funicular railway. From this position of safety she tracked one of the helicopters as it travelled south to north across the bay, appearing to bisect the diagonal lines in the sky. It was low enough to whip up sand from the beach, making a swirling trail in its wake like the train of a bride's gown. The deep thudding of its rotor blades was something she felt in her chest more than heard.

Perhaps it had been wrong to agree to Kit's suggestion that they split up. When they had left the hotel and seen the first of the street cordons and the army patrols, it had been a knee-jerk reaction that they oughtn't to risk being found together, in case anyone looked closely, spotted them as twins, then made a connection to January's missing Skin. The closer Caitlin came to the sea, the more densely packed the barriers became. The streets were entirely empty of pedestrians.

Further along the beachfront a group of soldiers marched in a ragged line. Most of the buildings were tourist businesses – ice cream parlours, amusements and souvenir shops – and none were open this early in the morning. Each time the officers reached a seafront hotel, one or two of them peeled away from the line to thump on the doors. Caitlin stepped from her hiding place to watch as a stream of confused people emerged from a cheap-looking hostel. She ducked into cover as a white van crawled along the seafront road. The soldiers bustled the families into the van – there were a dozen of them or more. The van was the type used by tradesmen, and Caitlin could see that it didn't even contain seats. Children's cries carried on the still air.

Taking advantage of the distraction, she left the ticket office and scurried along the road, keeping close to the overhanging foyer roofs. Now the soldiers and civilians were within earshot.

"But I don't understand!" one of the women being bundled into the van shouted.

"I told you," one of the pair of soldiers replied tersely. "It's a bloody radiation leak. Don't you care about those kids of yours? Now get in!"

The woman gazed up at the streaks in the sky. "But they're—"

Her answer was cut off as the soldier slammed the rear

door. Then the van sped away along the seafront.

"For pity's sake," the soldier said to his colleague. "How many more streets to go?"

The other man held up a hand to silence him. He was listening to an earpiece. His shoulders slumped. "You're not going to like this, Vern. Sounds as though the radius has got bigger again in the last half an hour, even though the ETA's still oh-eight-thirty. We're to keep going as far as the castle up on the hill there. Come on, we'd better catch up."

He set off at a jog after the line of soldiers. The other man stood for a moment with his hands on hips, shook his head, then set off in pursuit.

At least the soldiers' direction of travel made Caitlin's task easier. It would be far more difficult to reach the agreed rendezvous point if she were trying to make her way against the flow of oncoming soldiers. She winced as she realised that Kit must be doing exactly that, travelling south to the pier. Still, better Kit than her. The more time they spent together, the more Caitlin was convinced that Kit was the more resourceful of the two of them. She no longer felt any envy. She just wanted to survive whatever was happening and, somehow, find her way home.

She made her way cautiously along the seafront towards the pier. Though she kept checking the side streets to her left, her eyes were more often fixed on the green slashes above the sea. Around thirty trails were visible now, of varying intensities. Their reflections, in the calm between waves, made the water appear to be filled with spindly creatures.

When she came level with the pier she hurried out of cover

and across the road. Then she yelped and ducked right. Before the harbour wall stood a soldier in a black uniform, surveying the empty street. A long, black automatic firearm was slung around his neck and held in both his hands.

She looked up at the building that had provided her cover. The Museum of Automata sign was unlit. The thin lettering tubes that she had only ever seen burning with neon light were filthy black. Her dad had told her that the museum had closed the previous summer and that there had been local petitions to reopen it. Several times, she had daydreamed that they might raise the funds themselves, take it on as a family business. Now, it was grotesque in its abandoned state.

The padlocks made it clear that there would be no chance of entering by the front door. She slipped along the side of the building that wasn't visible to the armed soldier, then hugged the wall and watched the soldier carefully for any sign of movement as she teetered on the edge of the concrete pier at the rear of the museum. Sure enough, there was another door here. It hung ajar very slightly.

"Hey, slowcoach."

Caitlin started at the voice. "How did you get here so quickly?"

"How did you take so bloody long?" Then Kit's face crumpled. "It was terrifying. Patrols everywhere, and have you seen that maniac with the itchy trigger finger? I'm just glad we both made it without being spotted."

"But we were wrong," Caitlin said. "This isn't about us, really, is it?"

"All we can do is stay safe until it's over," Kit said. "Forget the plan to skip town for now. Everyone'll be waiting for the Fall, and when it ends they might well bugger off home."

She led the way deeper into the pitch-black museum. They had crept through the gift shop and emerged into the museum proper before Caitlin registered that something – some*one* – was moving in the darkness.

# SEVENTEEN

"It's a pleasure to meet you both, finally," Gerry said. "Hold on. I've been tinkering with the backup generator. Let there be light."

She tugged at the master switch behind the admissions desk. Lights flickered on, revealing the clouds of dust that hung in the still air of the museum. She checked that she hadn't also operated the outside lights and hoped that the shutters covering the museum front would hide any sign of illumination.

She crossed her arms and examined the two girls. They had done a reasonable job of appearing distinct from one another. The girl wearing the green dress appeared quite prim, whereas the other was more boyish in her tracksuit. Nobody would give them a second glance. In her teenage years, Gerry had had friends who dressed, looked and acted more like each other than these two girls.

"Who the hell are you?" the girl in the green dress said.

"I'm Gerry Chafik. I promise I'm here to help, so please don't do anything silly."

With the lights on she was able to take in her surroundings for the first time. The museum exhibits were cloaked in dust. There was more variety than she had expected – alongside the Victorian diorama cabinets there were more modern automata, including a spindly mechanical cat and a bald-headed robot on a plinth that had no eyes in its smooth face, but which had complex-looking hinged limbs and fingers. A giant Archimedes screw stretched from floor to ceiling with the purpose of transporting coloured balls from a pit and into plastic chutes.

"So. Are you going to tell me which of you is the Charmer, or shall I guess?" she said.

Both girls watched her warily.

"It's okay, I promise," Gerry said. "I'm not from the Party. I'm a journalist, or at least I was."

"Just as bad," the tracksuited girl said.

Gerry shook her head. "If there's a story to be written about all this, that's a discussion for another day. There are more pressing matters. Those meteors are still fairly high in the sky. We're okay here for a while."

All three of them stared up at the ceiling as the *thwack* of a helicopter grew in volume and then subsided.

The two girls exchanged glances. They both shrugged.

"I'm Caitlin Hext," the tracksuited girl said.

"I'm Kit," the other girl said.

"Kit *Hext*," Caitlin added. "We're family."

Kit responded with an appreciative grin.

"All right then," Gerry said. "So what I need to tell you affects both of you, because it's all about family too."

Gerry still found it difficult to know which of them to address. Flustered, she turned to examine the cabinet she was leaning against. Its crimson velour curtain was parted slightly. Inside, beneath a dark window, she could read an inscription: *Behind You! Or, The Snake-Charmer's Shock*. Inside the diorama she could make out the silhouette of a figure sitting at the foot of a bed. This must be the same cabinet where Janet Hext had gone missing, all those years ago.

"The Hext family aren't special only because they're Charmers," she said. "It's more than that. One of your ancestors was a shepherd in Ilam in 1808, at the time of the Fall."

"That doesn't sound all that special," Caitlin said scornfully.

Kit shushed her. Interesting that the Skin might be keener on family history than the Charmer.

"What's important is that this ancestor, or maybe his entire family, lived up on the mountainside. That is, far closer to the meteor strike than any of the villagers. I think the Fall affected your family differently to other people."

"Like how?"

Gerry frowned. "At first I thought it was about the longevity of your family's Snakeskins." Involuntarily, she glanced at Kit, who squirmed in discomfort. "I think I'm right in saying there's been evidence of that in the past. Is that right?"

The girls' eyes flicked to the automaton cabinet behind her. So she had been right about their memories of Janet.

"But it's not enough to explain all this," she continued.

"From what I know now, it seems that only a small proportion of Skins ash spontaneously."

The girls looked at each other. Gerry could imagine what they were thinking about. All those Skins in the January care home. The implications about how they might meet their end.

Kit, in particular, was deathly pale. "So what happens to them?"

"I'm sorry to tell you," Gerry replied, "that Dr Victoria Scaife is even less pleasant than she appears."

"They were going to kill me," Kit said quietly.

Gerry nodded. "You escaped in the nick of time."

A strange expression crossed Caitlin's face, and Kit shuffled awkwardly. Gerry had no idea what it meant.

"And it gets worse," she continued. "The decision to dispose of Skins that might cause any embarrassment is one that goes all the way to the top. The aim of some faction within our government is to keep Charmers' real potential as a resource only for themselves. They've been culling undesirable Skins for decades."

Caitlin chewed her lip. "But those trails out there in the sky. Isn't that—"

Gerry nodded. "Another Fall. And you can be certain that this time it won't be just a random collection of townspeople who'll benefit."

"That's what the barricades are for," Kit said. "Right?"

"Right. To keep people out – at least, the wrong types of people. I'd bet anything that Party officials, or whoever's paid the government handsomely for the chance to be here at the right moment, are making a beeline for Scarborough right at this moment."

Caitlin shook her head. "What makes you so sure the government could have prepared for this? How could they possibly know?"

"My guess is that all the space telescopes in the country have been pointing up there, waiting for this for generations," Gerry replied. "The real question is, why all the last-minute panic? The army have been announcing radiation leaks even while the meteors are visible in the sky above. It's all a bit crude."

Kit tapped her chin. "Because they knew *when* the Fall would be. They just didn't know *where*."

Gerry had been processing all these clues for many hours, but Kit had caught up with her immediately. Caitlin, the real human, was much slower on the uptake. Perhaps the Snakeskin's desperation made her synapses fire more quickly. Or perhaps Skins were superior to their originators.

"Not for want of trying, though," Gerry said.

Kit murmured, "Of course!"

"What?" Caitlin said indignantly. "Of course what? Want to let me in on the big secret?"

Kit turned to face her. "Don't you get it? We show up here in Scarborough and the authorities are hot on our trail. And then there's those bloody fireballs up in the sky. It's not a coincidence, Cait."

Now it was Caitlin's face that turned ashen. "They've been tracking us. Because they realised we're the key to predicting the location of the Fall."

Gerry was impressed. What she had told them was a huge amount to take in, but they were coping remarkably well. "I don't think they figured out Caitlin's significance right away. But when I was at your house I noticed the field behind your house was cordoned off – there were blue tarpaulins all over the place but no signs of building work. My guess is it was an attempt to secure as much of the area as possible around the projected location, ahead of time. And I believe that their tracking calculations would have been screwed up by the appearance of a brand-new Hext."

Caitlin looked as though she might be sick at any moment. "So you're sure that the Fall is being guided by something specific to members of my family?" When Gerry nodded, she breathed, "Because... because..."

Kit's eyes widened. "Shitting hell." She noticed Gerry's baffled expression. "Our uncle. He died. Just after our shedding."

"Yes, I heard. I'm sorry." Gerry realised that she had never had a chance to investigate the specifics of Toby Hext's death. "Was it in suspicious circumstances?"

"Swimming pool, alone, at night," Caitlin whispered.

Gerry had no idea what to say. Toby's death must have marked the point when the Party had identified the Hext family as crucial to determining the location of the Fall. Killing him would have been merely a convenience: one fewer data point screwing up the government's efforts at triangulation.

She was thankful that Kit broke the silence. "Hold on. You said that the appearance of a new Hext screwed up the calculations. So I count, even though I'm a Snakeskin? I'm partly responsible for drawing the meteors to Earth, along with Cait?"

Gerry nodded. It had been *after* Toby Hext's death that the Party had identified the urgent need to kill the Skin while she was held at the care home.

Caitlin looked thoughtful. "A couple of soldiers out there were talking about a deadline – something happening at half past eight – and they mentioned a radius getting bigger."

"And I'm guessing they weren't happy about it?" Gerry said.

Caitlin shook her head.

Gerry tapped her chin. "Did you guys split up at all over the last hour?"

Their wide-eyed expressions answered the question.

"There you go, then," she continued. "The further you are apart, the harder it is for them to be precise in their calculations."

Caitlin nodded. "But that must mean they're not able to track our locations, only the trajectory of the meteors. Now that they're close to the Earth, they must be monitoring what they call the 'luminous tracks'. I read about it somewhere. But it amounts to the same thing."

Gerry raised an eyebrow. Smart kid. Strange that the Skin hadn't made the same observation. Though they shared the same memories, the ways in which they applied their knowledge appeared to have diverged already.

Without warning, Kit turned and sprinted to the door.

Caitlin dived after her. "Where the hell are you going?"

Kit tried to struggle free. "Weren't you even listening to

what you just said? You guys had better come up with a plan right this second, because I'm out of here!"

Gerry leapt to her feet too. She was an utter fool. She had been so intent on piecing together the puzzle that she had been blind to the immediate danger.

"Kit's right," she said, running to shut off the lights. "The army's out there, and the Party, and God knows who else – not to mention a sky full of space-rocks all hurtling towards us. And every second that you two are in the same place means that they're all closing in on you!"

✳

Russell watched as Party employees continued lugging equipment from the rear of the minibus. He had offered to help – inwardly cursing himself for his meekness – but Ellis had instructed him to stay sitting at the counter of the seafront cafe. Now the tables of each booth were strewn with computer terminals and wires. Those employees who had finished installing their equipment now bent before their terminals, absorbed in dense onscreen text and abstract, flickering diagrams. Ellis paced around, peering over shoulders. He kneaded his hands constantly and kept looking at the wide window to see the meteor trails still hanging like paper streamers over the sea.

A police car screeched up at the kerb. A uniformed officer leapt out and immediately flung open the back door, then bent to pull out somebody who struggled and bit at him.

To Russell's surprise, he saw that it was Spencer Blackwood. The boy's hands were bound before him so that when he was pushed towards the cafe it looked as though he were praying to it.

Ellis saw him arrive, but he didn't go to greet him.

The moment he saw his father, the fight seemed to leave Spencer. His bound body slackened. It shook with heavy sobs.

Without thinking, Russell dashed over to him. When the police officer tried to obstruct his path he shoved the man away. He held Spencer's shoulders, first at arm's length, then in a full embrace. Judging from his expression the boy already understood what had happened to Nell.

"I'm so sorry," Russell whispered. "I'm so, so sorry."

The boy twisted awkwardly, trying to look up at Russell. Russell realised with a start that Spencer might well think that he had been complicit in Nell's murder and the deaths of Ellis's Skins.

"No," he whispered. "I didn't know. I swear."

Spencer gazed at him for a few seconds. Then, almost imperceptibly, he nodded and his eyes widened.

Russell frowned in confusion.

Spencer nodded again – or rather, he jerked his head to one side.

"Left pocket," he said under his breath.

Without releasing his embrace, Russell moved his hand down to the pocket of the boy's jacket. The police officer had turned his attention to Ellis. Russell reached into the pocket and pulled out something cuboid and cold. He put it behind his back and pressed it against his spine.

"Over there." The police officer pushed Spencer roughly

towards Ellis. "He fought hard, sir."

Ellis appeared momentarily impressed. He had always complained that Spencer wasn't a fighter.

The father and son stood facing each other. The nearby Party employees bent closer to their monitors to avoid appearing interested.

Russell took advantage of everyone's attention being elsewhere. As he sidled to the cafe counter he snuck a look at the object he now held in his hand. It must be another of Spencer's electronic projects, little more than a circuit board bulked out with wires and a steel chassis. Other than a nine-volt battery, only one of the components was at all familiar – a small nubbin with a wire-net hood. A microphone. With his hands bound, Spencer wouldn't have been able to operate the recording device himself.

He almost dropped the thing as he fumbled to turn it over, searching for the controls. It was too small to hold a tape, so he hoped that it contained one of the hard drives that Spencer had demonstrated at his home. There was only one switch, and when Russell pressed it an LED blinked. He palmed the device, microphone outward, and shrugged the arm of his jumper so that it was hidden from view.

The truth was the only weapon he and Spencer had, now.

Ellis glanced at Russell as he sidled up. But his attention was occupied with the boy, bound and dragged before him.

In a hoarse voice, Spencer said, "Why?"

Ellis took a breath before speaking, as though he had rehearsed his answer. "The world needs change, son, and we need the world. British isolationism is a dead end. The country has progressed as far as it's able. We must impress the world beyond our shores with our sole trump card – our unique abilities – before it loses currency. I believe that I, and others who think the same way as me, can lead a global government... a government comprised of Charmers, of course, but it's our duty to be selective this time. We have the opportunity to select those who deserve the gift. No random, chaotic elements. Charmers have enormous responsibilities, son, and few are capable of meeting those challenges."

So that was it. Up to now, Russell had been preoccupied with the idea of rival factions within the Great British Prosperity Party. But this was bigger. It would explain why he hadn't recognised many of the names in Ellis's file. Ellis and his fellow conspirators must have been offering Charmer powers to select people from around the world, presumably in return for substantial donations. All with the pretext of building a Charmer cartel that spanned far beyond Britain, and which would rule the world unchallenged.

"You think that's what I care about?" Spencer hissed. His eyes shone.

Ellis blinked. "Oh. Dear Nell. She—"

Spencer turned his head to one side and spat a gobbet of red phlegm. The police officer really must have had to fight him to bring him here. Good lad. "No. Don't you dare try and justify what you did to Mum and the others. You set fire to our house..." His voice faltered. "...and you burned her to death."

"I had to."

Russell stifled a gasp as he almost fumbled and dropped

the recording device. This clear admission of guilt was somehow more shocking than his detailing of the Charmer plot. He prayed that there would be an opportunity to use the audio recording against Ellis.

"But that's not what I meant either," Spencer said. "I'm asking: Why all this? Why bring me here? Is there any possible way you can make what you're doing any worse?"

Ellis's cheeks flushed. "It's for your own good, son."

He reeled in response to the hateful look that Spencer gave him.

"I'm a Charmer," Spencer muttered. "I wish to God I wasn't. It's a curse. If I could cut out whatever part of me will trigger the shedding in a couple of months – whatever part of me that was given by you – I would."

Ellis simply shook his head. He looked old and tired.

"You're not." He turned to look out at the green streaks in the sky. They were growing in intensity by the minute. "You're not a Charmer. But you will be. Then we'll be the same. Given time, you'll understand why it had to be this way."

Spencer looked as if he had been struck in the face. "But… how can I not be a Charmer? Mum was, and you are."

Ellis simply shrugged.

Spencer fell silent as he processed the information. "Oh. I get it now." A crooked grin spread over his face. "And you know what? It's more than I could have hoped for."

Russell saw Ellis's hands curl into fists.

"Who is it?" Spencer demanded. He writhed, pulling against the straps that bound his hands. "Or are you going to make me guess?"

After a few seconds' hesitation, Ellis replied, "Peter."

Russell frowned. The name rang a bell. Hadn't he met a Peter recently? He watched Spencer's reaction. An expression of delight flashed across the boy's face, then crushing regret.

Then Russell remembered the list of names: Jules, Peter, Lewis, Christopher and poor, brave Clive. Ellis's Snakeskins.

"Of course," Spencer whispered, speaking more to himself than to his father. "Your first. The one that Mum fell in love with. The reason she stayed." His eyes were wet with tears. "Peter. My dad. And you killed him."

Ellis turned his back on the boy. One of the technical operators looked up as he placed a hand on her shoulder. "The radius has narrowed once again, sir, as you hoped," she said. "Pinpointing the location is becoming more accurate as the meteors come nearer."

"And the Hext girls?"

"Even if they are detained at this point, we ought to keep them secure in their current position to avoid any last-minute swerves. With the additional visual information—" the operator indicated the streaks visible in the sky "—we're confident of the timing, too. Twenty-five minutes, with an error margin of only a minute either side."

Ellis stared out over the seafront. "And still definitely inland?"

"All current data suggest that will be the case, sir, though it's a close call."

"Inform me at once if there's any hint of movement east." Ellis flinched slightly as the door to the cafe opened and

Angela McKinney entered, scowling, flanked by men and women in business suits. Ellis's posture stiffened as she busied herself examining each of the terminal screens in turn.

As he waited for Angela to make her way over to him, Ellis turned to face Spencer. All of the emotion had drained from his face.

"It was a mistake," Ellis said to his son. "The child of a Skin isn't a Charmer. You received no gift. Not a single thing. But you should have been mine, Spencer, you should have been one of us. And now you can be."

\*

Caitlin waited and watched, measuring the passing of time by the regular thudding of boat hulls knocking together. The army had done a good job – there was nobody around. The desolation was eerie and the creep of the meteors across the sky gave the sense of an apocalypse already having occurred.

Kit had volunteered to be the one to return stealthily to the seafront shops and sneak, little by little, over to the far side of the harbour, keeping out of sight of the soldier guard. She had made it clear that there was no point in risking them both being on the move, as long as they kept their distance from one another. Caitlin suspected that Kit thought she might be a liability.

She tried to see Kit amongst the piles of crab cages where the harbour wall curved around the bay, but there was no sign of her. Nevertheless, she was certain that Kit could see her and was waiting for the signal.

When it came, Caitlin's sudden shift into alertness almost made her jump from her hiding place behind an A-board advertising pleasure-boat cruises.

The voice rang out again from behind Caitlin. "You're not taking me anywhere! I'm staying right here!"

The soldier's head whipped around in the direction of the Museum of Automata. Its rear door was wide open, now.

"Get your hands off me, or I swear to God you'll get a bullet between your eyes!"

Gerry was doing an excellent job. She sounded dangerous and desperate.

Both Caitlin and the soldier on the harbour wall flinched at a loud cracking sound that echoed off the seafront buildings. Caitlin wondered what Gerry had found within the museum to make such a noise.

Immediately, the soldier broke into a run. He sprinted past Caitlin's hiding place, making a beeline for the open back door of the museum.

Then Caitlin set off in the other direction. Kit appeared from nowhere and reached the harbour before her. They held hands for balance as they scurried down the stone steps to the jetty.

"Can you relax your grip a bit?" Kit said. "You're crushing my fingers."

"And your palm's all sweaty. Shut up."

They scurried along the jetty, ducking behind coils of rusted cable, keeping close to the water in order to examine the boats.

"That one," Kit said, pointing. "Look. It's named *Evie*."

Caitlin's immediate instinct was anger. Evie was her friend, not Kit's. In fact, Kit had only met her twice, technically, at the shedding and at the funeral.

"Don't be an idiot," she said. "It's a speedboat."

"I've always wanted to drive one. I mean, *you've* always wanted to. So now I want to, too. You can't blame me for that. I'm only a poor Snakeskin with no original thoughts of my own."

Caitlin tried to ignore her. What Kit said was true enough. Caitlin only had herself to blame for being so insufferable.

"You can't have that one," she hissed. "Even if you knew how to operate something that big, you don't have the keys. It has to be the kind with an outboard motor."

Kit lapsed into silence. Then, "There! And another close by!"

One of the boats was tied to the side of a much larger yacht, bumping against its white hull. The other was tied with a rope at the foot of a flight of moss-green steps that led down to the water.

"You can take the nearest one," Kit said, "but you'll have to drop me off at the other one. Hold on while I untie the rope."

As Kit bent to the task, Caitlin yanked at the starter cord. The motor coughed and fell silent. From here, the door of the museum was obscured. She prayed that the soldier was still searching the premises and wouldn't hear the engine. She gritted her teeth and pulled again. Nothing at all this time. She pulled with all her strength and the cord whipped out of her hand. She fell back, gasping.

Kit stood over her looking scornful. In one hand she

held the cut end of the rope, in the other a utility knife. She had come prepared. She tossed the rope away and turned to the engine.

"It's no good getting frustrated," she muttered.

With a single tug, the motor spluttered into life. Caitlin made a show of rubbing her spine where she had fallen, in an attempt to hide her annoyance.

Kit made short work of cutting the rope attaching the second boat to the yacht, and starting the second motor. She hopped between the boats and settled herself into position beside the outboard.

She grinned at Caitlin. "So this is it."

"I don't know what you're looking so pleased about."

"Give me a break. Compared to the way I thought I was going to die, this is a doddle. Out on the ocean waves. Way better than disappearing in a puff of ash. Should we hug or something?"

"I think you've had enough of me. Right?"

"Right. But hey. I'm sorry."

"For what?"

"I don't know." Then Kit exclaimed, "Oh! I've always wanted to say this. Synchronise watches."

Caitlin looked down at the wristwatch she had stolen from the museum gift shop. In its centre was a blank-faced automaton and part of the dial was cut away to reveal tiny cogs clicking. "Eight-thirteen. And five seconds... six, seven."

"Close enough," Kit said.

"It feels like we should take a second and say something profound."

"Figure it out later and assume I'd have said the same thing," Kit said with a grin. "Right. See you on the other side, then."

She swung the motor and her boat lurched towards the mouth of the harbour. Caitlin cursed as she struggled to keep up.

\*

Gerry stretched out her limbs, pressing herself onto the flat roof of the Museum of Automata. Gravel dug against her arms. She desperately wanted to scratch them, but she didn't dare disturb the camera she was holding against the lip of the roof. Beneath her, somewhere within the museum, she could hear the shuffling movements of the soldier, still searching for the source of the shouting.

Caitlin and Kit in their boats were now hidden behind the stone wall that cradled the harbour. Resourceful kids, both of them.

In the last ten minutes the sky had turned from peach to a sickly green. She could no longer look directly at the meteors or even their trails, due to their intensity. It was impossible to tell if they really were changing direction.

A squeal of tyres made her almost upset the camera. Carefully, she repositioned it so that it pointed towards the harbourside, where six cars had parked messily. The sound of doors slamming carried across the still air like distant gunshots. She pressed herself flatter as the soldier burst from the museum with his gun raised, and ran towards the cars.

The disposable camera had no zoom. She grimaced at the

thought of the high-end SLR still sitting on her coffee table at home. She ought to have recognised the limitations of the gift-shop camera earlier, should have hidden within the harbour itself, forfeiting the high angle this position gave her but lessening the distance. But it was too late now. She peered into the viewfinder, trying to make out the faces of the people emerging from the cars. Several more vehicles arrived. Soon, the harbourside was thronging with people.

Two strode ahead of the group and along the concrete jetty. She recognised them immediately. The man was Ellis Blackwood, the MP. Beside him stood another minister, Angela McKinney, who Gerry had recently, reluctantly, featured in an article about 'fashion secrets of the snappiest-dressing Party members'. Gerry took several shots and then trained the camera on the throng that followed them.

Several of the faces were immediately familiar. The Brinkley siblings, low-ranking cabinet ministers about whom there had always been rumours of attempted coups to seize power within the Party. Alvin Routledge, the fast-food millionaire. A Shepperton comedian turned producer whose name Gerry couldn't recall. Most of the group looked as though they were dressed for a party. Others wore the dull uniforms of drivers or the conservative attire of personal assistants. She gasped as she identified Zemma Finch at the rear of the group. Gerry swore and hammered at the shutter release button.

The members of the group pushed at each other for positions behind Ellis Blackwood and Angela McKinney as they strode along the harbour front. Ellis shouted something and pointed ahead to part of the harbour wall, which must be where Caitlin and Kit were hiding in their respective boats. His body language betrayed his anxiety: Gerry presumed that he had only moments ago reassured Angela that the Fall would occur on land, and this close to the seafront his certainty would be tested. He wouldn't have had time to requisition a boat large enough for his entourage.

She shielded the camera lens from the flickering of the sky. Eight-twenty-five. Any moment now.

She saw the boats before Ellis or Angela did. Caitlin and Kit – it was impossible to tell which was which – each steered their craft at forty-five degrees from the other, rapidly increasing the distance between them as they burst away from the harbour.

Even from this distance she could hear Ellis's roar. He stood with his back to Gerry, teetering on the edge of the jetty with his arms aloft as he bellowed at the departing girls. Angela clutched her head with both hands. The group behind her fragmented and turned to disarray as its members tried to understand what was happening. A few stumbled down to the collection of tiny boats moored in the harbour, but simply stared at them and shouted back up to the rest of the group.

Caitlin's and Kit's boats soon appeared to reach the horizon. They must be hundreds of metres apart by now. Their outlines shimmered, swallowed up by the bloom of light from the sky. The two girls were now stick figures with burning green halos that enveloped their bodies.

Gerry looked up at the fireballs hanging overhead. If she

squinted, she convinced herself that she could see kinks in the trails. It was working. The meteors were redirecting to follow the Hext girls.

Despite herself, she felt a pang of regret. All her life she had dreamed of being a Charmer, of rejuvenating and enjoying the status of those anointed for greatness. Today, a new image had occurred to her, a fantasy tinged with guilt, in which she commanded a gang of willing, subservient clones. Or perhaps her Skins might have been friends as much as lackeys. Either way, she had come within a hair's breadth of being granted that gift, and without paying for it as, presumably, the gaggle of people standing on the harbour front had. And she had sabotaged her chances. She had aided Caitlin and Kit in their plan. If she was ever miserable about her ordinariness in future, she had nobody to blame but herself.

She switched to a second disposable camera and took a dozen more photos.

At least she would have the story.

\*

The light from above was almost unbearable now. Caitlin could no longer make out the individual meteors or their trails. Their heat warmed the top of her head. The sea shone with green reflections and the lurch of the waves made her constantly disoriented. Her arm braced against the vibration of the outboard motor began to feel numb. She felt less and less as though she was on a boat and more as though she were falling, upwards, into the sun.

She twisted around. It was impossible to tell whether she was still heading in the agreed direction, but she was certainly travelling away from land. The beach was a thin stripe to her right, appearing more grey than sand-coloured in contrast to the vivid green light. As long as Kit acted as a mirror image, keeping the seafront to her left, they must both still be on track.

There. She could make out the other boat in the distance, if she screwed up her eyes against the brightness. Searing light slashed somewhere between the two craft, appearing to pierce the sea.

Kit was standing up in her boat. Her arms looked as thin as straws. She was waving.

Caitlin stood too. She raised both her arms.

She meant to shout 'Goodbye', but it came out as a wordless bellow.

The sea fizzed before her—

—and something plunged in—

—and then more and more and more—

—until all Caitlin could hear were stomach-punching thuds—

—and all she could see were plumes of rising water—

—and blinding, burning, strobing light—

—and then something pushed her off her feet and into the water—

—and then she was—

# EIGHTEEN

She was being watched.

"Come in if you're coming in," Caitlin said calmly to the wide mirror.

There was no response. She glanced at the speaker grille in the corner of the plain room. It hummed softly on standby.

"I can't talk to you like this," she said. "I get distracted by my reflection."

This was, in fact, true. During all of her sessions in the interview room, intermittently over the past three days, she had tried to avoid looking directly at herself in the one-way mirror. She looked alien in her pale scrubs, her hair hanging in clumps, having been offered no shower and no hairbrush since she had been pulled from the sea and into the helicopter. She was curiously unrecognisable, yet whenever she saw her reflection her instinctive reaction was that she was looking at Kit.

None of the interviewers had answered her questions about Kit's whereabouts. Caitlin had passed through grief and out the other side. Her initial triumph about altering the trajectory of the Fall had produced euphoria unimpeded by her certainty that she'd soon be disposed of, along with her Skin. But as the days passed the purpose of her imprisonment seemed less and less clear.

\*

On the first day, most of the questions had related to her physical state. She assured the serious-looking men that she felt quite normal, other than the scratchy throat and beginnings of a cold produced by having floundered in the water for so long. When she had found her way to the surface, the motorboat had disappeared. Presumably it had capsized and sunk.

She asked the men whether anybody had benefitted from the Fall. They refused to answer. She had no idea whether her questioners were Charmers at all. But they didn't look healthy and their expressions were permanently sour.

On the morning of the second day – at least, she thought of it as morning, because it had been soon after she had been woken by somebody hammering on the door of her bare cell – the questions had been about her family history. Then the men asked her about her contact and activities with Kit. Her resolve not to respond slipped; she begged to know whether Kit was alive. They didn't tell her, but in their hesitations Caitlin found hope.

On the afternoon of the second day they had changed tack and the intensity of their questioning increased. As well as seriousness, the men now exhibited hints of panic. They asked about her contact with other people. They asked whether she had shared what she knew with anybody other than Kit. Years ago, Caitlin played a game to infuriate Evie: She answered each question with a question of her own. She played it again now. She asked after Kit. She asked whether any single person had managed to throw themselves in the path of the Fall. She asked whether anything had changed in the world outside these walls. She asked whether her interviewers were worried about the truth getting out.

Her interviewers could barely disguise their agitation. After a round of relentless questioning, one man said, "But you already told us that—" and his partner shook his head and said, "That was the other one," and Caitlin leapt up whooping, and was still grinning when the chain around her wrists snapped taut and yanked her back down into the hard seat.

They showed her a picture and said a name: Gerry Chafik.

Caitlin smiled. "Has this Gerry Chafik gone and said something she shouldn't have said? Or shown somebody something she shouldn't have shown?" Then, when she registered a flinch, she said in a lower voice, "Are things beginning to look bad for you?"

\*

The speaker fizzled. Then a voice said, "You will be escorted back to your room momentarily."

Caitlin frowned. "But you haven't asked me anything. I've been sitting here like a lemon for maybe half an hour."

\*

The next time she was brought to the interview room, she didn't recognise the man and woman on the other side of the table. Rather than uniforms, they wore standard business attire.

"Can you confirm that you are Caitlin Hext?" the woman said.

"Yes. You already knew that."

"We have some questions before we proceed. You're free to answer them or to remain silent. But we would appreciate your cooperation."

Caitlin hesitated. This was new. "Okay."

"I'm going to read you a list of names. I'd like you to tell me which of them you recognise."

"Sounds fun. But if it's pop culture, I'm good on films but crap on sport, okay?"

The woman's expression was implacable. "Geraldine Chafik."

Caitlin tried to make an assessment about whether admitting to knowing Gerry would land the journalist – or herself – in further trouble. Her previous denial had prevented her from asking follow-up questions of her own. And if they'd caught Gerry, surely she couldn't be put in worse trouble. The same went for Caitlin.

"Sure. Gerry the journalist."

"You've met in person?"

"Once. She seemed all right. Did she do what she said she'd do?"

The woman looked again at her list. "Russell Handler."

"No."

"Clive Blackwood."

"Nope."

"Spencer Blackwood."

Caitlin grimaced. "Spencer Blackwood? From college?"

"I'd be grateful if you'd answer the question."

"Yes. We go to college together. Went. I guess you're not going to let me go back there, are you, or maybe go anywhere at all."

"What is the nature of your association? To what degree has Spencer Blackwood been aware of your activities during the last week?"

Caitlin tried to spread her arms wide, but the chain stopped her short. "Our association is Physics and English Lit and that's about it. He's not my friend, or fellow plotter, or anything. Seriously, what is all this?"

The woman looked to the man, who said, "One more question. Do you feel well? Have you experienced any unusual physical symptoms during the last three days? Nausea? Headaches? Bursts of adrenalin? Unusual sensations of well-being?"

Caitlin smiled. The scattershot nature of the questions suggested that they had no other data, nobody who might provide a comparison.

"I'm okay. No better than that and no worse, which is kind of amazing, considering the standards of bed and board here. How's everyone else looking?" She pointed at the wall to indicate the world outside.

The man's demeanour changed. His shoulders slackened. "It's too early to say. It appears that nobody has benefitted directly from the Fall. I understand that early reports have suggested measurable changes to the seawater, though dispersal has been fast. We don't know what that means, whether any benefits may be dispersed too." He leant forward. "Don't be alarmed. I'm going to remove your restraints."

And he did.

The woman reached into a slim case and pulled out glossy photos. They were screenshots of TV images. Caitlin saw the *Rise and Shine* ident in the bottom-left corner. In the main part of the image Gerry Chafik sat on a red sofa, hands clasped on her skirt. An inset picture floated above her head. The woman pushed the paper to one side; the photo underneath was a blow-up of the inset image. Caitlin recognised the harbour at Scarborough. She peered at the sea for a glimpse of herself on her boat, but the water was a dark mass and above it the sky was tinged green and the meteor trails looked like rips. A mass of figures hurried away from the camera. At the head of the group a man had turned to address them, his arms aloft in a gesture presumably intended to calm but which betrayed his panic. Caitlin didn't recognise him, but his facial features could be made out clearly.

"This photograph and others like it were broadcast on breakfast TV yesterday morning," the woman said. "And they appear to have triggered a chain of events."

She slid the photo aside. Beneath it another image showed three people, one of whom was Spencer Blackwood, standing on the steps of a grand building. Caitlin frowned at the man on the left, who appeared identical to the panicked man in the first photo, though this person leant heavily on a walking stick. In the foreground Caitlin could see the backs of heads, a crowd looking up at them. At the top of the photo a red horizontal strip and the lower parts of lettering suggested a banner. It appeared to be a rally of some sort, but weren't gatherings like that against the law?

The woman pointed at the man in the centre. "Late last night, Russell Handler broadcast a segment of covertly recorded audio on pirate radio. It relates to Ellis Blackwood and a great number of other government ministers. The footage has since been repeated many times on other stations and networks. It supports Gerry Chafik's story, and adds new details, and raises many more questions and implications. Spencer Blackwood and a Snakeskin who calls himself Clive Blackwood corroborate the account. We suspect that more witnesses will soon make themselves known."

Caitlin studied each of them in turn. "You're not from the government, are you?"

The man shook his head. "Temporarily, the Great British Prosperity Party has no jurisdiction over this facility. But we must work quickly and we must use our resources efficiently. So this is what we need to know. Are you prepared to testify, to add what you know to the information already available to the public?"

Caitlin remembered that her chains had been removed. She lifted her hands, stared at the lines on her palms, curled her fingers until her nails dug in, then watched as the elasticity of her skin erased the crescent-shaped dents.

"Try and stop me," she said.

She saw how it would be. The bursting of a dam. Testimonials and truth. The rage of the public, who would now be forced to look to the Snakeskins at the January care home, to relieved whistle-blowers within government, perhaps even to the world beyond the British coast, in the search for sources of trustworthy information. Things would be different.

She saw, too, what *wouldn't* occupy the attention of the public. The Fall would remain an unknown. The gift it bestowed would still be considered divine. Caitlin thought of her dad's telescope and wondered if he might allow her to borrow it.

"The truth is coming out, little by little," the woman said. "And we thank you in advance for the part you will play."

Caitlin stood, stretching out her spine. "There's something I need from you first."

"Anything."

"I need to see Kit."

The woman nodded, turned to the one-way mirror and nodded again.

## ABOUT THE AUTHOR

Tim Major is the author of *You Don't Belong Here*, *Blighters* and *Carus & Mitch*, YA novel *Machineries of Mercy*, short story collection *And the House Lights Dim* and a non-fiction book about the silent crime film, *Les Vampires*. Tim's short stories have appeared in *Interzone*, *Shoreline of Infinity* and *Not One of Us* and have been selected for *Best of British Science Fiction* and *Best Horror of the Year*. He is also co-editor of the British Fantasy Society's fiction journal, *BFS Horizons*. Find out more at www.cosycatastrophes.com

## ACKNOWLEDGEMENTS

Enormous, grateful thanks to the team at Titan Books – particularly my editor, Gary Budden, who took a chance on this novel and who has been supportive and critical at precisely the right moments.

Thanks to my literary agent, Alexander Cochran – here's to lots of exciting projects in the future.

Thanks to my many excellent writer friends, particularly the FantasyCon and Edge-Lit clan, for their support, enthusiasm and inspiration. Thanks to Dan Coxon for all of the above plus copyediting and, perhaps most importantly, resolving the *alright/all right* feud. Thanks to Aliya Whiteley for remaining cool in the face of unnerving coincidence.

Thanks to my young sons, Arthur and Joe, for forcing me to capitalise on available writing hours.

Thanks to my mum, who long ago let me use her fancy typewriter, which maybe started something.

Above all, thanks and love and everything, everything to my wife, Rose.

ALSO AVAILABLE FROM TITAN BOOKS

# THE RIFT

## NINA ALLAN

**WINNER OF THE 2017 BSFA AWARD FOR BEST NOVEL
WINNER OF THE KITSCHIES RED TENTACLE 2017**

Selena and Julie are sisters. As children they were close, but as they grow older, a rift develops between them. There are greater rifts, however. Julie goes missing aged seventeen. It will be twenty years before Selena sees her again. When Julie reappears, she tells Selena an incredible story about how she has spent time on another planet. Does Selena dismiss her sister as the victim of delusions, or believe her, and risk her own sanity?

**"Astonishing and brilliant, the best thing this
immensely gifted writer has yet done."**
Adam Roberts, author of *The Thing Itself*

**"A heart-rending novel about being believed, being trusted,
and the temptation to hide the truth. Of people going missing,
and their incomplete stories. A generous book, it leaves the
reader looking at the world anew. Dizzying stuff."**
Anne Charnock, author of *A Calculated Life*

TITANBOOKS.COM

ALSO AVAILABLE FROM TITAN BOOKS

# ZERO BOMB

## M.T. HILL

The near future. Following the death of his daughter Martha, Remi flees the north of England for London. Here he tries to rebuild his life as a cycle courier, delivering subversive documents under the nose of an all-seeing state.

But when a driverless car attempts to run him over, Remi soon discovers that his old life will not let him move on so easily. Someone is leaving coded messages for Remi across the city, and they seem to suggest that Martha is not dead at all. Unsure what to believe, and increasingly unable to trust his memory, Remi is slowly drawn into the web of a dangerous radical whose '70s sci-fi novel is now a manifesto for direct action against automation, technology, and England itself.

The deal? Remi can see Martha again – if he joins the cause.

**"One of the most innovative and outspoken new writers of British science fiction."**
Nina Allan, author of *The Rift*

**TITAN**BOOKS.COM

ALSO AVAILABLE FROM TITAN BOOKS

# THE RIG

## ROGER LEVY

Humanity has spread across the depths of space but is connected by AfterLife – a vote made by every member of humanity on the worth of a life. Bale, a disillusioned policeman on the planet Bleak, is brutally attacked, leading writer Razer on to a story spanning centuries of corruption. On Gehenna, the last religious planet, a hyperintelligent boy, Alef, meets psychopath Pellonhorc, and so begins a rivalry and friendship to last an epoch.

So many Lives, forever interlinked, and one structure at the center of it all: the rig.

"A triumph that is guaranteed to blow your mind."
Lavie Tidhar, author of *A Man Lies Dreaming*

"Roger Levy is SF's best kept secret, and *The Rig* is a tour de force: a darkly brilliant epic of life, death and huge drilling platforms. Read it and discover what you've been missing."
Adam Roberts

TITANBOOKS.COM

For more fantastic fiction, author events, exclusive
excerpts, competitions, limited editions and more

VISIT OUR WEBSITE
**titanbooks.com**

LIKE US ON FACEBOOK
**facebook.com/titanbooks**

FOLLOW US ON TWITTER
**@TitanBooks**

EMAIL US
**readerfeedback@titanemail.com**